BAD HUGH

BAD HUGH

Mary Jane Holmes

WILDSIDE PRESS

BAD HUGH

This edition published 2005 by Wildside Press, LLC.
www.wildsidepress.com

CHAPTER I

SPRING BANK

A large, old-fashioned, weird-looking wooden building, with strangely shaped bay windows and stranger gables projecting here and there from the slanting roof, where the green moss clung in patches to the moldy shingles, or formed a groundwork for the nests the swallows built year after year beneath the decaying eaves. Long, winding piazzas, turning sharp, sudden angles, and low, square porches, where the summer sunshine held many a fantastic dance, and where the winter storm piled up its drifts of snow, whistling merrily as it worked, and shaking the loosened casement as it went whirling by. Huge trees of oak and maple, whose topmost limbs had borne and cast the leaf for nearly a century of years, tall evergreens, among whose boughs the autumn wind ploughed mournfully, making sad music for those who cared to listen, and adding to the loneliness which, during many years, had invested the old place. A wide spreading grassy lawn, with the carriage road winding through it, over the running brook, and onward 'neath graceful forest trees, until it reached the main highway, a distance of nearly half a mile. A spacious garden in the rear, with bordered walks and fanciful mounds, with climbing roses and creeping vines showing that somewhere there was a taste, a ruling hand, which, while neglecting the somber building and suffering it to decay, lavished due care upon the grounds, and not on these alone, but also on the well-kept barns, and the whitewashed dwellings in front, where numerous, happy, well-fed negroes lived and lounged, for ours is a Kentucky scene, and Spring Bank a Kentucky home.

As we have described it so it was on a drear December night, when a fearful storm, for that latitude, was raging, and the snow lay heaped against the fences, or sweeping-down from the bending trees, drifted against the doors, and beat against the windows, whence a cheerful light was gleaming, telling of life and possible happiness within. There were no flowing curtains before the windows, no drapery sweeping to the floor, nothing save blinds without and simple shades within, neither of which were doing service now, for the master of the house would have it so in spite of his sister's remonstrances.

Some one might lose their way on that terrible night, he said, and the blaze of the fire on the hearth, which could be seen from afar, would be to them a beacon light to guide them on their way. Nobody would look in upon them, as Adaline, or 'Lina as she chose to be called, and as all did call her except himself, seemed to think there might, and even if they did, why need she care? To be sure she was not quite as fixey as she was on pleasant days when there was a possibility of visitors, and her cheeks were not quite so red, but she was looking well enough, and she'd undone all those little tags or braids which disfigured her so shockingly in the morning, but which, when brushed and carefully arranged, did give her hair that waving appearance she so much desired. As for himself, he never meant to do anything of which he was ashamed, so he did not care how many were watching him through the window, and stamping his heavy boots upon the rug, for he had just come in from the storm Hugh Worthington piled fresh fuel upon the fire, and, shaking back the mass of short brown curls which had fallen upon his forehead, strode across the room and arranged the shades to his own liking, paying no heed when his more fastidious sister, with a frown upon her dark, handsome face, muttered something about the "Stanley taste."

"There, Kelpie, lie there," he continued, returning to the hearth, and, addressing a small, white, shaggy dog, which, with a human look in its round, pink eyes, obeyed the voice it knew and loved, and crouched down in the corner at a safe distance from the young lady, whom it seemed instinctively to know as an enemy.

"Do, pray, Hugh, let the dirty things stay where they are," 'Lina exclaimed, as she saw her brother walk toward the dining-room, and guessed his errand. "Nobody wants a pack of dogs under their feet. I wonder you don't bring in your pet horse, saddle and all."

"I did want to when I heard how piteously he cried after me as I left the stable tonight," said Hugh, at the same time opening a door leading out upon a back piazza, and, uttering a peculiar whistle, which brought around him at once the pack of dogs which so annoyed his sister.

"I'd be a savage altogether if I were you!" was the sister's angry remark, to which Hugh paid no heed.

It was his house, his fire, and if he chose to have his dogs there, he should, for all of Ad, but when the pale, gentle-looking woman, knitting so quietly in her accustomed chair, looked up and said imploringly:

"Please turn them into the kitchen, they'll surely be comfortable there," he yielded at once, for that pale, gentle woman, was his mother, and, to her wishes, Hugh was generally obedient.

The room was cleared of all its canine occupants, save Kelpie, who Hugh insisted should remain, the mother resumed her knitting, and Adaline her book, while Hugh sat down before the blazing fire, and, with his hands crossed above his head, went on into a reverie, the nature of which his mother, who was watching him, could not guess; and when at last she asked of what he was thinking so intently, he made her no reply. He could hardly have told himself, so varied were the thoughts crowding upon his brain that wintry night. Now they were of the eccentric old man, who had been to him a father, and from whom he had received Spring Bank, together with the many peculiar ideas which made him the strange, odd creature he was, a puzzle and a mystery to his own sex, and a kind of terror to the female portion of the neighborhood, who looked upon him as a woman-hater, and avoided or coveted his not altogether disagreeable society, just as their fancy dictated. For years the old man and the boy had lived together alone in that great, lonely house, enjoying vastly the freedom from all restraint, the liberty of turning the parlors into kennels if they chose, and converting the upper rooms into a hay-loft, if they would. No white woman was ever seen upon the premises, unless she came as a beggar, when some new gown, or surplice, or organ, or chandelier, was needed for the pretty little church, lifting its modest spire so unobtrusively among the forest trees, not very far from Spring Bank. John Stanley didn't believe in churches; nor gowns, nor organs, nor women, but he was proverbially liberal, and so the fair ones of Glen's Creek neighborhood ventured into his den, finding it much pleasanter to do so after the handsome, dark-haired boy came to live with him; for about that frank, outspoken boy there was then something very attractive to the little girls, while their mothers pitied him, wondering why he had been permitted to come there, and watching for the change in him, which was sure to ensue.

Not all at once did Hugh conform to the customs of his uncle's household, and at first there often came over him a longing for something different, a yearning for the refinements of his early home among the Northern hills, and a wish to infuse into Chloe, the colored housekeeper, some of his mother's neatness. But a few attempts at reform had taught him how futile was the effort, Aunt Chloe always meeting him with the argument:

"'Taint no use, Mr. Hugh. A nigger's a nigger; and I spec' ef you're to talk to me till you was hoarse 'bout your Yankee ways of scrubbin', and sweepin', and moppin' with a broom, I shouldn't be an atomer white-folksey than I is now. Besides Mas'r John, wouldn't bar no finery; he's only happy when the truck is mighty nigh a foot thick, and his things is lyin' round loose and handy."

To a certain extent this was true, for John Stanley would have felt sadly out of place in any spot where, as Chloe said, "his things were not lying round loose and handy," and as habit is everything, so Hugh soon grew accustomed to his surroundings, and became as careless of his external appearance as his uncle could desire. Only once had there come to him an awakening—a faint conception of the happiness there might arise from constant association with the pure and refined, such as his uncle had labored to make him believe did not exist. He was thinking of that incident now, and as he thought the veins upon his broad, white forehead stood out round and full, while the hands clasped above the head worked nervously together, and it was not strange that he did not heed his mother when she spoke, for Hugh was far away from Spring Bank, and the wild storm beating against its walls was to him like the sound of the waves dashing against the vessel's side, just as they did years ago on that night he remembered so well, shuddering as he heard again the murderous hiss of the devouring flames, covering the fatal boat with one sheet of fire, and driving into the water as a safer friend the shrieking, frightened wretches who but an hour before had been so full of life and hope, dancing gayly above the red-tongued demon stealthily creeping upward from the hold below, where it had taken life. What a fearful scene that was, and the veins grew larger on Hugh's brow while his broad chest heaved with something like a stifled sob as he recalled the little childish form to which he had clung so madly until the cruel timber struck from him all consciousness, and he let that form go down—down 'neath the treacherous waters of Lake Erie never to come up again alive, for so his uncle told when, weeks after the occurrence, he awoke from the delirious fever which ensued and listened to the sickening detail.

"Lost, my boy, lost with many others," was what his uncle had said.

He heard the words as plainly now as when they first were spoken, remembering how his uncle's voice had faltered, and how the thought had flashed upon his mind that John Stanley's heart was not as hard toward womenkind as people had supposed. "Lost"—there was a world of meaning in that word to Hugh more than any one had ever guessed, and, though it was but a child he lost, yet in the quiet night, when all else around Spring Bank was locked in sleep, he often lay thinking of that child and of what she might perhaps have been had she been spared to him. He was thinking of her now, and as he thought visions of a sweet, pale face, shadowed with curls of golden hair, came up before his mind, and he saw again the look of bewildered surprise and pain which shone in the soft, blue eyes and illumined every feature when in an unguarded moment he gave vent to the half infidel principles he had learned from his uncle. Her creed was different from his, and she explained it to him so earnestly, so tearfully, that he had said to her at last he did but jest to hear what she would say, and, though she seemed satisfied, he felt there was a shadow between them—a shadow which was not swept away, even after he promised to read the little Bible she gave him and see for himself whether he or she were right. He had that Bible now hidden away where no curious eye could find it, and carefully folded between its leaves was a curl of golden hair. It was faded now, and its luster was almost gone, but as often as he looked upon it, it brought to mind the bright head it once adorned, and the fearful hour when he became its owner. That tress and the Bible which inclosed it had made Hugh Worthington a better man. He did not often read the Bible, it is true, and his acquaintances were frequently startled with opinions which had so pained the little girl on board the *St. Helena*, but this was merely on the surface, for far below the rough exterior there was a world of goodness, a mine of gems, kept bright by memories of the angel child which flitted for so brief a span across his pathway and then was lost forever. He had tried so hard to save her—had clasped her so fondly to his bosom when with extended arms she came to him for aid. He could save her, he said—he could swim to the shore with perfect ease and so without a moment's hesitation she had leaped with him into the surging waves, and that was about the last he could remember, save that he clutched frantically at the long, golden hair streaming above the water, retaining in his firm grasp the lock which no one at Spring Bank had ever seen, for this one romance of Hugh's seemingly unromantic life was a secret with himself. No one save his uncle had witnessed his emotions when told that she was dead; no one else had seen his bitter tears or heard the vehement exclamation: "You've tried to teach me there was no hereafter, no heaven for such as she, but I know better now, and I am glad there is, for she is safe forever."

These were not mere idle words, and the belief then expressed became with Hugh Worthington a firm, fixed principle, which his skeptical uncle tried in vain to eradicate. "There was a heaven, and she was there," comprised nearly the whole of Hugh's religious creed, if we except a vague, misty hope, that he, too, would some day find her, how or by what means he never seriously inquired; only this he knew, it would be through her influence, which even now followed him everywhere, producing its good effects. It had checked him many and many a time when his fierce temper was in the ascendant, forcing back the harsh words he would otherwise have spoken, and making him as gentle as a child; and when the temptations to which young men of his age are exposed were spread out alluringly before him, a single thought of her was sufficient to lead him from the forbidden ground.

Only once had he fallen, and that two years before, when, as if some demon had possessed him, he shook off all remembrances of the past, and yielding to the baleful fascinations of one who seemed to sway him at will, plunged into a tide of dissipation, and lent himself at last to an act which had since embittered every waking hour. As if all the events of his life were crowding upon his memory this night, he thought of two years ago, and the scene which transpired in the suburbs of New York, whither immediately after his uncle's death he had gone upon a matter of important business. In the gleaming fire before him there was now another face than hers, an older, a different, though not less beautiful face, and Hugh shuddered as he thought how it must have changed ere this—thought of the anguish which stole into the dark, brown eyes when first the young girl learned how cruelly she had been betrayed. Why hadn't he saved her? What had she done to him that he should treat her so, and where was she now? Possibly she was dead. He almost hoped she was, for if she were, the two were then together, his golden-haired and brown, for thus he designated the two.

Larger and fuller grew the veins upon his forehead, as memory kept thus faithfully at work, and so absorbed was Hugh in his reverie that until twice repeated he did not hear his mother's anxious inquiry:

"What is that noise? It sounds like some one in distress."

Hugh started at last, and, after listening for a moment he, too, caught the sound which had so alarmed his mother, and made 'Lina stop her reading. A moaning cry, as if for help, mingled with an infant's wail, now here, now there it seemed to be, just as the fierce north wind shifted its course and drove first at the uncurtained window of the sitting-room, and then at the ponderous doors of the gloomy hall.

"It is some one in the storm, though I can't imagine why any one should be abroad tonight," Hugh said, going to the window and peering out into the darkness.

"Lyd's child, most likely. Negro young ones are always squalling, and I heard her tell Aunt Chloe at supper time that Tommie had the colic," 'Lina remarked opening again the book she was reading, and with a slight shiver drawing nearer to the fire.

"Where are you going, my son?" asked Mrs. Worthington, as Hugh arose to leave the room.

"Going to Lyd's cabin, for if Tommie is sick enough to make his screams heard above the storm, she may need some help," was Hugh's reply, and a moment after he was ploughing his way through the drifts which lay between the house and the negro quarters.

"How kind and thoughtful he is," the mother said, softly, more to herself than to her daughter, who nevertheless quickly rejoined:

"Yes, kind to niggers, and horses, and dogs, I'll admit, but let me, or any other white woman come before him as an object of pity, and the tables are turned at once. I wonder what does make him hate women so."

"I don't believe he does," Mrs. Worthington replied. "His uncle, you know, was very unfortunate in his marriage, and had a way of judging all our sex by his wife. Living with him as long as Hugh did, it's natural he should imbibe a few of his ideas."

"A few," 'Lina repeated, "better say all, for John Stanley and Hugh Worthington are as near alike as an old and young man well could be. What an old codger he was though, and how like a savage he lived here. I never shall forget how the house looked the day we came, or how satisfied Hugh seemed when he met us at the gate, and said, 'everything was in spendid order,'" and closing her book, the young lady laughed merrily as she recalled the time when she first crossed her brother's threshold, stepping, as she affirmed, over half a dozen dogs, and as many squirming kittens, catching her foot in some fishing tackle, finding tobacco in the china closet, and segars in the knife box, where they had been put to get them out of the way.

"But Hugh really did his best for us," mildly interposed the mother. "Don't you remember what the servants said about his cleaning one floor himself because he knew they were tired!"

"Did it more to save the lazy negroes' steps than from any regard for our comfort," retorted 'Lina. "At all events he's been mighty careful since how he gratified my wishes. Sometimes I believe he perfectly hates me, and wishes I'd never been born," and tears, which arose from anger, rather than any wounded sisterly feeling, glittered in 'Lina's black eyes.

"Hugh does not hate any one," said Mrs. Worthington, "much less his sister, though you must admit that you try him terribly."

"How, I'd like to know?" 'Lina asked, and her mother replied:

"He thinks you proud, and vain, and artificial, and you know he abhors deceit above all else. Why, he'd cut off his right hand sooner than tell a lie."

"Pshaw!" was 'Lina's contemptuous response, then after a moment she continued: "I wonder how we came to be so different. He must be like his father, and I like mine—that is, supposing I know who he is. Wouldn't it be funny if, just to be hateful, he had sent you back the wrong child?"

"What made you think of that?" Mrs. Worthington asked, quickly, and 'Lina replied:

"Oh, nothing, only the last time Hugh had one of his tantrums, and got so outrageously angry at me, because I made Mr. Bostwick think my hair was naturally curly, he said he'd give all he owned if it were so, but I reckon he'll never have his wish. There's too much of old Sam about me to admit of a doubt," and half spitefully, half playfully she touched the spot in the center of her forehead known as her birthmark.

When not excited it could scarcely be discerned at all, but the moment she was aroused, the delicate network of veins stood out round and full, forming what seemed to be a tiny hand without the thumb. It showed a little now in the firelight, and Mrs. Worthington shuddered as she glanced at what brought so vividly before her the remembrance of other and wretched days. Adaline observed the shudder and hastened to change the conversation from herself to Hugh, saying by way of making some amends for her unkind remarks: "It really is kind in him to give me a home when I have no particular claim upon him, and I ought to respect him for that. I am glad, too, that Mr. Stanley made it a condition in his will that if Hugh ever married, he should forfeit the Spring Bank property, as that provides against the possibility of an upstart wife coming here some day and turning us, or at least me, into the street. Say, mother, are you not glad that Hugh can never marry even if he wishes to do so, which is not very probable."

"I am not so sure of that," returned Mrs. Worthington, smoothing, with her small, fat hands the bright worsted cloud she was knitting, a feminine employment for which she had a weakness. "I am not so sure of that. Suppose Hugh should fancy a person whose fortune was much larger than the one left him by Uncle John, do you think he would let it pass just for the sake of holding Spring Bank?"

"Perhaps not," 'Lina replied; "but there's no possible danger of any one's fancying Hugh."

"And why not?" quickly interrupted the mother. "He has the kindest heart in the world, and is certainly fine-looking if he would only dress decently."

"I'm much obliged for your compliment, mother," Hugh said, laughingly, as he stepped suddenly into the room and laid his hand caressingly on his mother's head, thus showing that even he was not insensible to flattery. "Have you heard that sound again?" he continued. "It wasn't Tommie, for I found him asleep, and I've been all around the house, but could discover nothing. The storm is beginning to abate, I think, and the moon is trying to break through the clouds," and, going again to the window, Hugh looked out into the yard, where the shrubbery and trees were just discernible in the grayish light of the December moon. "That's a big drift by the lower gate," he continued; "and queer shaped, too. Come see, mother. Isn't that a shawl, or an apron, or something blowing in the wind?"

Mrs. Worthington arose, and, joining her son, looked in the direction indicated, where a garment of some kind was certainly fluttering in the gale.

"It's something from the wash, I guess," she said. "I thought all the time Hannah had better not hang out the clothes, as some of them were sure to be lost."

This explanation was quite satisfactory to Mrs. Worthington, but that strange drift by the gate troubled Hugh, and the signal above it seemed to him like a signal of distress. Why should the snow drift there more than elsewhere? He never knew it do so before. He had half a mind to turn out the dogs, and see what that would do.

"Rover," he called, suddenly, as he advanced to the rear room, where, among his older pets, was a huge Newfoundland, of great sagacity. "Rover, Rover, I want you."

In an instant the whole pack were upon him, jumping and fawning, and licking the hands which had never dealt them aught save kindness. It was only Rover, however, who was this time wanted, and leading him to the door, Hugh pointed toward the gate, and bade him see what was there. Snuffing slightly at the storm, which was not over yet, Rover started down the walk, while Hugh stood waiting in the door. At first Rover's steps were slow and uncertain, but as he advanced they increased in rapidity, until, with a sudden bound and cry, such as dogs are wont to give when they have caught their destined prey, he sprang upon the mysterious ridge, and commenced digging it down with his paws.

"Easy, Rover—be careful," Hugh called from the door, and instantly the half savage growl which the wind had brought to his ear was changed into a piteous cry, as if the faithful creature were answering back that other help than his was needed there.

Rover had found something in that pile of snow.

CHAPTER II

WHAT ROVER FOUND

Unmindful of the sleet beating upon his uncovered head Hugh hastened to the spot, where the noble brute was licking a face, a baby face, which he had ferreted out from beneath the shawl trapped so carefully around it to shield it from the cold, for instead of one there were two in that rift of snow—a mother and her child! That stiffened form lying there so still, hugging that sleeping child so closely to its bosom, was no delusion, and his mother's voice calling to know what he was doing brought Hugh back at Last to a consciousness that he must act, and that immediately.

"Mother," he screamed, "send a servant here, quick! or let Ad come herself. There's a woman dead, I fear. I can carry her, but the child, Ad must come for her."

"The what?" gasped Mrs. Worthington, who, terrified beyond measure at the mention of a dead woman, was doubly so at hearing of a child. "A child," she repeated, "whose child?"

Hugh, made no reply save an order that the lounge should be brought near the fire and a pillow from his mother's bed. "From mine, then," he added, as he saw the anxious look in his mother's face, and guessed that she shrank from having her own snowy pillow come in contact with the wet, limp figure he was depositing upon the lounge. It was a slight, girlish form, and the long brown hair, loosened from its confinement, fell in rich profusion over the pillow which 'Lina brought half reluctantly, eying askance the insensible object before her, and daintily holding back her dress lest it should come in contact with the child her mother had deposited upon the floor, where it lay crying lustily.

The idea of a strange woman being thrust upon them in this way was highly displeasing to Miss 'Lina, who haughtily drew back from the little one when it stretched its arms out toward her, while its pretty lip quivered and the tears dropped over its rounded cheek.

Meantime Hugh, with all a woman's tenderness, had done for the now reviving stranger what he could, and as his mother began to collect her scattered senses and evince some interest in the matter, he withdrew to call the negroes, judging it prudent to remain away a while, as his presence might be an intrusion. From the first he had felt sure that the individual thrown upon his charity was not a low, vulgar person, as his sister seemed to think. He had not yet seen her face distinctly, for it lay in the shadow, but the long, flowing hair, the delicate hands, the pure white neck, of which he had caught a glimpse as his mother unfastened the stiffened dress, all these had made an impression, and involuntarily repeating to himself, "Poor girl, poor girl," he strode a second time across the drifts which lay in his back yard, and was soon pounding at old Chloe's cabin door, bidding her and Hannah dress at once and come immediately to the house.

An indignant growl at being thus aroused from her first sleep was Chloe's only response, but Hugh knew that his orders were being obeyed.

The change of atmosphere and restoratives applied had done their work, and Mrs. Worthington saw that the long eyelashes began to tremble, while a faint color stole into the hitherto colorless cheeks, and at last the large, brown eyes unclosed and looked into hers with an expression so mournful, so beseeching, that a thrill of yearning tenderness for the desolate young creature shot through her heart, and bending down she said, "Are you better now?"

"Yes, thank you. Where is Willie?" was the low response, the tone thrilling Mrs. Worthington again with emotion.

Even 'Lina started, it was so musical, and coming near she answered: "If it's the baby you mean, he is here, playing with Rover."

There was a look of gratitude in the brown eyes, which closed again wearily. With her eyes thus closed, 'Lina had a fair opportunity to scan the beautiful face, with its delicately-chiseled features, and the wealth of lustrous brown hair, sweeping back from the open forehead, on which there was perceptible a faint line, which 'Lina stooped down to examine.

"Mother, mother," she whispered, drawing back, "look, is not that a mark just like mine?"

Thus appealed to, Mrs. Worthington, too, bent down, but, upon a closer scrutiny, the mark seemed only a small, blue vein.

"She's pretty," she said. "I wonder why I feel so drawn toward her?"

'Lina was about to reply, when again the brown eyes looked up, and the stranger asked hesitatingly:

"Where am I? And is he here! Is this his house?"

"Whose house?" Mrs. Worthington asked.

The girl did not answer at once, and when she did her mind seemed wandering.

"I waited so long," she said, "but he never came again, only the letter which broke my heart. Willie was a baby then, and I almost hated him for a while, but he wasn't to blame. I wasn't to blame. I'm glad God gave me Willie now, even if he did take his father from me."

Mrs. Worthington and her daughter exchanged glances, and the latter abruptly asked:

"Where is Willie's father?"

"I don't know," came in a wailing sob from the depths of the pillow.

"Where did you come from?" was the next question. The young girl looked up in some alarm, and answered meekly:

"From New York. I thought I'd never get here, but everybody was so kind to me and Willie, and the driver said if 'twan't so late, and he so many passengers, he'd drive across the fields. He pointed out the way and I came on alone."

The color had faded from Mrs. Worthington's face, and very timidly she asked again:

"Whom are you looking for? Whom did you hope to find?"

"Mr. Worthington. Does he live here?" was the frank reply; whereupon 'Lina drew herself up haughtily, exclaiming:

"I knew it. I've thought so ever since Hugh came home from New York."

'Lina was about to commence a tirade of abuse, when the mother interposed, and with an air of greater authority than she generally assumed toward her imperious daughter, bade her keep silence while she questioned the stranger, gazing wonderingly from one to the other, as if uncertain what they meant.

Mrs. Worthington had no such feelings for the girl as 'Lina entertained.

"It will be easier to talk with you," she said, leaning forward, "if I know what to call you."

"Adah," was the response, and the brown eyes, swimming with tears, sought the face of the questioner with a wistful eagerness, as if it read there the unmistakable signs of a friend.

"Adah, you say. Well, then, Adah, why have you come to my son on such a night as this, and what is he to you?"

"Are you his mother?" and Adah started up. "I did not know he had one. Oh, I'm so glad. And you'll be kind to me, who never had a mother?"

A person who never had a mother was an anomaly to Mrs. Worthington, whose powers of comprehension were not the clearest imaginable.

"Never had a mother!" she repeated. "How can that be?"

A smile flitted for a moment across Adah's face, and then she answered:

"I never knew a mother's care, I mean."

"But your father? What do you know of him?" said Mrs. Worthington, and instantly a shadow stole into the sweet young face, as Adah replied:

"Only this, I was left at a boarding school."

"And Hugh? Where did you meet him? And what is he to you?"

"The only friend I've got. May I see him, please?"

"First tell what he is to you and to this child," 'Lina rejoined. Adah answered calmly:

"Your brother might not like to be implicated. I must see him first—see him alone."

"One thing more," and 'Lina held back her mother, who was starting in quest of Hugh, "are you a wife?"

"Don't, 'Lina," Mrs. Worthington whispered, as she saw the look of agony pass over Adah's face. "Don't worry her so; deal kindly by the fallen."

"I am not fallen!" came passionately from the quivering lips. "I am as true a woman as either of you—look!" and she pointed to the golden band encircling the third finger.

'Lina was satisfied, and needed no further explanations. To her, it was plain as daylight. In an unguarded moment, Hugh had set his uncle's will at naught, and married some poor girl, whose pretty face had pleased his fancy. How glad 'Lina was to have this hold upon her brother, and how eagerly she went in quest of him, keeping back old Chloe and Hannah until she had witnessed his humiliation.

Somewhat impatient of the long delay, Hugh sat in the dingy kitchen, when 'Lina appeared, and with an air of injured dignity, bade him follow her.

"What's up now that Ad looks so solemn like?" was Hugh's mental comment as he took his way to the room where, in a half reclining position sat Adah, her large, bright eyes fixed eagerly upon the door through which he entered, and a bright flush upon her cheek called up by the suspicions to which she had been subjected.

Perhaps they might be true. Nobody knew but Hugh, and she waited for him so anxiously, starting when she heard a manly step and knew that he was coming. For an instant she scanned his face curiously to assure herself that it was he, then with an imploring cry as if for him to save her from some dreaded evil, she stretched her little hands toward him and sobbed: "Mr. Worthington, was it true? Was it as his letter said?" and shedding back from her white face the wealth of flowing hair, Adah waited for the answer, which did not come at once. In utter amazement Hugh gazed upon the stranger, and then exclaimed:

"Adah, Adah Hastings, why are you here?"

In the tone of his voice surprise and pity were mingled with disapprobation, the latter of which Adah detected at once, and as if it had crushed out the last lingering hope, she covered her face with her hands and sobbed piteously.

"Don't you turn against me, or I'll surely die, and I've come so far to find you."

By this time Hugh was himself again. His rapid, quick-seeing mind had come to a decision, and turning to his mother and sister, he said:

"Leave us alone for a time."

Rather reluctantly Mrs. Worthington and her daughter left the room. Deliberately turning the key in the lock, Hugh advanced to her side, groaning as his eye fell upon the child, which had fallen asleep again.

"I hoped this might have been spared her," he thought, as, kneeling by the couch, he said, kindly: "Adah, I am more pained to see you here than I can express. Why did you come, and where is—"

The name was lost to 'Lina, and muttering to herself: "It does not sound much like a man and wife," she rather unwillingly quitted her position, and Hugh was really alone with Adah.

Never was Hugh in so awkward a position before, or so uncertain how to act. The sight of that sobbing, trembling wretched creature, whose heart he had helped to crush, had perfectly unmanned him, making him almost as much a woman as herself.

"Oh, what made you? Why didn't you save me?" she said, looking up to him with an expression of reproach.

He had no excuse. He knew how innocent she was, and he held her in his arms as he would once have held the Golden Haired, had she come to him with a tale of woe.

"Let me see that letter again," he said.

She gave it to him; and he read once more the cruel lines, in which there was still much of love for the poor thing, to whom they were addressed.

"You will surely find friends who will care for you, until the time when I may come to really make you mine."

Hugh repeated these words twice, aloud, his heart throbbing with the noble resolve, that the confidence she had placed in him by coming there, should not be abused, for he would be true to the trust, and care for the poor, little, half crazed Adah, moaning so piteously beside him, and as he read the last line, saying eagerly:

"He speaks of coming back. Do you think he ever will? or could I find him if I should try? I thought of starting once, but it was so far; and there was Willie. Oh, if he could see Willie! Mr. Worthington, do you believe he loves me one bit?"

Hugh said at last, that the letter contained many assurances of affection.

"It seems family pride has something to do with it. I wonder where his people live, or who they are? Did he never tell you?"

"No," and Adah shook her head mournfully.

"Would you go to them?" Hugh asked quickly; and Adah answered:

"Sometimes I've thought I would. I'd brave his proud mother—I'd lay Willie in her lap. I'd tell her whose he was, and then I'd go away and die." Then, after a pause, she continued: "Once, Mr. Worthington, I went down to the river, and said I'd end my wretched life, but God held me back. He cooled my scorching head—He eased the pain, and on the very spot where I meant to jump, I kneeled down and said: 'Our Father.' No other words would come, only these: 'Lead us not into temptation.' Wasn't it kind in God to save me?"

There was a radiant expression in the sweet face as Adah said this, but it quickly passed away and was succeeded by one of deep concern when Hugh abruptly said:

"Do you believe in God?"

"Oh, Mr. Worthington. Don't you? You do, you must, you will," and Adah shrank away from him as from a monster.

The action reminded him of the Golden Haired, when on the deck of the *St. Helena* he had asked her a similar question, and anxious further to probe the opinion of the girl beside him, he continued:

"If, as you think, there is a God who knew and saw when you were about to drown yourself, why didn't He prevent the cruel wrong to you? Why did He suffer it?"

"What He does we know not now, but we shall know hereafter," Adah said, reverently, adding: "If George had feared God, he would not have left me so; but he didn't, and perhaps he says there is no God—but you don't, Mr. Worthington. Your face don't look like it. Tell me you believe," and in her eagerness Adah grasped his arm beseechingly.

"Yes, Adah, I believe," Hugh answered, half jestingly, "but it's such as you that make me believe, and as persons of your creed think everything is ordered for good, so possibly you were permitted to suffer that you might come here and benefit me. I think I must keep you, Adah, at least, until he is found."

"No, no," and the tears flowed at once, "I cannot be a burden to you. I have no claim."

After a moment she grew calm again, and continued:

"You whispered, you know, that if I was ever in trouble, come to you, and that's why I remembered you so well, maybe. I wrote down your name, and where you lived, though why I did not know, and I forgot where I put it, but as if God really were helping me I found it in my old portfolio, and something bade me come, for you would know if it was true, and your words had a meaning of which I did not dream when I was so happy. George left me money, and sent more, but it's most gone now. I can take care of myself."

"What can you do?" Hugh asked, and Adah replied:

"I don't know, but God will find me something. I never worked much, but I can learn, and I can already sew neatly, too; besides that, a few days before I decided to come here, I advertised in the *Herald* for some place as governess or ladies' waiting maid. Perhaps I'll hear from that."

"It's hardly possible. Such advertisements are thick as blackberries," Hugh said, and then in a few brief words, he marked out Adah's future course.

George Hastings might or might not return to claim her, and

whether he did or didn't, she must live meantime, and where so well as at Spring Bank, or who, next to Mr. Hastings, was more strongly bound to care for her than himself?

"To be sure, he did not like women much," he said; "their artificial fooleries disgusted him. There wasn't one woman in ten thousand that was what she seemed to be. But even men are not all alike," he continued, with something like a sneer, for when Hugh got upon his favorite hobby, "women and their weaknesses," he generally grew bitter and sarcastic. "Now, there's the one of whom you are continually thinking. I dare say you have contrasted him with me and thought how much more elegant he was in his appearance. Isn't it so?" and Hugh glanced at Adah, who, in a grieved tone, replied:

"No, Mr. Worthington, I have not compared you with him—I have only thought how good you were."

Hugh knew Adah was sincere, and said:

"I told you I did not like women much, and I don't but I'm going to take care of you until that scoundrel turns up; then, if you say so, I'll surrender you to his care, or better yet, I'll shoot him and keep you to myself. Not as a sweetheart, or anything of that kind," he hastened to add, as he saw the flush on Adah's cheek. "Hugh Worthington has nothing to do with that species of the animal kingdom, but as my Sister Adah!" and as Hugh repeated that name, there arose in his great heart an indefinable wish that the gentle girl beside him had been his sister instead of the high-tempered Adaline, who never tried to conciliate or understand him, and whom, try as he might, Hugh could not love as brothers should love sisters.

He knew how impatiently she was waiting now to know the result of that interview, and just how much opposition he should meet when he announced his intention of keeping Adah. Hugh was master of Spring Bank, but though its rightful owner, Hugh was far from being rich, and many were the shifts and self-denials he was obliged to make to meet the increased expense entailed upon him by his mother and sister. John Stanley had been accounted very wealthy, and Hugh, who had often seen him counting out his gold, was not a little surprised when, after his death, no ready money could be found, or any account of the same—nothing but the Spring Bank property, consisting of sundry acres of nearly wornout land, the old, dilapidated house, and a dozen or more negroes. This to a certain extent was the secret of his patched boots, his threadbare coat and coarse pants, with which 'Lina so often taunted him, saying he wore them just to be stingy and mortify her, she knew he did, when in fact necessity rather than choice was the cause of his shabby appearance. He had never told her so, however, never said that the unfashionable coat so offensive to her fastidious vision was worn that she might be the better clothed and fed. But Hugh was capable of great self-sacrifices. He could manage somehow, and Adah should stay. He would say that she was a friend whom he had known in New York, that her husband had deserted her, and in her distress she had come to him for aid.

All this he explained to Adah, who assented tacitly, thinking within herself that she should not long remain at Spring Bank, a dependent upon one on whom she had no claim. She was too weak now, however, to oppose him, and merely nodding to his suggestions laid her head upon the arm of the lounge with a low cry that she was sick and warm. Stepping to the door Hugh turned the key, and summoning the group waiting anxiously in the adjoining room, bade them come at once, as Mrs. Hastings appeared to be fainting. Great emphasis he laid upon the Mrs. and catching it up at once 'Lina repeated, "Mrs. Hastings! So am I just as much."

"Ad," and the eyes which shone so softly on poor Adah flashed with gleams of fire as Hugh said to his sister, "not another word against that girl if you wish to remain here longer. She has been unfortunate."

"I guessed as much," sneeringly interrupted 'Lina.

"Silence!" and Hugh's foot came down as it sometimes did when chiding a refractory negro. "She is as true, yes, truer, than you. He who should have protected her has basely deserted her. There is a reason which I do not care to explain, why I should care for her and I shall do it. See that a fire is kindled in the west chamber, and go up yourself when it is made and see that all is comfortable. Do you understand?" and he gazed sternly at 'Lina, who was too much astonished to answer, even if she had been so disposed.

Quick as thought, 'Lina darted up a back stairway, and when, half an hour later, Hugh, hearing mysterious sounds above, and suspecting something wrong, went up to reconnoiter, he found Hannah industriously pulling the tacks from the carpet, preparatory to taking it up. In thunder tones, he demanded what she was doing, and with a start, which made her drop tacks, hammer, saucer and all, Hannah replied:

"Lor', Mas'r Hugh, how you skeered me! Miss 'Lina done order me to take up de carpet, 'case it's ole miss's, and she won't have no low-lived truck tramplin' over it. That's what Miss 'Lina say," and Hannah tossed her head quite conceitedly.

"Miss 'Lina be hanged," was Hugh's savage response; "and you, woman, do you hear?—drive those nails back faster than you took them out."

"Yes, mas'r," and Hannah hastened down. Whispering to her mistress, Hannah told what Hugh had said, and instantly there came over Mrs. Worthington's face a look of concern, as if she, too, objected to having the stranger occupy a room wherein an ex-governor had slept, but Hugh's wish was law to her, and she answered that all was ready. A moment after, Hugh appeared, and taking Adah in his arms, carried her to the upper chamber, where the fire was burning brightly, casting cheerful shadows upon the wall, and making Adah smile gratefully, as she looked up in his face, and murmured:

"God bless you, Mr. Worthington! Adah will pray for you tonight, when she is alone. It's all that she can do."

They laid her upon the bed, Hugh himself arranging her pillows, which no one else appeared inclined to touch.

Family opinion was against her, innocent and beautiful as she looked lying there—so helpless, so still, with her long-fringed lashes shading her colorless cheek, and her little hands folded upon her bosom, as if already she were breathing the promised prayer for Hugh. Only in Mrs. Worthington's heart was there a chord of sympathy. She couldn't help feeling for the desolate stranger; and when, at her own request, Hannah placed Willie in her lap, ere laying him by his mother, she gave him an involuntary hug, and touched her lips to his fat, round cheek.

"He looks as you did, Hugh, when you were a baby like him," she said, while Chloe rejoined:

"De very spawn of Mas'r Hugh, now. I 'tected it de fust minit. Can't cheat dis chile," and, with a chuckle, which she meant to be very expressive, the fat old woman waddled from the room.

Hugh and his mother were alone, and turning to her son, Mrs. Worthington said, gently:

"This is sad business, Hugh; worse than you imagine. Do you know how folks will talk?"

"Let them talk," Hugh growled. "It cannot be much worse than it is now. Nobody cares for Hugh Worthington; and why should they, when his own mother and sister are against him, in actions if not in words?—one sighing when his name is mentioned, as if he really were the most provoking son that ever was born, and the other openly berating him as a monster, a clown, a savage, a scarecrow, and all that. I tell you, mother, there is but little to encourage me in the kind of life I'm leading. Neither you nor Ad have tried to make anything of me."

Choking with tears, Mrs. Worthington said:

"You wrong me, Hugh; I do try to make something of you. You are a dear child to me, dearer than the other, but I'm a weak woman, and 'Lina sways me at will."

A kind word unmanned Hugh at once, and kneeling by his mother, he put his arms around her, and asked again her care for Adah.

"Hugh," and Mrs. Worthington looked him steadily in the face, "is Adah your wife, or Willie your child?"

"Great guns, mother!" and Hugh started to his feet as quick as if a bomb had exploded at his side. "No! Are you sorry, mother, to find me better than you imagined it possible for a bad boy like me to be?"

"No, Hugh, not sorry. I was only thinking that I've sometimes fancied that, as a married man, you might be happier, even if you did lose Spring Bank; and when this woman came so strangely, and you seemed so interested, I didn't know, I rather thought—"

"I know," and Hugh interrupted her. "You thought, maybe, I raised Ned when I was in New York; and, as a proof of said resurrection, Mrs. Ned and Ned, Junior, had come with their baggage."

If the hair was golden instead of brown, and the eyes a different shade, he shouldn't "make so tremendous a fuss," he thought; and, with a sigh to the memory of the lost Golden Hair, he turned abruptly to his mother, and as if she had all the while been cognizant of his thoughts, said:

"But that's nothing to do with the case in question. Will you be kind to Adah Hastings, for my sake? And when Ad rides her highest horse, as she is sure to do, will you smooth her down? Tell her Adah has as good a right here as she, if I choose to keep her."

"I never meddle with your affairs," and there was a tone of whining complaint in Mrs. Worthington's voice; "I never pry and you never tell, so I don't know how much you are worth, but I can judge somewhat, and I don't think you are able."

Mrs. Worthington was much more easily won over to Hugh's opinion than 'Lina. They'd be a county talk, she said; nobody would come near them; hadn't Hugh enough on his hands already without taking more?

"If my considerate sister really thinks so, hadn't she better try and help herself a little?" retorted Hugh in a blaze of anger.

'Lina began to cry, and Hugh, repenting of his harsh speech as soon as it was uttered, but far too proud to take it back, strode up and down the room, chafing like a young lion.

"Come children, it's after midnight, let us adjourn until tomorrow," Mrs. Worthington said, by way of ending the painful interview, at the same time handing a candle to Hugh, who took it silently and withdrew, banging the door behind him with a force which made 'Lina start and burst into a fresh flood of tears.

"I'm a brute, a savage, and want to kick myself," was Hugh's not very self-complimentary soliloquy, as he went up the stairs. "What did I want to twit Ad for? Confound my badness!" and having by this time reached his own door, Hugh sat down to think.

CHAPTER III

HUGH'S SOLILOQUY

"One, two three—yes, as good as four women and a child," he began, "to say nothing of the negroes, and that is not the worst of it; the hardest of all is the having people call me stingy, and the knowing that this opinion of me is encouraged and kept alive by the remarks and insinuations of my own sister," and in the red gleam of the firelight the bearded chin quivered for a moment as Hugh thought how unjust 'Lina was to him, and how hard was the lot imposed upon him.

Then shifting the position of his feet, which had hitherto rested upon the hearth, to a more comfortable and suggestive one upon the mantel, Hugh tried to find a spot in which he could economize.

"I needn't have a fire in my room nights," he said, as a coal fell into the pan and thus reminded him of its existence, "and I won't, either. It's nonsense for a great hot-blooded clown, like me to be babied with a fire. I've no tags to braid, no false switches to comb out and hide, no paint to wash off, only a few buttons to undo, a shake or so, and I'm all right. So there's one thing, the fire—quite an item, too, at the rate coal is selling. Then there's coffee. I can do without that, I suppose, though it will be perfect torment to smell it, and Hannah makes such splendid coffee, too; but will is everything. Fire, coffee—I'm getting on famously. What else?"

"Tobacco," something whispered, but Hugh answered promptly: "No, sir, I shan't! I'll sell my shirts, the new ones Aunt Eunice made, before I'll give up my best friend. It's all the comfort I have when I get a fit of the blues. Oh, you needn't try to come it!" and Hugh shook his head defiantly at his unseen interlocutor, urging that 'twas a filthy practice at best, and productive of no good.

Horses was suggested again. "You have other horses than Bet," and Hugh was conscious of a pang which wrung from him a groan, for his horses were his idols. The best-trained in the country, they occupied a large share of his affections, making up to him for the friendship he rarely sought in others, and parting with them would be like severing a right hand. It was too terrible to think about, and Hugh dismissed it as an alternative which might have to be considered another time. Then hope made her voice heard above the little blue imps tormenting him so sadly.

He should get along somehow. Something would turn up. Ad might marry and go away. What made her so different from his mother? He had loved her, and he thought of her now as she used to look when in her dainty white frocks, with the strings of coral he had bought with nuts picked on the New England hills.

He used to kiss those chubby arms—kiss the rosy cheeks, and the soft brown hair. But that hair had changed sadly since the days when its owner had first lisped his name, and called him "Ugh," for the bands and braids coiled around 'Lina's haughty head were black as midnight. Not less changed than 'Lina's tresses was 'Lina herself, and Hugh, strong man that he was, had often felt like crying for the little baby sister, so lost and dead to him in her young womanhood. What had changed Ad so?

There was many a tender spot in Hugh Worthington's heart, and shadow after shadow flitted across his face as he thought how cheerless was his life, and how little there was in his surroundings to make him happy. There was nothing he would not do for people if approached in the right way, but nobody cared for him, unless it were his mother and Aunt Eunice. They seemed to like him, and he reckoned they did, but for the rest, who was there that ever thought of doing him a kindness? Poor Hugh! It was a dreary picture he drew as he sat alone that night, brooding over his troubles, and listening to the moan of the wintry wind—the only sound he heard, except the rattling of the shutters and the creaking of the timbers, as the old house rocked in the December gale.

Suddenly there crept into his mind Adah's words, "I shall pray for you tonight." He never prayed, and the Bible given by Golden Hair had not been opened this many a day. Since his dark sin toward Adah he had felt unworthy to touch it, but now that he was doing what he could to atone, he surely might look at it, and unlocking the trunk where it was hidden, he took it from its concealment and opened it reverently, half wondering what he should read first, and if it would have any reference to his present position.

"Inasmuch as ye did it to the least of these ye did it unto Me."

That was what Hugh read in the dim twilight, that the passage on which the lock of hair lay, and the Bible dropped from his hands as he whispered:

"Golden Hair, are you here? Did you point that out to me? Does it mean Adah? Is the God you loved on earth pleased that I should care for her?"

To these queries, there came no answer, save the mournful wailing of the night wind roaring down the chimney and past the sleet-covered window, but Hugh was a happier man for reading that, and had there before existed a doubt as to his duty toward Adah, this would have swept it away.

CHAPTER IV

TERRACE HILL

The storm which visited Kentucky so wrathfully, and was far milder among the New England hills, and in the vicinity of Snowdon, whither our story now tends, was scarcely noticed, save as an ordinary winter's storm. As yet it had been comparatively warmer in New England than in Kentucky; and Miss Anna Richards, confirmed invalid though she was, had decided that inasmuch as Terrace Hill mansion now boasted a furnace in the cellar, it would hardly be necessary to take her usual trip to the South, so comfortable was she at home, in her accustomed chair, with her pretty crimson shawl wrapped gracefully around her. Besides that, they were expecting her Brother John from Paris, where he had been for the last eighteen months, pursuing his medical profession, and she must be there to welcome him.

Anna was proud of her young, handsome brother, as were the entire family, for on him and his success in life all their future hopes were pending. Aside from being proud, Anna was also very fond of John, because as all were expected to yield to her wishes, she had never been crossed by him, and because he was nearer to her own age, and had evidently preferred her to either of his more stately sisters, Miss Asenath and Miss Eudora, whose birthdays were very far distant from his.

John had never been very happy at home—never liked Snowdon much, and hence the efforts they were putting forth to make it attractive to him after his long absence. He could not help but like home now, the ladies said to each other, as, a few days before his arrival, they rode from the village, where they had been shopping, up the winding terraced hill, admiring the huge stone building embosomed in evergreens, and standing out so distinctly against the wintry sky. And indeed Terrace Hill mansion was a very handsome place, exciting the envy and admiration of the villagers, who, while commenting upon its beauty and its well-kept grounds, could yet remember a time when it had looked better even than it did now—when the house was oftener full of city company, of sportsmen who came up to hunt, and fish, and drink, as it was sometimes hinted by the servants, of whom there was then a greater number than at present—when high-born ladies rode up and down in carriages, or dashed on horseback through the park and off into the leafy woods—when sounds of festivity were heard in the halls from year's end to year's end, and the lights in the parlors were rarely extinguished, or the fires on the hearth put out. All this was during the lifetime of its former owner. With his death there had come a change to the inhabitants of Terrace Hill. In short it was whispered rather loudly now that the ladies of Terrace Hill were restricted in their means, that it was harder to collect a bill from them than it used to be, that there was less display of dress and style, fewer fires, and lights, and servants, and withdrawal from society, and an apparent desire to be left to themselves.

This was what the village people whispered, and none knew the truth of the whisperings better than the ladies in question. They knew they were growing poorer with each succeeding year, but it was not the less mortifying to be familiarly accosted by Mrs. Deacon Briggs, or invited to a sociable by Mrs. Roe.

How Miss Asenath and Miss Eudora writhed under the infliction, and how hard they tried to appear composed and ladylike just as they would deem it incumbent upon them to appear, had they been on their way to the gallows. How glad, too, they were when their aristocratic doors closed upon the little, talkative Mrs. Roe, and what a good time they had wondering how Mrs. Johnson, who really was as refined and cultivated as themselves, could associate with such folks to the extent she did. She was always present at the Snowdon sewing circles, they heard, and frequently at its tea-drinkings, while never was there a sickbed but she was sure to find it, particularly if the sick one were poor and destitute. This was very commendable and praiseworthy, they admitted, but they did not see how she could endure it. Once Miss Asenath had ventured to ask her, and she had answered that all her best, most useful lessons, were learned in just such places—that she was better for these visits, and found her purest enjoyments in them. To Miss Asenath and Miss Eudora, this was inexplicable, but Anna, disciplined by years of ill health, had a slight perception of higher, purer motives than any which actuated the family at Terrace Hill. On the occasion of little Mrs. Roe's call it was Anna who apologized for her presumption, saying that Mrs. Roe really had the kindest of hearts; besides, it was quite natural for the villagers not to stand quite so much in awe of them now that their fortune was declining, and as they could not make circumstances conform to them, they must conform to circumstances. Neither Asenath nor Eudora, nor the lady mother liked this kind of conformation, but Anna was generally right, and they did not annihilate Mrs. Roe with a contemptuous frown as they had fully intended doing. Mrs. Johnson and her daughter Alice had been present, they heard, the latter actually joining in some of the plays, and the new clergyman, Mr. Howard, had suffered himself to be caught by Miss Alice, who disfigured her luxuriant curls with a bandage, and played at blindman's buff. This proved conclusively to the elder ladies of Terrace Hill that ministers were no better than other people, and they congratulated themselves afresh upon their escape from having one of the brotherhood in thir family.

In this escape Anna was particularly interested, as it had helped to make her the delicate creature she was, for since the morning when she had knelt at her proud father's feet, and begged him to revoke his cruel decision, and say she might be the bride of a poor missionary, Anna had greatly changed, and the father, ere he died, had questioned the propriety of separating the hearts which clung so together. But the young missionary had married another, and neither the parents nor the sisters ever forgot the look of anguish which stole into Anna's face, when she heard the fatal news. She had thought herself prepared, but the news was just as crushing when it came, accompanied, though it was with a few last lines from him. Anna kept this letter yet, wondering if the missionary remembered her yet, and if they would ever meet again. This was the secret of the missionary papers scattered so profusely through the rooms at Terrace Hill. Anna was interested in everything pertaining to the work, though, it must be confessed, that her mind wandered oftenest to the banks of the Bosphorus, the City of Mosques and Minarets, where he was laboring. Neither the mother, nor Asenath, nor Eudora ever spoke to her of him, and so his name was never heard at Terrace Hill, unless John mentioned it, as he sometimes did, drawing comical pictures of what Anna would have been by this time had she married the missionary.

Anna only laughed at her wild brother's comments, telling him once to beware, lest he, too, follow her example, and was guilty of loving some one far beneath him. John Richards had spurned the idea. The wife who bore his name should be every way worthy of a Richards. This was John's theory, nursed and encouraged by mother and sisters, the former charging him to be sure and keep his heart from all save the right one. Had he done so?

A peep at the family as on the day of his expected arrival from Paris they sat waiting for him will enlighten us somewhat. Taken as a whole, it was a very pleasant family group, which sat there waiting for the foreign lion, waiting for the whistle of the engine which was to herald his approach.

"I wonder if he has changed," said the mother, glancing at the opposite mirror and arranging the puffs of glossy false hair which shaded her aristocratic forehead.

"Of course he has changed somewhat," returned Miss Asenath, rubbing together her white, bony hands, on one of which a costly diamond was flashing. "Nearly two years of Paris society must have imparted to him that *air distingué* so desirable in a young man who has traveled."

"He'll hardly fail of making a good match now," Miss Eudora remarked, caressing the pet spaniel which had climbed into her lap. "I think we must manage to visit Saratoga or some of those places next summer. Mr. Gardner found his wife at Newport, and they say she's worth half a million."

"But horridly ugly," and Anna looked up from the reverie in which she had been indulging. "Lottie says she has tow hair and a face like a fish. John would never be happy with such a wife."

"Possibly you think he had better have married that sewing girl about whom he wrote us just before going to Europe," Miss Eudora said spitefully, pinching the long silken ears of her pet until the animal yelled with pain.

There was a faint sigh from the direction of Anna's chair, and all knew she was thinking of the missionary. The mother continued:

"I trust he is over that fancy, and ready to thank me for the strong letter I wrote him."

"Yes, but the girl," and Anna leaned her white cheek in her whiter hand. "None of us know the harm his leaving her may have done. Don't you remember he wrote how much she loved him—how gentle and confiding her nature was, and how to leave her then might prove her ruin?"

"Our little Anna is growing very eloquent upon the subject of sewing girls," Miss Asenath said, rather scornfully, and Anna rejoined:

"I am not sure she was a sewing girl. He spoke of her as a schoolgirl."

"But it is most likely he did that to mislead us," said the mother. "The only boarding school he knows anything about is the one where Lottie was. If he were not her uncle by marriage I should not object to Lottie as a daughter," was the next remark, whereupon there ensued a conversation touching the merits and demerits of a certain Lottie Gardner, whose father had taken for a second wife Miss Laura Richards.

This Laura had died within a year of her marriage, but Lottie had claimed relationship to the family just the same, grandmaing Mrs. Richards and aunty-ing the sisters. John, however, was never called uncle, except in fun. He was too near her age, the young lady frequently declaring that she had half a mind to throw aside all family ties and lay siege to the handsome young man, who really was very popular with the fair sex. During this discussion of Lottie, Anna had sat listlessly looking up and down the columns of an old*Herald*, which Dick, Eudora's pet dog, had ferreted out from the table and deposited at her feet. She evidently was not thinking of Lottie, nor yet of the advertisements, until one struck her notice as being very singular. Holding it a little more to the light she said: "Possibly this is the very person I want—only the child might be an objection. Just listen," and Anna read as follows:

"Wanted—By an unfortunate young married woman, with a child a few months old, a situation in a private family either as governess, seamstress, or lady's maid. Country preferred. Address—"

Anna was about to say whom when a violent ringing of the bell announced an arrival, and the next moment a tall young man, exceedingly Frenchified in his appearance, entered the room, and was soon in the arms of his mother.

John, hastening to where Anna sat, wound his arms around her light figure, and kissed her white lips and looked into her face with an expression, which told that, however indifferent he might be to others, he was not so to Anna.

"You have not changed for the worse," he said. "You are scarcely thinner than when I went away."

"And you are vastly improved," was Anna's answer.

His mother continued: "I thought, perhaps, you were offended at my plain letter concerning that girl, and resented it by not coming, but of course you are glad now, and see that mother was right. What could you have done with a wife in Paris?"

"I should not have gone," John answered, moodily, a shadow stealing over his face.

It was not good taste for Mrs. Richards thus early to introduce a topic on which John was really so sore, and for a moment an awkward silence ensued, broken at last by the mother again, who, feeling that all was not right, and anxious to know if there was yet aught to fear from a poor, unknown daughter-in-law, asked, hesitatingly:

"Have you seen her since your return?"

"She's dead," was the laconic reply, and then, as if anxious to change the conversation, the young doctor turned to Anna and said: "Guess who was my fellow traveler from Liverpool?"

Anna never could guess anything, and after a little her brother said:

"The Rev. Charles Millbrook, missionary to Turkey, returning for his health."

For an instant Anna trembled as if she saw opening before her the grave which for fourteen years had held her buried heart. Charlie was breathing again the air of the same hemisphere with herself. She might, perhaps, see him once more, and Hattie, was she with him, or was there another grave made with the Moslem dead by little Anna's aide? She would not ask, for she felt the cold, critical eyes bent upon her from across the hearth, and a few commonplace inquiries was all she ventured upon. Had Mr. Millbrook greatly changed since he went away? Did he look very sick? And how had her brother liked him?

"I scarcely spoke to him," was John's reply. "I confess to a most lamentable ignorance touching the Rev. Mr. Millbrook and his family. He wore crape on his hat, I remember, but there was a lady with him to whom he was quite attentive, and who, I think, was called by his name."

"Tall, with black eyes, like Lottie's?" Anna meekly asked, and John replied: "Something after the Lottie order, though more like yourself."

"It's strange I never saw a notice of his expected return," was

Anna's next remark. "Perhaps it was in the last *Missionary Herald*. You have not found it yet, have you, mother?"

The ringing of the supper bell prevented Mrs. Richards from answering. How gracefully he did the honors, and how proud all were of him, as he repeated little incidents of Parisian life, speaking of the emperor and Eugenie as if they had been everyday sights to him. In figure and form the fair empress reminded him of Anna, he said, except that Anna was the prettier of the two—a compliment which Anna acknowledged with a blush and a trembling of her long eyelashes. It was a very pleasant family reunion, for John did his best to be agreeable.

"Oh, John, please be careful. There's an advertisement I want to save," Anna exclaimed, as she saw her brother tearing a strip from the *Herald* with which to light his cigar, but as she spoke, the flame curled around the narrow strip, and Dr. Richards had lighted his cigar with the name and address appended to the advertisement which had so interested Anna.

How disturbed she was when she found that nought was left save the simple wants of the young girl.

"Let's see," and taking the mutilated sheet, Dr. Richards read the "Wanted, by a young unfortunate married woman."

"That unfortunate may mean a great deal more than you imagine," he said.

"Yes, but she distinctly says married. Don't you see, and I had really some idea of writing to her."

"I'm sorry I was so careless, but there are a thousand unfortunate women who would gladly be your maid, little sister. I'll send you out a score, if you say so," and John laughed.

"Has anything of importance occurred in this slow old town?" he inquired, after Anna had become reconciled to her loss. "Are the people as odd as usual?"

"Yes, more so," Miss Eudora thought, "and more presuming," whereupon she rehearsed the annoyances to which they had been subjected from their changed circumstances, dwelling at length upon Mrs. Roe's tea drinking, and the insult offered by inviting them, when she knew there would be no one present with whom they associated.

"You forget Mrs. Johnson," interposed Anna. "We would be glad to know her better than we do, she is so refined and cultivated in all her tastes, while Alice is the sweetest girl I ever knew. By the way, brother, they have come here since you left, consequently you have a rare pleasure in store, the forming their acquaintance."

"Whose, the old or the young lady's?" John asked.

"Both," was Anna's reply. "The mother is very youthful in her appearance. Why, she scarcely looks older than I, and I, you know, am thirty-two."

As if fearful lest her own age should come next under consideration, Miss Eudora hastened to say:

"Yes, Mrs. Johnson does look very young, and Alice seems like a child. Such beautiful hair as she has. It used to be a bright yellow, or golden, but now it has a darker, richer shade, while her eyes are the softest, handsomest blue."

Alice Johnson was evidently a favorite, and this stamped her somebody, so John began to ask who the Johnsons were.

Mrs. Richards seemed disposed to answer, which she did as follows:

"Mrs. Johnson used to live in Boston, and her husband was grandson of old Governor Johnson."

"Ah, yes," and John began to laugh. "I see now what gives Miss Alice's hair that peculiar shade, and her eyes that heavenly blue; but go on, mother, and give her figure as soon as may be."

"What do you mean?" asked Anna. "I should suppose you'd care more for her face than her form."

John smiled mischievously, while his mother continued:

"I fancy that Mrs. Johnson's family met with a reverse of fortune before her marriage. I do not see her as often as I would like to, for I am greatly pleased with her, although she has some habits of which I cannot approve. Why, I hear that Alice had a party the other day consisting-wholly of ragged urchins."

"They were her Sabbath school scholars," interposed Anna.

"I vote that Anna goes on with Alice's history. She gives it best," said John, and so Anna continued:

"There is but little more to tell. Mrs. Johnson and her daughter are both nice ladies, and I am sure you will like them—everybody does; and rumor has already given Alice to our young clergyman, Mr. Howard."

"And she is worth fifty thousand dollars, too," rejoined Asenath.

"I have her figure at last," said John, winking slyly at Anna.

And, indeed, the fifty thousand dollars did seem to make an impression on the young man, who grew interested at once, making numerous inquiries, asking where he would be most likely to see her.

"At church," was Anna's reply. "She is always there, and their pew joins ours."

Dr. Richards was exceedingly vain, and his vanity manifested itself from the tie of his neckerchief down to the polish of his boots. Once, had Hugh Worthington known him intimately, he would have admitted that there was at least one man whose toilet occupied quite as much time as Adaline's. In Paris the vain doctor had indulged in the luxury of a valet, carefully keeping it a secret from his mother and sisters, who were often compelled to deny themselves that the money he asked for so often might be forthcoming. But that piece of extravagance was over now; he dared not bring his valet home, though he sadly wished him there as he meditated upon the appearance he would make in church next Sabbath. He was glad there was something new and interesting in Snowdon in the shape of a pretty girl, for he did not care to return at once to New York, where he had intended practicing his profession. There were too many sad memories clustering about that city to make it altogether desirable, but Dr. Richards was not yet a hardened wretch, and thoughts of another than Alice Johnson, with her glorious hair and still more glorious figure, crowded upon his mind as on that first evening of his return, he sat answering questions and asking others of his own.

It was late ere the family group broke up, and the storm, beating so furiously upon Spring Bank, was just making its voice heard around Terrace Hill mansion, when the doctor took the lamp the servant brought, and bidding his mother and sisters good-night, ascended the stairs whither Anna had gone before him. She was not, however, in bed, and called softly to him:

"John, Brother John, come in a moment, please."

CHAPTER V

ANNA AND JOHN

He found her in a tasteful gown, its heavy tassels almost sweeping the floor, while her long, glossy hair, loosened from its confinement of ribbon and comb, covered her neck and shoulders as she sat before the fire always kindled in her room.

"How picturesque you look," he said, gayly.

"John," and Anna's voice was soft and pleasing, "was Charlie greatly changed? Tell me, please."

"I was so young in the days when he came wooing that I hardly remember how he used to look. I should not have known him, but my impression is that he looks about as well as men of forty usually look."

"Not forty, John, only thirty-eight," Anna interposed.

"Well, thirty-eight, then. You remember his age remarkably well," John said, laughingly, adding: "Did you once love him very much?"

"Yes," and Anna's voice faltered a little.

"Why didn't you marry him, then?"

John spoke excitedly, and the flush deepened on his cheek when Anna answered meekly:

"Why didn't you marry that poor girl?"

"Why didn't I?" and John started to his feet; then he continued: "Anna, I tell you there's a heap of wrong for somebody to answer for, but it is not you, and it is not me—it's—it's mother!" and John whispered the word, as if fearful lest the proud, overbearing woman should hear.

"You are mistaken," Anna replied, "for as far as Charlie was concerned father had more to do with it than mother. I've never seen him since. He did marry another, but I've never quite believed that he forgot me."

Anna was talking now more to herself than to John, and Charlie, could he have seen her, would have said she was not far from the narrow way which leadeth unto life. To John her white face, irradiated with gleams of the soft firelight, was as the face of an angel, and for a time he kept silence before her, then suddenly exclaimed:

"Anna, you are good, and so was she, so good, so pure, so artless, and that made it hard to leave her, to give her up. Anna, do you know what my mother wrote me? Listen, while I tell, then see if she is not to blame. She cruelly reminded me that by my father's will all of us, save you, were wholly dependent upon her, and said the moment I threw myself away upon a low, vulgar, penniless girl, that moment she'd cast me off, and I might earn my bread and hers as best I could. She said, too, my sisters, Anna and all, sanctioned what she wrote, and your opinion had more weight than all the rest."

"Oh, John, mother could not have so misconstrued my words. Surely my note explained—I sent one in mother's letter."

"It never reached me," John said, while Anna sighed at this proof of her mother's treachery.

Always conciliatory, however, she soon remarked:

"You are sole male heir to the Richards name. Mother's heart and pride are bound up in you. A poor, unknown girl would only add to our expenses, and not help you in the least. What was her name? I've never heard."

John hesitated, then answered: "I called her Lily, she was so fair and pure."

Anna was never in the least suspicious, but took all things for granted, so now she thought within herself, "Lilian, most likely." Then she said: "You were not engaged to her, were you?"

John started forward, and gazed into his sister's face with an expression as if he wished she would question him more closely, but Anna never dreamed of a secret, and seeing him hesitate, she said:

"You need not tell me unless you like. I only thought, maybe, you and Lily were not engaged."

"We were. Anna, I'm a wretch—a miserable wretch, and have scarcely known an hour's peace since I left her."

"Was there a scene?" Anna asked; and John replied:

"Worse than that. Worse for her. She did not know I was going till I was gone. I wrote to her from Paris, for I could not meet her face and tell her how mean I was. I've thought of her so much, and when I landed in New York I went at once to find her, or at least to inquire, hoping she'd forgotten me. The beldame who kept the place was not the same with whom I had left Lily, but she know about her, and told me she died with cholera last September. She and—oh, Lily, Lily—" and hiding his face in Anna's lap, John Richards, whom we have only seen as a traveled dandy, sobbed like a little child.

"John," she said at last, when the sobbing had ceased, "You say this Lily was good. Do you mean she was a Christian, like Charlie?"

"Yes, if there ever was one. Why, she used to make a villain like me kneel with her every night, and say the Lord's Prayer."

For an instant, a puzzling thought crossed Anna's brain as to the circumstances which could have brought her brother every night to Lily's side, but it passed away immediately as she rejoined:

"Then she is safe in heaven, and there are no tears there. We'll try to meet her some day. You could not help her dying. She might have died had she been your wife, so I'd try to think it happened for the best, and you'll soon get to believing it did. That's my experience. You are young yet, and life has much in store for you. You'll find some one to fill Lily's place; some one whom we shall all think worthy of you, and *we'll* be so happy together."

She did not speak of Alice Johnson, but she thought of her. John, too, thought of Alice Johnson, wondering how she would look to him who might have married the daughter of a count. He had not told Anna of this, and he was about preparing to leave her, when, changing the conversation, she said:

"Did we ever write to you—no, we didn't—about that mysterious stranger, that man who stopped for a day or two at the hotel, nearly two years ago, and made so many inquiries about us and our place, pretending he wanted to buy it in exchange for city property, and that some one had told him it was for sale?"

"What man? Who was he?" John asked; and Anna replied:

"He called himself Bronson."

"Describe him," John said, settling back so that his face was partly concealed in the shadow.

"Rather tall, firmly-knit figure, with what I imagine people mean when they say a bullet-head, that is, a round, hard head, with keen gray eyes, sandy mustache, and a scar or something on his right temple. Are you cold?" and she turned quickly to her brother, who had shuddered involuntarily at her description, for well he knew now who that man was.

But why had he come there? This John did not know, and as it was necessary to appear natural, he answered to Anna's inquiry, that he thought he had taken cold, as the cars were badly warmed.

"But, go on; tell me more of this Bronson. He heard our house was for sale. How, pray?"

"From some one in New York; and the landlord suggested it might have been you."

"It's false. I never told him so," and John spoke savagely.

"Then you did know him? What was he? We were half afraid of him, he behaved so strangely," Anna said, looking wonderingly at her brother, whose face alternately flushed and then grew pale.

Simple little Anna, how John blessed her in his heart for possessing so little insight into the genuine springs of his character, for when he answered:

"Of course I don't know him—I mean that I never told any one that Terrace Hill was for sale."

She believed what he said, and very innocently continued:

"Had there been a trifle more of fun in my nature, I should, have teased Eudora, by telling her he came here to see her or Asenath. He was very curious for a sight of all of us."

"Did he come here—into the house?" John asked; and Anna replied:

"Why, yes. He was rather coarse looking, to be sure, with marks of dissipation, but very gentlemanly and even pleasing in his address."

Anna went on: "He was exceedingly polite—apologized for troubling me, and then stated his business. I told him he must have been misinformed, as we never dreamed of selling. He took his leave, looking back all the way through the park, and evidently examining minutely the house and grounds. Mother was so fidgety after it, declaring him a burglar, and keeping a watch for several nights after his departure."

"Undoubtedly he was," said John. "A burglar, I dare say, and you were fortunate, all of you, in not being stolen from your beds as you lay sleeping."

"Oh, we keep our doors locked," was Anna's demure reply.

"Midnight, as I live!" he exclaimed, and was glad of an excuse for retiring, as he wished now to be alone.

Anna had not asked him half what she had meant to ask concerning Charlie, but she would not keep him longer, and with a kiss upon his handsome brow she sent him away, herself holding the door a little ajar and listening to see what effect the new carpet would have upon him. It did not have any at first, so much was he absorbed in that man with the scar upon his temple. Why had he come there, and why had it not been told him before? His people were so stupid in their letters, never telling what was sure to interest him most. But what good could it have done had he known of the mysterious visit? None whatever—at least nothing particular had resulted from it, he was sure.

"It must have been just after one of his sprees, when he is always more than half befogged," he said to himself. "Possibly he was passing this way and the insane idea seized him to stop and pretend to buy Terrace Hill. The rascal!" and having thus satisfactorily settled it in his mind, the doctor did look at Anna's carpet, admiring its pattern, and having a kind of pleasant consciousness that everything was in keeping, from the handsome drapery which shaded the windows to the marble hearth on which a fire was blazing.

In Adah Hastings' dream that night there were visions of a little room far up in a fourth story, where her fair head was pillowed again upon the manly arm of one who listened while she chided him gently for his long delay, and then told him of their Willie boy so much like him, as the young mother thought.

In Dr. Richards' dreams, when at last he slept, there were visions of a lonely grave in a secluded part of Greenwood, and he heard again the startling words:

"Dead, both she and the child."

He did not know there was a child, and he staggered in his sleep, just as he staggered down the creaking stairs, repeating to himself:

"Lily's child—Lily's child. May Lily's God forgive me."

CHAPTER VI

ALICE JOHNSON

The Sabbath dawned at last. The doctor had not yet made his appearance in the village, and Saturday had been spent by him in rehearsing to his sisters and the servants the wonderful things he had seen abroad, and in lounging listlessly by a window which overlooked the town, and also commanded a view of the tasteful cottage by the riverside, where they told him Mrs. Johnson lived. One upper window he watched with peculiar interest, from the fact that, early in the day, a head had protruded from it a moment, as if to inhale the wintry air, and then been quickly withdrawn.

"Does Miss Johnson wear curls?" he asked, rather indifferently, with his eye still on the cottage by the river.

"Yes; a great profusion of them," was Mrs. Richards' reply, and then the doctor knew he had caught a glimpse of Alice Johnson, for the head he had seen was covered with curls, he was sure.

But little good did a view at that distance afford him. He must see her nearer ere he decided as to her merits to be a belle. He did not believe her face would at all compare with the one which continually haunted his dreams, and over which the coffin lid was shut weary months ago, but fifty thousand dollars had invested Miss Alice with that peculiar charm which will sometimes make an ugly face beautiful. The doctor was beginning to feel the need of funds, and now that Lily was dead, the thought had more than once crossed his mind that to set himself at once to the task of finding a wealthy wife was a duty he owed himself and his family. Had poor, deserted Lily lived; had he found her in New York, he could not tell what he might have done, for the memory of her sweet, gentle love was the one restraining influence which kept him from much sin. He never could forget her; never love another as he had once loved her, but she was dead, and it was better, so he reasoned, for now was he free to do his mother's will, and take a wife worthy of a Richards.

Anna was not with the party which at the usual hour entered the family carriage with Bibles and prayer books in hand. She seldom went out except on warm, pleasant days; but she stood in the deep bay window watching the carriage as it wound down the hill, thinking first how pleasant and homelike the Sabbath bells must sound to Charlie this day, and secondly, how handsome and stylish her young brother looked with his Parisian cloak and cap, which he wore so gracefully. Others than Anna thought so, too; and at the church door there was quite a little stir, as he gallantly handed out first his mother and then his sisters, and followed them into the church.

Dr. Richards had never enjoyed a reputation for being very

devotional, and the interval between his entrance and the commencement of the service was passed by him in a rather scornful survey of the timeworn house. With a sneer in his heart, he mentally compared the old-fashioned pulpit, with its steep flight of steps and faded trimmings, with the lofty cathedral he had been in the habit of attending in Paris, and a feeling of disgust and contempt was creeping over him, when a soft rustling of silk, and a consciousness of a delicate perfume, which he at once recognized as aristocratic, warned him that somebody was coming; somebody entirely different from the score of females who had distributed themselves within range of his vision, their countrified bonnets, as he termed them, trimmed outside and in without the least regard to taste, or combination of color. But the little lady, moving so quietly up the aisle—she was different. She was worthy of respect, and the Paris beau felt an inclination to rise at once and acknowledge her superior presence.

Wholly unconscious of the interest she was exciting, the lady deposited her muff upon the cushions, and then kneeling reverently upon the well-worn stool, covered her face with the hands which had so won the doctor's admiration. What a little creature she was, scarcely larger than a child twelve summers old, and how gloriously beautiful were the curls of indescribable hue, falling in such profusion from beneath the jaunty hat. All this Dr. Richards noted, marveling that she knelt so long, and wondering what she could be saying.

Alice's devotion ended at last, and the view so coveted was obtained; for in adjusting her dress Alice turned toward him, or rather toward his mother, and the doctor drew a sudden breath as he met the brilliant flashing of those laughing sunny blue eyes, and caught the radiant expression of that face, slightly dimpled with a smile. Beautiful, wondrously beautiful was Alice Johnson, and yet the features were not wholly regular, for the piquant nose had a slight turn up, and the forehead was not very high; but for all this, the glossy hair, the dancing blue eyes, the apple-blossom complexion, and the rosebud mouth made ample amends; and Dr. Richards saw no fault in that witching face, flashing its blue eyes for an instant upon him, and then modestly turning to the service just commencing. So absorbed was Dr. Richards as not to notice that the strain of music filling the old church did not come from the screeching melodeon he had so anathematized, but from an organ as mellow and sweet in its tone as any he had heard across the sea. He did not notice anything; and when his sister, surprised at his sitting posture, whispered to him of her surprise, he started quickly, and next time the congregation arose he was the first upon his feet, mingling his voice with that of Alice Johnson and even excelling her in the loudness of his reading!

As if divining his wishes in the matter, his mother turned to the eagerly expectant doctor, whom she introduced as "My son, Dr. Richards."

Alice had heard much of Dr. Richards from the young girls of Snowdon. She had heard his voice in the Psalter, his responses in the Litany, and accepted it as a sign of marked improvement. He could not be as irreverent and thoughtless as he had been represented by those who did not like him; he must have changed during his absence, and she frankly offered him her hand, and with a smile which he felt even to his finder tips, welcomed him home, making some trivial remark touching the contrast between their quiet town and the cities he had left.

"But you will help make it pleasanter for us this winter, I am sure," she continued, and the sweet blue eyes sought his for an answer as to whether he would desert Snowdon immediately.

What a weak, vacillating creature is man before a pretty woman like Alice Johnson. Twenty-four hours ago, and the doctor would have scoffed at the idea that he should tarry longer than a week or two at the farthest in that dull by-place, where the people were only half civilized; but now the tables were turned as by magic. Snowdon was as pretty a rural village as New England could boast, and he meant to enjoy it for a while. It would be a relief after the busy life he had led, and was just the change he needed! So, in answer to Alice's remark, he said he should probably remain at home some time, that he always found it rather pleasant at Snowdon, though as a boy he had, he supposed, often chafed at its dullness; but he saw differently now. Besides, it could not now be dull, with the acquisition it had received since he was there before; and he bowed gracefully toward the young lady, who acknowledged the compliment with a faint blush, and then turned toward the group of "noisy, ill-bred children," as Dr. Richards thought, who came thronging about her.

"My Sabbath school scholars," Alice said, as if in answer to these mental queries, "Ah, here comes my youngest—my pet," and Alice stooped to caress a little rosy-cheeked boy, with bright brown eyes and patches on both coat sleeves.

The doctor saw the patches, but not the handsome face, and with a gesture of impatience, turned to go, just as his ear caught another kiss, and he knew the patched boy received what he would have given much to have.

"Hanged if I don't half wish I was one of those ragged urchins," he said, after handing his mother and sisters to their carriage, and seating himself at their side. "But does not Miss Johnson display strange taste? Surely some other one less refined might be found to look after those brats, if they must be looked after, which I greatly doubt. Better leave them, as you find them; can't elevate them if you try. It's trouble thrown away."

Just before turning from the main road into the park which led to Terrace Hill, they met a stylish little covered sleigh. The colored driver politely touched big hat to the ladies, who leaned out a moment to look after him.

"That's Mrs. Johnson's turnout," said Eudora. "In the winter Martin always takes Alice to church and then returns for her."

"And folks say," interposed Asenath, "that if the walking is bad or the weather cold, both Alice and her mother go two miles out of their way to carry home some old woman or little child, who lives at a distance. I've seen Alice myself with half a dozen or more of these children, and she looked as proud and happy as a queen. Queer taste, isn't it?"

John thought it was, though he himself said: "It is like what Lily would have done, had she possessed the power and means."

"Well, brother, what of Miss Alice? Was she at church?" Anna asked softly. "I need not ask though, for of course she was. I should almost as soon think of hearing that Mr. Howard himself was absent as Alice."

"That reminds me," said John, "of what you said concerning Mr. Howard and Alice. There can't be any truth in it. She surely does not fancy him."

"Not as a lover," Anna replied. "She respects him greatly, however, because he is a clergyman."

"Is she then a very strong church woman?" John asked.

"Yes, but not a bit of a blue," Anna replied. "If all Christians were like Alice, religion would be divested of much of its supposed gloom. She shows it everywhere, and so does not have to wear it on set occasions to prove that she possesses it. How were you pleased with Miss Johnson?"

"How was I pleased with her? I felt like kissing the hem of her blue silk, of course! But I tell you, Anna, those ragged, dirty urchins who came trooping into that damask-cushioned pew, marred the picture terribly. What possible pleasure can she take in teaching them?"

Anna had an idea of the pleasure it might be to feel that one was doing good, but she could not explain lucidly, so she did not attempt it. She only said Miss Alice was very benevolent and received her reward in the love bestowed upon her so freely by those whom she befriended.

"And to win her good graces, must one pretend to be interested in those ragamuffins?" John asked, a little spitefully.

"Why, no, not unless they were. Alice could not wish you to be deceitful," was Anna's reply, after which a long silence ensued, and Anna dropped away to sleep, while her brother sat watching the fire blazing in the grate, and trying to decide as to his future course.

Should he return to New York, accept the offer of an old friend of his father's, an experienced practitioner, and thus earn his own bread honorably; or, should he remain a while at Snowdon and cultivate Alice Johnson? He had never yet failed when he chose to exert himself, and though he might, for a time, be compelled to adopt a different code of morality from that which he at present acknowledged, he would do it for once. He could be interested in those ragged children; he could encourage Sunday schools; he could attend church as regularly as Alice herself; and, better yet, he could doctor the poor for nothing, as that was sure to tell, and he would do it, too, if necessary. This was the finale which he reached at last by a series of arguments pro and con, and when it was reached, he was anxious to commence the task at once. He presumed he could love Alice Johnson; she was so pretty; but even if he didn't, he would only be doing what thousands had done before him. He should be very proud of her, and would certainly try to make her happy. One long, almost sobbing sigh to the memory of poor Lily, who had loved so much and been so cruelly betrayed, one faint struggle with conscience, which said that Alice Johnson was too pure a gem for him to trifle with, and then, the past, with its sad memories, was buried.

"Not going to church twice in one day!" Mrs. Richards exclaimed as the doctor threw aside the book he had been reading, and started for his cloak.

"Why, yes," he answered. "I liked that parson so much better than I expected, that I think I'll go again," and hurrying out, he was soon on his way to St. Paul's.

"Gone on foot, too, when it's so cold!" and the mother, who had risen and stood watching him from the window, spoke anxiously.

The service was commencing, but the doctor was in no hurry to take his seat. He would as soon be seen as not, and, vain fop that he was, he rather enjoyed the stirring of heads he felt would ensue when he moved up the aisle. At last he would wait no longer, and with a most deferential manner, as if asking pardon for disturbing the congregation, he walked to his pew door, and depositing his hat and cloak, sat down just where he meant to sit, next the little figure, at which he did not glance, knowing, of course, that it was Alice.

How then was he astonished and confounded when at the reading of the Psalter, another voice than hers greeted his ear!—a strange, sharp voice, whose tones were not as indicative of refinement as Alice's had been, and whose pronunciation, distinctly heard, savored somewhat of the so-called down East. He looked at her now, moving off a foot or more, and found her a little, odd, old woman, shriveled and withered, with velvet hat, not of the latest style, its well-kept strings of black vastly different from the glossy blue he had so much admired at an earlier period of the day. Was ever man more disappointed? Who was she, the old witch, for so he mentally termed the inoffensive woman devoutly conning her prayer book, unconscious of the wrath her presence was exciting in the bosom of the young man beside her! How he wished he had stayed at home, and were it not that he sat so far distant from the door, he would certainly have left in disgust. What a drawling tone was Mr. Howard's.

Such were the doctor's thoughts. But hark! Whose voice was that? The congregation seemed to hold their breath as the glorious singer warbled forth the birdlike strain, "Thou that takest away the sins of the world." She sang those words as if she felt them every one, and Dr. Richards' heart thrilled with an indefinable emotion us he listened. "Thou that sittest on the right hand of God the Father;" how rich and full her voice as she sang that alone; and when the final Amen was reached, and the grand old chant was ended, Dr. Richards sat like one entranced, straining his ear to catch the last faint echo of the sweetest music he had ever heard.

Could Alice sing like that, and who was this nightingale? How he wished he knew; and when next the people arose, obedient to the organ's call, he was of their number, and turning full about, looked up into the gallery, starting as he looked, and half uttering an exclamation of surprise. There was no mistaking the Russian sable fur, the wide blue ribbons thrown so gracefully back, the wealth of sunny hair, or the lustrous eyes, which swept for an instant over the congregation below, taking in him with the rest, and then were dropped upon the keys, where the snowy, ungloved hands were straying. The organist was Alice Johnson! There were no more regrets now that he had come to church, no more longings to be away, no more maledictions against Mr. Howard's drawling manner, no more invectives against the poor old woman, listening like himself with rapt attention, and wondering if the music of heaven could be sweeter than that her bonny Alice made. The doctor, too, felt better for such music, and he never remembered having been more attentive to a sermon in his life than to the one, which followed the evening service.

When it was ended, and the people dismissed, she came tripping down the stairs, flooding the dingy vestibule with a world of sunshine.

"Here, Aunt Densie, here I am. Martin is waiting for us," the doctor heard her say to the old lady, who was elbowing her way through the crowd, and who at last came to a standstill, apparently looking for something she could not find. "What is it, auntie?" Alice said again. "Lost something, have you? I'll be with you in a minute."

Two hours ago, and Dr. Richards would not have cared if fifty old women had lost their entire wardrobe. As an attache of some kind to Alice Johnson, Densie was an object of importance, and stepping forward, just as Alice had made her way to the distressed old lady's side, he very politely offered to assist in the search.

"Ah, Dr. Richards, thank you," Alice said, as the black kid was found, and passed to its anxious owner.

The doctor never dreamed of an introduction, for his practiced eye saw at once that however Alice might auntie her, the woman was still a servant. How then was he surprised when Alice said:

"Miss Densmore, this is Dr. Richards, from Terrace Hill," adding, in an aside to him: "My old nurse, who took care of both mother and myself when we were children."

They were standing in the door now, and the covered sleigh was drawn up just in front.

"Auntie first," she said, as they reached the carriage steps, and so the doctor was fain to help auntie in, whispering gallantly in an aside:

"Age before beauty always!"

"Thank you," and Alice's ringing laugh cut the winter air as she followed Densie Densmore, the doctor carefully wrapping her cloak about her, and asking if her fur was pulled up sufficiently around her neck.

"It's very cold," he said, glancing up at the glittering stars, scarcely brighter than the blue eyes flashing on him. "At least I found it so on my walk to church," and with a slight shiver the scheming doctor was bowing himself away, when Alice exclaimed:

"Did you walk this wintry night? Pray, gratify me then by accepting a seat in our sleigh. There's plenty of room without crowding auntie."

Happy Dr. Richards! How he exerted himself to be agreeable, talking about the singing, asking if she often honored the people as she had tonight.

"I take Miss Fisher's place when she is absent," Alice replied, whereupon, the doctor said he must have her up at Terrace Hill some day, to try Anna's long-neglected instrument. "It was once a most superb affair, but I believe it is sadly out of tune. Anna is very fond of you, Miss Johnson, and your visits would benefit her greatly. I assure you there's a duty of charity to be discharged at Terrace Hill as well as elsewhere. Anna suffers from too close confinement indoors, but, with a little skill, I think we can manage to get her out once more. Shall we try?"

Selfish Dr. Richards! It was all the same to him whether Anna went out once a day or once a year, but Alice did not suspect him and she answered frankly that she should have visited Terrace Hill more frequently, had she supposed his mothers and sisters cared particularly for society, but she had always fancied they preferred being alone.

CHAPTER VII

RIVERSIDE COTTAGE

Mrs. Johnson did not like Dr. Richards, and yet he became an almost daily visitor at Riverside Cottage, where one face at least grew brighter when he came, and one pair of eyes beamed on him a welcome. His new code of morality worked admirably. Mr. Howard himself was not more regular at church, or Alice more devout, than Dr. Richards. The children, whom he had denominated "ragged brats," were no longer spurned with contempt, but fed with peanuts and molasses candy. He was popular with the children, but the parents, clear sighted, treated him most shabbily at his back, accusing him of caring only for Miss Alice's good opinion.

This was what the poor said, and what many others thought. Even Anna, who took everything for what it seemed, roused herself and more than once remonstrated with her brother upon the course he was pursuing, if he were not in earnest, as something he once said to her made her half suspect.

She had become very intimate with Alice latterly, and as her health improved with the coming of spring, almost every fine day found her at Riverside Cottage, where once she and Mrs. Johnson stumbled upon a confidential chat, having for its subject John and Alice, Anna said nothing against her brother. She merely spoke of him as kind and affectionate, but the quick-seeing mother detected more than the words implied, and after that the elegant doctor was less welcome to her fireside than, he had been before.

As the winter passed away and spring advanced, he showed no intentions of leaving Snowdon, but on the contrary opened an office in the village, greatly to the surprise of the inhabitants, who remembered his former contempt for any one who could settle down in that dull town, and greatly to the dismay of old Dr. Rogers, who for years had blistered and bled the good people without a fear of rivalry.

"Does Dr. Richards intend locating permanently in Snowdon?" Mrs. Johnson asked of her daughter as they sat alone one pleasant spring evening.

"His sign would indicate as much," was Alice's reply.

"Mother," she said gently, "you look pale and worried. You have looked so for some time past. What is it, mother? Are you very sick, or are you troubled about me?"

"Is there any reason why I should be troubled about my darling?" asked the mother.

Alice never had any secrets from her mother, and she answered frankly: "I don't know, unless—unless—mother, why don't you like Dr. Richards?"

The ice was fairly broken now, and very briefly but candidly Mrs. Johnson told why she did not like him. He was handsome, refined, educated, and agreeable, she admitted, but still there was something lacking. The mask he was wearing had not deceived her, and she would have liked him far better without it. This she said to Alice, adding gently: "He may be all he seems, but I doubt it. I distrust him greatly. I think he fancies you and loves your money."

"Oh, mother," and in Alice's voice there was a sound of tears, "you do him injustice, and he has been so kind to us, while Snowdon is so much pleasanter since he came."

"Are you engaged to him?" was Mrs. Johnson's next question.

"No," and Alice looked up wonderingly. "I do not believe I like him well enough for that."

Alice Johnson was wholly ingenuous and would not for the world have concealed a thing from her mother, and very frankly she continued:

"I like Dr. Richards better than any gentleman I have ever met. I should have told you, mother."

"God bless my darling, and keep her as innocent as now," Mrs. Johnson murmured. "I am glad there is no engagement. Will you promise there shall not be for one year at least?"

"Yes, I will, I do," Alice said at last.

A second "God bless my darling," came from the mother's lips, and drawing her treasure nearer to her, she continued: "You have made me very happy, and by and by you'll be so glad. You may leave me now, for I am tired and sick."

It was long ere Alice forgot the expression of her mother's face or the sound of her voice, so full of love and tenderness, as she bade her good-night on that last evening they ever spent together alone. The indisposition of which Mrs. Johnson had been complaining for several days, proved to be no light matter, and when next morning Dr. Rogers was summoned to her bedside, he decided it to be a fever which was then prevailing to some extent in the neighboring towns.

That afternoon it was told at Terrace Hill that Mrs. Johnson was very sick, and half an hour later the Richards carriage, containing the doctor and his Sister Anna, wound down the hill, and passing through the park, turned in the direction of the cottage, where they found Mrs. Johnson even worse than they had anticipated. The sight of distress aroused Anna at once, and forgetting her own feebleness she kindly offered to stay until night if she could be of any service. Mrs. Johnson was fond of Anna, and she expressed her pleasure so eagerly that Anna decided to remain, and went with Alice to remove her wrappings.

"Oh, I forgot!" she exclaimed, as a sudden thought seemed to strike her. "I don't know as I can stay after all, though I might write it here, I suppose as well as at home; and as John is going to New

York tonight he will take it along."

"What is it?" Alice asked; and Anna replied:

"You'll think me very foolish, no doubt, but I want to know if you too think so. I'm so dependent on other's opinions," and, in a low tone, Anna told of the advertisement seen early last winter, how queerly it was expressed, and how careless John had been in tearing off the name and address, with which to light his cigar. "It seems to me," she continued, "that 'unfortunate married woman' is the very one I want."

"Yes; but how will you find her? I understand that the address was burned," Alice rejoined quickly, feeling herself that Anna was hardly sane in her calculations.

"Oh, I've used that in the wording," Anna answered. "I do not know as it will ever reach her, it's been so long, but if it does, she'll be sure to know I mean her, or somebody like her."

"I dislike writing very much," she said, as she saw the array of materials, "and I write so illegibly too. Please do it for me, that's a dear, good girl," and she gave the pen to Alice, who wrote the first word, "Wanted," and then waited for Anna to dictate.

"Wanted—By an invalid lady, whose home is in the country, a young woman, who will be both useful and agreeable, either as a companion or waiting maid. No objection will be raised if the woman is married, and unfortunate, or has a child a few months old. Address,

"A.E.R., Snowdon, Hampden Co., Mass."

Alice thought it the queerest advertisement she had ever seen, but Anna was privileged to do queer things, and folding the paper, she went out into the hall, where the doctor sat waiting for her.

John's mustached lip curled a little scornfully as he read it.

"Why, puss, that girl or woman is in Georgia by this time, and as the result of this, Terrace Hill will be thronged with unfortunate women and children, desiring situations. Better let me burn this, as I did the other, and not be foolish. She will never see it," and John made a gesture as if he would put it in the stove, but Anna caught his hand, saying imploringly: "Please humor me this once. She may see it, and I'm so interested."

Anna was always humored, and the doctor placed in his memorandum book the note, then turning to Alice he addressed her in so low a tone that Anna readily took the hint and left them together. Dr. Richards was not intending to be gone long, he said, though the time would seem a little eternity, so much was his heart now bound up in Snowdon.

Afraid lest he might say something more of the same nature, Alice hastened to ask if he had seen her mother, and what he thought of her.

"I stepped in for a moment while you were in the library," he replied. "She seemed to have a high fever, and I fancied it increased while I stood by her. I am sorry to leave while she is so sick, but remember that if anything happens you will be dearer to me than ever," and the doctor pressed the little hand which he took in his to say good-by, for now he must really go.

As the day and night wore on Mrs. Johnson grew worse so rapidly, that at her request a telegram was forwarded to Mr. Liston, who had charge of her moneyed affairs, and who came at once, for the kind old man was deeply interested in the widow and her lovely daughter. As Mrs. Johnson, could bear it, they talked alone together until he perfectly understood what her wishes were with regard to Alice, and how to deal with Dr. Richards, whom he had not yet seen. Then promising to return again in case the worst should happen, he took his leave, while Mrs. Johnson, now that a weight was lifted from her mind, seemed to rally, and the physician pronounced her better. But with that strange foreknowledge, as it were, which sometimes comes to people whose days are nearly numbered, she felt that she would die, and that in mercy this interval of rest and freedom from pain was granted her, in which she might talk with Alice concerning the arrangements for the future.

"Alice, darling," she said, when they were alone, "come sit by me here on the bed and listen to what I say."

Alice obeyed, and taking her mother's hot hands in hers she waited for what was to come.

"You have learned to trust God in prosperity, and He will be a thousandfold nearer to you in adversity. You'll miss me, I know, and be very lonely without me, but you are young, and life has many charms for you, besides God will never forget or forsake His covenant children."

Gradually as she talked the wild sobbing ceased, and when the white face lifted itself from its hiding place there was a look upon it as if the needed strength had been sought and to some extent imparted.

"My will was made some time ago," Mrs. Johnson continued, "and I need not tell you that with a few exceptions, such as legacies to Densie Densmore, and some charitable institutions, you are my sole heir. Mr. Liston is to be your guardian, and will look after your interests until you are of age, or longer if you choose. You know that as both your father and myself were the only children you have no near relatives on either side—none to whom you can look for protection.

"You will remember having heard me speak occasionally of some friends now living in Kentucky, a Mrs. Worthington, whose husband was a distant relative of ours. Ralph Worthington and your father were schoolboys together, and afterward college companions. Only once did anything come between them, and that was a young girl, a very young girl, whom both desired, and whom only one could have."

Alice was interested now, and forgetting in a measure her grief, she asked quickly: "Did my father love some one else than you?"

"I never knew he did," and a tear rolled down the faded cheek of the sick woman. "Ralph Worthington was true as steel, and when he found another preferred to himself, he generously yielded the contest."

"Oh, I shall like Mr. Worthington," Alice exclaimed, a desire rising in her heart to see the man who had loved and lost her mother.

"He was, at his own request, groomsman at our wedding, and the bridesmaid became his wife in little less than a year."

"Did he love her?" Alice asked, in some astonishment, and her mother replied evasively:

"He was kind and affectionate, while she loved him with all a woman's devotion. I was but sixteen when I became a bride, and several years elapsed ere God blessed me with a child. Your father was consumptive, and the chances were that I should early be left a widow. This it was which led to the agreement made by the two friends that if either died the living one should care for the widow and fatherless. To see the two you would not have guessed that the athletic Ralph would be the first to go, yet so it was. He died ere you were born."

"Then he is dead? Oh, I'm so sorry," Alice exclaimed.

"Yes, he's dead; and, as far as possible, your father fulfilled his promise to the widow and her child—a little boy, five years old, of whom Mrs. Worthington herself was appointed guardian. I never knew what spirit of evil possessed Eliza, but in less than a year after her husband's death, she made a second and most unfortunate marriage. Mr. Murdoch proved a greater scoundrel than we supposed, and when their little girl was nearly two years old, we heard of a divorce. Mr. Johnson's health was failing fast, and we were about to make the tour of Europe. Just before we sailed we visited poor Eliza, whom we found heartbroken, for the brutal wretch had managed to steal her daughter, and carried it no one knew whither. I never shall forgot the distress of the brother. Clasping my dress, he sobbed: 'Oh, lady, please bring back my baby sister, or Hugh will surely die.' I've often thought of him since, and wondered what he had grown to be. We comforted Eliza as best we could, and left money to be used for her in case she needed it. Then we embarked with you and Densie for Europe. You know how long we stayed there, how for a while, your father seemed to regain his strength, how he at last grew worse and hastened home to die. In the sorrow and excitement which followed, it is not strange that Eliza was for a time forgotten, and when I remembered and inquired for her again, I heard that Hugh had been adopted by some relation in Kentucky, that the stolen child had been mysteriously returned, and was living with its mother in Elmwood.

"At first Eliza appeared a little cool, but this soon wore off. She did not talk much of Hugh. Neither did she say much of Adaline, who was then away at school. Still my visit was a sadly satisfactory one, as we recalled old times when we were girls together, weeping over our great loss when our husbands were laid to rest. Then we spoke of their friendship, and lastly of the contract.

"'It sounds preposterous, in me, I know,' Mrs. Worthington said, when we parted, 'you are so rich, and I so poor, but if ever your Alice should want a mother's care, I will gladly give it to her.'

"This was nearly eight years ago. In my anxiety about you, I failed to write her for a long, long time, while she was long in answering, and then the correspondence ceased till just before her removal to Kentucky, when she apprised me of the change. You have now the history of Mrs. Worthington, the only person who comes to mind as one to whose care I can intrust you."

"But, mother, I may not be wanted there," and Alice's lip quivered painfully.

"You will not go empty-handed, nor be a burden to them. They are poor, and money will not come amiss. I said that Mr. Liston would attend to all pecuniary matters, paying your allowance quarterly; and I am sure you will not object when I tell you that I think it right to leave Adaline the sum of one thousand dollars. It will not materially lessen your inheritance, and it will do her a world of good. Mr. Liston will arrange it for you. You will remain here until you hear from Mrs. Worthington, and then abide by her arrangements. Will you go, my daughter—go cheerfully and do as I desire?"

"Yes, mother, I'll go," came gaspingly from Alice's lips. "I'll go; but, mother, oh, mother," and Alice's cry ended as it always did, "you will not, you must not die!"

But neither tears, nor prayers could avail to keep the mother longer. Her work on earth was done, and after this conversation with her daughter, she grew worse so rapidly that hope died out of Alice's heart, and she knew that soon she would be motherless. There were days and nights of pain and delirium in which the sick woman recognized none of those around her save Alice, whom she continually blessed as her darling, praying that God, too, would bless and keep His covenant child. At last there came a change, and one lovely Sabbath morning, ere the bell from St. Paul's tower sent forth its summons to the house of God, there rang from its belfry a solemn toll, and the villagers listening to it, said, as they counted forty-four, that Mrs. Johnson was dead.

CHAPTER VIII

MR. LISTON AND THE DOCTOR

Among Snowdon's poor that day, as well as among the wealthier class, there was many an aching heart, and many a prayer was breathed for the stricken Alice, not less beloved than the mother had been. At Terrace Hill mansion too, much sorrow was expressed. On the whole it was very unfortunate that Mrs. Johnson should have died so unexpectedly, and they did wish John was there to comfort the young girl who, they heard, refused to see any one except the clergyman and Mr. Liston.

"Suppose we telegraph for John," Eudora said, and in less than two hours thereafter, Dr. Richards in New York read that Alice was an orphan.

There was a pang as he thought of her distress, a wish that he were with her, and then in his selfish heart the thought arose, "What if she does not prove as wealthy as I have supposed? Will that make any difference?"

"I must do something," he soliloquized, "or how can I ever pay those debts in New York, of which mother knows nothing? I wish that widow—"

He did not finish his wishes, for a turn in the path brought him suddenly face to face with Mr. Liston, whom he had seen at a distance, and whom he recognized at once.

"I'll quiz the old codger," he thought. "He don't, of course, know me, and will never suspect my object."

Mistaken, doctor! The old codger was fully prepared. He did know Dr. Richards by sight, and was rather glad than otherwise when the elegant dandy, taking a seat upon the gnarled roots of the tree under which he was sitting, made some trivial remark about the weather, which was very propitious for the crowd who were sure to attend Mrs. Johnson's funeral.

Yes, Mr. Liston presumed there would be a crowd. It was very natural there should be, particularly as the deceased was greatly beloved and was also reputed wealthy, "It beats all what a difference it makes, even after death, whether one is supposed to be rich or poor," and the codger worked away industriously at the pine stick he was whittling.

"But in this case the supposition of riches must be correct, though I know people are oftener overvalued than otherwise," and with his gold-headed cane the doctor thrust at a dandelion growing near.

"Nothing truer than that," returned the whittler, brushing the litter from his lap. "Now I've no doubt that prig of a doctor, who they say is shining up to Alice, will be disappointed when he finds just how much she's worth. Let me see. What is his name? Lives up there," and with his jackknife Mr. Liston pointed toward Terrace Hill.

"The Richards family live there, sir. You mean their son, I presume."

"Ted, the chap that has traveled and come home so changed. They do say he's actually taken to visiting all the rheumatic old women in town, applying sticking-plasters to their backs and administering squills to their children, all free gratis."

Poor doctor! How he fidgeted, moving so often that his tormentor demurely asked him if he were sitting on a thistle or what!

"Does Miss Johnson remain here?" the doctor asked at last, and Mr. Liston replied by telling what he knew of the arrangements.

At the mention of Worthington the doctor looked up quickly. Whom had he known by that name, or where had he heard it before? "Mrs. Worthington, Mrs. Worthington," he repeated, unpleasant memories of something, he knew not what, rising to his mind. "Is he living in this vicinity?"

"In Elmwood. It's a widow and her daughter," Mr. Liston answered, wisely resolving to say nothing of a young man, lest the doctor should feel anxious.

"A widow and her daughter! I must be mistaken in thinking I ever knew any one by that name, though it seems strangely familiar," said the doctor, and as by this time he had heard all he wished to hear, he arose, and bidding Mr. Liston good-morning walked away in no enviable frame of mind.

Looking at his watch the doctor found that it lacked several hours yet ere the express from Boston was due. But this did not discourage him. He would stay in the fields or anywhere, and turning backward he followed the course of the river winding under the hill until he reached the friendly woods which shielded him from observation. How he hated himself hiding there among the trees, and how he longed for the downward train, which came at last, and when the village bell tolled out its summons to the house of mourning, he sat in a corner of the car returning to New York even faster than he had come.

Gradually the Riverside cottage filled with people assembling to pay the last tribute of respect to the deceased, who during her short stay among them had endeared herself to many hearts.

Slowly, sadly, they bore her to the grave. Reverently they laid her down to rest, and from the carriage window Alice's white face looked wistfully out as "earth to earth, ashes to ashes," broke the solemn stillness. Oh, how she longed to lay there, too, beside her mother! How the sunshine, flecking the bright June grass with gleams of gold, seemed to mock her misery as the gravelly earth rattled heavily down upon the coffin lid, and she knew they were covering up her mother. "If I, too, could die!" she murmured, sinking back in the carriage corner and covering her face with her veil. But not so easily could life be shaken off by her, the young and strong. She must live yet longer. She had a work to do—a work whose import she knew not; and the mother's death, for which she then could see no reason, though she knew well that one existed, was the entrance to that work. She must live and she must listen while Mr. Liston talked to her that night on business, arranging about the letter, which was forwarded immediately to Kentucky, and advising her what to do until an answer was received, when he would come up again and do whatever was necessary.

CHAPTER IX

MATTERS IN KENTUCKY

Backward now with our reader we turn, and take up the broken thread of our story at the point where we left Adah Hastings.

It was a bitter morning in which to face the fierce north wind, and plow one's way to the Derby cornfield, where, in a small, dilapidated building, Aunt Eunice Reynolds, widowed sister of John Stanley, had lived for many years, first as a pensioner upon her brother's bounty, and next as Hugh's incumbent. At the time of her brother's death Aunt Eunice had intended removing to Spring Bank, but when Hugh's mother wrote, asking for a home, she at once abandoned the plan, and for two seasons more lived alone, watching from her lonely door the tasseled corn ripening in the August sun. Of all places in the world Hugh liked the cottage best, particularly in summer. Few would object to it then with its garden of gayly colored flowers, its barricades of tasseled corn and the bubbling music of the brook, gushing from the willow spring a few rods from the door. But in the winter people from the highway, as they caught from across the field the gleam of Aunt Eunice's light, pitied the lonely woman sitting there so solitary beside her wintry fire. But Aunt Eunice asked no pity. If Hugh came once a week to spend the night, and once a day to see her, it was all that she desired, for Hugh was her darling, her idol, the object which kept her old heart warm and young with human love. For him she would endure any want or encounter any difficulty, and so it is not strange that in his dilemma regarding Adah Hastings, he intuitively turned to her, as the one of all others who would lend a helping hand. He had not been to see her in two whole days, and when the gray December morning broke, and he looked out upon the deep, untrodden snow, and then glanced across the fields to where a wreath of smoke, even at that early hour, was rising slowly from her chimney, he frowned impatiently, as he thought how bad the path must be between Spring Bank and the cornfield, whither he intended going, as he would be the first to tell what had occurred. 'Lina's fierce opposition to and his mother's apparent shrinking from Adah had convinced him how hopeless was the idea that she could stay at Spring Bank with any degree of comfort to herself or quiet to him. Aunt Eunice's house was the only refuge for Adah, and there she would be comparatively safe from censorious remarks.

"Inasmuch as ye did it to the least of these ye did it unto Me," kept ringing in Hugh's ears, as he hastily dressed himself, striking his benumbed fingers together, and trying hard to keep his teeth from chattering, for Hugh was beginning his work of economy, and when at daylight Claib came as usual to build his master's fire, he had sent him back, saying he did not need one, and bidding him go, instead, to Mrs. Hastings' chamber.

"Make a hot one there," he said. "Pile the coals on high, so as to heat up quick."

As Hugh passed through the hall on his way downstairs, he could not refrain from pausing a moment at the door of Adah's room. The fire was burning, he knew, for he heard the kindling coals sputtering in the flames, and that was all he heard. He would look in an instant, he said, to see if all were well, and carefully turning the knob he entered the chamber where the desolate Adah lay sleeping, her glossy brown hair falling like a veil about her sweet pale face, on which the tear stains still were visible.

As she lay with the firelight falling full upon her forehead, Hugh, too, caught sight of the mark which had attracted 'Lina's curiosity, and starting forward, bent down for a nearer view.

"Strange that she should have that mark. Oh Heaven!" and Hugh staggered against the bedpost as a sudden thought flashed upon him. "Was that polished villain who had led him into sin anything to Adaline, anything to his mother? Poor girl, I am sorry if you, too, have been contaminated, however slight the contamination may be," he said, softly, glancing again at Adah, about whose lips a faint smile was playing, and who, as he looked, murmured faintly:

"Kiss me, George, just as you used to do."

"Rascally villain!" Hugh muttered, clinching his fist involuntarily. "You don't deserve that such as she should dream of you. I'd kiss her myself if I was used to the business, but I should only make a bungle, as I do with everything, and might kiss you, little shaver," and Hugh bent over Willie.

There was something in Hugh which won his confidence at once, and stretching-out his dimpled arms, he expressed his willingness to be taken up. Hugh could not resist Willie's appeal, and lifting him gently in his arms, he bore him off in triumph, the little fellow patting his cheek, and rubbing his own against it.

"I don't know what I'll do with you, my little man," he said, as he reached the lower hall; then suddenly turning in the direction of his mother's room, he walked deliberately to the bedside, and ere the half awakened 'Lina was aware of his intention, deposited his burden between her and his mother.

"Here, Ad, here's something that will raise you quicker than yeast," he said, beating a hasty retreat, while the indignant young lady verified his words by leaping halfway across the floor, her angry tones mingling with Willie's crowing laugh, as the child took the whole for fun, meant expressly for his benefit.

Hugh knew that Willie was safe with his mother, and hurried out to the kitchen, where only a few of his negroes were yet stirring.

"Ho, Claib!" he called, "saddle Rocket quick and bring him to the door. I'm going to the cornfield."

"Lor' bless you, mas'r, it's done snow higher than Rocket's head. He never'll stand it nohow."

"Do as I bid you," was Hugh's reply, and indolent Claib went shivering to the stable where Hugh's best horses were kept.

A whinnying sound of welcome greeted him as he entered, but was soon succeeded by a spirited snort as he attempted to lead out a most beautiful dapple gray, Hugh's favorite steed, his pet of pets, and the horse most admired and coveted in all the country.

"None of yer ars," Claib said, coaxingly, as the animal threw up its graceful neck defiantly. "You've got to git along, 'case Mas'r Hugh say so. You knows Mas'r Hugh."

"What is it?" Hugh asked, coming out upon the stoop, and comprehending the trouble at a glance. "Rocket, Rocket," he cried, "easy, my boy," and in an instant Rocket's defiant attitude changed to one of perfect obedience.

"There, my beauty," he said, as the animal continued to prance around him, now snuffing at the snow, which he evidently did not fancy, and then pawing at it with his forefeet. "There, my beauty, you've showed off enough. Come, now, I've work for you to do."

Docile as a lamb when Hugh commanded, he stood quietly while Claib equipped him for his morning's task.

"Tell mother I shan't be back to breakfast," Hugh said, as he sprang into the saddle, and giving loose rein to Rocket went galloping through the snow.

Under ordinary circumstances that early ride would have been vastly exhilarating to Hugh, who enjoyed the bracing air, but there was too much now upon his mind to admit of his enjoying anything. Thoughts of Adah, and the increased expense her presence would necessarily bring, flitted across his mind, while Barney's bill, put over once, and due again ere long, sat like a nightmare on him, for he saw no way in which to meet it. No way save one, and Rocket surely must have felt the throbbing of Hugh's heart as that one way flashed upon him, for he gave a kind of coaxing whine, and dashed on over the billowy drifts faster than before.

"No, Rocket, no," and Hugh patted his glossy neck. He'd never part with Rocket, never. He'd sell Spring Bank first with all its incumbrances.

It was now three days since Hugh had gladdened Aunt Eunice's cottage with the sunshine of his presence, and when she awoke that morning, and saw how high the snow was piled around her door, she said to herself, "The boy'll be here directly to know if I'm alive," and this accounted for the round deal table drawn so cozily before the blazing fire, and looking so inviting with its two plates and cups, one a fancy china affair, sacredly kept for Hugh, whose coffee always tasted better when sipped from its gilded side, the lightest of egg bread was steaming on the hearth, the tenderest of steak was broiling on the griddle, while the odor of the coffee boiling on the coals came tantalizingly to Hugh's olfactories as Aunt Eunice opened the door, saying pleasantly:

"I told 'em so. I felt it in my bones, and the breakfast is all but ready. Put Rocket up directly, and come in to the fire."

Fastening Rocket in his accustomed place in the outer shed, Hugh stamped the snow from his heavy boots, and then went in to Aunt Eunice's cheerful kitchen-parlor, as she called it, where the tempting breakfast stood upon the table.

"No coffee! What new freak is that?" and Aunt Eunice gazed at him in astonishment as he declined the cup she had prepared with so much care, dropping in the whitest lumps of sugar, and stirring in the thickest cream.

It cost Hugh a terrible struggle to refuse that cup of coffee, but if he would retrench, he must begin at once, and determining to meet it unflinchingly he replied that "he had concluded to drink water for a while, and see what that would do; much was said nowadays about coffee being injurious, and he presumed it was."

"There's something on your mind," she said, observing his abstraction. "Have you had another dunning letter, or what?"

Aunt Eunice had made a commencement, and in his usual impulsive way Hugh began by asking if "she ever knew him tell a lie?"

No, Aunt Eunice never did. Nobody ever did, bad as some folks thought him.

"Do they think me very bad?" and Hugh spoke so mournfully that Aunt Eunice tried to apologize.

"She didn't mean anything, only folks sometimes said he was cross and rough, and—and—"

"Stingy," he suggested, supplying the word she hated to say.

Yes, that was what Ellen Tiffton said, because he refused to go to the Ladies' Fair, where he was sure to have his pockets picked. But, law, she wasn't worth minding, if she was Colonel Tiffton's girl, and going to have a big party one week from the next Monday. Had Hugh heard of it?

Hugh believed Ad said something about it yesterday, but he paid no attention, for, of course, he should not go even if he were invited, as he had nothing fit to wear.

"But why did you ask if I ever knew you tell a lie?" Aunt Eunice said, and then in a low tone, as if afraid the walls might hear, Hugh told the whole story of Adah.

"'Twas a mighty mean trick, I know," he said, as he saw Aunt Eunice's look of horror when he confessed the part he had had in wronging the poor girl, "but, Aunt Eunice, that villain coaxed me into drinking wine, which you know I never use, and I think now he must have drugged it, for I remember a strange feeling in my head, a feeling not like drunkenness, for I knew perfectly well what was transpiring around me, and only felt a don't-care-a-tive-ness which kept me silent when I should have spoken. She has come to me at last. She believes God sent her, and if He did He'll help me take care of her. I shall not turn her off."

"But, Hugh," and Aunt Eunice spoke earnestly, "you cannot afford the expense. Think twice before you commit yourself."

"I have thought twice, the last time just as I did the first. Adah shall stay, and I want you to take her. You need some one these winter nights. There's the room you call mine. Give her that. Will you, Aunt Eunice?" and Hugh wound his arm around Aunt Eunice's ample waist, while he pleaded for Adah Hastings.

Aunt Eunice was soon won over, as Hugh knew she would be, and it was settled that she should come that very day, if possible.

"Look, the sky is clearing," and he pointed to the sunshine streaming through the window.

"We'll have her room fixed before I go," and with his own hands Hugh split and prepared the wood which was to kindle Adah's fire, then with Aunt Eunice's help sundry changes were made in the arrangement of the rather meager furniture, which never seemed so meager to Hugh as when he looked at it with Adah's eyes and wondered how she'd like it.

"Oh, I wish I were rich," he sighed mentally, and taking out his well-worn purse he carefully counted its contents.

Aunt Eunice, who had stepped out for a moment, reappeared, bringing a counterpane and towel, one of which was spread upon the bed, while the other covered the old pine stand, marred and stained with ink and tallow, the result of Hugh's own carelessness.

"What a heap of difference that table cloth and pocket hand-kerchief do make," was Hugh's manlike remark, his face brightening with the improved appearance of things, and his big heart grew warm with the thought that he might keep his twenty-five dollars and Adah be comfortable still.

"Ad may pick Adah's eyes out before I get home," was his laughing remark as he vaulted into his saddle and dashed off across the fields, where, beneath the warm Kentucky sun, the snow was already beginning to soften.

Breakfast had been rather late at Spring Bank that morning, for the strangers had required some care, and Miss 'Lina was sipping her coffee rather ill-naturedly when a note was handed her, and instantly her mood was changed.

"Splendid, mother!" she exclaimed, glancing at the tiny, three-cornered thing; "an invitation to Ellen Tiffton's party. I was half afraid she would leave me out after Hugh's refusal to attend the Ladies' Fair, or buy a ticket for her lottery. It was only ten dollars either, and Mr. Harney spent all of forty, I'm sure, in the course of the evening. I think Harney is splendid."

"Hugh had no ten dollars to spare," Mrs. Worthington said,

apologetically, "though, of course, he might have been more civil than to tell Ellen it was a regular swindle, and the getters-up ought to be indicted. I almost wonder at her inviting him, as she said she'd never speak to him again."

"Invited him! Who said she had? It's only one card for me," and with a most satisfied expression 'Lina presented the rote to her mother, whose pale face flushed at the insult thus offered her son—an insult which even 'Lina felt, but would not acknowledge, lest it should interfere with her going.

"You won't go, of course," Mrs. Worthington said, quietly. "You'll resent her slighting Hugh."

"Indeed I shan't," the young lady retorted. "I hardly think it fair in Ellen, but I shall accept, of course, and I must go to town today to see about having my pink silk fixed. I think I'll have some black lace festooned around the skirt. How I wish I could have a new one. Do you suppose Hugh has any money?"

"None for new dresses or lace flounces, either," Mrs. Worthington replied, "I fancy he begins to look old and worn with this perpetual call for money from us. We must economize."

"Never mind, when I get Bob Harney I'll pay off old scores," 'Lina said, laughingly, as she arose from the table, and went to look over her wardrobe.

Meanwhile Hugh had returned, meeting in the kitchen with Lulu.

"Well, Lu, what is it? What's happened?" Hugh asked, as he saw she was full of some important matter.

In an instant the impetuous Lulu told him of the party to which he was not invited, together with the reason why, and the word she had sent back.

"I'll give 'em a piece of my mind!" she said, as she saw Hugh change color. "She may have old Harney. His man John told Claib how his a master said he meant to get me and Rocket, too, some day; me for her waiting maid, I reckon. You won't sell me, Master High, will you?" and Lulu's soft black eyes looked pleadingly up to Hugh.

"Never!" and Hugh's riding whip came down upon the table with a force which made Lulu start.

Satisfied that she was safe from Ellen Tiffton's whims, Lulu darted away, singing as she went, while Hugh entered the sitting-room, where 'Lina sat, surrounded by her party finery, and prepared to do the amiable to the utmost.

"That really is a handsome little boy upstairs," she said, as if she supposed it were her mother who came in; then with an affected start she added, "Oh, it's you! I thought 'twas mother. Don't you think, Ellen has not invited you. Mean, isn't it?"

"Ellen can do as she likes," Hugh replied, adding, as he guessed the meaning of all that finery, "you surely are not going?"

"Why not?" and 'Lina's black eyes flashed full upon him.

"I thought perhaps you would decline for my sake," he replied.

An angry retort trembled on 'Lina's lip, but she had an object to attain, so she restrained herself and answered that "she had thought of it, but such a course would do no good, and she wanted to go so much, the Tifftons were so exclusive and aristocratic."

Hugh whistled a little contemptuously, but 'Lina kept her temper, and continued, coaxingly:

"Everybody is to be there, and after what has been said about —about—your being rather—close, you'd like to have your sister look decent, I know; and really, Hugh, I can't unless you give me a little money. Do, Hugh, be good for once."

"Ad, I can't," and Hugh spoke sorrowfully, for a kind word from 'Lina always touched his weaker side. "I would if I could, but honestly I've only twenty-five dollars in the world, and I've thought of a new coat. I don't like to look so shabby. It hurts me worse than it does you," and Hugh's voice trembled as he spoke.

Any but a heart of stone would have yielded at once, but 'Lina was too supremely selfish. Hugh had twenty-five dollars. He might give her half, or even ten. She'd be satisfied with ten. He could soon make that up. The negro hire came due ere long. He must have forgotten that.

No, he had not; but with the negro hire came debts, thoughts of which gave him the old worn look his mother had observed. Only ten dollars! It did seem hard to refuse, and if 'Lina went Hugh wished her to look well, for underneath his apparent harshness lurked a kind of pride in his dark sister, whose beauty was of the bold, dashing style.

"Take them," he said at last, counting out the ten with a half regretful sigh. "Make them go as far as you can, and, Ad, remember, don't get into debt."

"I won't," and with a civil "Thank you," 'Lina rolled up her bills, while Hugh sought his mother, and sitting down beside her said, abruptly:

"Mother, are you sure that man is dead?—Ad's father I mean?"

There was a nervous start, a sudden paling of Mrs. Worthington's cheek, and then she answered, sadly:

"I suppose so, of course. I received a paper containing a marked announcement of his death, giving accurately his name and age. There could be no mistake. Why do you ask that question?"

"Nothing, only I've been thinking of him this morning. There's a mark on Adah's temple similar to Ad's, only not so plain, and I did not know but she might possibly be related. Have you noticed it?"

"'Lina pointed it out last night, but to me it seemed a spreading vein, nothing more. Hugh!" and Mrs. Worthington grasped his arm with a vehemence unusual to her accustomed quiet manner, "you seem to know Adah's later history. Do you know her earlier? Who is she? Where did she come from?"

"I'm going to her now; will you come, too?" she said, and accordingly both together ascended to the chamber where Adah sat before the fire with Willie on her lap, her glossy hair, which Lulu's skillful fingers had arranged, combed smoothly down upon her forehead, so as to hide the mysterious mark, if mark there were, on that fair skin.

Something in the expression of her face as she turned toward Mrs. Worthington made that lady start, while her heart throbbed with an indefinable emotion. Who was Adah Hastings, and why was she so drawn toward her?

Addressing to her some indifferent remark, she gradually led the conversation backward to the subject of her early home, asking again what she could remember, but Adah was scarcely more satisfactory than on the previous night. Memories she had of a gentle lady, who must have been her mother, of a lad who called her sister, and kissed her sometimes, of a cottage with grass and flowers, and bees buzzing beneath the trees.

"Are you faint?" Hugh asked, quickly, as his mother turned white as ashes, and leaned against the mantel.

She did not seem to hear him, but continued questioning Adah.

"Did you say bees? Were there many?"

"Oh, yes, so many, I remember, because they stung me once," and Adah gazed dreamily into the fire, as if listening again to the musical hum heard in that New England home, wherever it might have been.

"Go on, what more can you recall?" Mrs. Worthington said, and Adah replied:

"Nothing but the waterfall in the river. I remember that near our door."

During this conversation, Hugh had been standing by the table, where lay a few articles which he supposed belonged to Adah. One of these was a small double locket, attached to a slender chain.

"The rascal's, I presume," he said to himself, and taking it in his hand, he touched the spring, starting quickly as the features of a young-girl met his view. How radiantly beautiful the original of that picture must have been, and Hugh gazed long and earnestly upon the sweet young face, and its soft, silken curls, some shading the open brow, and others falling low upon the uncovered neck. Adah, lifting up her head, saw what he was doing, and said:

"Don't you think her beautiful?"

"Who is she?" Hugh asked, coming to her side, and passing her the locket.

"I don't know," Adah replied. "She came to me one day when Willie was only two weeks old and my heart was so heavy with pain. She had heard I did plain sewing and wanted some for herself. She seemed to me like an angel, and I've sometimes thought she was, for she never came again. In stooping over me the chain must have been unclasped. I tried to find her when I got well, but my efforts were all in vain, and so I've kept it ever since. It was not stealing, was it?"

"Of course not," Hugh said, while Adah, opening the other side, showed him a lock of dark brown hair, tied with a tiny ribbon, in which was written, "*In memoriam*, Aug. 18."

As Hugh read the date his heart gave one great throb, for that was the summer, that the month when he lost the Golden Haired. Something, too, reminded him of the warm moonlight night, when the little snowy fingers, over which the fierce waters were soon to beat, had strayed through his heavy locks, which the girl had said were too long to be becoming, playfully severing them at random, and saying "she means to keep the fleece to fill a cushion with."

"I wonder whose it is?" Adah said; "I've thought it might have been her mother's."

"Her lover's more likely," suggested Hugh, glancing once more at the picture, which certainly had in it a resemblance to the Golden Haired, save that the curls were darker, and the eyes a deeper blue.

"Will mas'r have de carriage? He say something 'bout it," Cæsar said, just then thrusting his woolly head in at the door, and thus reminding Hugh that Adah had yet to hear of Aunt Eunice and his plan of taking her thither.

With a burst of tears, Adah listened to him, and then insisted upon going away, as she had done the previous night. She had no claim on him, and she could not be a burden.

"You, madam, think it best, I'm sure," she said, appealing to Mrs. Worthington, whose heart yearned strangely toward the unprotected stranger, and who answered, promptly:

"I do not, I am willing you should remain until your friends are found."

Adah offered no further remonstrance, but turning to Hugh, said, hesitatingly:

"I may hear from my advertisement. Do you take the *Herald*?"

"Yes, though I can't say I think much of it," Hugh replied, and Adah continued:

"Then if you ever find anything for me, you'll tell me, and I can go away. I said, 'Direct to Adah Hastings.' Somebody will be sure to see it. Maybe George, and then he'll know of Willie," and the white face brightened with eager anticipation as Adah thought of George reading that advertisement, a part of which had lighted Dr. Richards' cigar.

With a muttered invective against the "villain," Hugh left the room to see that the carriage was ready, while his mother, following him into the hall, offered to go herself with Adah if he liked. Glad to be relieved, as he had business that afternoon in Versailles, and was anxious to set off as soon as possible, Hugh accepted at once, and half an hour later, the Spring Bank carriage drove slowly from the door, 'Lina calling after her mother to send Cæsar back immediately.

CHAPTER X

'LINA'S PURCHASE AND HUGH'S

There were piles of handsome dress goods upon the counter at Harney's that afternoon, and Harney was anxious to sell. It was not always that he favored a customer with his own personal services, and 'Lina felt proportionably flattered when he came forward and asked what he could show her. Of course, a dress for the party—he had sold at least a dozen that day, but fortunately he still had the most elegant pattern of all, and he knew it would exactly suit her complexion and style.

Deluded 'Lina! Richard Harney, the wealthy bachelor merchant, did not mean one word he said. He had tried to sell that dress a dozen times, and been as often refused, no one caring just then to pay fifty dollars for a dress which could only be worn on great occasions. But 'Lina was easily flattered, while the silk was beautiful. But ten dollars was all she had, and turning away from the tempting silk she answered faintly, that "it was superb, but she could not afford it, besides, she had not the money today."

"Not the slightest consequence," was Harney's quick rejoinder. "Not the slightest consequence. Your brother's credit is good—none better in the country, and I'm sure he'll be proud to see you in it. I should, were I your brother."

'Lina blushed, while the wish to possess the silk grew every moment stronger.

"If it were only fifty dollars, it would not seem so bad," she thought. Hugh could manage it some way, and Mr. Harney was so good natured; he could wait a year, she knew. But the making would cost ten dollars more, for that was the price Miss Allis charged, to say nothing of the trimmings. "No, I can't," she said, quite decidedly, at last, asking for the lace with which she at first intended renovating her old pink silk, "She must see Miss Allis first to know how much she wanted," and promising to return, she tripped over to Frankfort's fashionable dressmaker, whom she found surrounded with dresses for the party.

As some time would elapse ere Miss Allis could attend to her, she went back to Harney's just for one more look at the lovely fabric. It was, if possible, more beautiful than before, and Harney was more polite, while the result of the whole was that, when 'Lina at four o'clock that afternoon entered her carriage to go home, the despised pink silk, still unpaid on Haney's books, was thrown down anywhere, while in her hands she carefully held the bundle Harney brought himself, complimenting her upon the sensation she was sure to create, and inviting her to dance the first set with him. Then with a smiling bow he closed the door upon her, and returning to his books wrote down Hugh Worthington his debtor to fifty dollars more.

"That makes three hundred and fifty," he said to himself. "I know he can't raise that amount of ready money, and as he is too infernal proud to be sued, I'm sure of Rocket or Lulu, it matters but little which," and with a look upon his face which made it positively hideous, the scheming Harney closed his books, and sat down to calculate the best means of managing the rather unmanageable Hugh!

It was dark when 'Lina reached home, but the silk looked well by firelight, better even than in the light of day, and 'Lina would have been quite happy but for her mother's reproaches and an occasional twinge as she wondered what Hugh would say. He had not yet returned, and numerous were Mrs. Worthington's surmises as to what was keeping him so late. A glance backward for an hour or so will let us into the secret.

It was the day when a number of negroes were to be sold in the courthouse. There was no trouble in disposing of them all, save one, a white-haired old man, whom they called Uncle Sam.

With tottering steps the old man took his place, while his dim eyes wandered wistfully over the faces around him congregated, as if seeking for their owner. But none was found who cared for Uncle Sam.

"Won't nobody bid for Sam? I fetched a thousan' dollars onct," and the feeble voice trembled as it asked this question.

"What will become of him if he is not sold?" Hugh asked of a bystander, who replied, "Go back to the old place to be kicked and cuffed by the minions of the new proprietor, Harney. You know Harney, of Frankfort?"

Yes, Hugh did know Harney as one who was constantly adding to his already large possessions houses and lands and negroes without limit, caring little that they came to him laden with the widow's curse and the orphan's tears. This was Harney, and Hugh always felt exasperated whenever he thought of him. Advancing a step or two he came nearer to the negro, who took comfort at once from the expression of his face, and stretching out his shaking hand he said, beseechingly:

"You, mas'r, you buy old Sam, 'case it 'ill be lonesome and cold in de cabin at home when they all is gone. Please, mas'r."

"What can you do?" was Hugh's query, to which the truthful negro answered:

"Nothin' much, 'cept to set in the chimbly corner eatin' corn bread and bacon—or, yes," and an expression of reverence and awe stole over the wrinkled face, as in a low tone he added, "I can pray for young mas'r, and I will, only buy me, please."

Hugh had not much faith in praying negroes, but something in old Sam struck him as sincere. His prayers might do good, and be needed somebody's, sadly. But what should he offer, when fifteen dollars was all he had in the world, and was it his duty to encumber himself with a piece of useless property? Visions of the Golden Haired and Adah both arose up before him. They would say it was right. They would tell him to buy old Sam, and that settled the point with him.

"Five dollars," he called out, and Sam's "God bless you," was sounding in his ears, when a voice from another part of the building doubled the bid, and with a moan Uncle Sam turned imploringly toward Hugh.

"A leetle more, mas'r, an' you fotches 'em; a leetle more," he whispered, coaxingly, and Hugh faltered out "Twelve."

"Thirteen," came again from the corner, and Hugh caught sight of the bidder, a sour-grained fellow, whose wife had ten young children, and so could find use for Sam.

"Thirteen and a half," cried Hugh.

"Fourteen," responded his opponent.

"Leetle more, mas'r, berry leetle," whispered Uncle Sam.

"Fourteen and a quarter," said Hugh, the perspiration starting out about his lips, as he thought how fast his pile was diminishing, and that he could not go beyond it.

"Fourteen and a half," from the corner.

"Leetle more, mas'r," from Uncle Sam.

"Fourteen, seventy-five," from Hugh.

"Fifteen," from the man in the corner, and Hugh groaned aloud.

"That's every dime I've got."

Quick as thought an acquaintance beside him slipped a bill into his hand, whispering as he did so:

"It's a V. I'll double it if necessary. I'm sorry for the darky."

It was very exciting now, each bidder raising a quarter each time, while Sam's "a leetle more, mas'r," and the vociferous cheers of the crowd, whenever Hugh's voice was heard, showed him to be the popular party.

"Nineteen, seventy-five," from the corner, and Hugh felt his courage giving way as he faintly called out:

"Twenty."

Only an instant did the auctioneer wait, and then his decision, "Gone!" made Hugh the owner of Uncle Sam, who, crouching down before him, blessed him with tears and prayers.

"I knows you're good," he said; "I knows it by yer face; and mebby, when the rheumatics gits out of my ole legs I kin work for mas'r a heap. Does you live fur from here?"

"Look here, Sam," and Hugh laughed heartily at the negro's forlorn appearance, as, regaining his feet, he assumed a most deprecating attitude, asking pardon for tumbling down, and charging it all to his shaky knees. "Look here, there's no other way, except for you to ride, and me to walk. Rocket won't carry double," and ere Sam could remonstrate, Hugh had dismounted and placed him in the saddle.

Rocket did not fancy the exchange, as was manifest by an indignant snort, and an attempt to shake Sam off, but a word from Hugh quieted him, and the latter offered the reins to Sam, who was never a skillful horseman, and felt a mortal terror of the high-mettled steed beneath him. With a most frightened expression upon his face, he grasped the saddle pommel with both hands, and bending nearly double, gasped out:

"Sam ain't much use't to gemman's horses. Kind of bold me on, mas'r, till I gits de hang of de critter. He hists me around mightily."

So, leading Rocket with one hand, and steadying Sam with the other, Hugh got on but slowly, and 'Lina had looked for him many times ere she spied him from the window as he came up the lawn.

"Who is he, and what did you get him for?" Mrs. Worthington asked, as Hugh led Sam into the dining-room.

Briefly Hugh explained to her why he had bought the negro.

"It was foolish, I suppose, but I'm not sorry yet," he added, glancing toward the corner where the poor old man was sitting, warming his shriveled hands by the cheerful fire, and muttering to himself blessings on "young mas'r."

But for the remembrance of her dress, 'Lina would have stormed, but as it was, she held her peace, and even asked Sam some trivial question concerning his former owners. Supper had been delayed for Hugh, and as he took his seat at the table, he inquired after Adah.

"Pretty well when I left," said his mother, adding that Lulu had been there since, and reported her as looking pale and worn, while Aunt Eunice seemed worried with Willie, who was inclined to be fretful.

"They need some one," Hugh said, refusing the coffee his mother passed him on the plea that he did not feel like drinking it tonight. "They need one of the servants. Can't you spare Lulu?"

Mrs. Worthington did not know, but 'Lina, to whom Lulu was a kind of waiting maid, took the matter up alone, and said:

"Indeed they couldn't. There was no one at Spring Bank more useful, and it was preposterous for Hugh to think of giving their best servant to Adah Hastings. Let her take care of her baby herself. She guessed it wouldn't hurt her. Anyway, they couldn't afford to keep a servant for her."

With a long-drawn sigh, Hugh finished his supper, and was about lighting his cigar when he felt some one touching him, and turning around he saw that Sam had grasped his coat. The negro had heard the conversation, and drawn correct conclusions. His new master was not rich. He could not afford to buy him, and having bought him could not afford to keep him. There was a sigh in the old man's heart, as he thought how useless he was, but when he heard about the baby, his spirits arose at once. In all the world there was nothing so precious to Sam as a child, a little white child, with waxen hands to pat his old black face, and his work was found.

"Mas'r," he whispered, "Sam kin take keer that baby. He knows how, and the little children in Georgy, whar I comed from, used to be mighty fond of Sam. I'll tend to the young lady, too. Is she yourn, mas'r?"

'Lina laughed aloud, while Hugh replied:

"She's mine while I take care of her."

Then, turning to his sister, he asked if she procured what she wanted.

With a threatening frown at Lulu, who had seen and gone into ecstasies over the rose silk, 'Lina answered that she was fortunate enough to get just what she wanted, adding quickly:

"It's to be a much gayer affair than I supposed. They are invited from Louisville, and even from Cincinnati, so Mr. Harney says."

"Harney, did you trade there?" Hugh asked.

"Why, yes. It's the largest and best store in town. Why shouldn't I?" 'Lina replied, while Sam, catching at the name, put in:

"Hartley's the man what foreclosed the mortgage. You orto hear ole mas'r cuss him oncet. Sharp chap, dat Harney; mighty hard on de blacks, folks say," and glad to have escaped from his clutches, Sam turned again to his dozing reverie, which was broken at last by Hugh's calling Claib, and bidding him show Sam where he was to sleep.

How long Hugh did sit up that night, and 'Lina, who wanted so much to see once more just how her rose silk looked by lamp-light, thought he never would take her broad hints and leave. He dreaded to go—dreaded to exchange that warm, pleasant room for the cold, cheerless chamber above, where he knew no fire would greet him, for he had told Claib not to make one, and that was why he lingered as long below. But the ordeal must be met, and just as the clock was striking eleven, he bade his mother and sister good-night, whistling as he bounded up the stairs, by way of keeping up his spirits. How dreary and dark it looked in his room, as with a feeling akin to homesickness Hugh set his candle down and glanced at the empty hearth.

"After all, what does it matter?" he said. "I only have to hurry and get in bed the sooner," and tossing one boot here and another there, he was about to finish undressing when suddenly he remembered the little Bible, and the passage read last night. Would there be one for him tonight? He meant to look and see, and all cold and shivery as he was, Hugh lifted the lid of the trunk which held his treasure, and taking it out, opened to the place where the silken curl was lying. There was a great throb at his heart when he saw that the last coil of the tress lay just over the words, "Whosoever shall give to drink unto one of these little ones a cup of cold water in the name of a disciple, verily, I say unto you, he shall in no wise lose his reward."

"It does seem as if this was meant to encourage me," Hugh said, reading the passage twice. "I don't much believe, though, I bought old Sam in the name of a disciple, though I do think his telling me he prayed had a little to do with it. It's rather pleasant to think there's two to pray for me now, Adah and Sam. I wonder if it makes any difference with God that one prayer is white and the other black? Golden Hair said it didn't when we talked about the negroes," and shutting the Bible, Hugh was about to put it up when something whispered of his resolution to commence reading it through.

"It's too confounded cold. I'll freeze to death, I tell you," he said, as if arguing the point with some unseen presence. "Get into bed and read it then, hey? It's growing late and my candle is most burned out. The first chapter of Genesis is short, is it? Won't take one over three minutes? Stick like a chestnut burr, don't you," and as if the matter were decided, Hugh sprang into bed, shivering as if about to take a cold plunge bath. How then was he disappointed to find the sheets as nice and warm as Aunt Chloe's warming pan of red-hot coals could make them.

And so he fell away to sleep, dreaming that Golden Hair had come back, and that he held her in his arms, just as he held the Bible he had unconsciously taken from the pillow beneath his head.

CHAPTER XI

SAM AND ADAH

It was Saturday night again, and Adah, with heavy eyes and throbbing head, sat bending over the dazzling silk, which 'Lina had coaxed her to make.

'Lina could be very gracious when she chose, and as she saw a way by which Adah might be useful to her, she chose to be so now, and treated the unsuspecting girl so kindly, that Adah promised to undertake the task, which proved a harder one than she had anticipated. Anxious to gratify 'Lina, and keep what she was doing a secret from Hugh, who came to the cottage often, she was obliged to work early and late, bending over the dress by the dim candle-light until her head seemed bursting with pain, and rings of fire danced before her eyes. She never would have succeeded but for Uncle Sam, who proved a most efficient member of the household, fitting in every niche and corner, until Aunt Eunice, with all her New England aversion to negroes, wondered how she had ever lived without him. Particularly did he attach himself to Willie, relieving Adah from all care, and thus enabling her to devote every spare moment to the party dress.

"You'se workin' yourself to death," he said to her, as late on Saturday night she sat bending to the tallow candle, her hair brushed back from her forehead and a purplish glow upon her cheek.

"I know I'm working too hard," she said. "I'm very tired, but Monday is the party. Oh, I am so hot and feverish," and, as if even the slender chain of gold about her neck were a burden, she undid the clasp, and laid upon the stand the locket which had so interested Hugh.

Naturally inquisitive Sam took it in his hand, and touching the spring held it to the light, uttering an exclamation of surprise.

"Dat's de bery one, and no mistake," he said, his old withered face lighting up with eager joy.

"Who is she, Sam?" Adah asked, forgetting her work in her new interest.

"Miss Ellis. I done forgot de other name. Ellis they call her way down thar whar Sam was sold, when dat man with the big splot on his forerd like that is on your'n steal me away and sell me in Virginny. Miss, ever hearn tell o' dat? We thinks he's takin' a bee line for Canada, when fust we knows we's in ole Virginny, and de villain not freein' us at all. He sell us. Me he most give away, 'case I was so old, and the mas'r who buy some like Mas'r Hugh, he pity, he sorry for ole shaky nigger. Sam tell him on his knees how he comed from Kaintuck, but Mas'r Sullivan say he bought 'em far, and that the right mas'r sell 'em sneakin' like to save rasin' a furse, and he show a bill of sale. They believe him spite of dis chile, and so Sam 'long to anodder mas'r."

"Yes; but the lady, Miss Ellis. Where did you find her?" Adah asked, and Sam replied:

"I'se comin' to her d'rectly. Mas'r Fitzhugh live on big plantation—big house, too, with plenty company; and one day she comed, with great trunk, a visitin' you know. She'd been to school with Miss Mabel, Mas'r Fitzhugh's daughter."

"Are you sure it's the same?" Adah asked.

"Yes, miss, Sam sure, he 'members them curls—got a heap of 'em; and that neck—oh, wear that neck berry low, so low, so white, it make even ole Sam feel kinder, kinder, yes, Sam feel very much that way."

Adah could not repress a smile, but she was too much interested to interrupt him, and he went on:

"They all think heap of Miss Ellis, and I hear de blacks tellin' how she berry rich, and comed from way off thar wher white niggers live—Masser-something."

"Massachusetts?" suggested Adah.

"Yes; that's the very mas'r, I 'member dat."

"Was Ellis her first or last name?" Adah asked, and Sam replied:

"It was neider, 'twas her Christian name. I'se got mizzable memory, and I disremembers her last name. The folks call her Ellis, and the blacks Miss Ellis."

"A queer name for a first one," Adah thought, while Sam continued:

"She jest like bright angel, in her white gownds and dem long curls, and Sam like her so much. She promise to write to Mas'r Browne and tell him whar I is. I didn't cry loud then—heart too full. I cry whimperin' like, and she cry, too. Then she tell me about God, and Sam listen, oh, listen so much, for that's what he want to hear so long. Miss Nancy, in Kuntuck, be one of them that reads her pra'rs o' Sundays, and ole mas'r one that hollers 'em. Sam liked that way best, seemed like gettin' along and make de Lord hear, but it don't show Sam the way, and when the ministers come in, he listen, but they that reads and them that hollers only talk about High and Low—Jack and the Game, or something, Sam disremembers so bad; got mizzable memory. He only knows he not find the way, 'till Miss Ellis tells him of Jesus, once a man and always God. It's very queer, but Sam believe it, and then she sing, 'Come unto me.' You ever hear it?"

Adah nodded, and Sam went on.

"But you never hear Miss Ellis sing it. Oh, so fine, the very rafters hold their breff, and Sam find the way at last."

"Where is Miss Ellis now?" Adah asked, and Sam replied:

"Gone to Masser—what you say once. She gived me five dollars and then ask what else. I look at her and say, 'Sam wants a spear or two of yer shinin' hair,' and Miss Mabel takes shears and cut a little curl. I'se got 'em now. I never spend the money," and from an old leathern wallet Sam drew a bill and a soft silken curl, which he laid across Adah's hand.

"Yes, that is like her hair," Adah said, gazing fondly upon the tiny lock which was Sam's greatest earthly treasure; then, returning it to him, she asked: "And where is that Sullivan?" a chill creeping over her as she remembered how about four years ago the man she called her guardian was absent for some time, and came back to her with colored hair and whiskers.

"Oh, he gone long before, nobody know whar. Sam b'lieves, though, he hear they tryin' to cotch him, but disremembers, got such mizzable memory."

"You say he had a mark like mine?" Adah continued.

"Yes, berry much, but more so. Show plainer when he cussin' mad, just as yours show more when you tired. Whar you git dat?" and Sam bent down to inspect more closely Adah's birthmark.

"I don't know. I was born with it," and Adah half groaned aloud at the sad memories which Sam's story had awakened within her.

She could scarcely doubt that Sullivan, the negro-stealer, and Monroe, her guardian, were the same, but where was he now, and why had he treated her so treacherously, when he had always seemed so kind?

"Miss Adah prays," the old man answered. "Won't she say 'Our Father' with Sam?"

Surely Hugh's sleep was sweeter that night for the prayer breathed by the lowly negro, and even the wild tumult in Adah's heart was hushed by Sam's simple, childlike faith that God would bring all right at last.

Early on Monday afternoon 'Lina, taking advantage of Hugh's absence, came over for her dress, finding much fault, and requiring some of the work to be done twice ere it suited her. Without a murmur Adah obeyed, but when the last stitch was taken and the party dress was gone, her overtaxed frame gave way, and Sam himself helped her to her bed, where she lay moaning, with the blinding pain in her head, which increased so fast that she scarcely saw the tempting little supper which Aunt Eunice brought, asking her to eat. Of one thing, however, she was conscious, and that of the dark form bending over her pillow and whispering soothingly the passage which had once brought Heaven to him, "Come unto me, come unto me, and I will give you rest."

The night had closed in dark and stormy, and the wintry rain beat fiercely against the windows; but for this Sam did not hesitate a moment when at midnight Aunt Eunice, alarmed at Adah's rapidly increasing fever, asked if he could find his way to Spring Bank.

"In course," he could, and in a few moments the old, shriveled form was out in the darkness, groping its way over fences, and through the pitfalls, stumbling often, and losing his hat past recovery, so that the snowy hair was dripping wet when at last Spring Bank was reached and he stood upon the porch.

In much alarm Hugh dressed himself and hastened to the cottage. But Adah did not know him and only talked of dresses and parties, and George, whom she begged to come back and restore her good name.

CHAPTER XII

WHAT FOLLOWED

There was a bright light in the sitting-room, and through the half closed shutters Hugh caught glimpses of a blazing fire. 'Lina had evidently come home, and half wishing she had stayed a little longer, Hugh entered the room.

Poor 'Lina! The party had proved a most unsatisfactory affair. She had not made the sensation she expected to make. Harney had scarcely noticed her at all, having neither eyes nor ears for any one save Ellen Tiffton, who surely must have told that Hugh was not invited, for, in no other way could 'Lina account for the remark she overheard touching her want of heart in failing to resent a brother's insult. In the most unenviable of moods, 'Lina left at a comparatively early hour. She bade Cæsar drive carefully, as it was very dark, and the rain was almost blinding, so rapidly it fell.

"Ye-es, mis-s, Cæs—he—done been to party fore now. Git 'long dar, Sorrel," hiccoughed the negro, who, in Colonel Tiffton's kitchen had indulged rather too freely to insure the safety of his mistress.

Still the horses knew the road, and kept it until they left the main highway and turned into the fields. Even then they would probably have made their way in safety, had not their drunken driver persisted in turning them into a road which led directly through the deepest part of the creek, swollen now by the melted snow and the vast amount of rain which had fallen since the sunsetting. Not knowing they were wrong, 'Lina did not dream of danger until she heard Cæsar's cry of "Who'a dar, Sorrel. Git up, Henry. Dat's nothin' but de creek," while a violent lurch of the carriage sent her to the opposite side from where she had been sitting.

A few mad plunges, another wrench, which pitched 'Lina headlong against the window, and the steep, shelving bank was reached, but in endeavoring to climb it the carriage was upset, and 'Lina found herself in pitchy darkness. Perfectly sobered now, Cæsar extricated her as soon as possible. The carriage was broken and there was no alternative save for 'Lina to walk the remaining distance home. It was not far, for the scene of the disaster was within sight of Spring Bank, but to 'Lina, bedraggled with mud and wet to the skin, it seemed an interminable distance, and her strength was giving out just as she reached the friendly piazza, and called on her mother for help, sobbing hysterically as she repeated her story, but dwelling most upon her ruined dress.

"What will Hugh say? It was not paid for, either. Oh, dear, oh, dear, I most wish I was dead!" she moaned, as her mother removed one by one the saturated garments.

The sight of Hugh called forth her grief afresh, and forgetful of her dishabille, she staggered toward him, and impulsively winding her arms around his neck, sobbed out:

"Oh, Hugh, Hugh! I've had such a doleful time. I've been in the creek, the carriage is broken, the horses are lamed, Cæsar is drunk, and—and—oh, Hugh, I've spoiled my dress!"

Laughing merrily Hugh held her off at a little distance, likening her to a mermaid fresh from the sea, and succeeding at last in quieting her down until she could give a more concise account of the catastrophe.

"Never mind the dress," he said, good-humoredly, as she kept recurring to that. "It isn't as if it were new. An old thing is never so valuable."

Alas, that 'Lina did not then confess the truth. Had she done so he would have forgiven her freely, but she let the golden opportunity pass, and so paved the way for much bitterness of feeling in the future.

During the gloomy weeks which followed, Hugh's heart and hands were full, inclination tempting him to stay by the moaning Adah, who knew the moment he was gone, and stern duty, bidding him keep with delirious 'Lina, who, strange to say, was always more quiet when he was near, taking readily from him the medicine refused when offered by her mother. Day after day, week after week, Hugh watched alternately at the bedsides, and those who came to offer help felt their hearts glow with admiration for the worn, haggard man, whose character they had so mistaken, never dreaming what depths of patient, all-enduring tenderness were hidden beneath his rough exterior. Even Ellen Tiffton was softened, and forgetting the Ladies' Fair, rode daily over to Spring Bank, ostensibly to inquire after 'Lina, but really to speak a kindly word to Hugh, to whom she felt she had done a wrong. How long those fevers ran, and Hugh began to fear that 'Lina's never would abate, sorrowing much for the harsh words which passed between them, wishing they had been unsaid, for he would rather that none but pleasant memories should be left to him of this, his only sister. But 'Lina did not die, and as her disease had from the first assumed a far more violent form than Adah's, so it was the first to yield, and February found her convalescent. With Adah it was different. But there came a change at last, a morning when she awoke from a deathlike stupor which had clouded her faculties so long, as the attending physician said to Hugh that his services would be needed but a little longer. Physicians' bills, together with that of Harney's yet unpaid, for Harney, villain though he was, would not present it when Hugh was full of trouble; but the hour was coming when it must be settled, and Hugh at last received a note, couched in courteous terms, but urging immediate payment.

"I'll see him today. I'll know the worst at once," he said, and mounting Rocket, who never looked more beautiful than he did that afternoon, he dashed down the Frankfort turnpike, and was soon closeted with Harney.

CHAPTER XIII

HOW HUGH PAID HIS DEBTS

The perspiration was standing in great drops about Hugh's quivering lips, and his face was white as ashes, as, near the close of that interview, he hoarsely asked:

"Do I understand you, sir, that Rocket will cancel this debt and leave you my debtor for one hundred dollars?"

"Yes, that was my offer, and a most generous one, too, considering how little horses are bringing," and Harney smiled villainously as he thought within himself: "Easier to manage than I supposed. I believe my soul I offered too much. I should have made it an even thing."

Hugh knew how long this plan had been premeditated, and his blood boiled madly when he heard it suggested, as if that moment had given it birth. Still he restrained himself, and asked the question we have recorded, adding, after Harney's reply:

"And suppose I do not care to part with Rocket?"

Harney winced a little, but answered carelessly:

"Money, of course, is just as good. You know how long I've waited. Few would have done as well."

Yes, Hugh knew that, but Rocket was as dear to him as his right eye, and he would almost as soon have plucked out the one as sold the other.

"I have not the money," he said, frankly, "and I cannot part with Rocket. Is there nothing else? I'll give a mortgage on Spring Bank."

Harney did not care for a mortgage, but there was something else, and the rascally face brightened, as, stepping back, while he made the proposition, he faintly suggested "Lulu." He would give a thousand dollars for her, and Hugh could keep his horse. For a moment the two young men regarded each other intently, Hugh's eyes flashing gleams of fire, and his whole face expressive of the contempt he felt for the wretch who cowed at last beneath the look, and turned away muttering that "he saw nothing so very heinous in wishing to purchase a nigger wench."

Then, changing his tone to one of defiance, he added:

"Since you are not inclined to part with either of your pets, you'll oblige me with the money, and before tomorrow night. You understand me, I presume?"

"I do," and bowing haughtily, Hugh passed through the open door.

In a kind of desperation he mounted Rocket, and dashed out of town at a speed which made more than one look after him, wondering what cause there was for his headlong haste. A few miles from the city he slacked his speed, and dismounting by a running brook, sat down to think. The price offered for Lulu would set him free from every pressing debt, and leave a large surplus, but not for a moment did he hesitate.

"I'd lead her out and shoot her through the heart, before I'd do that thing," he said.

Then turning to the noble animal cropping the grass beside him, he wound his arms around his neck, and tried to imagine how it would seem to know the stall at home was empty, and his beautiful Rocket gone.

"If I could pawn him," he thought, just as the sound of wheels was heard, and he saw old Colonel Tiffton driving down the turnpike.

Between the colonel and his daughter Ellen there had been a conversation that very day touching the young man Hugh, in whom Ellen now felt a growing interest. Seated in their handsome parlor, with her little hands folded listlessly one above the other, Ellen was listening, while her father told her mother.

"He didn't see how that chap was ever to pay his debts. One doctor twice a day for three months was enough to ruin anybody, let alone having two," and the sometimes far-seeing old colonel shook his head doubtfully.

"Father," and Ellen stole softly to his side, "if Mr. Worthington wants money so badly, you'll lend it to him, won't you?"

Again a doubtful shake as the prudent colonel replied: "And lose every red I lend, hey? That's the way a woman would do, I s'pose, but I am too old for that. Now, if he could give good security, I wouldn't mind, but what's he got, pray, that we want?"

Ellen's gray eyes scanned his face curiously a moment, and then Ellen's rather pretty lips whispered in his ear: "He's got Rocket, pa."

"Yes, yes, so he has; but no power on earth could make him part with that nag. I've always liked that boy, always liked old John, but the plague knows what he did with his money."

"You'll help Hugh?" and Ellen returned to the attack.

"Well," said the old man, "we'll see about this Hugh matter," and the colonel left the house, and entered the buggy which had been waiting to take him to Frankfort.

"That's funny that I should run a-foul of him," he thought, stopping suddenly as he caught sight of Hugh, and calling out cheerily: "How d'ye, young man? That's a fine nag of yours. My Nell is nigh about crazy for me to buy him. What'll you take?"

"What'll you give?" was Hugh's Yankeelike response, while the colonel, struck by Hugh's peculiar manner, settled himself back in his buggy and announced himself ready to trade.

Hugh knew he could trust the colonel, and after a moment's hesitation told of his embarrassments, and asked the loan of five hundred dollars, offering Rocket as security, with the privilege of redeeming him in a year.

"You ask a steep sum," he said, "but I take it you are in a tight spot and don't know what else to do. That girl in the snow bank—I'll be hanged if that was ever made quite clear to me."

"It is to me, and that is sufficient," Hugh answered, while the old colonel replied:

"Good grit, Hugh. I like you for that. In short, I like you for everything, and that's why I was sorry about that New York lady. You see, it may stand in the way of your getting a wife by and by, that's all."

"I shall never marry," Hugh answered, thinking of the Golden Haired.

"No?" the colonel replied. "Well, there ain't many good enough for you, that's a fact, and so I tell 'em when they get to—get to—"

Hugh looked up inquiringly, his face flashing as he guessed at what they got.

"Bless me, there's ain't many girls good for anybody. I never saw but one, except my Nell, that was worth a picayune, and that was Alice Johnson."

"Who? Who did you say?" And Hugh grew white as marble.

The colonel replied: "I said Alice Johnson, twentieth cousin of mine—blast that fly!—lives in Massachusetts; splendid girl—hang it all can't I hit him?—there, I've killed him." And the colonel put up his whip, never dreaming of the effect that name had produced on Hugh, whose heart gave one great throb of hope, and then grew heavy and sad as he thought how impossible it was that the Alice Johnson the colonel knew could be the Golden Haired.

"There are fifty by that name, no doubt," he said, "and if there were not, she is dead."

Hugh dared not question the colonel further, and was only too glad when the latter said: "If I understand you, I can have Rocket for five hundred dollars, provided I let you redeem him within a year. Now that's equivalent to my lending you five hundred dollars out and out. I see, but seeing it's you, I reckon I'll have to do it. As luck will have it, I was going down to Frankfort this very day to put some money in the bank, and if you say so, we'll clinch the bargain at once," and the colonel began to count the amount.

Alice Johnson was forgotten in that moment when Hugh felt as if his very life was dying out. Then chiding himself as weak, he lifted up his head and said: "Rocket is yours."

The words were like a sob; and the generous old man hesitated. But Hugh was in earnest. His debts must be paid, and that five hundred dollars would do it.

"I'll bring him around tomorrow. Will that be time enough?" he asked, as he rolled up the bills.

"Yes, oh, yes," the colonel replied, while Hugh continued:

"And, colonel, you'll—you'll be kind to Rocket. He's never been struck a blow since he was broken to the saddle. He wouldn't know what it meant."

"Oh, yes, I see—Rarey's method. Now I never could make that work. Have to lick 'em sometimes, but I'll remember Rocket. Good-day," and gathering up his reins Colonel Tiffton rode slowly away.

Hugh rode back to Frankfort and dismounted at Harney's door.

In silence Harney received the money, gave his receipt, and then watched Hugh as he rode again from town, muttering: "I shall remember that he knocked me down, and some time I'll repay it."

It was dark when Hugh reached home, his flashing eyes indicating the storm which burst forth the moment he entered the room where 'Lina was sitting. In tones which made even her tremble he accused her of her treachery, pouring forth such a torrent of wrath that his mother urged him to stop, for her sake if no other. She could always quiet Hugh, and he calmed down at once, hurling but one more missile at his sister, and that in the shape of Rocket, who, he said, was sold for her extravagance.

'Lina was proud of Rocket, and the knowledge that he was sold touched her far more than all Hugh's angry words. But her tear a were of no avail; the deed was done, and on the morrow Hugh, with an unflinching hand, led his idol from the stable and rode rapidly across the fields, leading another horse which was to bring him home.

The next morning Lulu came running up the stairs, exclaiming:

"He's done come home, Rocket has. He's at the kitchen door."

It was even as Lulu, said, for the homesick brute, suspecting something wrong, had broken from his fastenings, and bursting the stable door had come back to Spring Bank, his halter dangling about his neck, and himself looking very defiant, as if he were not again to be coaxed away. At sight of Hugh he uttered a sound of joy, and bounding forward planted both feet within the door ere Hugh had time to reach it.

"Thar's the old colonel now," whispered Claib, just as the colonel himself appeared to claim his runaway.

"I'll take him home myself," he said to the old colonel, emerging from his hiding place behind the leach, and bidding Claib follow with another horse Hugh went a second time to Colonel Tiffton's farm.

CHAPTER XIV

MRS. JOHNSON'S LETTER

The spring had passed away, and the warm June sun was shining over Spring Bank, whose mistress and servants were very lonely now, for Hugh was absent, and with him the light of the house had departed. Business of his late uncle's had taken him to New Orleans, where he might possibly remain all the summer. 'Lina was glad, for since the fatal dress affair there had been but little harmony between herself and her brother. The tenderness awakened by her long illness seemed to have been forgotten, and Hugh's manner toward her was cold and irritating to the last degree, so that the young lady rejoiced to be freed from his presence.

"I do hope he'll stay all summer," she said one morning, when speaking of him to her mother. "I think it's a heap nicer without him, though dull enough at the best. I wish we could go somewhere, some watering place I mean. There's the Tifftons, just returned from New York, and I don't much believe they can afford it more than we, for I heard their place was mortgaged, or something. Oh, bother, to be so poor," and the young lady gave a little angry jerk at the tags she was unbraiding.

"Whar's ole miss's?" asked Claib, who had just returned from Versailles. "Thar's a letter for you," and depositing it upon the bureau, he left the room.

"Whose writing is that?" 'Lina said, catching it up and examining the postmark. "Shall I open it?" she called, and ere her mother could reply, she had broken the seal, and held in her hand the draft which made her the heiress of one thousand dollars.

Had the fabled godmother of Cinderella appeared to her suddenly, she would scarcely have been more bewildered.

"Mother," she screamed again, reading aloud the " 'Pay to the order of Adaline Worthington,' etc. Who is Alice Johnson? What does she say? 'My dear Eliza, feeling that I have not long to live—' What—dead, hey? Well, I'm sorry for that, but, I must say, she did a very sensible thing at the last, sending me a thousand dollars. We'll go somewhere now, won't we?" and clutching fast the draft, the heartless girl yielded the letter to her mother, who, burying her face in her hands, sobbed bitterly as the past came back to her, when the Alice, now at rest and herself were girls together.

'Lina took up the letter her mother had dropped and read it through. "Wants you to take her daughter, Alice. Is the woman crazy? And her nurse, Densie, Densie Densmore. Where have I heard that name before? Say, mother, let's talk the matter over. Shall you let Alice come? Ten dollars a week, they'll pay. Let me see. Five hundred and twenty dollars a year. Whew! We are rich as Jews. Our ship is really coming in," and 'Lina rang the bell and ordered Lulu to bring "a lemonade with ice cut fine and a heap of sugar in it."

By this time Mrs. Worthington was able to talk of a matter which had apparently so delighted 'Lina. Her first remark, however, was not very pleasant to the young lady:

"I would willingly give Alice a home, but it's not for me to say. Hugh alone can decide it."

"You know he'll refuse," was 'Lina'a angry reply. "He hates young ladies. So you may as well save your postage to New Orleans, and write at once to Miss Johnson that she cannot come on account of a boorish clown."

"'Lina," feebly interposed Mrs. Worthington, "'Lina, we must write to Hugh."

"Mother, you shall not," and 'Lina spoke determinedly. "I'll send an answer to this letter myself, this very day. I will not suffer the chance to be thrown away. Hugh may swear a little at first, but he'll get over it."

"Hugh never swears," and Mrs. Worthington spoke up at once.

"He don't hey? Maybe you've forgotten when he came home from Frankfort, that time he heard about my dress!"

"I know he swore then; but he never has since, I'm sure, and I think he is better, gentler, more refined than he used to be, since—since—Adah came."

A contemptuous "Pshaw!" came from 'Lina's lips. "Say," she continued, "wouldn't you rather Adah were your child than me? Then you'd be granny, you know." And a laugh came from 'Lina's lips.

Mrs. Worthington did not reply; and 'Lina proceeded to speak of Alice Johnson, asking for her family. Were they aristocratic? Were they the F.F.V.'s of Boston? and so forth.

"Now let us talk a little about the thousand dollars. What shall I do with it?" 'Lina said, for already the money was beginning to burn in her hands.

"Redeem Rocket with half of it," Mrs. Worthington said, "and that will reconcile Hugh to Alice Johnson."

"Do you think I've taken leave of my senses?" 'Lina asked, with unaffected surprise. "Buy Rocket for five hundred dollars! Indeed, I shall do no such thing. If Hugh had not sworn so awfully, I might; but I remember what he said too well to part with half of my inheritance for him. I'm going to Saratoga, and you are going, too. We'll have heaps of dresses, and—oh, mother, won't it be grand! We'll take Lu for a waiting maid. That will be sure to make a sensation at the North. I can imagine just how old Deacon Tripp of Elwood, would open his eyes when he heard 'Mrs. Square Worthington and darter' had come back with a 'nigger.' It would furnish him with material for half a dozen monthly concerts, and I'm not sure but he'd try to run her off, if he had a chance. But Lu likes Hugh too well ever to be coaxed away; so we're safe on that score. 'Mrs. Worthington, daughter, and colored servant, Spring Bank, Kentucky.' I can almost see that on the clerk's books at the United States. Then I can manage to let it be known that I'm an heiress, as I am. We needn't tell that it's only a thousand dollars, most of which I have on my back, and maybe I'll come home Adaline somebody else. There are always splendid matches at Saratoga. We'll go North the middle of July, just three weeks from now."

'Lina had talked so fast that Mrs. Worthington had been unable to put in a word; but it did not matter. 'Lina was invulnerable to all she could say, and it was in vain that she pleaded for Rocket, or reminded the ungrateful girl of the many long, weary nights, when Hugh had sat by her bedside, holding her feverish hands and bathing her aching head. This was very kind and brotherly, 'Lina admitted; but she steeled her heart against the still, small voice, which whispered to her: "Redeem Rocket, and let Hugh find him here when he gets home."

'Lina wrote to Alice Johnson herself that morning, went to Frankfort that afternoon, to Versailles and Lexington the next day, and on the morning of the third day after the receipt of Mrs. Johnson's letter, Spring Bank presented the appearance of one vast show-room, so full it was of silks and muslins and tissues and flowers and ribbons and laces, while amid it all, in a maze of perplexity as to what was required of her, or where first to commence, Adah Hastings sat, a flush on her fair cheeks, and a tear half dimming the luster of her eyes as thoughts of Willie crying for mamma at home, and refusing to be comforted even by old Sam came to her.

When 'Lina first made known her request to Adah, to act as her dressmaker, Aunt Eunice had objected, on the ground of Adah's illness having been induced by overwork, but 'Lina insisted so strenuously, promising not to task her too much, and offering with an air of extreme generosity to pay three shillings a day, that Adah had consented, for pretty baby Willie wanted many little things which Hugh would never dream of, and for which she could not ask him. Three shillings a day for twelve days or more seemed like a fortune to Adah, and so she tore herself away from Willie's clinging arms and went willingly to labor for the capricious 'Lina, ten times more impatient and capricious since she "had come into possession of property."

Womanlike, the sight of 'Lina's dresses awoke in Adah a thrill of delight, and she entered heartily into the matter without a single feeling of envy.

"I's goin', too. Did you know that?" Lulu said to her as she sat bending over a cloud of lace and soft blue silk.

"Do you want to go?" Adah asked, and Lulu replied:

"Not much. Miss 'Lina will be so lofty. Jes' you listen and hear her call me oncet. 'Ho Loo-loo, come quick,' jes' as if she done nothin' all her life but order a nigger 'round. I knows better. I knows how she done made her own bed, combed her own ha'r, and like enough washed her own rags afore she comed here. Yes, 'Loo-loo is coming,'" and the saucy wench darted off to 'Lina screaming loudly for her.

"Miss Worthington," Adah said, timidly, as 'Lina came near, "Lulu tells me she is going North with you. Why not take me instead of her?"

"You!" and 'Lina's black eyes flashed scornfully. "What in the world could I do with you and that child, and what would people think? Why, I'd rather have Lulu forty times. A negro gives an*éclat*to one's position which a white servant cannot. By the way, here is Miss Tiffton's square-necked bertha. She's just got home from New York, and says they are all the fashion. You are to cut me a pattern. There's a paper, the Louisville *Journal*, I guess, but nobody reads it, now Hugh is gone," and with a few more general directions, 'Lina hurried away leaving Adah so hot, so disappointed, that the hot tears fell upon the paper she took in her hand, the paper containing Anna Richards' advertisement, intended solely for the poor girl sitting so lonely and sad at Spring Bank that summer morning.

In spite of the doctor's predictions and consignment of that girl to Georgia, or some warmer place, it had reached her at last. She did not see it at first, so fast her tears fell, but just as her scissors were raised to cut the pattern her eyes fell on the spot headed, "A Curious Advertisement," and suspending her operations for a moment, she read it through, a feeling rising in her heart that it was surely an answer to her own advertisement, sent forth months ago, with tearful prayers that it might be successful.

At the table she heard 'Lina say that Claib was going to town that afternoon, and thinking within herself. "If a letter were only ready, he could take it with him," she asked permission to write a few lines. It would not take her long, she said, and she could work the later to make it up.

'Lina did not refuse, and in a few moments Adah penned a note to A.E.R.

"It's an answer to an advertisement for a governess or waiting maid," she said, as 'Lina glanced carelessly at the superscription.

"It will do no harm, or good either, I imagine," was 'Lina'a reply, and placing the letter in her pocket, she was about returning to her mother, when she spied Ellen Tiffton dismounting at the gate.

Ellen was delighted to see 'Lina, and 'Lina was delighted to see Ellen, leading her at once into the work-room, where Adah sat by the window, busy on the bertha, and looking up quietly when Ellen entered, as if half expecting an introduction. But 'Lina did not deign to notice her, save in an aside to Ellen, to whom she whispered softly:

"That girl, Adah, you know."

Reared in a country where the menials all were black, Ellen knew no such marked distinction among the whites, and walked directly up to Adah, whose face seemed to puzzle her. It was the first time they had met, and Adah turned crimson beneath the close scrutiny to which she was subjected. Noticing her embarrassment, and wishing to relieve it, Ellen addressed to her some trivial remark concerning her work, complimenting her skill, asking some questions about Willie, whom she had seen, and then leaving her for a girlish conversation with 'Lina, to whom she related many particulars of her visit to New York. Particularly was she pleased with a certain Dr. Richards, who was described as the most elegant young man at the hotel.

"There was something queer about him too," she said, in a lower tone, and drawing nearer to 'Lina. "He seemed so absent-like, as if there were something on his mind—some heart trouble, you know; but that only made him more interesting; and such an adventure as I had, too. Send her out of the room, please," and nodding toward Adah, Ellen spoke beneath her breath.

'Lina comprehended her meaning, and turning to Adah said rather haughtily:

"It's cool on the west end of the piazza. You may go and sit there a while."

With a heightened color at being thus addressed before a stranger, Adah withdrew, and Ellen continued:

"It's so strange. I found in the hall, near my door, a tiny ambrotype of a young girl, who must have been very beautiful—such splendid hair, soft brown eyes, and cheeks like carnation pinks. I wondered much whose it was, for I knew the owner must be sorry to lose it. Father suggested that we put a written notice in the business office, and that very afternoon Dr. Richards knocked at our door, saying the ambrotype was his. 'I would not lose it for the world,' he said, 'as the original is dead,' and he looked so sad that I pitied him so much; but I have the strangest part yet to tell. You are sure she cannot hear?" and walking to the open window, Ellen glanced down the long piazza to where Adah's dress was visible.

"I looked at the face so much that I never can forget it, particularly the way the hair was worn, combed almost as low upon the forehead as you wears yours, and just as that Mrs. Hastings wears hers. I noticed it the moment I came in; and, 'Lina, Mrs. Hastings is the original of that ambrotype, I'm sure, only the picture was younger, fresher-looking, than she. But they are the same, I'm positive, and that's why I started so when I first saw this Adah. Funny, isn't it?"

'Lina knew just how positive Ellen was with regard to any opinion she espoused, and presumed in her own mind that in this point, as in many others, she was mistaken. Still she answered that it was queer, though she could not understand what Adah could possibly be to Dr. Richards.

"Call her in for something and I'll manage to question her. I'm so curious and so sure," Ellen said, while 'Lina called: "Adah, Miss Tiffton wishes to see how my new blue muslin fits. Come help me try it on."

Obedient to the call Adah came, and was growing very red in the face with trying to hook 'Lina's dress, when Ellen casually remarked:

"You lived in New York, I think?"

"Yes, ma'am," was the reply, and Ellen continued:

"Maybe I saw some of your acquaintances. I was there a long time."

Oh, how eagerly Adah turned toward her now, the glad thought flashing upon her that possibly she meant George. Maybe he'd come home.

"Whom did you see?" she asked, her eyes fixed wistfully on Ellen, who replied:

"Oh, a great many. There was Mr. Reed, and Mr. Benedict, and Mr. Ward, and—well, I saw the most of Dr. Richards, perhaps. Do you know either of them?"

"No, I never heard of them before," was the reply, so frankly spoken that Ellen was confounded, for she felt sure that Dr. Richards was a name entirely new to Adah.

"I thought you were mistaken," 'Lina said, when the dress was taken off and Adah gone. "A man such as you describe the doctor would not care for a poor girl like Adah. Is his home at New York, and are you sure he'll be at Saratoga?"

"He said so; and I think he told me his mother and sisters were in some such place as Snow-down, or Snow-something."

"Snowdon," suggested 'Lina. "That's where Alice Johnson lives. I must tell you of her."

"Alice Johnson," Ellen repeated; "why, that's the girl father says so much about. Of course I fell in the scale, for there was nothing like Alice, Alice—so beautiful, so religious."

"Religious!" and 'Lina laughed scornfully. "Adah pretends to be religious, too, and so does Sam, while Alice will make three. Pleasant prospects ahead. I wonder if she's the blue kind—thinks dancing wicked, and all that."

Ellen could not tell. She thought it queer that Mrs. Johnson should send her to a stranger, as it were, when they would have been so glad to receive her. "Pa won't like it a bit, and she'd be so much more comfortable with us," and Ellen glanced contemptuously around at the neat but plainly-furnished room.

It was not the first time Ellen had offended by a similar remark, and 'Lina flared up at once. Mrs. Johnson knew her mother well, and knew to whom she was committing her daughter.

"Did she know Hugh, too?" hot-tempered Ellen asked, sneeringly, whereupon there ensued a contest of words touching Hugh, in which Rocket, the Ladies' Fair, and divers other matters figured conspicuously, and when, ten minutes later, Ellen left the house, she carried with her the square-necked bertha, together with sundry other little articles of dress, which she had lent for patterns, and the two were, on the whole, as angry as a sandy-haired and black-eyed girl could be.

"What a stupid I was to say such hateful things of Hugh, when I really do like him," was Ellen's comment as she galloped away, while 'Lina muttered: "I stood up for Hugh once, anyhow. To think of her twitting me about our house, when everybody says the colonel is likely to fail any day," and 'Lina ran off upstairs to indulge in a fit of crying over what she called Nell Tiffton's meanness.

One week later and there came a letter from Alice herself, saying that at present she was stopping in Boston with her guardian, Mr. Liston, who had rented the cottage in Snowdon, but that she would meet Mrs. Worthington and daughter at Saratoga. Of course she did not now feel like mingling in gay society and should consequently go to the Columbian, where she could be comparatively quiet; but this need not in the least interfere with their arrangements, as the United States was very near, and they could see each other often.

The same day also brought a letter from Hugh, making many kind inquiries after them all, saying his business was turning out better than he expected, and inclosing forty dollars, fifteen of which, he said, was for Adah, and the rest for Ad, as a peace offering for the harsh things he had said to her. Forty dollars was just the price of a superb pearl bracelet in Lexington, and if Hugh had only sent it all to her instead of a part to Adah! The letter was torn in shreds, and 'Lina went to Lexington next day in quest of the bracelet, which was pronounced beautiful by the unsuspecting Adah, who never dreamed that her money had helped to pay for it. Truly 'Lina was heaping up against herself a dark catalogue of sin to be avenged some day, but the time was not yet.

Thus far everything went swimmingly. The dresses fitted admirably, and nothing could exceed the care with which they had been packed. Her mother no longer bothered her about Hugh. Lulu was quite well posted with regard to her duty.

Thus it was in the best of humors, that 'Lina tripped from Spring Bank door one pleasant July morning, and was driven with her mother and Lulu to Lexington, where they intended taking the evening train for Cincinnati.

CHAPTER XV

SARATOGA

"Mrs. Worthington, daughter, and colored servant, Spring Bank, Kentucky."

"Dr. John Richards and mother, New York City."

"Irving Stanley, Esq., Baltimore."

These were the last entries the flaxen-haired clerk at Union Hall had made, feeling sure, as he made them, that each one had been first to the United States, and failing to find accommodations there, had come down to Union Hall.

The Union was so crowded that for the newcomers no rooms were found except the small, uncomfortable ones far up in the fourth story of the Ainsworth block, and thither, in not the most amiable mood, 'Lina followed her trunks, and was followed in turn by her mother and Lulu, the crowd whom they passed deciphering the name upon the trunks and whispering to each other: "From Spring Bank, Kentucky. Haughty-looking girl, wasn't she?"

From his little twelve by ten apartment, where the summer sun was pouring in a perfect blaze of heat, Dr. Richards saw them pass, and after wondering who they were, and hoping they would be comfortable in their pen, gave them no further thought, but sat jamming his penknife into the old worm-eaten table, and thinking savage thoughts against that capricious lady, Fortune, who had compelled him to come to Saratoga, where rich wives were supposed to be had for the asking. In Dr. Richard's vest pocket there lay at this very moment a delicate little note, the meaning of which was that Alice Johnson declined the honor of becoming his wife. Now he was ready for the first chance that offered, provided that chance possessed a certain style, and was tolerably good-looking.

This, then, was Dr. Richards' errand to Saratoga, and one cause of his disgust at being banished from the United States, where heiresses were usually to be found in such abundance.

From his pleasanter, airier apartment, on the other side of the narrow hall, Irving Stanley looked out through his golden glasses, pitying the poor ladies condemned to that slow roast.

How hot, and dusty, and cross 'Lina was, and what a look of dismay she cast around the room, with its two bedsteads, its bureau, its table, its washstand, and its dozen pegs for her two dozen dresses, to say nothing of her mother's.

How tired and faint poor Mrs. Worthington was, sinking down upon the high-post bed! How she wished she had stayed at home, like a sensible woman, instead of coming here to be made so uncomfortable in this hot room. But it could not now be helped, 'Lina said; they must do the best they could; and with a forlorn glance at the luxuriant patch of weeds, the most prominent view from the window, 'Lina opened one of her trunks, and spreading a part of its contents upon the bed, began to dress for dinner. The dinner bell had long since ceased ringing, and the tread of feet ceased in the halls below ere she descended to the deserted parlor, followed by her mother, nervous and frightened at the prospect of this, her first appearance at Saratoga.

"Pray, rouse yourself," 'Lina whispered, "and not let them guess you were never at a watering place before," and 'Lina thoughtfully smoothed her mother's cap by way of reassuring her.

But even 'Lina herself quailed when she reached the door and caught a glimpse of the busy life within, the terrible ordeal she must pass.

"Oh, for a pair of pantaloons to walk beside one, even if Hugh were in them," she thought, as her own and her mother's lonely condition arose before her.

"Courage, mother," she whispered again, and then advanced into the room, growing bolder at every step, for with one rapid glance she had swept the hall, and felt that amid that bevy of beauty and fashion there were few more showy than 'Lina Worthington in her rustling dress of green, with Ellen Tiffton's bracelet on one arm and the one bought with Adah's money on the other.

Not having been an heiress long enough to know just what was expected of her, and fancying it quite in character to domineer over every colored person just as she did over Lulu, 'Lina issued her commands with a dignity worthy of the firm of Mrs. Worthington & Daughter. Bowing deferentially, the polite attendant quickly drew back her chair, while she spread out her flowing skirts to an extent which threatened to envelop her mother, sinking meekly into her seat, not confused and flurried. But alas for 'Lina. The servant did not calculate the distance aright, and my lady, who had meant to do the thing so gracefully, who had intended showing the people that she had been to Saratoga before, suddenly found herself prostrate upon the floor, the chair some way behind her, and the plate, which, in her descent, she had grasped unconsciously, flying off diagonally past her mother's head, and fortunately past the head of her mother's left-hand neighbor.

Poor 'Lina! How she wished she might never get up again.

At first, 'Lina thought nothing could keep her tears back, they gathered so fast in her eyes, and her voice trembled so that she could not answer the servant's question:

"Soup, madam, soup?"

But he of the white hand did it for her.

"Of course she'll take soup," then in an aside, he said to her gently: "Never mind, you are not the first lady who has been served in that way. It's quite a common occurrence."

There was something reassuring in his voice, and turning toward him for the first time, 'Lina caught the gleam of the golden glasses, and knew that her*vis-à-vis*upstairs was also her right-hand neighbor. Who was he, and whom did he so strikingly resemble? Suddenly it came to her. Saving the glasses, he was very much like Hugh. No handsomer, not a whit, but more accustomed to society, easier in his manners and more gallant to ladies. Could it be Irving Stanley? she asked herself, remembering now to have heard that he did resemble Hugh, and also that he wore glasses. Yes, she was sure, and the red which the doctor had pronounced "well put on," deepened on her cheeks, until her whole face was crimson with mortification, that such should have been her first introduction to the aristocratic Irving.

Kind and gentle as a woman, Irving Stanley was sometimes laughed at by his own sex, as too gentle, too feminine in disposition; but those who knew him best loved him most, and loved him, too, just because he was not so stern, so harsh, so overbearing as lords of creation are wont to be.

Such was Irving Stanley, and 'Lina might well be thankful that her lot was cast so near him. He did not talk to her at the table further than a few commonplace remarks, but when, after dinner was over, and his Havana smoked, he found her sitting with her mother out in the grove, apart from everybody, and knew instantly that they were there alone, he went to them at once, and ere many minutes had elapsed discovered to his surprise that they were his so-called cousins from Kentucky. Nothing could exceed 'Lina's delight. He was there unfettered by mother or sister or sweetheart, and of course would attach himself exclusively to her. 'Lina was very happy, and more than once her loud laugh rang out so loud that Irving, with all his charity, had a faint suspicion that around his Kentucky cousin, brilliant though she was, there might linger a species of coarseness, not altogether agreeable to one of his refinement. Still he sat chatting with her until the knowing dowagers, who year after year watch such things at Saratoga, whispered behind their fans of a flirtation between the elegant Mr. Stanley and that dark, haughty-looking girl from Kentucky.

"I never saw him so familiar with a stranger upon so short an acquaintance," said fat Mrs. Buford.

"Is that Irving Stanley, whom Lottie Gardner talks so much about?" And Mrs. Richards leveled her glass again, for Irving Stanley was not unknown to her by reputation. "She must be somebody, John, or he would not notice her," and she spoke in an aside, adding in a louder tone: "I wonder who she is? There's their servant. I mean to question her," and as Lulu came near, she said: "Girl, who do you belong to?"

"'Longs to them," answered Lulu, jerking her head toward 'Lina and Mrs. Worthington.

"Where do you live?" was the next query, and Lulu replied:

"Spring Bank, Kentucky. Missus live in big house, 'most as big as this;" then anxious to have the ordeal passed, and fearful that she might not acquit herself satisfactorily to 'Lina, who, without seeming to notice her, had drawn near enough to hear, she added: "Miss 'Lina is an airey, a very large airey, and has a heap of—of—" Lulu hardly knew what, but finally in desperation added: "a heap of a'rs," and then fled away ere another question could be asked her.

"What did she say she was?" Mrs. Richards asked, and the doctor replied:

"She said an airey. She meant an heiress."

Money, or the reputation of possessing money, is an all-powerful charm, and in few places does it show its power more plainly than at Saratoga, where it was soon known that the lady from Spring Bank, with pearls in her hair, and pearl bracelets on her arms, was heiress to immense wealth in Kentucky, how immense nobody knew, and various were the estimates put upon it. Among Mrs. Bufort's clique it was twenty thousand, farther away in another hall it was fifty, while Mrs. Richards, ere the supper hour arrived, had heard that it was at least a hundred thousand dollars. How or where she heard it she hardly knew, but she indorsed the statement as current, and at the tea table that night was exceedingly gracious to 'Lina and her mother, offering to divide a little private dish which she had ordered for herself, and into which poor Mrs. Worthington inadvertently dipped, never dreaming that it was not common property.

"It was not of the slightest consequence, Mrs. Richards was delighted to share it with her," and that was the way the conversation commenced.

'Lina knew now that the proud man whose lip had curled so scornfully at dinner was Ellen's Dr. Richards, and Dr. Richards knew that the girl who sat on the floor was 'Lina Worthington, from Spring Bank, where Alice Johnson was going.

CHAPTER XVI

THE COLUMBIAN

It was very quiet at the Columbian, and the few gentlemen seated upon the piazza seemed to be of a different stamp from those at the more fashionable houses, as there were none of them smoking, nor did they stare impertinently at the gayly-dressed lady coming-up the steps, and inquiring of the clerk if Miss Alice Johnson were there.

Yes, she was, and her room was No. ——. Should he send the lady's card? Miss Johnson had mostly kept her room.

'Lina had brought no card, but she gave her name, and passed on into the parlor, which afforded a striking contrast to the beehive downtown. In a corner two or three were sitting; another group occupied a window; while at the piano were two more, an old and a young lady; the latter of whom was seated upon the stool, and with her foot upon the soft pedal, was alternately striking a few sweet, musical chords, and talking to her companion, who seemed to be a little deaf.

"This is Miss Johnson," and the waiter bowed toward the musician, who, quick as thought, seized upon the truth, and springing to Mrs. Worthington's side, exclaimed:

"It's Mrs. Worthington, I know, my mother's early friend. Why did you sit here so long without speaking to me? I am Alice Johnson," and overcome with the emotions awakened by the sight of her mother's early friend, Alice hid her face with childlike confidence in Mrs. Worthington's bosom, and sobbed for a moment bitterly.

Then growing calm, she lifted up her head and smiling through her tears said:

"Forgive me for this introduction. It is not often I give way, for I know and am sure it was best and right that mother should die. I am not rebellious now, but the sight of you brought it back so vividly. You'll be my mother, won't you?" and kissing the fat white hands involuntarily smoothing her bright hair, the impulsive girl nestled closer to Mrs. Worthington, looking up into her face with a confiding affection which won a place for her at once in Mrs. Worthington's heart.

"My darling," she said, winding her arm around her waist, "as far as I can I will be to you a mother, and 'Lina shall be your sister. This is 'Lina, dear," and she turned to 'Lina, who, piqued at having been so long unnoticed, was frowning gloomily.

But 'Lina never met a glance purer or more free from guile than that which Alice gave her, and it disarmed her at once of all jealousy, making her return the orphan's kisses with as much apparent cordiality as they had been given. During this scene the woman of the snowy hair and jet black eyes had stood silently by, regarding 'Lina with that same curious expression which had so annoyed the young lady, and from which she now intuitively shrank.

"My nurse, Densie Densmore," Alice said at last, adding in an aside: "She is somewhat deaf and may not hear distinctly, unless you speak quite loud. Poor old Densie," she continued, as the latter bowed to her new acquaintances, and then seated herself at a respectful distance. "She has been in our family for a long time." Then changing the conversation, Alice made many inquiries concerning Kentucky, startling them with the announcement that she had that day received a letter from Colonel Tiffton, who she believed was a friend of theirs, urging her to spend a few weeks with him. "They heard from you what were mother's plans for my future, and also that I was to meet you here. They must be very thoughtful people, for they seem to know that I cannot be very happy here."

For a moment 'Lina and her mother looked aghast, and neither knew what to say. 'Lina, as usual, was the first to rally and calculate results.

They were very intimate at Colonel Tiffton's. She and Ellen were fast friends. It was very pleasant there, more so than at Spring Bank; and all the objection she could see to Alice's going was the fear lest she should become so much attached to Mosside, the colonel's residence, as to be homesick at Spring Bank.

"If she's going, I hope she'll go before Dr. Richards sees her, though perhaps he knows her already—his mother lives in Snowdon," 'Lina thought, and rather abruptly she asked if Alice knew Dr. Richards, who was staying at the Union.

Alice blushed crimson as she replied:

"Yes, I know him very well and his family, too. Are either of his sisters with him?"

"His mother is here," 'Lina replied, "and I like her so much. She is very familiar and friendly; don't you think so?"

Alice would not tell a lie, and she answered frankly:

"She does not bear that name in Snowdon. They consider her very haughty there. I think you must be a favorite."

"Are they very aristocratic and wealthy?" 'Lina asked, and Alice answered:

"Aristocratic, not wealthy. They were very kind to me, and the doctor's sister, Anna, is one of the sweetest ladies I ever knew. She may possibly be here during the summer. She is an invalid, and has been for years."

Suddenly Ellen Tiffton's story of the ambrotype flashed into 'Lina's mind. Alice might know something of it, and after a little she asked if the doctor had not at one time been engaged.

Alice did not know. It was very possible. Why did Miss

Worthington ask the question?

'Lina did not stop to consider the propriety or impropriety of making so free with a stranger, and unhesitatingly repeated what Ellen Tiffton had told her of the ambrotype. This, of course, compelled her to speak of Adah, who, she said, came to them under very suspicious circumstances, and was cared for by her eccentric brother, Hugh.

In spite of the look of entreaty visible on Mrs. Worthington's face, 'Lina said:

"To be candid with you, Miss Johnson, I'm afraid you won't like Hugh. He has many good traits, but I am sorry to say we have never succeeded in cultivating him one particle, so that he is very rough and boorish in his manner, and will undoubtedly strike you unfavorably. I may as well tell you this, as you will probably hear it from Ellen Tiffton, and must know it when you see him. He is not popular with the ladies; he hates them all, he says. Mother, Looloo, come," and breaking off from her very sisterly remarks concerning Hugh, 'Lina sprang up in terror as a large beetle, attracted by the light, fastened itself upon her hair.

Mrs. Worthington was the first to the rescue, while Lulu, who had listened with flashing eye when Hugh was the subject of remark, came laggardly, whispering slyly to Alice:

"That's a lie she done tell you about Mas'r Hugh. He ain't rough, nor bad, and we blacks would die for him any day."

Alice was confounded at this flat contradiction between mistress and servant, while a faint glimmer of the truth began to dawn upon her. The "horn-bug" being disposed of, 'Lina became quiet, and might, perhaps, have taken up Hugh again, but for a timely interruption in the shape of Irving Stanley, who had walked up to the Columbian, and seeing 'Lina and her mother through the window, sauntered leisurely into the parlor.

"Ah, Mr. Stanley," and 'Lina half arose from her chair, thus intimating that he was to join them. "Miss Johnson, Mr. Stanley," and 'Lina watched them closely.

"You have positively been smitten by Miss Johnson's pretty face," said 'Lina, laughing a little spitefully, as they parted at the piazza, Irving to go after his accustomed glasses of water, and 'Lina to seek out Dr. Richards in the parlor. "Yes, I know you are smitten, and inasmuch as we are cousins, I shall expect to see you at Spring Bank some day not far in the future."

"It is quite probable you will," was Irving's reply, as he walked away, his head and heart full of Alice Johnson.

Meantime "Mrs. Worthington, daughter and servant," had entered the still crowded parlors, where Mrs. Richards sat fanning herself industriously, and watching her John with motherly interest as he sauntered from one group of ladies to another, wondering what made Saratoga so dull, and where Miss Worthington had gone. It is not to be supposed that Dr. Richards cared a fig for Miss Worthington as Miss Worthington. It was simply her immense figure he admired, and as, during the evening he had heard on good authority that said figure was made up mostly of cotton growing on some Southern field, the exact locality of which his informant did not know, he had decided that, of course, Miss 'Lina's fortune was over-estimated. Such things always were, but still she must be wealthy. He had no doubt of that, and he might as well devote himself to her as to wait for some one else. Accordingly the moment he spied her in the crowd he joined her, asking if they should not take a little turn up and down the piazza.

"Wait till I ask mamma's permission to stay up a little longer. She always insists upon my keeping such early hours," was 'Lina's very filial and childlike reply, as she walked up to mamma, not to ask permission, but to whisper rather peremptorily, "Dr. Richards wishes me to walk with him, and as you are tired, you may as well go to bed!"

Meantime the doctor and 'Lina were walking up and down the long piazza, chatting gayly, and attracting much attention from 'Lina's loud manner of talking and laughing.

"By the way, I've called on Miss Johnson, at the Columbian," she said. "Beautiful, isn't she?"

"Ra-ather pretty, some would think," and the doctor had an uncomfortable consciousness of the refusal in his vest pocket.

If Alice had told. But no, he knew her better than that. He could trust her on that score, and so the dastardly coward affected to sneer at what he called her primness, charging 'Lina to be careful what she did, if she did not want a lecture, and asking if there were any ragged children in Kentucky, as she would not be happy unless she was running a Sunday school!

"She can teach the negroes! Capital!" and 'Lina laughed so loudly that Mrs. Richards joined them, laughing, too, at what she did not know, only—Miss Worthington had such spirits; it did one good; and she wished Anna was there to be enlivened.

"Write to her, John, won't you?"

John mentally thought it doubtful. Anna and 'Lina would never assimilate, and he would rather not have his pet sister's opinion to combat until his own was fully made up.

"Anna—oh, yes!" 'Lina exclaimed. "Miss Johnson spoke of her as the sweetest lady she ever saw. I wish she would come. I'm so anxious to see her. An invalid, I believe?"

Yes, dear Anna was a sad invalid, and cared but little to go from home, though if she could find a waiting maid, such as she had been in quest of for the last six months she might perhaps be persuaded.

"A waiting maid," 'Lina repeated to herself, remembering the forgotten letter in her dress pocket, wondering if it could be Anna

Richards, whose advertisement Adah had answered, and if it were, congratulating herself upon her thoughtlessness in forgetting it, as she would not for the world have Adah Hastings, with her exact knowledge of Spring Bank, in Mrs. Richards' family. It passed her mind that the very dress had been given to Adah, who might find the letter yet. She only reflected that the letter never was sent, and felt glad accordingly. Very adroitly she set herself at work to ascertain if Anna Richards and "A.E.R." were one and the same individual.

If Anna wished for a waiting maid, she could certainly find one, she should suppose. She might advertise.

"She has," and the doctor began to laugh. "The most ridiculous thing. I hardly remember the wording, but it has been copied and recopied, for its wording, annoying Anna greatly, and bringing to our doors so many unfortunate women in search of places, that my poor little sister trembles now every time the bell rings, thinking it some fresh answer to her advertisement."

"I've seen it," and 'Lina very unconsciously laid her hand on his arm. "It was copied and commented upon by Prentice, and my sewing woman actually thought of answering it, thinking the place would suit her. I told her it was preposterous that 'A.E.R.' should want her with a child."

"The very one to suit Anna," and the doctor laughed again. "That was one of the requirements, or something. How was it, mother? I think we must manage to get your sewing woman. What is her name?"

'Lina had trodden nearer dangerous ground than she meant to do, and she veered off at once, replying to the doctor:

"Oh, she would not suit at all. She's too—I hardly know what, unless I say, lifeless, or insipid. And then, I could not spare my seamstress. She cuts nearly all my dresses."

"She must be a treasure. I have noticed how admirably they fitted," and old Mrs. Richards glanced again at the blue silk, half wishing that Anna had just such a waiting maid, they could all find her so useful. "If John succeeds, maybe Miss Worthington will bring her North," was her mental conclusion, and then, as it was growing rather late, she very thoughtfully excused herself, saying, "It was time old people retired; young ones, of course, could act at their own discretion. She would not hurry them," and hoping to see more of Miss Worthington tomorrow, she bowed good-night, and left the doctor alone with 'Lina.

"In the name of the people, what are you sitting up for?" was 'Lina's first remark when she went upstairs, followed by a glowing account of what Dr. Richards had said, and the delightful time she'd had. "Only play our cards well, and I'm sure to go home the doctor's *fiancée*. Won't Ellen Tiffton stare when I tell her, mother?" and 'Lina spoke in a low tone. "The doctor thinks I'm very rich. So do all the people here. Lulu has told that I'm an heiress; now don't you upset it all with your squeamishness about the truth. Nobody will ask you how much I'm worth, so you won't be compelled to a lie direct. Just keep your tongue between your teeth, and leave the rest to me. Will you?"

There was, as usual, a feeble remonstrance, and then the weak woman yielded so far as promising to keep silent was concerned.

Meantime the doctor sat in his own room nearby, thinking of 'Lina Worthington, and wishing she were a little more refined.

"Where does she get that coarseness?" he thought. "Not from her mother, certainly. She seems very gentle and ladylike. It must be from the Worthingtons," and the doctor wondered where he had heard that name before, and why it affected him rather unpleasantly, bringing with it memories of Lily. "Poor Lily," he sighed mentally. "Your love would have made me a better man if I had not cast it from me. Dear Lily, the mother of my child," and a tear half trembled in his eyelashes, as he tried to fancy that child; tried to hear the patter of the little feet running to welcome him home, as they might have done had he been true to Lily; tried to hear the baby voice calling him "papa;" to feel the baby hands upon his face—his bearded face where the great tears were standing now. "I did love Lily," he murmured; "and had I known of the child I never could have left her. Oh, Lily, my lost Lily, come back to me, come!" and his arms were stretched out into empty space, as if he fain would encircle again the girlish form he had so often held in his embrace.

It was very late ere Dr. Richards slept that night, and the morning found him pale, haggard and nearly desperate. Thoughts of Lily were gone, and in their place was a fixed determination to follow on in the course he had marked out, to find him a rich wife, to cast remorse to the winds, and be as happy as he could.

How anxious the doctor was to have Alice go; how fearful lest she should not; and how relieved when asked by 'Lina one night to go with her the next morning and see Miss Johnson off. There were Mrs. Worthington and 'Lina, Dr. Richards and Irving Stanley, and a dozen more admirers, who, dazzled with Alice's beauty, were dancing attendance upon her to the latest moment, but none looked so sorry as Irving Stanley, or said good-by so unwillingly, and 'Lina, as she saw the wistful gaze he sent after the receding train, playfully asked him if he did not feel some like the half of a pair of scissors.

The remark jarred painfully on Irving's finer feelings, while the doctor, affecting to laugh and ejaculate "pretty good," wished so much that his black-eyed lady were different in some things.

CHAPTER XVII

HUGH

An unexpected turn in Hugh's affairs made it no longer necessary for him to remain in the sultry climate of New Orleans,
and just one week from his mother's departure from Spring Bank
he reached it, expressing unbounded surprise when he heard from
Aunt Eunice where his mother had gone, and how she had gone.

"Fool and his money soon parted," Hugh said. "I can fancy just
the dash Ad is making. But who sent the money?"

"A Mrs. Johnson, an old friend of your mother's," Aunt
Eunice replied, while Hugh looked up quickly, wondering why the
Johnsons should be so continually thrust upon him, when the only
Johnson for whom he cared was dead years ago.

"And the young lady—what about her?" he asked, while Aunt
Eunice told him the little she knew, which was that Mrs. Johnson
wished her daughter to come to Spring Bank, but she did not know
what they had concluded upon.

"That she should not come, of course," Hugh said. "They had
no right to give her a home without my consent, and I've plenty of
young ladies at Spring Bank now. Oh, it was such a relief when I
was gone to know that in all New Orleans there was not a single
hoop annoyed on my account. I had a glorious time doing as I
pleased."

"And yet you've improved, seems to me," Aunt Eunice said.

"Oh, I'll turn out a polished dandy by and by, who knows?"
Hugh answered, laughingly; then helping his aunt to mount the
horse which had brought her to Spring Bank, he returned to the
house, which seemed rather lonely, notwithstanding that he had so
often wished he could once more be alone, just as he was before his
mother came.

On the whole, however, he enjoyed his freedom from restraint,
and very rapidly fell back into his old loose way of living, bringing
his dogs even into the parlor, and making it a repository for both
his hunting and fishing apparatus.

"It's splendid to do as I'm mind to," he said, one hot August
morning, nearly three weeks after his mother's departure.

"Hello, Mug, what do you want?" he asked, as a very bright-
looking little mulatto girl appeared in the door.

"Claib done buyed you this yer," and the child handed him the
letter from his mother.

The first of it was full of affection for her boy, and Hugh felt his
heart growing very tender as he read, but when he reached the
point where poor, timid Mrs. Worthington tried to explain about
Alice, making a wretched bungle, and showing plainly how much
she was swayed by 'Lina, it began to harden at once.

"What the plague!" he exclaimed as he read on. "Suppose I remember having heard her speak of her old school friend, Alice Morton? I don't remember any such thing. Her daughter's name's Alice—Alice Johnson," and Hugh for an instant turned white, so powerfully that name always affected him.

"She is going to Colonel Tiffton's first, though they've all got the typhoid fever, I hear, and that's no place for her. That fever is terrible on Northerners—terrible on anybody. I'm afraid of it myself, and I wish this horrid throbbing I've felt for a few days would leave my head. It has a fever feel that I don't like," and the young man pressed his hand against his temples, trying to beat back the pain which so much annoyed him.

Just then Collonel Tiffton was announced, his face wearing an anxious look, and his voice trembling as he told how sick his Nell was, how sick they all were, and then spoke of Alice Johnson.

"She's the same girl I told you about the day I bought Rocket; some little kin to me, and that makes it queer why her mother should leave her to you. I knew she would not be happy at Saratoga, and so we wrote for her to visit us. She is on the road now, will be here day after tomorrow, and something must be done. She can't come to us without great inconvenience to ourselves and serious danger to her. Hugh, my boy, there's no other way—she must come to Spring Bank," and the old colonel laid his hand on that of Hugh, who looked at him aghast, but made no immediate reply.

"A pretty state of things, and a pretty place to bring a lady," he muttered, glancing ruefully around the room and enumerating the different articles he knew were out of place. "Fish worms, fishhooks, fishlines, bootjack, boot-blacking, and rifle, to say nothing of the dogs—and me!"

The last was said in a tone as if the "me" were the most objectionable part of the whole, as, indeed, Hugh thought it was.

"I wonder how I do look to persons wholly unprejudiced!" Hugh said, and turning to Muggins he asked what she thought of him.

"I thinks you berry nice. I likes you berry much," the child replied, and Hugh continued:

"Yes; but how do I look, I mean? What do I look like, a dandy or a scarecrow?"

Muggins regarded him for a moment curiously, and then replied:

"I'se dunno what kind of thing that dandy is, but I 'members dat yer scarecrow what Claib make out of mas'r's trouse's and coat, an' put up in de cherry tree. I thinks da look like Mas'r Hugh—yes, very much like!"

Hugh laughed long and loud, pinching Mug's dusky cheek, and bidding her run away.

"Pretty good," he exclaimed, when he was left alone, "That's

Mug's opinion. Look like a scarecrow. I mean to see for myself," and going into the sitting-room, where the largest mirror was hung, he scanned curiously the figure which met his view, even taking a smaller glass, and holding it so as to get a sight of his back. "Tall, broad-shouldered, straight, well-built. My form is well enough," he said. "It's the clothes that bother. I mean to get some new ones. Then, as to my face," and Hugh turned himself around, "I never thought of it before; but my features are certainly regular, teeth can't be beaten, good brown skin, such as a man should have, eyes to match, and a heap of curly hair. I'll be hanged if I don't think I'm rather good-looking!" and with his spirits proportionately raised, Hugh whistled merrily as he went in quest of Aunt Chloe, to whom he imparted the startling information that on the next day but one, a young lady was coming to Spring Bank, and that, in the meantime, the house must be cleaned from garret to cellar, and everything put in order for the expected guest.

With growing years, Aunt Chloe had become rather cross and less inclined to work than formerly, frequently sighing for the days when "Mas'r John didn't want no clarin' up, but kep' things lyin' handy." With her hands on her fat hips she stood, coolly regarding Hugh, who was evidently too much in earnest to be opposed. Alice was coming, and the house must be put in order.

The cleaning and arranging was finished at last, and everything within the house was as neat and orderly as Aunt Eunice and Adah could make it, even Aunt Chloe acknowledging that "things was tiptop," but said, "it was no use settin' 'em to rights when Mas'r Hugh done onsot 'em so quick;" but Hugh promised to do better. He would turn over a new leaf, so by way of commencement, on the morning of Alice's expected arrival he deliberately rolled up his towel and placed it under his pillow instead of his nightshirt, which he hung conspicuously over the washstand. His boots were put behind the fire-board, his every day hat jammed into the bandbox where 'Lina kept her winter bonnet, and then, satisfied that so far as his room was concerned, everything was in order, he descended the stairs and went into the garden to gather fresh flowers with which still further to adorn Alice's room. Hugh was fond of flowers, and two most beautiful bouquets were soon arranged and placed in the vases brought from the parlor mantel, while Muggins, who trotted beside him, watching his movements and sometimes making suggestions, was told to see that they were freshly watered, and not allowed to stand where the sun could shine on them, as they might fade before Miss Johnson came.

During the excitement of preparing for Alice, the pain in his head had in a measure been forgotten, but it had come back this morning with redoubled force, and the veins upon his forehead looked almost like bursting with their pressure of feverish blood. Hugh had never been sick in his life, and he did not think it possible for him to be so now, so he tried hard to forget the giddy, half blinding pain warning him of danger, and after forcing himself to sip a little coffee in which he would indulge this morning, he ordered Claib to bring out the covered buggy, as he was going up to Lexington.

CHAPTER XVIII

MEETING OF ALICE AND HUGH

Could 'Lina have seen Hugh that morning as he emerged from a fashionable tailor's shop, she would scarcely have recognized him. The hour passed rapidly away, and its close found Hugh waiting at the terminus of the Lexington and Cincinnati Railroad. He did not have to wait there long ere a wreath of smoke in the distance heralded the approach of the train, and in a moment the broad platform was swarming with passengers, conspicuous among whom were an old lady and a young, both entire strangers, as was evinced by their anxiety to know where to go.

"There are ours," the young lady said, pointing to a huge pile of trunks, distinctly marked "A.J.," as she held out her checks in her ungloved hand.

Hugh noticed the hand, saw that it was very small and white and fat, but the face he could not see, and he looked in vain for the magnificent hair about which even his mother had waxed eloquent, and which was now put plainly back, so that not a vestige of it was visible. Still Hugh felt sure that this was Alice Johnson, so sure that when he had ascertained the hotel where she would wait for the Frankfort train, he followed on, and entering the back parlor, the door of which was partly closed, sat down as if he, too, were a traveler, waiting for the train.

Meantime, in the room adjoining, Alice, for it was she, divested herself of her dusty wrappings, and taking out her combs and brushes, began to arrange her hair, talking the while to Densie, reclining on the sofa.

It would seem that Alice's own luxuriant tresses suggested her first remark, for she said to Densie: "That Miss Worthington has beautiful hair, so black, so glossy, and so wavy, too. I wonder she never curls it. It looks as if she might."

Densie did not know. It had struck her as singular taste, unless it were done to conceal a scar, or something of that kind.

"I did not like that girl," she said, "and still she interested me more than any person I ever met. I never went near her without experiencing a strange sensation, neither could I keep from watching her continually, although I knew as well as you that it annoyed her, Alice," and Densie lowered her voice almost to a whisper, "I cannot account for it, but I had queer fancies about that girl. Try now and bring her distinctly to your mind. Did you ever see any one whom she resembled; any other eyes like hers?" and Densie's own fierce, wild orbs flashed inquiringly upon Alice, who could not remember a face like 'Lina Worthington's.

"I did not like her eyes much," she said; "they were too intensely black, too much like coals of fire, when they flashed angrily on that poor Lulu, who evidently was not well posted in the duties of a waiting maid, auntie," and Alice's voice was lowered, too. "If mother had not so decided, I should shrink from being an inmate of Mrs. Washington's family. I like her very much, but 'Lina—I am afraid I shall not get on with her:"

"I know you won't. I honor your judgment," was Hugh's mental comment, while Alice went on:

"And what she told me of her brother was not calculated to impress me favorably."

Nervously Hugh's hands grasped each other, and he could distinctly hear the beating of his heart as he leaned forward so as not to lose a single word.

"She seemed trying to prepare me for him by telling how rough he was; how little he cared for etiquette; and how constantly he mortified her with his uncouth manners."

Alice did not hear the sigh of pain or see the mournful look which stole over Hugh's face. She did not even suspect his presence, and she went on to speak of Spring Bank, wondering if Hugh would be there before his mother returned, half hoping he would not, as she rather dreaded meeting him, although she meant to like him if she could.

Alice's long, bright hair, was arranged at last, and the soft curls fell about her face, giving to it the same look it had worn in childhood—the look which was graven on Hugh's heart, as with a pencil of fire; the look he never had forgotten through all the years which had come and gone since first it shone on him; the look he had never hoped to see again, so sure was he that it had long been quenched by the waters of Lake Erie. Alice's face was turned fully toward him. Through the open window at her back the August sunlight streamed, falling on her chestnut hair, and tinging it with the yellow gleam which Hugh remembered so well. For an instant the long lashes shaded the fair round cheek, and then were uplifted, disclosing the eyes of lustrous blue, which, seen but once, could never be mistaken, and Hugh was not mistaken. One look of piercing scrutiny at the face unconsciously confronting him, one mighty throb, which seemed to bear away his very life, one rapid passage of his hand before his eyes to sweep away the mist, if mist there were, and then Hugh knew the grave had given up its dead, mourned for so long as only he could mourn. She was not lost. Some friendly hand had saved her; some arm had borne her to the shore.

Golden Hair had come back to him, but, alas, prejudiced against him. She hoped he might be gone. She would be happier if he never crossed her path. "And I never, never will," Hugh thought, as with one farewell glance at her dazzling beauty, he staggered noiselessly from the room, and sought a small outer court, whose locality he knew, and where he could be alone to think.

"Oh, Adaline," he murmured, "what made you so cruel to me? I would not have served you so."

There was a roll of wheels before the door, and Hugh knew by the sound that it was the carriage for the cars. She was going. They would never meet again, Hugh said, and she would never know that the youth who saved her life was the same for whose coming they would wait and watch in vain at Spring Bank—the Hugh for whom his mother would weep a while; and for whose dark fate even Ad might feel a little sorry. She was not wholly depraved—she had some sisterly feeling, and his loss would waken it to life. They would appreciate him after he was gone, and the poor heart which had known so little love throbbed joyfully, as Hugh thought of being loved at last even by the selfish 'Lina.

Meantime Alice and Densie proceeded on their way to the Big Spring station, where Colonel Tiffton was waiting for them, according to his promise. There was a shadow in the colonel's good-humored face, and a shadow in his heart. His idol, Nellie, was very, very sick, while added to this was the terrible certainty that he and he alone must pay that $10,000 note on which he had foolishly put his name, because Harney had preferred it. He was talking with Harney when the cars came up, and the villain, while expressing regret that the colonel should be compelled to pay so much for what he never received, had said, with a relentless smile: "But it's not my fault, you know. I can't afford to lose it."

From that moment the colonel felt he was a ruined man, but he would not allow himself to appear at all discomposed.

"Wait a while," he said; "do nothing till my Nell lives or dies," and with a sigh as he thought how much dearer to him was his youngest daughter than all the farms in Woodford, he went forward to meet Alice, just appearing upon the platform.

The colonel explained to Alice why she must go to Spring Bank, adding, by way of consolation, that she would not be quite as lonely now Hugh was at home.

"Hugh at home!" and Alice shrank back in dismay, feeling for a moment that she could not go there.

But there was no alternative, and after a few tears, which, she could not repress, she said, timidly:

"What is this Hugh? What kind of a man, I mean?"

She could not expect the colonel to say anything bad of him, but she was not prepared for his frank response.

"The likeliest chap in Kentucky. Nothing dandified about him, to be sure. Wears his trouser legs in his boots as often as any way, and don't stand about the very latest cut of his coat, but he's got a heart bigger than an ox—yes, big as ten oxen! I'd trust him with my life, and know it was just as safe as his own. You'll like Hugh—Nell does."

The colonel never dreamed of the comfort his words gave

Alice, or how they changed her feelings with regard to one whom she had so dreaded to meet.

"There 'tis; we're almost there," the colonel said at last, as they turned off from the highway, and leaning forward Alice caught sight of the roofs and dilapidated chimneys of Spring Bank. "'Taint quite as fixey as Yankee houses, that's a fact, but we that own niggers never do have things so smarted up," the colonel said, guessing how the contrast must affect Alice, who felt so desolate and homesick as she drew up in front of what, for a time at least, was to be her home.

"Where is Hugh?" Alice asked.

Aunt Eunice would not say he had gone to Lexington for the sake, perhaps, of seeing her, so she replied:

"He went to town this morning, but he'll be back pretty soon. He has done his best to make it pleasant for you, and I do believe he doted on your coming after he got a little used to thinking about it. You'll like Hugh when you get accustomed to him. There, try to go to sleep," and kind Aunt Eunice bustled from the room just as poor Densie, who had been entirely overlooked, entered it, together with Aunt Chloe. The old negress was evidently playing the hostess to Densie, for she was talking quite loud, and all about "Mas'r Hugh." "Pity he wasn't thar, 'twould seem so different; 'tain't de same house without him. You'll like Mas'r Hugh," and she, too, glided from the room.

Was this the password at Spring Bank, "You'll like Mas'r Hugh?" It would seem so, for when at last Hannah brought up the waffles and tea, which Aunt Eunice had prepared, she set down her tray, and after a few inquiries concerning Alice's head, which was now aching sadly, she, too, launched forth into a panegyric on Mas'r Hugh, ending, as the rest had done, "You'll like Mas'r Hugh."

CHAPTER XIX

ALICE AND MUGGINS

Had an angel appeared suddenly to the blacks at Spring Bank they would not have been more surprised or delighted than they were with Alice when she came down to breakfast, looking so beautiful in her muslin wrapper, with a simple white blossom and geranium leaf twined among her flowing curls, and an expression of content upon her childish face, which said that she had resolved to make the best of the place to which Providence had so clearly led her for some wise purpose of his own. She had arisen early and explored the premises in quest of the spots of sunshine which she knew were there as well as elsewhere, and she had found them, too, in the grand old elms and maples which shaded the wooden building, in the clean, grassy lawn and the running brook, in the well-kept garden of flowers, and in the few choice volumes arranged in the old bookcase at one end of the hall. Who reads those books, her favorites, every one of them? Not 'Lina, most assuredly, for Alice's reminiscences of her were not of the literary kind; nor yet Mrs. Worthington, kind, gentle creature as she seemed to be. Who then but Hugh could have pored over those pages? And Alice felt a thrill of joy as she felt there was at least one bond of sympathy between them. There was no Bible upon the shelves, no religious book of any kind, if we except a work of infidel Tom Paine, at sight of which Alice recoiled as from a viper. Could Hugh believe in Tom Paine? She hoped not, and with a sigh she was turning from the corner, when the patter of little naked feet was heard upon the stairs, and a bright mulatto child, apparently seven or eight years old, appeared, her face expressive of the admiration with which she regarded Alice, who asked her name.

Curtseying very low, the child replied:

"I dunno, missus; I 'spec's I done lost 'em, 'case heap of a while ago, 'fore you're born, I reckon, they call me Leshie, but Mas'r Hugh done nickname me Muggins, and every folks do that now. You know Mas'r Hugh? He done rared when he read you's comin'; do this way with his boot, 'By George, Ad will sell the old hut yet without 'sultin' me,'" and the little darky's fist came down upon the window sill in apt imitation of her master.

A crimson flush overspread Alice's face as she wondered if it were possible that the arrangements concerning her coming there had been made without reference to Hugh's wishes.

"It may be, he was away," she sighed; then feeling an intense desire to know more, and being only a woman and mortal, she said to Muggins walking around her in circles, with her fat arms folded upon her bosom. "Your master did not know I was coming till he returned from New Orleans and found his mother's letter?"

"Who tole you dat ar?" and Muggins' face was perfectly comical in its bewilderment at what she deemed Alice's foreknowledge. "But dat's so, dat is. I hear Aunt Chloe say so, and how't was right mean in Miss 'Lina. I hate Miss 'Lina! Phew-ew!" and Muggins' face screwed itself into a look of such perfect disgust that Alice could not forbear laughing outright.

"You should not hate any one, my child," she said, while Muggins rejoined:

"I can't help it—none of us can; she's so—mean—and so—so—you mustn't never tell, 'case Aunt Chloe get my rags if you do—but she's so low-flung, Claib say. She hain't any bizzens orderin' us around nuther, and I will hate her!"

"But, Muggins, the Bible teaches us to love those who treat us badly, who are mean, as you say."

"Who's he?" and Muggins looked up quickly. "I never hearn tell of him afore, or, yes I has. Thar's an old wared-out book in Mas'r Hugh's chest, what he reads in every night, and oncet when I axes him what was it, he say, 'It's a Bible, Mug.' Dat's what he calls me for short; Mug!"

"Well," Alice said, "be a good girl, Muggins. God will love you if you do. Do you ever pray?"

"More times I do, and more times when I'se sleepy I don't," was Muggins' reply.

Here was a spot where Alice might do good; this half heathen, but sprightly, African child needed her, and she began already to get an inkling of her mission to Kentucky. She was pleased with Muggins, and suffered the little dusky hands to caress her curls as long as they pleased, while she questioned her of the bookcase and its contents, whose was it, 'Lina's or Hugh's?

"Mas'r Hugh's, in course. Miss 'Lina can't read!" was Muggins' reply, which Alice fully understood.

'Lina was no reader, while Hugh was, it might be said, and she continued to speak of him. Did he read much, ever evenings to his mother, or did 'Lina mother, or did 'Lina play often to them?

"More'n we wants, a heap!" and Muggins spoke scornfully. "We can't bar them rang-tang-em-er-digs she thumps out. Now, we likes Mas'r Hugh's the best—got good voice, sing Dixie, oh, splendid! Mas'r Hugh loves flowers, too. Tend all them in the garden."

"Did he?" and Alice spoke with great animation, for she had supposed that 'Lina's, or at least Mrs. Worthington's hands had been there.

But it was Hugh, all Hugh, and in spite of what Muggins had said concerning his aversion to her coming there, she felt a great desire to see him. She could understand in part why he should be angry at not having been consulted, but he was over that, she was sure from what Aunt Eunice said, and if he were not, it behooved her to try her best to remove any wrong impression he might have formed of her. "He shall like me," she thought; "not as he must like that golden-haired maiden whose existence this sprite of a negro has discovered, but as a friend, or sister," and a softer light shone in Alice's blue eyes, as she foresaw in fancy Hugh gradually coming to like her, to be glad that she was there, and to miss her when she was gone.

CHAPTER XX

POOR HUGH

Could Hugh have known the feelings with which Alice Johnson already regarded him, and the opinion she had expressed to Muggins, it would perhaps have stilled the fierce throbbings of his heart, which sent the hot blood so swiftly through his veins, and made him from the first delirious. They had found him in the quiet court, just after the sunsetting, and his uncovered head was already wet with the falling dew, and with the profuse perspiration induced by his long, heavy sleep. They could not arouse him to a distinct consciousness as to where he was or what had happened. He only talked of Ad and the Golden Haired, asking that they would take him anywhere, where neither could ever see him again. He was well known at the hotel, and measures were immediately taken for apprising his family of the sudden illness, and for removing him to Spring Bank as soon as possible.

Breakfast was not yet over at Spring Bank, and Aunt Eunice was just wondering what could have become of Hugh, when from her position near the window she discovered a horseman riding across the lawn at a rate which betokened some important errand. Alice spied him, too, and the same thought flashed over both herself and Aunt Eunice. "Something had befallen Hugh."

Alice was the first upon the piazza, where she stood waiting till the rider came up, his horse covered with foam, and himself flurried and excited.

"Are you Miss Worthington?" he asked, doffing his soft hat, and feeling a thrill of wonder at sight of her marvelous beauty.

"Miss Worthington is not at home," she said, going down the steps and advancing closer to him, "but I can take your message. Is anything the matter with Mr. Worthington?"

Aunt Eunice had now joined her, and listened breathlessly while the young man told of Hugh's illness, which threatened to be the prevailing fever.

"They were bringing him home," he said—"were now on the way, and he had ridden in advance to prepare them for his coming."

Aunt Eunice seemed literally stunned and wholly incapable of action, while the negroes howled dismally for Mas'r Hugh, who, Chloe said, was sure to die.

"She'd felt it all along. She knew dem dogs hadn't howled for nothing, nor them deathwatches ticked in the wall. Mas'r Hugh was gwine to die, and all the blacks would be sold—down the river, most likely, if Harney didn't get 'em," and crouching by the kitchen fire old Chloe bewailed the calamity she knew was about to befall them.

Alice alone was calm and capable of action. A room must be prepared, and somebody must direct, but to find the somebody was a most difficult matter. Chloe couldn't, Hannah couldn't, Aunt Eunice couldn't, and consequently it all devolved upon herself.

They carried Hugh to the room designated by Densie, and into which he went very unwillingly.

It was not his den, he said, drawing back with a bewildered look; his was hot, and close, and dingy, while this was nice and cool—a room such as women had—there must be a mistake, and he begged of them to take him away.

"No, no, my poor boy. This is right; Miss Johnson said you must come here just because it is cool and nice. You'll get well so much faster," and Aunt Eunice's tears dropped on Hugh's flushed face.

"Miss Johnson!" and the wild eyes looked up eagerly at her. "Who is she? Oh, yes, I know, I know," and a moan came from his lips as he whispered: "Does she know I've come? Does it make her hate me worse to see me in such a plight? Ho, Aunt Eunice, put your ear down close while I tell you something. Ad said—you know Ad—she said I was—I was—I can't tell you what she said for this buzzing in my head. Am I very sick, Aunt Eunice?" and about the chin there was a quivering motion, which betokened a ray of consciousness, as the brown eyes scanned the kind, motherly face bending over him.

"Yes, Hugh, you are very sick," and Aunt Eunice's tears dropped upon the face of her boy, so fearfully changed since yesterday.

He wiped them away himself, and looked inquiringly at her.

"Am I so sick that it makes you cry? Is it the fever I've got?"

"Yes, Hugh, the fever," and Aunt Eunice bowed her face upon his burning hands.

For a moment he lay unconscious, then raising himself up, he fixed his eyes piercingly upon her, and whispered, hoarsely:

"Aunt Eunice, I shall die! I have never been sick in my life; and the fever goes hard with such. I shall surely die. It's been days in coming on, and I thought to fight it off; I don't want to die. I'm not prepared."

He was growing terribly excited now, and Aunt Eunice hailed the coming of the doctor with delight. Hugh knew him, offering his pulse and putting out his tongue of his own accord. The doctor counted the rapid pulse, numbering even then 130 per minute, noted the rolling eyeballs and the dilation of the pupils, felt the fierce throbbing of the swollen veins upon the temple, and then gravely shook his head. Half conscious, half delirious, Hugh watched him nervously, until the great fear at his heart found utterance in words.

"Must I die?"

"We hope not. We'll do what we can to save you. Don't think of dying, my boy," was the physician's reply, as he turned to Aunt Eunice, and gave out the medicine, which must be most carefully administered.

Too much agitated to know just what he said, Aunt Eunice listened, as one who heard not, noticing which, the doctor said:

"You are not the right one to take these directions. Is there nobody here less nervous than yourself? Who was that young lady standing by the door when I came in? The one in white, I mean, with such a quantity of curls?"

"Miss Johnson—our visitor. She can't do anything," Aunt Eunice replied, trying to compose herself enough to know what she was doing.

But the doctor thought differently. Something of a physiognomist, he had been struck with the expression of Alice's face, and felt sure that she would be more efficient aid than Aunt Eunice herself. "I'll speak to her," he said, stepping to the hall. But Alice was gone. She had stood by the sickroom door long enough to hear Hugh's impassioned words concerning his probable death—long enough to hear him ask that she might pray for him; and then she stole away to where no ear, save that of God, could hear the earnest prayer that Hugh Worthington might live—or that dying, there might be given him a space in which to grasp the faith, without which the grave is dark indeed.

Meantime, the Hugh for whom the prayer was made had fallen into a heavy sleep, and Aunt Eunice noiselessly left the room, meeting in the hall with Alice, who asked permission to go in and sit by him at least until he awoke. Aunt Eunice consented, and with noiseless footsteps Alice advanced into the darkened room, and after standing still for a moment to assure herself that Hugh was really sleeping, stole softly to his bedside and bent down to look at him, starting quickly at the strong resemblance to somebody seen before. Who was it? Where was it? she asked herself, her brain a labyrinth of bewilderment as she tried in vain to recall the time or place where a face like this reposing upon the pillow before her had met her view. Suddenly she remembered Irving Stanley, and that between him and Hugh there was a relationship, and then she knew it was the likeness to Irving Stanley, which she so plainly traced. Alice hardly cared to acknowledge it, but as she looked at Hugh she felt that his was really the handsomer, the more attractive face of the two. It certainly was, as he lay there asleep, his long eyelashes resting upon his flushed cheek, his dark hair curling in soft rings about his high, white brow, his rich, brown beard glistening with perspiration, and his lips slightly apart, showing a row of even teeth.

There were others than Alice praying for Hugh that summer

afternoon, for Muggins had gone from the brook to the cornfield, startling Adah with the story of Hugh's sickness, and then launching out into a glowing description of the new miss, "with her white gown and curls as long as Rocket's tail."

"She talked with God, too," she said, "like what you does, Miss Adah. She axes Him to make Mas'r Hugh well, and He will, won't He?"

"I trust so," Adah answered, her own heart going silently up to the Giver of life and health, asking, if it were possible, that her noble friend might be spared.

Old Sam, too, with streaming eyes, stole out to his bethel by the spring, and prayed for the dear "Massah Hugh" lying so still at Spring Bank, and insensible to all the prayers going up in his behalf.

How terrible that deathlike stupor was, and the physician, when later in the afternoon he came again, shook his head sadly.

"I'd rather see him rave till it took ten men to hold him," he said, feeling the wiry pulse, which was now beyond his count.

"Is there nothing that will arouse him?" Alice asked, "no name of one he loves more than another?"

The doctor answered "no; love for womankind, save as he feels it for his mother or his sister, is unknown to Hugh Worthington."

Alice said softly, lest she should be heard:

"Hugh, shall I call Golden Haired?"

"Yes, yes, oh, yes," and the heavy lids unclosed at once, while the eyes, in which there was no ray of consciousness, looked wistfully into the lustrous blue orbs above him.

"Are you the Golden Haired?" and he laid his hand caressingly over the shining tresses just within his reach.

Alice was about to reply, when an exclamation from those near the window, and the heavy tramp of horse's feet, arrested her attention, and drew her also to the window, just as a most beautiful gray, saddled but riderless, came dashing over the gate, and tearing across the yard, until he stood panting at the door. Rocket had come home for the first time since his master had led him away!

Hearing of Hugh's illness, the old colonel had ridden over to inquire how he was, and fearing lest it might be difficult to get Rocket away if once he stood in the familiar yard, he had dismounted in the woods, and fastening him to a tree, walked the remaining distance. But Rocket was not thus to be cheated. Ever since turning into the well-remembered lane he had seemed like a new creature, pricking up his ears, and, dancing and curvetting daintily along, as he had been wont to do on public occasions when Hugh was his rider instead of the fat colonel. In this state of feeling it was quite natural that he should resent being tied to a tree, and as if divining why it was done, he broke his halter the moment the colonel was out of sight, and went galloping through the woods like lightning, never for an instant slackening his speed until he stood at Spring Bank door, calling, as well as he could call, for Hugh, who heard and recognized that call.

Throwing his arms wildly over his head, he raised himself in bed, and exclaimed joyfully:

"That's he! that's Rocket! I knew he'd come. I've only been waiting for him to start on that long journey. Ho! Aunt Eunice! Pack my clothes. I'm going away, where I shan't mortify Ad any more. Hurry up. Rocket is growing impatient. Don't you hear him pawing the turf? I'm coming, my boy, I'm coming!" and he attempted to leap upon the floor, but the doctor's strong arm held him down, while Alice, whose voice alone he heeded, strove to quiet him.

"I wouldn't go away today," she said soothingly. "Some other time will do as well, and Rocket can wait."

"Will you stay with me?" Hugh asked.

"Yes, I'll stay," was Alice's reply.

"I'm glad he's roused up," the doctor said, "though I don't like the way his fever increases," and Alice knew by the expression of his face that there was but little hope, determining not to leave him during the night.

Densie or Aunt Eunice might sleep on the lounge, she said, but the care, the responsibility shall be hers. To this the doctor willingly acceded, thinking that Hugh was safer with her than any one else. Exchanging the white wrapper she had worn through the day for one more suitable, Alice, after an hour's rest in her own room, returned to Hugh, who had missed her sadly, and who knew the moment she came back to him, even though his eyes were closed, and he seemed to be half asleep.

"Mas'r Hugh won't die," and Muuggins' faith came to the rescue, throwing a ray of hope into the darkness. "Miss Alice axed God to spar' him, and so did I; now He will, won't He, miss?" and she turned to Adah, who, with Sam, had just come up to Spring Bank, and hearing voices in the kitchen had entered there first. "Say, Miss Adah, won't God cure Mas'r Hugh—'ca'se I axed Him oncet?"

"You must pray more than once, child; pray many, many times," was Adah's reply; whereupon Mug looked aghast, for the idea of praying a second time had never entered her brain.

Still, if she must, why, she must, and she stole quietly from the kitchen. But it was now too dark to go down in the woods by the running brook, and remembering Alice had said that God was everywhere, she first cast around her a timid glance, as if fearful she should see Him, and then kneeling in the grass, wet with the heavy night dew, the little negro girl prayed again for Master Hugh, starting as she prayed at the sound which met her ear, and which came from the spot where Rocket still was standing by the block, waiting for his master.

Claib had offered him food and offered him drink, but both had been refused, and opening the stable door so that he could go in whenever he chose, Claib had left him there alone, solitary watcher of the night, waiting for poor Hugh.

Returning to the house, Mug stole upstairs to the door of the sickroom, where Alice was now alone with Hugh.

He was awake, and for an instant seemed to know her, for he attempted to speak, but the rational words died on his lips, and he only moaned, as if in distress.

"What is it?" Alice said, bending over him.

"Are you the Golden Haired?" he asked again, as her curls swept his face.

"Who is Golden Hair?" Alice asked, and instantly the great tears gathered in Hugh's dark eyes as he replied:

"Don't say who is she, but who was she. I've never told a living being before. Golden Hair was a bright angel who crossed my path one day, and then disappeared forever, leaving behind the sweetest memory a mortal man ever possessed. She's dead, Chestnut Locks," and he twined one of Alice's curls around his finger. "It's weak for men to cry, but I have cried many a night for her, when the clouds were crying, too, and I heard against my window the rain which I knew was falling upon her little grave."

He was growing rather excited, and thinking he had talked too much, Alice was trying to quiet him, when the door opened softly and Adah herself came in. Bowing politely to Alice she advanced to Hugh's bedside, and bending over him spoke his name. He knew her, and turning to Alice said: "This is Adah; you will like each other; you are much alike."

For an instant the two young girls gazed at each other as if trying to account for the familiar look each saw in the other's face. Adah was the first to remember, and when at last Hugh was asleep she unclasped from her neck the slender chain she had worn so long, and passing the locket to Alice, asked if she ever saw it before.

"Yes, oh, yes, it's I, it's mine, though not a very natural one. I never knew where I lost it. Where did you find it?" and opening the other side Alice looked to see if the lock of hair was safe.

Adah explained how it came into her possession, asking if Alice remembered the circumstances.

"Yes, and I thought of you so often, never dreaming that we should meet here as we have. You were so sick then, and I pitied you so much. Your husband was gone, you said. Was it long ere he came back?"

"He never came back," and the great brown eyes filled with tears.

"Never came? Do you think him dead?"

"No, no! oh, no! He's—Oh, Miss Johnson, I'll tell you some

time. Nobody here knows but Hugh how I was deceived, but I'll tell you. I can trust you," and Adah involuntarily laid her head in Alice's lap, sobbing bitterly.

In the hall without there was a shuffling step which Adah knew was Sam's, and remembering the conversation once held with him concerning that golden locket, whose original Sam was positive he had seen, Alice waited curious for his entrance. With hobbling steps the old man came in, scarcely noticing either of them, so intent was he upon the figure lying so still and helpless before him.

"Massah Hugh, my poor, dear Massah Hugh," he cried, bending over his young master. "I wish 'twas Sam had all de pain an' all de aches you feels. I'd b'ar it willingly, massah, I would. Dear massah, kin you hear Sam talkin' to you?"

Sam had turned away from Hugh, and with his usual politeness was about making his obeisance to Alice, when the words, "Your servant, miss," were changed into a howl of joy, and falling upon his knees, he clutched at Alice's dress, exclaiming:

"Now de Lord be praised, I'se found her again. I'se found Miss Ellis, I has, an' I feels like singin' 'Glory Hallelujah.' Does ye know me, lady? Does you 'member shaky ole darky, way down in Virginny? You teached him de way, an' he's tried to walk dar ever sence. Say, does you know ole Sam?" and the dim eyes looked eagerly into Alice's face.

She did remember him, and for a moment seemed speechless with surprise, then, stooping beside him, she took his shriveled hand and pressed it between her own, asking how he came there, and if Hugh had always been his master.

"You 'splain, Miss Adah. You speaks de dictionary better than Sam," the old man said, and thus appealed to, Adah told what she knew of Sam's coming into Hugh's possession.

"He buy me just for kindness, nothing else, for Sam ain't wo'th a dime, but Massah Hugh so good. I prays for him every night, and I asks God to bring you and him together. Miss Ellis will like Massah Hugh much, so much, and Massah Hugh like Miss Ellis. Oh, I'se happy chile tonight. I prays wid a big heart, 'case I sees Miss Ellis again," and in his great joy Sam kissed the hem of Alice's dress, crouching at her feet and regarding her with a look almost idolatrous.

They watched together that night, attending Hugh so carefully that when the morning broke and the physician came, he pronounced the symptoms so much better that there was much hope, he said, if the faithful nursing were continued.

CHAPTER XXI

ALICE AND ADAH

At Alice's request, Adah and Sam stayed altogether at Spring Bank, but Alice was the ruling power—Alice, the one whom Chloe and Claib consulted; one concerning the farm, and the other concerning the kitchen—Alice, to whom Aunt Eunice looked for counsel, and Densie for comfort—Alice, who remembered all the doctor's directions, taking the entire charge of Hugh's medicines herself—and Alice, who wrote to Mrs. Worthington, apprising her of Hugh's serious illness. They hoped he was not dangerous, she said, but he was very sick, and Mrs. Worthington would do well to come at once. She did not mention 'Lina, but the idea never crossed her mind that a sister could stay away from choice when a brother was so ill; and it was with unfeigned surprise that she one morning saw Mrs. Worthington and Lulu alighting at the gate, but no 'Lina with them.

"She was so happy at Saratoga," Mrs. Worthington said, when a little over the first flurry of her arrival. "So happy, too, with Mrs. Richards that she could not tear herself away, unless her mother should find Hugh positively dangerous, in which case she should, of course, come at once."

This was the mother's charitable explanation, made with a bitter sigh as she recalled 'Lina's heartless anger when the letter was received, as if Hugh were to blame, as, indeed, 'Lina seemed to think he was.

Meantime Alice, in her own room, was reading 'Lina's note, containing a most glowing description of the delightful time she was having at Saratoga, and how hard it would be to leave.

"I know dear Hugh is in good hands," she wrote, "and it is so pleasant here that I really do want to stay a little longer. Pray write to me just how Hugh is, and if I must come home. What a delightful lady that Mrs. Richards is—not one bit stiff as I can see. I don't know what people mean to call her proud. She has promised, if mamma will leave me here, to be my chaperon, and it's possible we may visit New York together, so as to be there when the prince arrives. Won't that be grand? She talks so much of you that sometimes I'm really jealous. Perhaps I may go to Terrace Hill before I return, but rather hope not, it makes me fidgety to think of meeting the Misses Richards, though, of course, I know I shall like them, particularly Anna. Oh, I most forgot! Irving is here yet, and has a sister, Mrs. Ellsworth, with him now. She is very elegant, and very much admired. Tell Adah I heard Mrs. Ellsworth say she wished she could find some young person as governess for her little girl, and kind of companion for her. I did not speak of Adah, but I thought of her, knowing she desired some such situation. She might write to Mrs. Ellsworth here, but I'd rather she should not refer to me as having known her. You see Mrs. Ellsworth would directly inquire about her antecedents, and to a stranger it would not sound well that she came to us one stormy night with that child, whose father we know nothing about, and if I told the truth, as I always try to do, I should have to tell this. So it will be better for Adah not to know us, even if she should come to Mrs. Ellsworth. You will understand me, I am sure, and believe that I am actuated by the kindest of motives. She can direct to Mrs. Julia Ellsworth, Union Hall, Saratoga Springs. By the way, tell mother not to forget that dress. She'll know what you mean.

"Mr. Stanley seemed quite blue after you went away. I should not be surprised to hear of his being at Spring Bank some day. Isn't it funny that you had to go right there? Perhaps it's as well for you that Hugh is sick. You will got a better impression. *Au revoir.*"

Not a word was there in this letter of the doctor, but Alice understood it all the same. He was the attraction which kept the selfish girl from her brother's side. "May she be happy with him, if, indeed, he has a right to win her," was Alice's mental comment, shuddering as she recalled the time when she was pleased with the handsome doctor, and silently thanking God, who had saved her from much sorrow. Hearing Mrs. Worthington in the hall, and remembering what 'Lina said concerning the dress, she stepped to the door and delivered the message, wondering that Mrs. Worthington should seem so confounded, and stammer so, as she turned to Adah, just coming up the stairs, and said:

"Have you ever done anything with that old muslin 'Lina gave you?"

"Never till today," Adah replied; "when it occurred to me that if this hot weather lasted, I might find it comfortable, provided I could fix it, so I sent Mug for it, and she is ripping the waist."

Mrs. Worthington was not a good dissembler, and her next question was:

"Did you find anything in the pocket?"

"Yes, my letter, written weeks ago. Your daughter must have forgotten it. I intrusted it to her care the day Miss Tiffton called."

Adah was just thinking of speaking freely to Alice Johnson concerning her future course, when Mrs. Worthington met her in the upper hall.

"I'll go to her now," she said, as Mrs. Worthington left her, and knocking timidly at Alice's door, she asked permission to enter.

"Oh, certainly, I have something to tell you," Alice said, motioning her to a chair, and sitting down beside her. "Miss Worthington sent me a note in which she speaks of you."

"Of me?" and Adah colored slightly. "I did not know she ever thought of me. Why did she not come with her mother?"

"She is enjoying herself so much is the reason she gives, though

I fancy there is another more powerful one. Perhaps the note will enlighten you," and Alice passed it to Adah, not so much to show her how heartless 'Lina was, as to see if in what she had said of the Richards family there was not something which Adah would recognize.

That look in Willie's face had almost grown to a certainty with Alice, who saw Anna, or Asenath, or Eudora, and sometimes John himself in every move of the little fellow. Silently Adah read the note, her paled cheeks turning scarlet at what 'Lina had said of herself and Mrs. Ellsworth. The Richards family were nothing to her. She only seized upon and treasured up the words "with a child about whose father we know nothing." Slowly the tears gathered in her eyes and finally fell in torrents as Alice asked:

"What made her cry?"

"Oh, Miss Johnson," and Adah hid her face in Alice's lap, "I'm thinking of George—of Willie's father. Will he never come back, or the world know that I thought I was a lawful wife? Yes, and I sometimes believe so now, or I should surely go wild, Miss Johnson," and Adah lifted up her head, disclosing a face which Alice scarcely recognized, for the strange expression there. "Miss Johnson, if I knew that George deliberately planned my ruin under the guise of a mock marriage, and then when it suited him deserted me as a toy of which he was tired, I should hate him!—hate him!"

"I frighten you, Miss Johnson," she said, as she saw how Alice shrank away from the dark eyes in which there was a fierce, resentful gleam, unlike sweet Adah Hastings. "I used to frighten myself when I saw in my eyes the demon which whispered suicide."

"Oh, Adah," said Alice, "you could not have dreamed that!"

"I did," and Adah spoke sadly now. "It was kind in God to save me, and I've tried to love Him better since; but there's something savage in my nature, something I must have inherited from one of my parents, and sometimes my heart, which at first was full of love for George, goes out against him for his base treachery."

"And yet you love him still?" Alice said, as she smoothed the beautiful brown hair.

"I suppose I do. A kind word from him would bring me back, but will it ever be spoken? Shall we ever meet again?"

"Where did he go?" Alice asked.

"He went to Europe, so he said."

There was a voluntary shudder as Alice recalled the time when Dr. Richards came home from Europe, and she had been flattered with his attentions.

"I may be unjust to him," she thought, then to Adah she said: "As you have told me your story in part, will you tell me the whole?"

There was no vindictiveness now in Adah's face, nothing save a calm, gentle expression such as it was used to wear, and the soft brown eyes drooped mournfully beneath the heavy lashes as she told the story of her wrongs.

"And Hugh?" Alice said. "Why did you come to him? Had you known him before?"

"Hugh was the other witness, bribed by my guardian to lend himself a party to the deception! I never saw him till that night; neither, I think, did George. My guardian planned the whole."

"Hugh Worthington is not the man I took him for," and Alice spoke bitterly.

"You mistake him," she cried eagerly. "My guardian, Mr. Monroe, was pleased with the young Kentuckian, and led him easily. He coaxed him to drink a glass of wine, which Hugh says must have been drugged, for it took away his power to act as he would otherwise have done, and when in this condition he consented to whatever Mr. Monroe proposed, keeping silent while the horrid farce went on. But he has repented so bitterly, and been so kind to me and Willie."

"And your guardian," interrupted Alice, "is it not strange that he should have acted so cruel a part?"

"Yes, that's the strangest part of all, and he was so kind to me. I cannot understand it, or where he is, though I've sometimes imagined he must be dead; or in prison," and Adah thought of what Sam had said concerning Sullivan, the negro-stealer.

"What do you mean; why should he be in prison?" Alice asked, and Adah replied by telling her what Sam had said, and the reason she had for thinking Sullivan and her guardian, Monroe, one and the same.

"I too am marked," and with a quick, nervous motion, she touched the spot where the blue lines were faintly visible. "I know not how I came by it, but it annoys me terribly. Mr. Monroe knew how I felt about it, and the day before that marriage he said to me: 'It will disappear with your children. They will not be marked,' and Willie isn't."

Just then Willie's voice was heard in the hall, and Alice admitted him into the room. She kissed his rosy cheek, and said to Adah: "Do you know I think he looks like Hugh."

"Yes," and Adah spoke sadly. "I know he does, and I am sorry for Hugh's sake, as it must annoy him. Neither can I account for it, for I am certainly nothing to Hugh. But there's another look in Willie's face, his father's. Oh, Miss Johnson, George was handsome."

"Can you describe him, or will it be too painful?" Alice asked, and Adah told how George Hastings looked, while Alice's handy worked nervously together, for Adah was describing Dr. Richards.

"And you've never seen him since, nor guessed where his proud mother lived?"

"Never, and when only the wrong is remembered, I think I never care to see or hear from him again. But the noble, self-denying Hugh! I would almost die for him; I ask God every day to bring him some good fortune at last. He will, I know He will, and Hugh shall yet—"

She stopped short, struck with an idea which had never before entered her mind. Hugh and Alice! Oh, if that could be.

"Why do you look at me?" Alice asked, as Adah sat drinking in the dazzling beauty which she wished might one day shine for Hugh.

"I am thinking how beautiful you are, and wondering if you ever loved any one; did you?"

"Not like you," Alice answered frankly. "When a little girl of thirteen I owed my life to a youth with many characteristics like Hugh Worthington. I liked him, and wanted so much to find him, but could not. Then I grew to womanhood, and another crossed my path, well skilled in finding every avenue to a maiden's heart. I did not love him. I am glad that I did not, for he was unworthy of my love; but I fancied him a while, and my heart did ache a little when mother on her deathbed talked to me against him. It was my money he wanted most, and when he thought I had none, he left me, saying as I heard, that I 'was a nice-ish kind of girl, rather good-looking, but too blue for him.'"

"And the other, the boy like Hugh, have you met him again?" Adah asked, feeling a little disappointed, when Alice replied:

"Once, I am very sure."

Alice heard the faint sigh, and hope died out for Hugh. Poor Hugh! Alice was thinking of him, too, and said at last: "Was Rocket sold to Colonel Tiffton for debt?"

"Yes, for 'Lina's debts, contracted at Harney's. I've heard of his boasting that Hugh should yet be compelled to see him galloping down the pike upon his idol."

"He never shall!" and Alice spoke under her breath, asking further questions concerning the sale of Colonel Tiffton's house, and now much Mosside was worth.

Adah did not know. She was only posted with regard to Rocket, who was pawned for five hundred dollars. "Once I insanely hoped that I might help redeem him—that God would find a work for me to do—and my heart was so happy for a moment."

"What did you think of doing?" Alice asked, glancing at the delicate young girl, who looked so unaccustomed to toil of any kind.

"I thought to be a governess or waiting maid," and Adah's lip began to quiver. Then she told how her letter had been carelessly forgotten.

"Do you remember the address?" and Alice waited curiously for the answer.

"Yes, 'A.E.R. Snowdon.' You came from Snowdon Miss Johnson, and I've wanted so much to ask if you knew 'A.E.R.,' but have never dared talk freely with you till today."

Alice was confounded. Surely the leadings of Providence were too plainly evident to be unnoticed. There was a reason why Adah Hastings must go to Anna Richards, and Alice hastened to reply: "'A.E.R.' is no less a person than Anna Richards whose mother and brother are now at Saratoga."

"Oh, I can't go there. They are too proud. They would hate me for Willie, and ask me for his father."

Very gently Alice talked to her of Snowdon and Anna Richards, whom Adah was sure to like.

"I'm so glad for your sake that it has come around at last," she said. "Will you write to her today, or shall I for you? Perhaps I had better!"

"Oh, no, I would rather go unannounced—rather Miss Anna should like me for my self, if I go," and Adah's voice trembled, for she shrank nervously from the thought of meeting the Richards family.

If 'Lina liked the old lady, she certainly could not, and the very thought of these elder sisters, in all their primness, dismayed and disheartened her.

While this was passing through her mind, she sat twining Willie's silken curls around her finger, and apparently listening to what Alice was now saying of Dr. Richards; but Alice might as well have talked to the winds for any impression she made. Adah was looking far into the future, wondering what it had in store for her, as if in Anna Richards she would indeed find the sympathizing friend which Alice said she would. Gradually, as she thought of Anna, her heart went out strangely toward her.

"I will go to Miss Richards," she said at last; "but I cannot go till Hugh is better, till he knows and approves. I must take his blessing with me. Do you think it will be long before he regains his reason?"

Alice could not tell.

"Do you correspond with Miss Richards?" Adah suddenly asked.

"No. I will send a note of introduction by you, though."

"Please don't," and Adah spoke pleadingly. "I should have to give it if you did, and I'd rather go by myself. I know it would be better to have your influence, but it is a fancy of mine not to say that I ever knew you or any one at Spring Bank."

Now it was settled that Adah should go, she felt a restless, impatient desire to be gone, questioning the doctor closely with regard to Hugh, who, it seemed to her, would never awaken from the state of unconsciousness into which he had fallen, and from which he only rallied for an instant, just long enough to recognize his mother, but never Alice or herself, both of whom watched over him day and night.

CHAPTER XXII

WAKING TO CONSCIOUSNESS

The sultry August glided by, and in the warm, still days of late September Hugh awoke from the sleep which had so long hung over him. Raising himself upon his elbow, he glanced around the room. There were the table, the stand, the mirror, the curtains, the vases, and the flowers, but what—did he see aright, or did his eyes deceive him? and the perspiration stood thickly about his mouth, as in the bouquet, that morning arranged, he recognized the gay flowers of autumn, not such as he had gathered for Alice, delicate summer flowers, but rich and gorgeous with a later bloom.

"I must have been sick," he whispered, and pressing his hand to his still throbbing head, he tried to reveal and form into some definite shape the events which had seemed, and which seemed to him still, like so many phantoms of the brain.

Was it a dream—his mother's tears upon his face, his mother's voice calling him her Hughey boy, his mother's sobs beside him? Was it, could it be all a dream that she, the Golden Haired, had been with him constantly? No that was not a dream. She did not hate him, else she had not prayed, and words of thanksgiving were going up to Golden Hair's God, when a footstep in the hall announced the approach of some one. Alice, perhaps, and Hugh lay very still, with half shut eyes, until Muggins, instead of Alice, appeared.

He was asleep, she said, as, standing on tiptoe, she scanned his face. He was asleep, and in her own dialect Muggins talked to herself about him as he lay there so still.

"Nice Mas'r Hugh—pretty Mas'r Hugh!" and Mug's little black hand was laid caressingly on the face she admired so much. "I mean to ask God about him, just like I see Miss Alice do," she continued, and stealing to the opposite side of the room, Muggins kneeled down, and with her face turned toward Hugh, she said: "If God is hearin' me, will He please do all dat Miss Alice ax him 'bout curin' Mas'r Hugh."

This was too much for Hugh. The sight of that ignorant negro child, kneeling by the window unmanned him entirely, and hiding his head beneath the sheets, he sobbed aloud. With a nervous start, Mug arose from her knees, and stood for an instant gazing in terror at the trembling of the bedclothes.

"I'll bet he's in a fit. I mean to screech for Miss Alice," and Muggins was about darting away, when Hugh's long arm caught and held her fast. "Oh, de gracious, Mas'r Hugh," she cried, "you skeers me so. Does you know me, Mas'r Hugh?" and she took a step toward him.

"Yes, I know you, and I want to talk a little. Where am I, Mug?

What room, I mean?"

"Why, Miss Alice's, in course. She 'sisted, and 'sisted, till 'em brung you in here, 'case she say it cool and nice. Oh, Miss Alice so fine."

"In Miss Johnson's room," and Hugh looked perfectly bewildered. In the room he had taken so much pains to have in order; it could not be; and he passed his hand up and down the comfortable mattress, striking it once with his fist, to see if it would sink in, and then, in a perplexed whisper, he asked: "This is her room, you say; but, Mug, where are the two feather beds?"

In a most aggrieved tone, Mug explained how Miss Adah and Aunt Eunice had spoiled their handiwork, but could not talk long of anything without bringing in Miss Alice.

"Where does Miss Alice pray for me?" he asked, and Muggins replied:

"Oh here, when she bese alone, and downstairs, and everywhere. You wants to hear her?"

Yes, Hugh did.

"Mug," he said. "I am going to be crazy as a loon. I have not been rational a bit, and you must not say I have. You must not say anything. Do you understand?"

Mug didn't at first, but after a little it came to her that "Mas'r Hugh was goin' to play 'possum. That Miss Alice and all dem would think him ravin' and only she would know the truth." It would be rare sport for Mug, and after giving her promise, she waited anxiously for some one to come. At last another footstep sounded in the hall.

"That's her'n," Muggins whispered. "Is you crazy, Mas'r Hugh?"

"Hush-sh!" came warningly from Hugh, who, the next moment had turned his head away from the fading light, and with eyes closed, pretended to be asleep.

Softly, on tiptoe as it were, Alice approached the bedside, bending so low to see if he were sleeping that he felt her fragrant breath, and a most delicious thrill ran through his frame, when a little, soft, warm hand was laid upon his brow, where the veins were throbbing wildly—so wildly that the unsuspecting maiden wet the linen napkin used for such a purpose, and bathed the feverish skin, pushing back, with a half caressing motion, the rings of damp, brown hair, and still the wicked Hugh never moved, nor winked, nor gave the slightest token of the ecstatic bliss he was enjoying.

"What a consummate hypocrite I am, to lie here and let her do what money could not tempt her to do, if she knew that I was conscious, but hanged if I don't like it," was Hugh's mental comment, while Alice's was: "Poor Hugh, the doctor said he would probably be better when he waked from this sleep, better or worse. Oh, what if he should die, and leave no sign of repentance," and by the rustling movement, Hugh knew that Alice Johnson was kneeling at his side, and with his hot hands in hers was praying for him, that he might not die.

"Spare him for his mother, he is her only boy," he heard her say, and on the pillow, where his face was lying, the great tear drops fell, as he thought how unworthy he was that she should pray for him.

He knew the pillow was wet, and shuddered when Alice attempted to fix his head, turning it more to the light. She saw the tear stains, and murmured to herself: "I did not think it was so warm." Then, sitting down beside him, she fanned him gently, occasionally feeling for his pulse to see if it were as rapid as ever. Once, as she touched his wrist, his fingers closed involuntarily around her little hand and held it a prisoner. He could not help it; the temptation was too strong to be resisted, and then he reflected that a crazy man was not responsible for his actions! As rational Hugh, he could never hope to touch that little soft hand trembling in his like a frightened bird, so he would as crazy Hugh improve his opportunity; and he did, holding fast the hand, and when she attempted to draw it away, pressing it tighter and muttering:

"No, no; mother, no."

"He thinks I am you," Alice whispered, as Mrs. Worthington came in, and Hugh's heart gave one great throb of filial love when his mother stooped over him, and 'mid a shower of tears kissed his forehead and lips, murmuring:

"Darling boy, he'll never know how much his poor mother loved him, or how her heart will break with missing him if he dies."

It was with the utmost difficulty that Hugh could restrain himself then, from assuring his mother that the crisis was passed and he was out of danger.

"I've gone too far now, the hypocrite that I am," he thought. "Alice Johnson never would forgive me. I can't retract now, not yet; I'm in a pretty fix."

As the twilight gathered in the room he lay, listening while his mother and Alice talked together, some times of him, sometimes of Colonel Tiffton, whose embarrassments were now generally known, and again of 'Lina, who, he heard, had chosen to remain at Saratoga, where she was enjoying herself so much with dear Mrs. Richards.

It was Alice who sat up that night, and Hugh, as he lay watching her with half closed eyes, as in her loose plain wrapper, with her luxuriant curls, coiled in a large square knot at the back of her head, she moved noiselessly around the room, felt a pang of remorse at his own duplicity, one moment resolving to give up the part he was playing and bid her leave him alone, and seek the rest she needed. But the temptation to keep her there was strong. He would be very quiet, he said to himself, and he kept his word, remaining so still and apparently sleeping so soundly, that Alice lay down upon the lounge on the opposite side of the room, where she had lain many a night, but never as now, with Hugh's eyes upon her, watching her so eagerly as she fell away to sleep, her soft, regular, childlike breathing awaking a thrill in Hugh's heart, and sending the blood in little, tingling throbs through every vein.

The drops and powders on the table remained undisturbed that night, for the patient was too quiet, and the watcher was so tired, that the latter never woke until the daylight was breaking, and Adah came to relieve her. With a frightened start she arose, astonished to find it was morning.

"I wonder if he had suffered from my neglect?" she said, stealing up to Hugh, who had schooled himself to meet her gaze with wide, open eyes, which certainly had in them no delirium, and which puzzled Alice somewhat, making her blush and turn away.

The old doctor, too, was puzzled, when, later in the morning, he came in, feeling his patient's pulse, examining his tongue, and pronouncing him decidedly out of danger. The fever had left him, he said—the crisis was past—Hugh was a heap better, and for his part he could not understand why the mind should not also come clear, or what it was which made his hitherto talkative subject so silent. He never had such a case—he didn't believe his books had one on record; and the befogged old man hurried home to see if, in all his musty volumes, unopened for many a year, there was a parallel case to Hugh Worthington's.

CHAPTER XXIII

'LINA'S LETTER

Wicked Hugh! How he did enjoy it, for days seeing the family come in and out, talking as freely of him as if he were a log of wood, and how perfectly happy he was when, one morning Alice came in and sat by him, placing her tiny gold thimble upon her delicate finger, and bending over her bit of dainty embroidery, humming occasionally a sweet, mournful air, which showed that her thoughts were wandering back to the cottage by the river, where her mother lived and died. While she was sitting there Mrs. Worthington joined her, and a moment after a letter was brought in from 'Lina, containing on the corner, "In haste."

Mrs. Worthington's eyesight had always been poor, and latterly it was greatly impaired, making glasses indispensable. Unfortunately, she had that very morning broken one of the eyes, and consequently could not use them at all.

"What is that?" she asked, pointing out the words, "In haste," to Alice, who explained what it was, while Mrs. Worthington, fearing lest something had befallen her daughter, could scarcely tear open the envelope. Then, when it was open, she could not read it, for 'Lina's writing was never very plain, and passing it to Alice, she said, entreatingly:

"Please read it for me. There is no secret, I presume."

Glancing at Hugh, who had purposely turned his face to the wall, Alice commenced as follows:

"Fifth Avenue Hotel, New York,
October, 1860."

"Dear Mother: What a little eternity it is since I heard from you, and how am I to know that you are not all dead and buried. Were it not that no news is good news, I should sometimes fancy that Hugh was worse, and feel terribly for not having gone home when you did.

"Now, then, to business, and firstly, as Parson Brown, of Elm wood, used to say, I want Hugh to send me some money, or all is lost. Tell him he must either beg, borrow, pawn or steal, for the rhino I must have. Let me explain.

"Here I am at Fifth Avenue Hotel, as good as any lady, if my purse is almost empty. Plague on it, why didn't that Mrs. Johnson send me two thousand instead of one? It would not hurt her, and them I should get through nicely."

"Oh, I ought not to read this—I cannot," and Alice threw the letter from her, and hurried from the room.

"The way of the transgressor is hard," groaned Hugh, and the groan caught the ear of his mother.

"What is it, Hugh?" she asked, coming quickly to his side. "Are you worse? Do you want anything?"

"No, I'm better, I reckon—the cobwebs are gone. I am myself again. What have you here?" and Hugh grasped the closely written sheet.

In her delight at having her son restored to his reason so suddenly, so unexpectedly, as the poor, deluded woman believed, Mrs. Worthington forgot for a moment the pain, and clasped her arms about him, sobbing like a child.

"Oh, my boy, I am so glad, so glad!" and her tears dropped fast, as like a weary child, which wanted to be soothed, she laid her head upon his bosom, crying quietly.

And Hugh, stronger now than she, held the poor, tired head there, and kissed the white forehead, where there were more wrinkles now than when he last observed it. His mother was growing old with care rather than with years, and Hugh shuddered, as, for the first time in his life, he thought how dreadful it would be to have no mother. Folding his weak arms about her, mother and son wept together in that moment of perfect understanding and union with each other. Hugh was the first to rally. It seemed so pleasant to lean on him, to know that he cared so much for her, that Mrs. Worthington would gladly have rested on his bosom longer, but Hugh was anxious to know the worst, and brought her back to something of the old, sad life, by asking if the letter were from 'Lina.

"Yes; I can't make it out, for one of my glasses is broken, and you know she writes so blind."

"It never troubles me," and taking the letter from her unresisting hand, Hugh asked that another pillow should be placed beneath his head, while he read it aloud.

"You see that thousand is almost gone, and as board is two and a half dollars per day, I can't stay long and shop in Broadway with old Mrs. Richards, as I am expected to do in my capacity of heiress. I tell you, Spring Bank, Kentucky—crazy old rat trap as it is, has done wonders for me in the way of getting me noticed. If I had any soul, big enough to find with a microscope, I believe I should hate the North for cringing so to anything from Dixie. Let the veriest vagabond in all the South, so ignorant that he can scarcely spell baker correctly, to say nothing of biscuit, let him, I say, come to any one of the New York hotels, and with something of a swell write himself from Charleston, or any other Southern city, and bless me, what deference is paid to my lord!

"You see I am a pure Southern woman here; nobody but Mrs. Richards knows that I was born, mercy knows where. But for you, she never need have known it either, but you must tell that we had not always lived in Kentucky.

"But to do Mrs. Richards justice, she never alludes to my birth. She takes it for granted that I moved, like Douglas, when I was very young, and you ought to hear her introduce me to some of her aristocratic friends. 'Mrs. So and So, Miss Worthington, from Spring Bank, Kentucky,' then in an aside, which I am not supposed to hear, she adds, 'A great heiress, of a very respectable family. You may have heard of them.' Somehow, this always makes me uncomfortable, as it brings up certain cogitations touching that scamp you were silly enough to marry, thereby giving me to the world, which my delectable brother no doubt thinks would have been better off without me. How is Hugh? And how is that Hastings woman? Are you both as much in love with her as ever? Well, so be it. I do not know as she ever harmed me, and she did fit my dresses beautifully. Even Mrs. Richards, who is a judge of such things, says they display so much taste, attributing it, of course, to my own directions. I am so glad now that I forgot to send her letter, as I would not for the world have Adah in the Richards' family. It would ruin my prospects for becoming Mrs. Dr. Richards sure, and allow me to say they are not inconsiderable."

"What does she mean? What letter? Who is Dr. Richards?" Hugh asked, his face a purplish red, and contrasting strikingly with the one of ashen hue still resting on his shoulder.

Mrs. Worthington explained as well as she could, and Hugh went on:

"Old Mrs. Richards would, of course, question Adah, and as Adah has some foolish scruples about the truth, she would be very apt to let the cat out of the bag.

"We left Saratoga a week ago—old lady Richards wanted to go to Terrace Hill a while and show me to Anna, who, it seems, is a kind of family oracle. After counting the little gold eagles in my purse, I said perhaps I'd go for a few days, though I dreaded it terribly, for the doctor had not yet bound himself fast, and I did not know what the result of those three old maid sisters, sitting on me, would be. Old lady was quite happy in prospect of going home, when one day a letter came from Anna. I happened to have a headache, and was lying on madam's bed, when the dinner bell happened to ring. I just peeped into the letter, feeling like stealing sheep, but being amply rewarded by the insight I obtained into the family secrets.

"They are poorer than I supposed, but that does not matter, position is what I want, and that they can give me. Anna, it seems, has an income of her own, and, generous soul that she is, gives it out to her mother. She sent fifty dollars in the letter, and in referring to it, said, 'Much as I might enjoy it, dear mother, I cannot afford to come where you are, I can pay your bills for some time longer, if you really think the water a benefit, but my presence would just double the expense. Then, if brother does marry, I wish to surprise him with a handsome set of pearls for his bride, and I am economizing to do so.'" (Note by 'Lina)—"Isn't she a clever old soul? Don't she deserve a better sister-in-law than I shall make, and won't I find the way to her purse often?"

Hugh groaned aloud, and the letter dropped from his hand.

"Mother," he gasped, "it must not be. 'Lina shall not thrust herself upon them. This Anna shall not be so cruelly deceived. I don't care a picayune for the doctor or the old lady. They are much like 'Lina, I reckon, but this Anna awakens my sympathy. I mean to warn her."

Hugh read on, feeling as if he, too, were guilty, thus to know what sweet Anna Richards had intended only for her mother's eye.

"'From some words you have dropped, I fancy you are not quite satisfied with brother's choice—that Miss Worthington does not suit you in all respects, and you wish me to see her. Dear mother, John marries for himself, not for us. I have got so I can drive myself out in the little pony phaeton which Miss Johnson was so kind as to leave for my benefit. Darling Alice, how much I miss her. She always did me good in more ways than one. She found the germ of faith which I did not know I possessed. She encouraged me to go on. She told me of Him who will not break the bruised reed. She left me, as I trust, a better woman than she found me. Precious Alice! how I loved her. Oh, if she could have fancied John, as at one time I hoped she would.'

(Second note by 'Lina.) "How that made me gnash my teeth, for I had suspected that I was only playing second fiddle for Alice Johnson, 'darling, precious Alice,' as Anna calls her."

"Oh, I am so glad Alice didn't read this letter," Mrs. Worthington cried, while something which sounded much like a bit of an oath dropped from Hugh's white lips, and then he continued:

"'When will you come? Asenath has sent the curtains in the north chamber to the laundress, but will go no farther until we hear for certain that Miss Worthington is to be our guest. Write immediately.

"'Yours affectionately,

"'Anna.

"'Remember me to John and Miss W——.

"'P.S.—I still continue to be annoyed with women answering that advertisement. Sometimes I'm half sorry I put it in the paper, though if the right one ever comes, I shall think there was a Providence in it.'

"Mother, I am resolved now to win Dr. Richards at all hazards. Only let me keep up the appearance of wealth, and the thing is easily accomplished; but I can't go to Terrace Hill yet, cannot meet this Anna, for, kindly as she spoke of me, I dread her decision more than all the rest, inasmuch as I know it would have more weight with the doctor.

"But to come back to the madam, showing her point-lace cap

at dinner, and telling Mrs. ex-Governor Somebody how Miss Worthington had a severe headache. I was fast asleep when she returned. Had not read Anna's letter, nor anything! You should have seen her face when I told her I had changed my mind, that I could not go to Terrace Hill, that mamma (that's you!) did not think it would be proper, inasmuch as I had no claim upon them. You see, I made her believe I had written to you on the subject, receiving a reply that you disapproved of my going, and Brother Hugh, too, I quote him a heap, making madam laugh till she cried with repeating his odd speeches, she does so want to see that eccentric Hugh, she says."

Another groan from Mrs. Worthington, another something like an oath from that eccentric Hugh, and he went on:

"I said, brother was afraid it was improper under the circumstances for me to go, afraid lest people should talk; that I preferred going at once to New York. So it was finally decided, to the doctor's relief, I fancied, that we come here, and here we are—hotel just like a beehive, and my room is in the fifth story.

"John had come on the day before to secure rooms, so madam and I were alone, occupying two whole seats, madam and myself on one, madam's feet, two satchels, two silk umbrellas, one fan, one bouquet, and a book in the other. Several tired-looking folks glanced wistfully in that direction, but madam frowned so majestically that they passed on into another car, leaving us to our extra seat. At Rhinebeck, however, she found her match in a very fine-looking man, apparently forty or thereabouts, with a weed on his hat and a certain air, which savored strongly of psalms and hymns and extempore praying. In short, I guessed at once that he was a Presbyterian minister, old school at that. Now, madam, you know, is true blue—apostolically descended, and cannot tolerate anything like a dissenter. But I do not give her credit for having sufficient sagacity to detect the heretic in this handsome, pleasant-faced stranger, who stood looking this way and that for a seat. Madam, I saw, grew very red in the face, and finally threw down her veil, but not till the minister saw it, and half started forward as if about to speak. The movement showed him one extra seat, and very politely he laid his hand upon it, saying:

"'Pardon me, ladies, this, I believe, is unoccupied, and I can find no other.'

"Madam's feet came down with a jerk, ditto madam's portion of the traps, although the stranger insisted that they did not trouble him, while again his mild but expressive eyes scanned the brown veil as if he would know whose face was under it. When we reached New York, he bowed to us again, as if to offer us assistance, but the doctor himself appeared, so that his services were unnecessary.

"'Did you see him?' madam whispered to John, who answered:

"'See who?'

"'Millbrook! He sat right there!'

"'What, the parson? Where is he going?'

"'I don't know. I'm so glad Anna was not here.'

"All this was in an aside, but I heard it, and here are the conclusions. Parson Millbrook has been and wants to be again a lover of Anna Richards, but madam has shut up her bowels of compassion against him for some reason to this deponent unknown. Poor Anna, I am sorry for her, and as her sister, may perhaps help her; but shall I ever be her sister? Ay, there's the rub, and now, honor bright, I reach the point at last.

"I am determined to bring the doctor to terms, and so rid you and Hugh of myself. To do this I must at some rate keep up the appearance of wealth. Perhaps Hugh never knew that Nell Tiffton lent me that elegant pearl bracelet, bought by her father at Ball & Black's. Night before last the doctor took me to hear Charlotte Cushman as *Meg Merrilies*. I wore all the jewelery for which I could find a place, Nell's bracelet with the rest. The doctor and madam have both admired it very much, never dreaming that it was borrowed. In the jam coming out it must have unclasped and dropped off, for it's not to be found high nor low, and you can fancy the muss I am in. Down at Ball & Black's there fortunately is another exactly like Nell's, and this I must buy at any rate. I can perhaps pay my board bills four or five weeks longer, but Hugh must send me fifty dollars with which to replace the bracelet. It must be done.

"Don't for mercy's sake, let Alice Johnson get a sight of this letter. I wonder if Dr. Richards did fancy her. Send the money, send the money.

"Your distracted

"'Lina.

"P.S.—One day later. Rejoice, oh, rejoice! and give ear. The doctor has actually asked the question, and I blushingly referred him to mamma, but he seemed to think this unnecessary, took alarm at once, and pressed the matter until I said yea. Aren't you glad? But one thing is sure—Hugh must sell a nigger to get me a handsome outfit. There's Mug, always under foot, doing no one any good. She'll bring six hundred any day, she's so bright and healthy. Lulu he must give out and out for a waiting maid. Madam expects it. And now one word more; if Adah Hastings has not got over her idea of going to Terrace Hill, she must get over it. Coax, advise, plead with, threaten, or even throttle her, if necessary—anything to keep her back.

"Yours, in ecstatic distress,

"'Lina"

CHAPTER XXIV

FORESHADOWINGS

So absorbed were Hugh and his mother in that letter as not to hear the howl of fear echoing through the hall, as Mug fled in terror from the dreaded new owner to whom Master Hugh was to sell her. Neither did they hear the catlike tread with which Lulu glided past the door, taking the same direction Mug had gone, namely, to Alice Johnson's room.

Lulu had been sitting by the open window at the end of the hall, and had heard every word of this letter, while Mug had reached the threshold in time to hear all that was said about selling her. Instinctively both turned for protection to Alice, but Mug was the first to reach her. Throwing herself upon her knees, she sobbed frantically.

"You buys me, Miss Alice. You give Mar's Hugh six hundred dollars for me, so't he can get Miss 'Lina's weddin' finery. I'll be good, I will. I'll learn do Lord's Prar, an' de Possums Creed, ebery word on't; will you, Miss Alice, say?"

Alice tried to wrest her muslin dress from the child's grasp, asking what she meant.

"I know, I'll tell," and Lulu, scarcely less excited, but far more capable of restraining herself, advanced into the room, and ere the bewildered Alice could well understand what it all meant, or make more than a feeble attempt to stop her, she had repeated rapidly the entire contents of 'Lina's letter.

Too much amazed at first to speak, Alice sat motionless, then she said to Lulu.

"I am sorry that you told me this. It was wrong in you to listen, and you must not repeat it to any one else. Will you promise?"

Lulu gave the required promise, then with terror in every lineament of her face she said:

"But, Miss Alice, must I be Miss 'Lina's waiting maid? Will Master Hugh permit it?"

Alice did not know Hugh as well as we do, and in her heart there was a fear lest for the sake of peace he might be overruled, so she replied evasively. It was no easy task to sooth Muggins, and only Alice's direct avowal, that if possible she would herself become her purchaser, checked her cries at all, but the moment this was said her sobbing ceased, and Alice was able to question Lulu as to whether Hugh had read the letter.

"He must be rational," she said, "but it is so sudden," and a painful uneasiness crept over her as she recalled the look which several times had puzzled her so much.

"You can go now," Alice said, sitting down to reflect as to her next best course.

Adah must go to Terrace Hill at once, and Alice's must be the purse which defrayed all the expense of fitting her up. If ever Alice felt thankful to God for having made her rich in this world's goods, it was that morning. Only the previous night she had heard from Colonel Tiffton that the day was fixed for the sale of his house and that Nell had nearly cried herself into a second fever at the thoughts of leaving Mosside. "Then there's Rocket," the colonel had said, "Hugh cannot buy him back, and he's so bound up in him too, poor Hugh, poor all of us," and the colonel had wrung Alice's hand, hurrying off ere she had time to suggest what all along had been in her mind.

"It does not matter," she thought. "A surprise will be quite as pleasant, and then Mr. Liston may object to it as a silly girl's fancy."

This was the previous night, and now this morning another demand had come in the shape of Muggins weeping in her lap, of Lulu begging to be saved from 'Lina Worthington, and from 'Lina herself asking Hugh for the money Alice knew he had not got.

"But I have," she whispered, "and I will send it too."

Just then Adah came up the stairs, and Alice called her in, asking if she still wished to go to Terrace Hill.

"Yes, more than ever," Adah replied. "Hugh is rational, I hear, so I can talk to him about it before long. You must be present, as I'm sure he will oppose it."

Meantime in the sickroom there was an anxious consultation between mother and son touching the fifty dollars which must be raised for Nellie Tiffton's sake.

"Were it not that I feel bound by honor to pay that debt, 'Lina might die before I'd send her a cent," said Hugh, his eyes blazing with anger as he recalled the contents of 'Lina's letter.

But how should they raise the fifty? Alice's bills had been paid regularly thus far, paid so delicately too, so as a matter of right, that Mrs. Worthington, who knew how sadly it was needed in their present distress, had accepted it unhesitatingly, but Hugh's face flushed with a glow of shame when he heard from his mother's lips that Alice was really paying them her board.

"It makes me hate myself," he said, groaning aloud, "that I should suffer a girl like her to pay for the bread she eats. Oh, poverty, poverty! It is a bitter drug to swallow." Then like a brave man who saw the evil and was willing to face it, Hugh came back to the original point, "Where should they get the money?"

"He might borrow it of Alice, as 'Lina suggested," Mrs. Worthington said, timidly, while Hugh almost leaped upon the floor.

"Never, mother, never! Miss Johnson shall not be made to pay our debts. There's Uncle John's gold watch, left as a kind of heirloom, and very dear on that account. I've carried it long, but now it must go. There's a pawnbroker's office opened in Frankfort—take it there this very afternoon, and get for it what you can. I never shall redeem it. There's no hope. It was in my vest pocket when I was taken sick."

"No, Hugh, not that. I know how much you prize it, and it's all the valuable thing you have. I'll take in washing first," Mrs. Worthington said.

But Hugh was in earnest, and his mother brought the watch from the nail over the mantel, where, all through his sickness it had ticked away the weary hours, just as it ticked the night its first owner died, with only Hugh sitting near, and listening as it told the fleeting moments.

"If I could only ask Alice what it was worth," she thought—and why couldn't she? Yes, she would ask Alice, and with the old hope strong at her heart, she went to Alice, whom she found alone.

"Did you wish to tell me anything? Hugh is better, I hear," Alice said, observing Mrs. Worthington's agitation, and then the whole came out.

"'Lina must have fifty dollars. The necessity was imperative, and they had not fifty to send unless Hugh sold his uncle's watch, but she did not know what it was worth—could Alice tell her?"

"Worth more than you will get," Alice said, and then, as delicately as possible she offered the money from her own purse, advancing so many reasons why they should take it, that poor Mrs. Worthington began to feel that in accepting it, she would do Alice a favor.

"She was willing," she stammered, "but there was Hugh—what could they do with him?"

"I'll manage that," Alice said, laughingly. "I'll engage that he eats neither of us up. Suppose you write to 'Lina now, saying that Hugh is better, and inclosing the money. I have some New York money still," and she counted out, not fifty, but seventy-five dollars, thinking within herself, "she may need it more than I do."

Easily swayed, Mrs. Worthington took the pen which Alice offered, but quickly put it from her, saying, with a little rational indignation, as she remembered 'Lina's heartlessness:

"I won't write her a word. She don't deserve it. Inclose the amount, and direct it, please."

Placing the money in an envelope, Alice directed it as she was bidden, without one word of Hugh, and without the slightest congratulation concerning the engagement; nothing but the money, which was to replace Ellen Tiffton's bracelet.

Claib was deputed as messenger to take it to the office, together with a hastily-written note to Mr. Liston, and then Alice sat down to consider the best means of breaking it to Hugh. Would he prove as gentle as when delirium was upon him; or would he be greatly changed? And what would he think of her? Alice would not have confessed it, but this really was the most important query of all.

Alice was not well pleased with her looks that morning. She was too pale, too languid, and the black dress she wore only increased the difficulty by adding to the marble hue of her complexion. Even her hair did not curl as well as usual, though Mug, who had dried her tears and come back to Alice's room, admired her so much, likening her to the apple blossoms which grew in the lower orchard.

"Is you gwine to Mas'r Hugh?" she asked, as Alice passed out into the hall. "I'se jest been dar. He's peart as a new dollar—knows everybody. How long sense, you 'spec'?" and Mug looked very wise, as she thus skirted around what she was forbidden to divulge on pain of Hugh's displeasure.

But Alice had no suspicions, and bidding Mug go down, she entered Hugh's presence with a feeling that it was to all intents and purposes their first meeting with each other.

CHAPTER XXV

TALKING WITH HUGH

"This is Miss Johnson," Mrs. Worthington said, as Alice drew near, her pallor giving place to a bright flush.

"I fancy I am to a certain degree indebted to Miss Johnson for my life," Hugh said. "I was not wholly unconscious of your presence," he continued, still holding her hand. "There were moments when I had a vague idea of somebody different from those I have always known bending over me, and I fancied, too, that this somebody was sent to save me from some great evil. I am glad you were here, Miss Johnson; I shall not forget your kindness."

He dropped her hand then, while Alice attempted to stammer out some reply.

"Adah, too, had been kind," she said, "quite as kind as herself."

"Yes, Hugh knew that Adah was a dear, good girl. He was glad they liked each other."

Alice thought of Terrace Hill, but this was hardly the time to worry Hugh with that, so she sat silent a while, until Mrs. Worthington, growing very fidgety and very anxious to have the money matter adjusted, said abruptly:

"You must not be angry, Hugh. I asked Alice what that watch was worth, and somehow the story of the lost bracelet came out, and—and—she—Alice would not let me sell the watch. Don't look so black, Hugh, don't—oh, Miss Johnson, you must pacify him," and in terror poor Mrs. Worthington fled from the room, leaving Alice and Hugh alone.

"My mother told you of our difficulties! Has she no discretion, no sense?" and Hugh's face grew dark with the wrath he dared not manifest with Alice's eyes upon him.

"Mr. Worthington," she said, "you have thanked me for caring for you when you were sick. You have expressed a wish to return in some way what you were pleased to call a kindness. There is a way, a favor you can grant me, a favor we women prize so highly; will you grant it? Will you let me do as I please? that's the favor."

She looked a very queen born to be obeyed as she talked thus to Hugh. She did not make him feel small or mean, only submissive, while her kindness touched a tender chord, which could not vibrate unseen. Hugh was very weak, very nervous, too, and turning his head away so that she could not see his face, he let the hot tears drop upon his pillow; slowly at first they came, but gradually as everything—his embarrassed condition, Rocket's loss, 'Lina's selfishness, and Alice's generosity, came rushing over him—they fell in perfect torrents, and Alice felt a keen pang of pity, as sob after sob smote upon her ear, and she knew the shame it must be to him thus to give away before her.

"I did not mean to distress you so. I am sorry if I have done a wrong," she said to him softly, a sound of tears in her own voice.

He turned his white, suffering face toward her, and answered with quivering lip:

"It is not so much that. It is everything combined. I am weak, I'm sick, I'm discouraged," and Hugh could not restrain the tears. Soon rallying, however, he continued:

"You think me a snivelling coward, no doubt, but believe me, Miss Johnson, it is not my nature thus to give way. Tears and Hugh Worthington are usually strangers to each other. I am a man, and I will prove it to you, when I get well, but now I am not myself, and I grant the favor you ask, simply because I can't help it. You meant it in kindness. I take it as such. I thank you, but it must not be repeated. You have come to be my friend, my sister, you say. God bless you for that. I need a sister's love so much, and Adah has given it to me. You like Adah?" and he fixed his eyes inquiringly on Alice, who answered:

"Yes, very much."

Now that the money matter was settled Hugh did not care to talk longer of that or of himself, and eagerly seized upon Adah as a topic interesting to both, and which would be likely to keep Alice with him for a while at least, so, after a moment's silence, during which Alice was revolving the expediency of leaving him lest he should become too weary, he continued:

"Miss Johnson, you don't know how much I love Adah Hastings; not as men generally love," he hastily added, as he caught an expression of surprise on Alice's face, "not as that villain professed to love her, but, as it seems to me, a brother might love an only sister. I mean no disrespect to 'Lina," and his chin quivered a little, "but I have dreamed of a different, brotherly love from what I feel toward her, and my heart has beaten so fast when I built castles of what might have been had we both been different, I, more forbearing, more even tempered, more like the world in general, and she, more—more"—he knew not what, for he would not speak against her, so he finally added, "had she known, just how to take me—just how to make allowances for my rough, uncouth ways, which, of course, annoy her."

Poor Hugh! he was trying now to smooth over what 'Lina had told Alice of himself—trying to apologize for them both, and he did it so skillfully, that Alice felt an increased respect for the man whose real character she had so misunderstood. She, knew, however, that it could not be pleasant for him to speak of 'Lina, and so she led him back to Adah by saying:

"I had thought to talk with you of a plan which Mrs. Hastings has in view, but think, perhaps, I had better wait till you are stronger."

"I am strong enough now—stronger than you think. Tell me of

the plan," and Hugh urged the request until Alice told him of Terrace Hill and Adah's wish to go there.

"I have heard something of this plan before," he said at last. "Ad spoke of it in her letter. Miss Johnson, you know Dr. Richards, I believe. Do you like him? Is he a man to be trusted?"

"Yes, I know Dr. Richards. He is said to be fine looking. I suspect there is a liking between him and your sister. Suppose for your benefit I describe him," and without waiting for permission, Alice portrayed the doctor, feature by feature, watching Hugh narrowly the while, to see if aught she said harmonized with any likeness he might have in his mind.

But Hugh was not thinking of that night which ruined Adah, and Alice's description awakened no suspicion. She saw it did not, and thought once to tell him frankly all she feared, but was deterred from doing so by a feeling that possibly she might be wrong in her conjectures. Adah's presence at Terrace Hill would set that matter right, and she asked if Hugh did not think it best for her to go.

Hugh could only talk in a straightforward manner, and after a moment he answered:

"Yes, best on some accounts. Her going may do good and prevent a wrong. Yes, Adah may go."

He continued: "she surely cannot go alone. Would Sam do? I hear her now. Call her while I talk with her."

Adah came at once, and heard from Hugh that he was willing she should go, provided Spring Bank were still considered her home, the spot to which she could always turn for shelter as to a brother's house.

"You seem so like a sister," he said, smoothing her soft brown hair, "that I shall be sorry to lose you, and shall miss you so much, but Miss Johnson thinks it right for you to go. Will you take Sam as an escort?"

"Oh, no, no; I don't want anybody," Adah cried, "Keep Sam with you, and if in time I should earn enough to buy him, to free him. Oh, will you sell him to me,—not to keep," she added, quickly, as she saw the quizzical expression of Hugh's face,—"not to keep. I would not own a slave—but to free, to tell him he's his own master. Will you, Hugh?"

He answered with a smile:

"I thought once as you do, that I would not own my brother, but we get hardened to these things. I've never sold one yet."

"But you will. You'll sell me Sam," and Adah, in her eagerness, grasped his hand.

"I'll give him to you," Hugh said. "Call him, Miss Johnson."

Alice obeyed, and Sam came hobbling in, listening in amazement to Hugh's question.

"Would you like to be free, my boy?"

There was a sudden flush on the old man's cheek, and then he answered, meekly:

"Thanky', Mas'r Hugh. It comed a'most too late. Years ago, when Sam was young and peart, de berry smell of freedom make de sap bump through de veins like trip-hammer. Den, world all before, now world all behind. Nothing but t'other side of Jordan before. 'Bleeged to you, berry much, but when mas'r bought ole Sam for pity, ole Sam feel in his bones that some time he pay Mas'r Hugh; he don't know how, but it be's comin'. Sam knows it. I'm best off here."

"But suppose I died, when I was so sick, what then?" Hugh asked, and Sam replied:

"I thinks that all over on dem days mas'r so rarin'. I prays many times that God would spar' young mas'r, and He hears ole Sam. He gives us back our mas'r."

There were tears in Hugh's eyes, but he again urged upon him his freedom, offering to give him either to Adah or Alice, just which he preferred.

"I likes 'em both," Sam said, "but I likes Mas'r Hugh de best, 'case, scuse me, mas'r, he ain't in de way, I feared, and Sam hope to help him find it. Sam long's to Mas'r Hugh till dat day comes he sees ahead, when he pays off de debt."

With another blessing on Mas'r Hugh Sam left the room.

"What can he mean about a coming day when he can pay his debt?" Hugh asked, but Alice could not enlighten him.

Adah, however, after hesitating a moment, replied:

"During your illness you have lost the newspaper gossip to the effect that if Lincoln is elected to the presidential chair, civil war is sure to be the result. Now, what Sam means is this, that in case of a rebellion or insurrection, which he fully expects, he will in some way save your life, he don't know how, but he is sure."

To Alice the word rebellion or insurrection had a dreadful sound, and her cheek paled with fear, but the feeling quickly passed away, as, like many other deluded ones she thought how impossible it was that our fair republic should be compelled to lay her dishonored head low in the dust.

It was settled finally that Adah should go as soon as the necessary additions could be made to her own and Willie's wardrobe, and then Alice adroitly led the conversation to Colonel Tiffton and his embarrassments. What did Hugh think Mosside worth, and who would probably be most anxious to secure it? There were livid spots on Hugh's face now, and a strange gleam in his dark eyes as he answered between his teeth, "Harney," groaning aloud as he remembered Rocket, and saw him in fancy the property of his enemy.

CHAPTER XXVI

THE DAY OF THE SALE

It was strange Hugh did not improve faster, the old doctor thought. There was something weighing on his mind, he said, something which kept him awake, and the kind man set himself to divine the cause. Thinking at last he had done so, he said to him one day, the last before the sale:

"My boy, you don't get on for worrying about something. I don't pretend to second sight, but I b'lieve I've got on the right track. It's my pesky bill. I know it's big, for I've been here every day this going on three months, but I'll cut it down to the last cent, see if I don't; and if it's an object, I'll wait ten years, so chirk up a bit," and wringing his hand, the well-meaning doctor hurried off, leaving Hugh alone with his sad thoughts.

It was not so much the bill which troubled him—it was Rocket, and the feeling sure that he should never own him again. Heretofore there had at intervals been a faint hope in his heart that by some means he might redeem him, but that was over now. The sale of Colonel Tiffton's effects occurred upon the morrow, and money stood waiting for Rocket, while Harney, with a fiendish, revengeful disposition, which was determined to gain its point at last, had been heard to say that "rather than lose the horse or let it pass back to its former owner, he believed he would give a thousand dollars."

That settled it, Hugh had no thousand dollars; he had not even ten, and with a moan of pain, he tried to shut out Rocket from his mind. And this it was which kept him so nervous and restless, dreading yet longing for the eventful day, and feeling glad when at last he could say—

"Tomorrow is the sale."

The next morning was cold and chilly, making Hugh shiver as he waited for the footstep which he had learned to know so well. She had not come to see him the previous night, and he waited for her anxiously now, feeling sure that on this day of all others she would stay with him. How, then, was he disappointed when at last she came to him, cloaked and hooded as for a ride.

"Are you going out today again?" he asked, his tone that of a pleading child.

"It does not seem right to leave you alone, I know," she said, "but poor Ellen needs me sadly, and I promised to be there."

"At Mosside, with all those rough men, oh, Alice, don't go!" and Hugh grasped the little hand.

"It may appear unladylike, I know, but I think it right to stay by Ellen. By the way," and Alice spoke rapidly now, "the doctor says you'll never get well so long as you keep so closely in the house. You are able to ride, and I promised to coax you out tomorrow, if the day is fine. I shall not take a refusal," she continued, as he shook his head. "I am getting quite vain of my horsemanship. I shall feel quite proud of your escort, even if I have to tease for it; so, remember, you are mine for a part of tomorrow."

She drew her hand from his, and with another of her radiant smiles, swept from the room, leaving him in a maze of blissful bewilderment. Never till this morning had a hope entered Hugh's heart that Alice Johnson might be won. Except her, there was not a girl in all the world who had ever awakened the slightest emotion within his heart, and Alice had seemed so far removed from him that to dream of her was worse than useless. She would never esteem him save as a friend, and until this morning Hugh had fancied he could be satisfied with that, but there was something in the way her little fingers twined themselves around his, something in her manner, which prompted the wild hope that in an unguarded moment she had betrayed herself, had permitted him a glimpse of what was in her mind, only a glimpse, but enough to make the poor deluded man giddy with happiness. She, the Golden Haired, could be won, and should be won.

"My wife, my Alice, my Golden Hair," he kept repeating to himself, until, in his weak state, the perspiration dropped from every pore, and his mother, when she came to him, asked in much alarm what was the matter.

He could not tell her of his newly-born joy, so he answered evasively:

"Rocket is sold today. Is not that matter enough?"

"Poor Hugh, I wish so much that I was rich!" the mother sighed, as she wiped the sweat drops from his brow, arranged his pillows more comfortably, and then, sitting down beside him, said, hesitatingly—"I have another letter from 'Lina. Can you hear it now, or will you read it for yourself?"

It was strange how the mention of 'Lina embittered at once Hugh's cup of bliss, making him answer pettishly:

"She has waited long enough, I think. Give it to me, please," and taking the letter that morning received, he read first that 'Lina was much obliged for the seventy-five dollars, and thought they must be growing generous, as she only asked for fifty.

"What seventy-five dollars? What does she mean?" Hugh exclaimed, but his mother could not tell, unless it were that Alice, unknown to them, had sent more than 'Lina asked for.

This seemed probable, and as it was the only solution of the mystery, he accepted it as the real one, and returned to the letter, learning that the bracelet was purchased, that it could not be told from the lost one, that she was sporting it on Broadway every day, that she did not go to the prince's ball just for the doctor's meanness in not procuring a ticket when he had one offered to him for eighty dollars!

"I don't really suppose he could afford it," she wrote, "but it made me mad just the same, and I pouted all day. I saw the ladies, though, after they were dressed, and that did me some good, particularly as the Queen of the South, Madam Le Vert, asked my opinion of her chaste, beautiful toilet, just as if she had faith in my judgment.

"Well, after the fortunate ones were gone, I went to my room to pout, and directly Mother Richards sent Johnny up to coax me, whereupon there ensued a bit of a quarrel, I twitting him about that ambrotype of a young girl, which Nell Tiffton found at the St. Nicholas, and which the doctor claimed, seeming greatly agitated, and saying it was very dear to him, because the original was dead. Well, I told him of it, and said if he loved that girl better than me, he was welcome to have her. 'Lina Worthington had too may eligible offers to play second fiddle to any one.

"''Lina,' he said, 'I will not deceive you, though I meant to do so. I did love another before ever I heard of you, a fair young girl, as pure, as innocent as the angels. She is an angel now, for she is dead. Do not ask further of her. Let it suffice that I loved her, that I lost her. I shall never tell you more of her sad story. Let her never be named to me again. It was long ago. I have met you since, have asked and wish you to be my wife,'—and so we made it up, and I promised not to speak of my rival. Pleasant predicament, I am in, but I'll worm it out of him yet. I'll haunt him with her dead body."

"Oh, mother," and Hugh gasped for breath. "Is Ad—can she be anything to us? Is my blood in her veins?"

"Yes, Hugh, she's your half sister. Forgive me that I made her so," and the poor mother wept over the heartless girl. "But go on," she whispered. "See where 'Lina is now," and Hugh read on, learning that old Mother Richards had returned home, that Anna had written a sweet, sisterly note, welcoming her as John's bride to their love, that she had answered her in the same gracious strain, heightening the effect by dropping a few drops of water here and there, to answer for tears wrung out by Anna's sympathy, that Mrs. Ellsworth and her brother, Irving Stanley, came to the hotel, that Irving had a ticket to the ball offered him, but declined, just because he did not believe in balls, that having a little 'axe to grind,' she had done her best to cultivate Mrs. Ellsworth, presuming a great deal on their courtship, and making herself so agreeable to her child, a most ugly piece of deformity, that cousin Carrie, who had hired a furnished house for the winter, had invited her to spend the season with her, and she was now snugly ensconced in most delightful quarters on Twenty-second Street, between Fifth and Sixth Avenues.

"Sometimes," she wrote, "I half suspect Mrs. Ellsworth did not think I would jump at her invitation so quick, but I don't care. The doctor, for some reason or other, has deferred our marriage until spring, and dear knows I am not coming back to horrid Spring Bank any sooner than I can help.

"By the way, I'm somewhat haunted with the dread that, after all, Adah may take it into her willful head to go to Terrace Hill, and I would not have her for the world. How does Alice get on with Hugh? I conclude he must be well by this time. Does he wear his pants inside his cowhides yet, or have Alice's blue eyes had a refining effect upon his pantaloons? Tell him not to set his heart upon her, for, to my certain knowledge, Irving Stanley, Esq., has an interest in that quarter, while she is not indifferent.

"He has his young sister Augusta here now. She has come on to do her shopping in New York, and is stopping with Mrs. Ellsworth. A fine little creature, quite stylish, but very puritanical. Through Augusta I have got acquainted with Lottie Gardner, a kind of stepniece to the doctor, and excessively aristocratic. You ought to have seen how coolly her big, proud, black eyes inspected one. I rather like her, though. She and Augusta Stanley were together at Madam ——'s school in the city.

"Didn't Adah say she went there once? Again I charge you, don't let her go to Terrace Hill on any account.

"And one other thing. I shall buy my bridal trousseau under Mrs. Ellsworth's supervision. She has exquisite taste, and Hugh must send the money. As I told him before, he can sell Mug. Harney will buy her. He likes pretty darkies."

"Oh, horror! can Ad be a woman, with womanly feelings?" Hugh exclaimed, feeling as if he hated his sister.

But after a moment he was able to listen while his mother asked if it would not be better to persuade Adah not to go to Terrace Hill.

"It may interfere with 'Lina's plans," she said, "and now it's gone so far, it seems a pity to have it broken up. It's—it's very pleasant with 'Lina gone," and with a choking sob, Mrs. Worthington laid her face upon the pillow, ashamed and sorry that the real sentiments of her heart were thus laid bare.

It was terrible for a mother to feel that her home would be happier for the absence of a child, and that child an only daughter, but she did feel so, and it made her half willing that Dr. Richards should be deceived. But Hugh shrank from the dishonorable proceeding.

Mrs. Worthington always yielded to Hugh, and she did so now, mentally resolving, however, to say a few words to Adah, relative to her not divulging anything which could possibly harm 'Lina, such as telling how poor they were, or anything like that. This done, Mrs. Worthington felt easier, and as Hugh looked tired and worried, she left him for a time, having first called Muggins to gather up the fragments of 'Lina's letter which Hugh had thrown upon the carpet.

"Yes, burn every trace of it," Hugh said, watching the child as she picked up piece by piece, and threw them into the grate.

"I means to save dat ar. I'll play I has a letter for Miss Alice," Mug thought, as she came upon a bit larger than the others, and unwittingly she hid in her bosom that portion of the letter referring to herself and Harney! This done, she too left the room, and Hugh was at last alone.

He had little hope now that he would ever win Alice, so jealously sure was he that Irving was preferred before him, and he whispered sadly to himself:

"I can live on just the same, I suppose. Life will be no more dreary than it was before I knew her. No, nor half so dreary, for 'it is better to have loved and lost than not to have loved at all.' That is what Adah said once when I asked what she would give never to have met that villain."

As it frequently happens that when an individual is talked or thought about, that individual appears, so Adah now came in, asking how Hugh was, and if she should not sit a while with him.

Hugh's face brightened at once, for next to Alice he liked best to have Adah with him. With 'Lina's letter still fresh in his mind it was very natural for him to think of what was said of Augusta Stanley, and after Adah had sat a moment, he asked if she remembered such a person at Madam Dupont's school, or Lottie Gardner either.

"Yes, I remember them both," and Adah looked up quickly. "Lottie was proud and haughty, though quite popular with most of the girls, I believe; but Augusta—oh, I liked her so much. Do you know her?"

"No; but Ad, it seems, has ingratiated herself into the good graces of Mrs. Ellsworth, this Augusta's sister. There's a brother, too'—"

"Yes, I remember. He came one day with Augusta, and all the girls were so delighted. I hardly noticed him myself, for my head was full of George. It was there I met him first, you know."

There was a shadow now on Adah's face, and she sat silent for some time, thinking of the past, while Hugh watched the changes of her beautiful face, wondering what was the mystery which seemed to have shrouded the whole of her young life.

"You have done me a great deal of good," he said; "and sometimes I think it's wrong in me to let you go away, when, if I kept you, you might teach me how to be a good man—a Christian man, I mean."

"Oh, if you only would be one," and the light which shone in Adah's eyes seemed born of Heaven. "I am going, it is true, but there is One who will stay with you—One who loves you so much."

He thought she meant Alice, and he grasped her hand, and exclaimed:

"Loves me, Adah, does she? Say it again! Does Alice Johnson love me, me? Hugh? Did she tell you so? Adah," and Hugh spoke vehemently, "I have admitted to you what an hour ago I fancied nothing could wring from me, but I trust to your discretion not to betray it; certainly not to her, not to Alice, for, of course, there is no hope. You do not think there is? You know her better than I," and he looked wistfully at Adah, who felt constrained to answer:

"There might have been, I'm sure, if she had seen no one else."

"Then she has—she does love another?" and Hugh's face was white as ashes.

"I do not know that she loves him; she did not say so," Adah replied, thinking it better for Hugh that he should know the whole. "There was a boy or youth, who saved her life at the peril of his own, and she remembered him so long, praying for him daily that God would bring him to her again, so she could thank him for his kindness."

Poor Hugh. He saw clearly now how it all was. He had suffered his uncle, who affected a dislike for "Hugh," to call him "Irving." He had also, for no reason at all, suffered Alice to think he was a Stanley, and this was the result.

"I can live on just as I did before," was again the mental cry of his wrung heart.

How changed were all things now, for the certainty that Alice never would be his had cast a pall over everything, and even the autumnal sunshine streaming through the window seemed hateful to him. Involuntarily his mind wandered to the sale and to Rocket, perhaps at that very moment upon the block.

"If I could have kept him, it would have been some consolation," he sighed, just as the sound of hoofs dashing up to the door met his ear.

It was Claib, and just as Hugh was wondering at his headlong haste, he burst into the room, exclaiming:

"Oh, Mas'r Hugh, 'tain't no use now. He'd done sold, Rocket is. I hearn him knocked down, and then I comed to tell you, an' he looked so handsome, too,—caperin' like a kitten. They done made me show him off, for he wouldn't come for nobody else, but the minit he fotched a sight of dis chile, he flung 'em right and left. I fairly cried to see how he went on."

There was no color now in Hugh's face, and his voice trembled as he asked:

"Who bought him?"

"Harney, in course, bought him for five-fifty. I tells you they runs him up, somebody did, and once, when he stood at four hundred and fifty, and I thought the auction was going to say 'Gone,' I bids myself."

"You!" and Hugh stared blankly at him.

"I know it wan't manners, but it came out 'fore I thought, and Harney, he hits me a cuff, and tells me to hush my jaw. He got paid, though, for jes' then a voice I hadn't hearn afore, a wee voice like a girl's, calls out five hundred, and ole Harney turn black as tar. 'Who's that?' he said, pushin' inter the crowd, and like a mad dog yelled out five-fifty, and then he set to cussin' who 'twas biddin' ag'in him. I hearn them 'round me say, 'That fetches it. Rocket's a goner,' when I flung the halter in Harney's ugly face, and came off home to tell you. Poor Mas'r, you is gwine to faint," and the well-meaning, but rather impudent Claib, sprang forward in time to catch and hold his young master, who otherwise might have fallen to the floor.

Hugh had borne much that day. The sudden hope that Alice might be won, followed so soon by the certainty that she could not, had shaken his nerves and tried his strength cruelly, while the story Claib had told unmanned him entirely, and this it was which made him grow so cold and faint, reeling in his chair, and leaning gladly for support against the sturdy Claib, who led him to the bed, and then went in quest of Adah.

CHAPTER XXVII

THE SALE

There was a crowd of people out that day to attend the sale of Colonel Tiffton's household effects. Even fair ladies, too, came in their carriages, holding high their aristocratic skirts as they threaded their way through the rooms where piles of carpeting and furniture of various kinds lay awaiting the shrill voice and hammer of the auctioneer, a portly little man, who felt more for the family than his appearance would indicate.

There had been a long talk that morning between himself and a young lady, a stranger to him, whose wondrous beauty had thrilled his heart just as it did every heart beating beneath a male's attire. The lady had seemed a little worried, as she talked, casting anxious glances up the Lexington turnpike, and asking several times when the Lexington cars were due.

"It shan't make no difference. I'll take your word," the auctioneer had said in reply to some doubts expressed by her. "I'd trust your face for a million," and with a profound bow by way of emphasizing his compliment, the well-meaning Skinner went out to the group assembled near Rocket while the lady returned to the upper chamber where Mrs. Tiffton and Ellen were assembled.

Once Harney's voice, pitched in its blandest tone, was heard talking to the ladies, and then Ellen stopped her ears, exclaiming passionately:

"I hate that man, I hate him. I almost wish that I could kill him."

"Hush, Ellen; remember! 'Vengeance is mine, I will repay, saith the Lord,'" Alice whispered to the excited girl who answered hastily:

"Don't preach to me now. I'm too wretched. Wait till you lose everything by one man's villainy, then see if you won't curse him."

There was an increased confusion in the yard below, and Alice knew the sale was about to commence. The white-haired colonel kept watch while one after another of his household goods were sold. Inferior articles they were at first, and the crowd were not much disposed to bid, but all were dear to the old man, who groaned each time an article was knocked off, and so passed effectually from his possession.

The crowd grew weary at last—they must have brisker sport than that, if they would keep warm in that chilly November wind, and cries for the "horses" were heard.

"Your crack ones, too. I'm tired of this," growled Harney, and Ellen's riding pony was led out. The colonel saw the playful animal, and tottered to Ellen's chamber, saying:

"They're going to sell Beauty, Nell. Poor Nellie, don't cry," and the old man laid his hand on his weeping daughter's head.

"Colonel Tiffton, this way please," and Alice spoke in a whisper. "I want Beauty. Couldn't you bid for me, bid all you would be willing to give if you were bidding for Ellen?"

The colonel looked at her in a kind of dazed, bewildered way, as if not fully comprehending her, till she repeated her request; then mechanically he went back to his post on the balcony, and just as Harney's last bid was about to receive the final "gone," he raised it twenty dollars, and ere Harney had time to recover his astonishment, Beauty was disposed of, and the colonel's servant Ham led her in triumph back to the stable.

With a fierce scowl of defiance Harney called for Rocket. Suspecting something wrong the animal refused to come out, and planting his fore feet firmly upon the floor of the stable, kept them all at bay. With a fierce oath, the brutal Harney gave him a stinging blow, which made the tender flesh quiver with pain, but the fiery gleam in the noble animal's eye warned him not to repeat it. Suddenly among the excited group of dusky faces he spied that of Claib, and bade him lead out the horse.

"I can't. Oh, mas'r, for the dear—" Claib began, but Harney's riding whip silenced him at once, and he went submissively in to Rocket, who became as gentle beneath his touch as a lamb.

Did the sagacious creature think then of Hugh, and fancy Claib had come to lead him home? We cannot tell. We only know how proudly he arched his graceful neck, as with dancing, mincing steps, he gamboled around Claib, rubbing his nose against the honest black face, where the tears were standing, and trying to lick the hands which had fed him so often at Spring Bank.

Loud were the cries of admiration which hailed his appearance.

The bids were very rapid, for Rocket was popular, but Harney bided his time, standing-silently by, with a look on his face of cool contempt for those who presumed to think they could be the fortunate ones. He was prepared to give more than any one else. Nobody would go above his figure, he had set it so high—higher even than Rocket was really worth. Five hundred and fifty, if necessary. No one would rise above that, Harney was sure, and quietly waited until the bids were far between, and the auctioneer still dwelling upon the last, seemed waiting expectantly for something.

"I believe my soul the fellow knows I mean to have that horse," thought Harney, and with an air which said, "that settles it," he called out in loud, clear tones, "Four hundred," thus adding fifty at one bid.

There was a slight movement then in the upper balcony, an opening of the glass door, and a suppressed whisper ran through the crowd, as Alice came out and stood by the colonel's aide.

The bidding went on briskly now, each bidder raising a few

dollars, till four hundred and fifty was reached, and then there came a pause, broken only by the voice of the excited Claib, who, as he confessed to Hugh, had ventured to speak for himself, and was rewarded for his temerity by a blow from Harney. With that blow still tingling about his ears and confusing his senses, Claib could not well tell whence or from whom came that silvery, half tremulous voice, which passed so like an electric shock through the eager crowd, and rousing Harney to a perfect fury.

"Five hundred."

There was no mistaking the words, and with a muttered curse at the fair bidder shrinking behind the colonel, and blushing, as if in shame, Harney yelled out his big price, all he had meant to give. He was mad with rage, for he knew well for whom that fair Northern girl was interested. He had heard much of Alice Johnson—had seen her occasionally in the Spring Bank carriage as she stopped in Frankfort; and once she had stopped before his store, asking, with such a pretty grace, that the piece of goods she wished to look at might be brought to her for inspection, that he had determined to take it himself, but remembered his dignity as half millionaire, and sent his head clerk instead.

Beneath Harney's coarse nature there was a strange susceptibility to female beauty, and neither the lustrous blue of Alice's large eyes, nor yet the singular sweetness of her voice, as she thanked the clerk for his trouble, had been forgotten. He had heard that she was rich—how rich he did not know—but fancied she might possibly be worth a few paltry thousands, not more, and so, of course, she was not prepared to compete with him, who counted his gold by hundreds of thousands. Five hundred was all she would give for Rocket. How, then was he surprised and chagrined when, with a coolness equal to his own, she kept steadily on, scarcely allowing the auctioneer to repeat his bid before she increased it, and once, womanlike, raising on her own.

"Fie, Harney! Shame to go against a girl! Better give it up, for don't you see she's resolved to have him? She's worth half Massachusetts, too, they say."

These and like expressions met Harney on every side, until at last, as he paused to answer some of them, growing heated in the altercation, and for the instant forgetting Rocket, the auctioneer brought the hammer down with a click which made Harney leap from the ground, for by that sound he knew that Rocket was sold to Alice Johnson for six hundred dollars!

Meantime Alice had sought the friendly shelter of Ellen's room, where the tension of nerve endured so long gave way, and sinking upon the sofa she fainted, just as down the Lexington turnpike came the man looked for so long in the earlier part of the day. She could not err, in Mr. Liston's estimation, and Alice grew calm again, and in a hurried consultation explained to him more definitely than her letter had done, what her wishes were—Colonel Tiffton must not be homeless in his old age. There were ten thousand dollars lying in the—— Bank in Massachusetts, so she would have Mosside purchased in her name for Colonel Tiffton, not as a gift, for he would not accept it, but as a loan, to be paid at his convenience. This was Alice's plan, and Mr. Liston acted upon it at once. Taking his place in the motley assemblage, he bid quietly, steadily, until at last Mosside, with its appurtenances, belonged ostensibly to him, and the half-glad, half-disappointed people wondered greatly who Mr. Jacob Liston could be, or from what quarter of the globe he had suddenly dropped into their midst.

Colonel Tiffton knew that nearly everything had been purchased by him, and felt glad that a stranger rather than a neighbor was to occupy what had been so dear to him, and that his servants would not be separated. With Ellen it was different. A neighbor might allow them to remain there a time, she said, while a stranger would not, and she was weeping bitterly, when, as the sound of voices and the tread of feet gradually died away from the yard below, Alice came to her side, and bending over her, said softly, "Could you bear some good news now—bear to know who is to inhabit Mosside?"

"Good news?" and Ellen looked up wonderingly.

"Yes, good news, I think you will call it," and then as deliberately as possible Alice told what had been done, and that the colonel was still to occupy his old home, "As my tenant, if you like," she said to him, when he began to demur.

When at last it was clear to the old man, he laid his hand upon the head of the young girl and whispered huskily, "I cannot thank you as I would, or tell you what's in my heart, God bless you, Alice Johnson."

Alice longed to say a word to him of the God to whom he had thus paid tribute, but she felt the time was hardly then, and after a few more assurances to Ellen started for Spring Bank, where Mrs. Worthington and Adah were waiting for her.

CHAPTER XXVIII

THE RIDE

They had kept it all from Hugh, telling him only that a stranger had purchased Mosside. He had not asked for Rocket, or even mentioned him, though his pet was really uppermost in his mind, and when he awoke next morning from his feverish sleep and remembered Alice's proposal to ride, he said to himself, "I cannot go, much as I might enjoy it. No other horse would carry me as gently as Rocket. Oh! Rocket!"

It was a bright, balmy morning, and Hugh, as he walked slowly to the window and inhaled the fragrant air, felt that it would do him good, "But I shan't go," he said, and when, after breakfast was over, Alice came, reminding him of the ride, he began an excuse, but his resolution quickly gave way before her sprightly arguments, and he finally assented, saying, however: "You must not expect a gay cavalier, for I am still too weak, and I have no horse fit to ride with you, at least."

"Yes, I know," and Alice ran gayly to her room and donned her riding dress, wondering what Hugh would say and how Rocket would act.

He was out in the back yard now, pawing and curvetting, and rubbing his nose against all who came near him, while Claib was holding him by his new bridle and talking to him of Mas'r Hugh.

Even an ugly woman is improved by a riding costume, and Alice, beautiful though she was, looked still more beautiful in her closely-fitting habit.

"There, I'm ready," she said, running down to Hugh.

At sight of her his face flushed, while a half sigh escaped him as he thought how proud he would once have been to ride with her; but that was in the days of Rocket, when rider and horse were called the best in the county.

"Where's Jim?" Hugh asked, glancing around in quest of the huge animal he expected to mount, and which he had frequently likened to a stone wall.

"Claib has your horse. He's coming," and with great apparent unconcern Alice worked industriously at one of her fairy gantlets.

Suddenly Adah flew to Hugh's side, and said, eagerly:

"Hugh, please whistle once, just as you used to do for Rocket—just once, and let Miss Johnson hear you."

Hugh felt as if she were mocking him, but he yielded, while like a gleam of lightning the shadow of a suspicion flitted across his mind. It was a loud, shrill whistle, penetrating even to the woods, and the instant the old familiar sound fell on Rocket's ear he went tearing around the house, answering that call with the neigh he had been wont to give when summoned by his master. Utterly speechless, Hugh stood gazing at him as he came up, his neck arched proudly, and his silken mane flowing as gracefully as on the day when he was led away to Colonel Tiffton's stall.

"Won't somebody tell me what it means?" Hugh gasped, stretching out his hands toward Rocket, who even attempted to lick them.

At this point Alice stepped forward, and taking Rocket's bridle, laid it across Hugh's lap, saying, softly:

"It means that Rocket is yours, purchased by a friend, saved from Harney, for you. Mount him, and see if he rides as easily as ever. I am impatient to be off."

But had Hugh's life depended upon it, he could not have mounted Rocket then. He knew the friend was Alice, and the magnitude of the act overpowered him.

"Oh, Miss Johnson," he cried, "what made you do it? It must not be. I cannot suffer it."

"Not to please me?" and Alice's face wore its most winning look. "It's been my fixed determination ever since I heard of Rocket, and knew how much you loved him. I was never so happy doing an act in my life, and now you must not spoil it all by refusing."

"As a loan, then, not as a gift," Hugh whispered. "It shall not be a gift."

"It need not," Alice rejoined, as a sudden plan for carrying out another project crossed her mind. "You shall pay for Rocket if you like, and I'll tell you how on our ride. Shall we go?"

Once out upon the highway, where there were no mud holes to shun, no gates to open and shut, Hugh broached the subject of Rocket again, when Alice told him unhesitatingly how he could, if he would, pay for him and leave her greatly his debtor. The scrap of paper, which Muggins had saved from the letter thrown by Hugh upon the carpet, had been placed by the queer little child in an old envelope, which she called her letter to Miss Alice. Handing it to her that morning with the utmost gravity, she had asked her to read "Mug's letter," and Alice had read the brief lines written by 'Lina: "Hugh must send the money, as I told him before. He can sell Mug; Harney likes pretty darkies." There was a cold, sick feeling at Alice's heart, a shrinking with horror from 'Lina Worthington, and then she came to a decision. Mug should be hers, and so, as skillfully as she could she brought it around, that having taken a great fancy both to Lulu and Muggins, she wished to buy them both, giving whatever Hugh honestly thought they were worth. Rocket, if he pleased, should be taken as part or whole payment for Mug, and so cease to be a gift.

"I have no mercenary motives in the matter," she said, "With me they will be free, and this, I am sure, will be an inducement for you to consent to my proposal."

A slave master can love his bond servant, and Hugh loved the little Mug so much that the idea of parting with her as he surely must at some future time if he assented to Alice's plan, made him hesitate. But he decided at last, influenced not so much by need of money as by knowing how much real good the exchange of owner-ship would be to the two young girls. In return for Rocket, Alice should have Muggins, while for Lulu she might give what she liked.

"Heaven knows," he added, "it is not my nature to hold any one in bondage, and I shall gladly hail the day which sees the negro free. But our slaves are our property. Take them from us and we are ruined wholly. Miss Johnson, do you honestly believe that one in forty of those Northern abolitionists would deliberately give up ten—twenty—fifty thousand dollars, just because the thing valued at that was man and not beast? No, indeed. Southern people, born and brought up in the midst of slavery, can't see it as the North does, and there's where the mischief lies."

He had wandered from Lulu and Muggins to the subject which then, far more than the North believed, was agitating the Southern mind. Then they talked of 'Lina, Hugh telling Alice of her intention to pass the winter with Mrs. Ellsworth, and speaking also of Irving Stanley.

"By the way, Ad writes that Irving was interested in you, and you in him," Hugh said, rather abruptly, stealing a glance at Alice, who answered frankly:

"I can hardly say that I know much of him, though once, long ago—"

She paused here, and Hugh waited anxiously for what she would say next. But Alice, changing her mind, only added:

"I esteem Mr. Stanley very highly. He is a gentleman, a scholar and a Christian."

"You like him better for that, I suppose—better for being a Christian, I mean," Hugh replied, a little bitterly.

"Oh, yes, so much better," and reining her horse closer to Hugh, Alice rode very slowly, while in earnest tones she urged on Hugh the one great thing he needed. "You are not offended?" she asked, as he continued silent.

"No, oh, no. I never had any religious teaching, only once; an angel flitted across my path, leaving a track of glorious sunshine, but the clouds have been there since, and the sunshine is most all gone."

Alice knew he referred to the maiden of whose existence Mug had told her, and she longed to ask him of her. Who was she, and where was she now? Alas, that she should have been so deceived, or that Hugh, when she finally did ask, "Who was the angel that crossed his path?" should answer evasively.

Just before turning into the Spring Bank fields, a horseman came dashing down the pike, checking his steed a moment as he drew near, and then, with a savage frown, spurring on his foam-covered horse, muttering between his teeth a curse on Hugh Worthington.

"That was Harney?" Alice said, stopping a moment outside the gate to look after him as he went tearing down the pike.

"Yes, that was Harney," Hugh replied. "There's a political meeting of some kind in Versailles today, and I suppose he is going there to raise his voice with those who are denouncing the Republicans so bitterly, and threatening vengeance if they succeed."

"The South will hardly be foolish enough to secede. Why, the North would crush them at once," returned Alice, still looking after Harney, as if she knew she were gazing after one destined to figure conspicuously in the fast approaching rebellion, his very name a terror and dread to the loyal, peace-loving citizens of Kentucky.

CHAPTER XXIX

HUGH AND ALICE

Three weeks had passed away since that memorable ride. Mr. Liston, after paying to the proper recipients the money due for Mosside, had returned to Boston, leaving the neighborhood to gossip of Alice's generosity, and to wonder how much she was worth. It was a secret yet that Lulu and Muggins were hers, but the story of Rocket was known, and numerous were the surmises as to what would be the result of her daily, familiar intercourse with Hugh. Already was the effect of her presence visible in his improved appearance, his gentleness of manner, his care to observe all the little points of etiquette never practiced by him before, and his attention to his own personal appearance. His trousers were no longer worn inside his boots, or his soft hat jammed into every conceivable shape, while Ellen Tiffton, who came often to Spring Bank, and was supposed to be good authority, pronounced him almost as stylish looking as any man in Woodford.

To Hugh, Alice was everything, and he did not know himself how much he loved her, save when he thought of Irving Stanley, and then the keen, sharp pang of jealous pain which wrung his heart told him how strong was the love he bore her. And Alice, in her infatuation concerning the mysterious Golden Hair, did much to feed the flame. He was to her like a beloved brother; indeed, she had one day playfully entered into a compact with him that she should be his sister, and never dreaming of the mischief she was doing, she treated him with all the familiarity of a pure, loving sister. It was Alice who rode with him almost daily. It was Alice who sang his favorite songs. It was Alice who brought his armchair in the evening when his day's work was over; Alice who worked his slippers; Alice who brushed his coat when he was going to town; Alice who sometimes tied his cravat, standing on tiptoe, with her fair face so fearfully near to his that all his powers of self-denial were needed to keep from touching his lips to the smooth brow gleaming so white and fair before his eyes.

Sometimes the wild thought crossed his mind that possibly he might win her for himself, but it was repudiated as soon as formed, and so, between hope and a kind of blissful despair, blissful so long as Alice stayed with him as she was now, Hugh lived on, until at last the evening came when Adah was to leave Spring Bank on the morrow. She had intended going immediately after the sale at Mosside, but Willie had been ailing ever since, and that had detained her. Everything which Alice could do for her had been done. Old Sam, at thoughts of parting with his little charge, had cried his dim eyes dimmer yet. Mrs. Worthington, too, had wept herself nearly sick, for now that the parting drew near she began to feel how dear to her was the young girl who had come to them so strangely.

"More like a daughter you seem to me," she had said to Adah, in speaking of her going; "and once I had a wild—" here she stopped, leaving the sentence unfinished, for she did not care to tell Adah of the shock it had given her when Hugh first pointed out to her the faint mark on Adah's forehead.

It was fainter now even than then, for with increasing color and health it seemed to disappear, and Mrs. Worthington could scarcely see it, when with a caressing movement of her hand she put the silken hair back from Adah's brow and kissed the bluish veins.

"There is none there. It was all a fancy," she murmured to herself, and then thinking of 'Lina, she said to Adah what she had all along meant to say, that if the Richards' family should question her of 'Lina, she was to divulge nothing to her disparagement, whether she were rich or poor, high or low. "You must not, of course, tell any untruths. I do not ask that, but I—oh, I sometimes wish they need not know that you came from here, as that would save all trouble, and 'Lina is so—so—"

Mrs. Worthington did not finish the sentence, for Adah instantly silenced her by answering frankly:

"I do not intend they shall know, not at present certainly."

Adah retired early, as did both Mrs. Worthington and Densie, for all were unusually tired; only Hugh, as he supposed, was up, and he sat by the parlor fire where they had passed the evening. He was very sorry Adah was going, but it was not so much of her he was thinking as of Alice. Had she dreamed of his real feelings, she never would have done what she did, but she was wholly unconscious of it, and so, when, late that night, she returned to the parlor in quest of something she had left, and found him sitting there alone, she paused a moment on the threshold, wondering if she had better join him or go away. His back was toward her, and he did not hear her light step, so intently was he gazing into the burning grate, and trying to frame the words he should say if ever he dared tell Alice Johnson of his love.

There was much girlish playfulness in Alice's nature, and sliding across the carpet, she clasped both her hands before his eyes, and exclaimed:

"A penny for your thoughts."

Hugh started as suddenly as if some apparition had appeared before him, and blushing guiltily, clasped and held upon his face the little soft, warm hands which did not tremble, but lay still beneath his own. It was Providence which sent her there, he thought; Providence indicating that he might speak, and he would.

"I am glad you have come. I wish to talk with you," he said, drawing her down into a chair beside him, and placing his arm lightly across its back. "What sent you here, Alice? I supposed you had retired," he continued, bending upon her a look which made her slightly uncomfortable.

But she soon recovered, and answered laughingly:

"I, too, supposed you had retired. I came for my scissors, and finding you here alone, thought I would startle you, but you have not told me yet of what you were thinking."

"Of the present, past and future," he replied; then, letting his hand drop from the back of the chair upon her shoulder, he continued: "May I talk freely with you? May I tell you of myself, what I was, what I am, what I hope to be?"

Her cheeks burned dreadfully, and her voice was not quite steady, as, rising from her seat, she said:

"I like a stool better than this chair. I'll bring it and sit at your feet. There, now I am ready," and seating herself at a safe distance from him, Alice waited for him to commence.

She grew tired of waiting, and turning her lustrous eyes upon him, said gently:

"You seem unhappy about something. Is it because Adah leaves tomorrow? I am sorry, too; sorry for me, sorry for you; but, Hugh, I will do what I can to fill her place. I will be the sister you need so much. Don't look so wretched; it makes me feel badly to see you."

Alice's sympathy was getting the better of her again, and she moved her stool a little nearer to Hugh, while she involuntarily laid her hand upon his knee. That decided him; and while his heart throbbed almost to bursting, he began by saying:

"I am in rather a gloomy mood tonight, I'll admit. I do feel Adah's leaving us very much; but that is not all. I have wished to talk with you a long time—wished to tell you how I feel. May I, Alice?—may I open to you my whole heart, and show you what is there?"

For a moment Alice felt a thrill of fear—a dread of what the opening of his heart to her might disclose. Then she remembered Golden Hair, whose name she had never heard him breathe, save as it passed his delirious lips. It was of her he would talk; he would tell her of that hidden love whose existence she felt sure was not known at Spring Bank. Alice would rather not have had this confidence, for the deep love-life of such as Hugh Worthington seemed to her a sacred thing; but he looked so white, so careworn, so much as if it would be a relief, that Alice answered at last:

"Yes, Hugh, you may tell, and I will listen."

He began by telling Alice first of his early boyhood, uncheered by a single word of sympathy save as it came from dear Aunt Eunice, who alone understood the wayward boy whom people thought so bad.

"Even she did not quite understand me," he said; "she did not dream of that hidden recess in my heart which yearned so terribly for a human love—for something or somebody to check the evil passions so rapidly gaining the ascendant. Neither did she know how often, in the silent night, the boy they thought so flinty, so averse to womankind, wept for the love he had no hope of gaining.

"Then mother and Ad came to Spring Bank, and that opened to me a new era. In my odd way, I loved my mother so much—so much; but Ad—say, Alice, is it wicked in me if I can't love Ad?"

"She is your sister," was Alice's reply; and Hugh rejoined:

"Yes—my sister. I'm sorry for it, even, if it's wicked to be sorry. She gave me back only scorn and bitter words, until my heart closed up against her, and I harshly judged all others by her—all but one!" and Hugh's voice grew very low and tender in its tone, while Alice felt that now he was nearing the Golden Hair.

"Away off in New England, among the Yankee hills, there was a pure, white blossom growing; a blossom so pure, so fair, that few, very few, were worthy even so much as to look upon it, as day by day it unfolded some new beauty. There was nothing to support this flower but a single frail parent stalk, which snapped asunder one day, and Blossom was left alone. It was a strange idea, transplanting it to another soil; for the atmosphere of Spring Bank was not suited to such as she. But she came, and, as by magic, the whole atmosphere was changed—changed at least to one—the bad, wayward Hugh, who dared to love this fair young girl with a love stronger than his life. For her he would do anything, and beneath her influence he did improve rapidly. He was conscious of it himself—conscious of a greater degree of self-respect—a desire to be what she would like to have him.

"She was very, very beautiful; more so than anything Hugh had ever looked upon. Her face was like an angel's face, and her hair—much like yours, Alice;" and he laid his hand on the bright head, now bent down, so that he could not see that face so like an angel's.

The little hand, too, had slid from his knee, and, fastlocked within the other, was buried in Alice's lap, as she listened with throbbing heart to the story Hugh was telling.

"In all the world there was nothing so dear to Hugh as this young girl. He thought of her by day and dreamed of her by night, seeing always in the darkness her face, with its eyes of blue bending over him—hearing the music of her voice, like the falling of distant water, and even feeling the soft touch of her hands as he fancied them laid upon his brow. She was good, too, as beautiful; and it was this very goodness which won on Hugh so fast, making him pray often that he might be worthy of her—for, Alice, he came at last to dream that he could win her; she was so kind to him—she spoke to him so softly, and, by a thousand little acts, endearing herself to him more and more.

"Heaven forgive her if she misled him all this while; but she did not. It were worse than death to think she did—to know I've told you this in vain—have offered you my heart only to have it thrust back upon me as something you do not want. Speak, Alice! in mercy, speak! Can it be that I'm mistaken?"

Alice saw how she had unwittingly led him on, and her white lips quivered with pain. Lifting up her head at last, she exclaimed:

"You don't mean me, Hugh! Oh, you don't mean me?"

"Yes, darling," and he clasped in his own the hand raised imploringly toward him. "Yes, darling, I mean you. Will you be my wife?"

Alice had never before heard a voice so earnest, so full of meaning, as the one now pleading with her to be what she could not be. She must do something, and sliding from her stool she sank upon her knees—her proper attitude—upon her knees before Hugh, whom she had wronged so terribly, and burying her face in Hugh's own hands, she sobbed:

"Oh, Hugh, Hugh! you don't know what you ask. I love you dearly, but only as my brother—believe me, Hugh, only as a brother. I wanted one so much—one of my own, I mean; but God denied that wish, and gave me you instead. I'm sorry I ever came here, but I cannot go away. I've learned to love my Kentucky home. Let me stay just the same. Let me really be what I thought I was, your sister. You will not send me away?"

She looked up at him now, but quickly turned away, for the expression of his white, haggard face was more than she could bear, and she knew there was a pang, keener even than any she had felt, a pang which must be terrible, to crush a strong man as Hugh was crushed.

"Forgive me, Hugh," she said, as he did not speak, but sat gazing at her in a kind of stunned bewilderment. "You would not have me for your wife, if I did not love you?"

"Never, Alice, never!" he answered. "But it is not any easier to bear. I don't know why I asked you, why I dared hope that you could think of me. I might have known you could not. Nobody does. I cannot win their love. I don't know how."

Alice neither looked up nor moved, only sobbed piteously, and this more than aught else helped Hugh to choke down his own sorrow for the sake of comforting her. The sight of her distress moved him greatly, for he knew it was grief that she had so cruelly misled him.

"Alice, darling," he said again, this time as a mother would soothe her child. "Alice, darling, it hurts me more to see you thus than your refusal did. I am not wholly selfish in my love. I'd rather you should be happy than to be happy myself. I would not for the world take to my bosom an unwilling wife. I should be jealous even of my own caresses, jealous lest the very act disgusted her more and more. You did not mean to deceive me. It was I that deceived myself. I forgive you fully, and ask you to forget that tonight has ever been. It cut me sorely at first, Alice, to hear you tell me so, but I shall get over it; the wound will heal."

"Oh, Hugh, don't; you break my heart. I'd rather you should scorn, or even hate me, for the sorrow I have brought. Such unselfish kindness will kill me," Alice sobbed, for never had she been so touched as by this insight into the real character of the man she had refused.

He would not hold her long in his arms, though it were bliss to do so, and putting her gently in the chair, he leaned his own poor sick head upon the mantel, while Alice watched him with streaming eyes and an aching heart, which even then half longed to give itself into his keeping. At last it was her turn to speak, hers the task to comfort. The prayer she had inwardly breathed for guidance to act aright had not been unheard, and with a strange calmness she arose, and laying her hand on Hugh's arm, bade him be seated, while she told him what she had to say. He obeyed her, sinking into the offered chair, and then standing before him, she began:

"You do not wish me to go away, you say. I have no desire to go, except it should be better for you. Even though I may not be your wife, I can, perhaps, minister to your happiness; and, Hugh, we will forget tonight, forget what has occurred, and be to each other what we were before, brother and sister. There must be no particular perceptible change of manner, lest others should suspect what has passed between us. Do you agree to this?"

He bowed his head, and Alice drew a step nearer to him, hesitating a moment ere she continued:

"You speak of a rival. I do not know that you have one. Sure it is I am bound to no one by any pledge, or promise, or tie, unless it be a tie of gratitude."

Hugh glanced up quickly now, and the words, "You are mistaken; it was not Irving Stanley," trembled on his lips, but his strong will fought them back, and Alice went on.

"I will be frank with you, and say that I have seen one who pleased me, both for the noble qualities he possessed, and because I had thought so much of meeting him, of expressing to him my thanks for a great favor done when I was only a child. There's a look in your face like his; you remind me of him often; and, Hugh—" the little hand pressed more closely on Hugh's shoulder, while Alice's breath came heavily, "And, Hugh, it may be, that in time I can conscientiously give you a different answer from what I did tonight. I may love as your wife should love you; and—and, Hugh, if I do, I'll tell you so at the proper time."

There was a gleam of sunshine now to illumine the thick darkness, and, in the first moments of his joy Hugh wound his arm around the slight form, and tried to bring it nearer to him. But Alice stepped back and answered:

"No, Hugh, that would be wrong. It may be I shall never come to love you save as I love you now, but I'll try—I will try," and unmindful of her charge to him, Alice parted the damp curls clustering around his forehead, and looked into his face with an expression which made his heart bound and throb with the sudden hope that even now she loved him better than she supposed.

It was growing very late, and the clock in the adjoining room struck one ere Alice bade Hugh good-night, saying to him:

"No one must know of this. We'll be just the same to each other as we have been."

"Yes, just the same, if that can be," Hugh answered, and so they parted.

CHAPTER XXX

ADAH'S JOURNEY

The night express from Rochester to Albany was crowded. Every car was full, or seemed to be, and the clamorous bell rang out its first summons for all to get on board, just as a pale, frightened-looking woman, bearing in her slender arms a sleeping boy, whose little face showed signs of suffering, stepped upon the platform of the rear carriage, and looked wistfully in at the long, dark line of passengers filling every seat. Wearily, anxiously, she had passed through every car, beginning at the first, her tired eyes scanning each occupant, as if mutely begging some one to have pity on her ere exhausted nature failed entirely, and she sank fainting to the floor. None had heeded that silent appeal, though many had marked the pallor of her girlish face, and the extreme beauty of the baby features nestling in her bosom. She could not hold out much longer, and when she reached the last car and saw that, too, was full, the delicate chin quivered perceptibly, and a tear glistened in the long eyelashes, sweeping the colorless cheek.

Slowly she passed up the aisle until she came to where there was indeed a vacant seat, only a gentleman's shawl was piled upon it, and he, the gentleman, looking so unconcernedly from the window, and apparently oblivious of her close proximity to him, would not surely object to her sitting there. How the tired woman did wish he would turn toward her, would give some token that she was welcome, would remove his heavy plaid, and say to her courteously, "Sit here, madam." But no, his eyes were only intent on the darkness without; he had no care for her, Adah, though he knew she was there.

The oil lamp was burning dimly, and the girl's white face was lost in the shadow, when the young man first glanced at her, so he had no suspicion of the truth, though a most indefinable sensation crept over him as he heard the timid footfall, and the rustling of female garments as Adah Hastings drew near with her boy in her arms. He knew she stopped before him; he knew, too, why she stopped, and for a brief instant his better nature bade him be a man and offer her what he knew she wanted. But only for an instant, and then his selfishness prevailed. "He would not seem to see her, he would not be bothered by a woman with a brat. If there was anything he hated it was a woman traveling with a young one, a squalling young one. They would never catch his wife, when he had one, doing a thing so unladylike. A car was no place for children. He hated the whole of them."

Adah passed on, her weary sigh falling distinctly on his ear, but falling to awaken a feeling of remorse for his unmanly conduct.

"I'm glad she's gone. I can't be bothered," was his mental comment as he settled himself more comfortably, feeling a glow of satisfaction when the train began to move, and he knew no more women with their babies would be likely to trouble him.

With that first heavy strain of the machinery Adah lost her balance, and would have fallen headlong but for the friendly hand put forth to save the fall.

"Take my seat, miss. It is not very convenient, but it is better than none. I can find another."

It was the friendliest voice imaginable which said these words to Adah, and the kind tone in which they were uttered wrung the hot tears at once from her eyes. She did not look up at him. She only knew that some one, a gentleman, had arisen and was bending over her; that a hand, large, white and warm, was laid upon her shoulder, putting her gently into the narrow seat next the saloon; that the same hand took from her and hung above her head the little satchel which was so much in her way, and that the manly voice, so sympathetic in its tone, asked if she would be too warm so near the fire.

She did not know there was a fire. She only knew that she had found a friend, and with the delicious feeling of safety which the knowledge brought, the tension of her nerves gave way, and burying her head on Willie's face she wept for a moment silently. Then, lifting it up, she tried to thank her benefactor, looking now at him for the first time, and feeling half overawed to find him so tall, so stylish, so exceedingly refined and aristocratic in every look and action.

Irving Stanley was a passenger on that train, bound for Albany. Like Dr. Richards, he had hoped to enjoy a whole seat, even though it were not a very comfortable one, but when he saw how pale and tired Adah was, he arose at once to offer his seat. He heard her sweet, low voice as she tried to thank him. He saw, too, the little, soft, white hands, holding so fast to Willie. Was he her brother or her son? She was young to be his mother. Perhaps she was his sister; but, no, there was no mistaking the mother-love shining out from the brown eyes turned so quickly upon the boy when he moaned, as if in pain, and seemed about to waken.

"He's been sick most all the way," she said. "There's something the matter with his ear, I think, as he complains of that. Do children ever die with the earache?"

Irving Stanley hardly thought they did. At all events, he never heard of such a case, and then, after suggesting a remedy, should the pain return, he left his new acquaintance.

"A part of your seat, sir, if you please," and Irving's voice was rather authoritative than otherwise, as he claimed the half of what the doctor was monopolizing.

It was of no use for Dr. Richards to pretend he was asleep, for Irving spoke so like a man who knew what he was doing, that the doctor was compelled to yield, and turning about, recognized his Saratoga acquaintance. The recognition was mutual, and after a few natural remarks, Irving explained how he had given his seat to a lady, who seemed ready to drop with fatigue and anxiety concerning her little child, who was suffering from the earache.

"By the way, doctor," he added, "you ought to know the remedy for such ailments. Suppose you prescribe in case it returns. I do pity that young woman."

Dr. Richards stared at him in astonishment.

"I know but little about babies or their aches," he answered at last, just as a scream of pain reached his ear, accompanied by a suppressed effort on the mother's part to soothe her suffering child.

The pain must have been intolerable, for the little fellow, in his agony, writhed from Adah's lap and sank upon the floor, his waxen hand pressed convulsively to his ear, and his whole form quivering with anguish as he cried, "Oh, ma! ma! ma! ma!"

The hardest heart could scarce withstand that scene, and many now gathered near, offering advice and help, while even Dr. Richards turned toward the group gathering by the door, experiencing a most unaccountable sensation as that baby cry smote on his ear. Foremost among those who offered aid was Irving Stanley. His was the voice which breathed comfort to the weeping Adah, his the hand extended to take up little Willie, his the arms which held and soothed the struggling boy, his the mind which thought of everything available that could possibly bring ease.

"Who'll give me a cigar? I do not use them myself. Ask him," he said, pointing to the doctor, who mechanically took a fine Havana from the case and half grudgingly handed it to the lady, who hurried back with it to Irving Stanley.

To break it up and place it in Willie's ear was the work of a moment, and ere long the fierce outcries ceased as Willie grew easier and lay quietly in Irving Stanley's arms.

"I'll take him now," and Adah put out her hands; but Willie refused to go, and clung closer to Mr. Stanley, who said, laughingly: "You see that I am preferred. He is too heavy for you to hold. Please trust him to me, while you get the rest you need."

And Adah yielded to that voice as if it were one which had a right to say what she must do, and leaning back against the window, rested her tired head upon her hand, while Irving carried Willie to his seat beside the doctor! There was a slight sneer on the doctor's face as he saw the little boy.

"You don't like children, I reckon," Irving said, as the doctor drew back from the little feet which unconsciously touched his lap.

"No, I hate them," was the answer, spoken half savagely, for at that moment a tiny hand was deliberately laid on his, as Willie showed a disposition to be friendly. "I hate them," and the little hand was pushed rudely off.

Wonderingly the soft, large eyes of the child looked up to his. Something in their expression riveted the doctor's gaze as by a spell. There were tears in the baby's eyes, and the pretty lip began to quiver at the harsh indignity. The doctor's finer feelings, if he had any, were touched, and muttering to himself, "I'm a brute," he slouched his riding cap still lower down upon his forehead, and turning away to the window, relapsed into a gloomy reverie.

As they drew near to Albany, another piercing shriek from Willie arose even above the noise of the train. The paroxysms of pain had returned with such severity that the poor infant's face became a livid purple, while Adah's tears dropped upon it like rain. Again the sympathetic women gathered around, again Dr. Richards, aroused from his uneasy sleep, muttered invectives against children in general and this one in particular, while again Irving Stanley hastened to the rescue, his the ruling mind which overmastered the others, planning what should be done, and seeing that his plans were executed.

"You cannot go on this morning. Your little boy must have rest and medical advice," he said to Adah, when at last the train stopped in Albany. "I have a few moments to spare. I will see that you are comfortable. You are going to Snowdon, I think you said. There is an acquaintance of mine on board who is also bound for Snowdon. I might—"

Irving Stanley paused here, for certain doubts arose in his mind, touching the doctor's willingness to be troubled with strangers.

"Oh, I'd rather go on alone," Adah exclaimed, as she guessed what he had intended saying.

"It's quite as well, I reckon," was Mr. Stanley's reply, and taking Willie in his arms, he conducted Adah to the nearest hotel.

"If you please, you will not engage a very expensive room for me. I can't afford it," Adah said, timidly, as she followed her conductor into the parlor of the Delavan.

She was poor, then. Irving would hardly have guessed it from her appearance, but this frank avowal which many would not have made, only increased his respect for her, while he wished so much that she might have one of the handsome sitting-rooms, of whose locality he knew so well.

It was a cozy, pleasant little chamber into which she was finally ushered, too nice, Adah feared, half trembling for the bill when she should ask for it, and never dreaming that just one-half the price had been paid by Irving, whose kind heart prompted him to the generous act.

There were but a few moments now ere he must leave, and standing by her side, with her little hand in his, he said:

"The meeting with you has been to me a pleasant incident, and I shall not soon forget it. I trust we may meet again. There is my card. I am acquainted North, South, East and West. Perhaps I know your husband. You have one?" he added quickly, as he saw the hot blood stain her face and neck to a most unnatural color.

He had not the remotest suspicion that she had never been a wife; he only thought from her agitation that she possibly was a widow, and unconsciously to himself the idea was fraught with a vague feeling of gladness, for, to most men, it is pleasanter knowing they have been polite to a pretty girl, or even a pretty widow, than to a wife, whose lord might object, and Irving was not an exception. Was she a widow, and had he unwittingly touched the half healed wound? He wished he knew, and he stood waiting for her answer to his question, "You have a husband?"

At a glance Adah had read the name upon the card, knowing now who had befriended her. It was Irving Stanley, Augusta's brother, second cousin to Hugh, and 'Lina was with his sister in New York. He was going there, he might speak of her, and if she told her name, her miserable story would be known to more than it was already. It was a false pride which kept Adah silent when she knew that Irving Stanley was waiting for her to speak, wondering at her agitated manner. He was looking at her eyes, her large brown eyes, which dared not meet his, and as he looked a terrible suspicion crept over him. Involuntarily he felt for her third finger. It was ringless, and he dropped it suddenly, but with a feeling that he might be unjust, that all were not of his church and creed, he took it again, and said his parting words. Then, turning to Willie, he smoothed the silken curls, praised the beauty of the sleeping child, and left the room.

Adah knew that he was gone, that she should not see him again, and that, at the very last, there had arisen some misunderstanding, she hardly knew what, for the shock of finding who he was had prevented her from fully comprehending the fact that he had asked her for her husband. She never dreamed of the suspicion which, for an instant, had a lodgment in his breast, or she would almost have died where she stood, gazing at the door through which he had disappeared.

"I ought to have told him my name, but I could not," she sighed, as the sound of his rapid footsteps died upon the stairs.

They ceased at last, and with a feeling of utter desolation, as if she were now indeed alone, Adah sank upon her knees, and covering her face with her hands, wept bitterly. Anon, however, holier, calmer feelings swept over her. She was not alone. They who love God can never be alone, however black the darkness be around them. And Adah did love Him, thanking Him at last for raising her up this friend in her sore need, for putting it into Irving Stanley's heart to care for her, a stranger, as he had done. And as she prayed, the wish arose that George had been, more like him. He would not then have deserted her, she sobbed, while again her lips breathed a prayer for Irving Stanley, thoughts of whom even then made her once broken heart beat as she had never expected it to beat again.

So absorbed was Adah that she did not hear the returning footsteps as Irving came across the hall. He had remembered some directions he would give her, and at the risk of being left, had come back a moment. She did not hear the turning of the knob, the opening of the door, or know that he for whom she prayed was standing so near to her that he heard distinctly what she said, kneeling there by the chair where he had sat, her fair head bent down and her face concealed from view.

"God in heaven bless and keep the noble Irving Stanley."

In the office below, Dr. Richards, who had purposely stopped for the day in Albany, smoked his expensive cigars, ordered oysters and wine sent to his room—the very one adjoining Adah's—made two or three calls, wrote an explanatory note to 'Lina—feeling half tempted to leave out the "Dear," with which he felt constrained to preface it—thought again of Lily—poor Lily, as he always called her—thought once of the strange woman and the little boy, in whom Irving Stanley had been so interested, wondered where they were going, and who it was the boy looked a little like—thought somehow of Anna in connection with that boy; and then, late in the afternoon, sauntered down to the Boston depot, and took his seat in the car, which, at about ten o'clock that night would deposit him at Snowdon. There were no "squalling brats" to disturb him, for Adah, unconscious of his proximity, was in the rear car—pale, weary, and nervous with the dread which her near approach to Terrace Hill inspired. What, if after all, Anna, should not want her? And this was a possible contingency, notwithstanding Alice had been no sanguine.

Darkly the December night closed in, and still the train kept on, until at last Danville was reached, and she must alight, as the express did not stop again until it reached Worcester. With a chill sense of loneliness, and a vague, confused wish for the one cheering voice which had greeted her ear since leaving Spring Bank, Adah stood upon the snow-covered platform, holding Willie in her arms, and pointing out her trunk to the civil baggage man, who, in answer to her inquiries as to the best means of reaching Terrace Hill, replied: "You can't go there tonight; it is too late. You'll have to stay in the tavern kept right over the depot, though if you'd kept on the train there might have been a chance, for I see the young Dr. Richards aboard; and as he didn't get out, I guess he's coaxed or hired the conductor to leave him at Snowdon."

The baggage man was right in his conjecture, for the doctor had persuaded the polite conductor, whom he knew personally, to stop the train at Snowdon; and while Adah, shivering with cold, found her way up the narrow stairs into the rather comfortless quarters where she must spend the night, the doctor was kicking the snow from his feet and talking to Jim, the coachman from Terrace Hill.

CHAPTER XXXI

THE CONVICT

It was a sad morning at Spring Bank, that morning of Adah's leaving, and many a tear was shed as the last good-by was spoken. Mrs. Worthington, Alice and Hugh accompanied Adah to Frankfort, and Alice had never seemed in better spirits than on that winter's morning. She would be gay; it was a duty she owed Hugh, and Adah, too. So she talked and laughed as if there was no load upon her heart, and no cloud on Adah's spirits. Outwardly Mrs. Worthington suffered most, wondering why she should cling so to Adah, and why this parting was so painful. All the farewell words had been spoken, for Adah would not leave them to the chance of a last moment. She seemed almost too pretty to send on that long journey alone, and Hugh felt that he might be doing wrong in suffering her to depart without an escort. But Adah only laughed at his fears. Willie was her protector, she said, and then, as the train came up she turned to Mrs. Worthington, who, haunted with the dread lest something should happen to prevent 'Lina's marriage, said softly:

"You'll be careful about 'Lina?"

Yes, Adah would be careful, and to Alice she whispered:

"I'll write after I get there, but you must not answer it at least not till I say you may. Good-by."

"Come, mother, we are waiting for you," Hugh said.

At the sound of Hugh's voice she started and replied:

"Oh, yes, I remember—we are to visit the penitentiary. Dear me," and in a kind of absent way, Mrs. Worthington took Hugh's arm, and the party proceeded on their way to the huge building known as the Frankfort Penitentiary. Hugh was well acquainted with the keeper, who admitted them cheerfully, and ushered them at once into the spacious yard.

Pleased with Alice's enthusiastic interest in everything he said, the keeper was quite communicative, pointing out the cells of any noted felons, repeating little incidents of daring attempts to escape, and making the visit far more entertaining than the party had expected.

"This," he said, opening a narrow door, "this belongs to the negro stealer, Sullivan. You know him, Mrs. Worthington. He ran off the old darky you now own, old Sam, I mean."

"I'd like to see Mr. Sullivan," Alice said. "I saw old Sam when he was in Virginia."

"We'll find him on the ropewalk. We put our hardest customers there. Not that he gives us trouble, for he does not, and I rather like the chap, but we have a spite against these Yankee negro stealers," was the keeper's reply, as he led the way to the long low room, where groups of men walked up and down—up and down—holding the long line of hemp, which, as far as they were concerned, would never come to an end until the day of their release.

"That's he," the keeper whispered to Alice, who had fallen behind Hugh and his mother. "That's he, just turning this way—the one to the right."

Alice nodded in token that she understood, and then stood watching while he came up. Mrs. Worthington and Hugh were watching too, not him particularly, for they did not even know which was Sullivan, but stood waiting for the whole long line advancing slowly toward them, their eyes cast down with conscious shame, as if they shrank from being seen. One of them, however, was wholly unabashed. He thought it probable the keeper would point him out; he knew they used to do so when he first came there, but he did not care; he rather liked the notoriety, and when he saw that Alice seemed waiting for him, he fixed his keen eyes on her, starting at the sight of so much beauty, end never even glancing at the other visitors, at Mrs. Worthington and Hugh, who, a little apart from each other, saw him at the same moment, both turning cold and faint, the one with surprise, and the other with a horrid, terrible fear.

It needed but a glance to assure Hugh that he stood in the presence of the man who with strangely winning powers had tempted him to sin—the villain who had planned poor Adah's marriage—Monroe, her guardian, whose sudden disappearance had been so mysterious. Hugh never knew how he controlled himself from leaping into that walk and compelling the bold wretch to tell if he knew aught of the base deserter, Willie Hastings' father. He did, indeed, take one forward step while his fist clinched involuntarily, but the next moment fell powerless at his side as a low wail of pain reached his ear and he turned in time to save his fainting mother from falling to the floor.

She, too, had seen the ropemaker, glancing at him twice ere sure she saw aright, and then, as if a corpse buried years ago had arisen to her view, the blood curdled about her heart which after one mighty throe lay heavy and still as lead. He was not dead; that paragraph in the paper telling her so was false; he did not die, such as he could not die; he was alive—alive—a convict within those prison walls; a living, breathing man with that same look she remembered so well, shuddering as she remembered it, 'Lina's father and her own husband!

"It was the heat, or the smell, or the parting with Adah, or something," she said, when she came back to consciousness, eagerly scanning Hugh's face to see if he knew too, and then glancing timidly around as if in quest of the phantom which had so affected her.

"Let's go home, I'm sorry I came to Frankfort," she whispered, while her teeth chattered and her eyes wore a look of terror for which Hugh could not account.

He never thought of associating her illness with the man who had so affected himself. It was overexertion, he said. His mother could not bear much, and with all the tenderness of an affectionate son he wrapped her shawl about her and led her gantry from the spot which held for her so great a terror. It was not physical fear; she had never been afraid of bodily harm, even when fully in his power. It was rather the olden horror stealing back upon her, the pain which comes from the slow grinding out of one's entire will and spirit. She had forgotten the feeling, it was so long since it had been experienced, but one sight of him brought it back, and all the way from Frankfort to Spring Bank she lay upon Hugh's shoulder quiet, but sick and faint, with a shrinking from what the future might possibly have in store for her.

In this state of mind she reached Spring Bank, where by some strange coincidence, if coincidence it can be called, old Densie Densmore was the first to greet her, asking, with much concern, what was the matter. It was a rare thing for Densie to be at all demonstrative, but in the suffering expression of Mrs. Worthington's face she recognized something familiar, and attached herself at once to the weak, nervous woman, who sought her bed, and burying her face in the pillow cried herself to sleep, while Densie, like some white-haired ghost, sat watching her silently.

"The poor thing has had trouble," she whispered, "trouble in her day, and it has left deep furrows in her forehead, but it cannot have been like mine. She surely, was never betrayed, or deserted, or had her only child stolen from her. The wretch! I cursed him once, when my heart was harder than it is now. I have forgiven him since, for well as I could, I loved him."

There was a moaning sound in the winter wind howling about Spring Bank that night, but it suited Densie's mood, and helped to quiet her spirits, as, until a late hour, she sat by Mrs. Worthington, who aroused up at intervals, saying, in answer to Densie's inquiries, she was not sick, she was only tired—that sleep would do her good.

And while they were thus together a convict sought his darkened cell and laid him down to rest upon the narrow couch which had been his bed so long. Drearily to him the morning broke, and with the struggling in of the daylight he found upon his floor the handkerchief dropped inadvertently by Mrs. Worthington, and unseen till now. He knew it was not unusual for strangers to visit the cells, and so he readily guessed how it came there, holding it a little more to the light to see the name written so plainly upon it.

"Eliza Worthington." That was what the convict read, a blur

before his eyes, and a strange sensation at his heart. "Eliza Worthington."

How came she there, and when? Suddenly he remembered the event of yesterday, the woman who fainted, the tall man who carried her out, the beautiful girl who had looked at him so pityingly, and then, while every nerve quivered with intense excitement, he whispered:

"That was my wife! I did not see her face, but she saw me, fainting at the sight."

Hard, and villainous, and sinful as that man had been, there was a tender chord beneath the villain exterior, and it quivered painfully as he said "fainted at the sight." This was the keenest pang of the whole, for as Densie Densmore had moaned the previous night, "I loved him once," so he now, rocking to and fro on his narrow bed, with that handkerchief pressed to his throbbing heart, murmured hoarsely:

"I loved Eliza once, though she would not believe it."

Then the image of the young man and the girl came up before him, making him start again, for he guessed that man was Hugh, his stepson, while the girl—oh, could that beautiful creature—be—his—daughter!

"Not Adaline, assuredly," he whispered, "nor Adah, my poor darling Adah. Oh, where is she this morning? I did love Adah," and the convict moistened Eliza Worthington's handkerchief with the tears he shed for sweet Adah Hastings.

Outwardly, that day the so-called Sullivan was the same, as he paced up and down the walk, but never since first he began the weary march, had his brain been the seat of thoughts so tumultuous as those stirring within him, the day succeeding Mrs. Worthington's visit. Where were his victims now? Were they all alive? And would he meet them yet? Would Eliza Worthington ever come there again, or Hugh, and would he see them if they did? Perhaps not, but some time, a few months hence, he would find them, would find Hugh at least, and ask if he knew aught of Adah—Adah, more terribly wronged than even the wife had been.

And while he thus resolved, poor Mrs. Worthington at home moved nervously around the house, casting uneasy glances backward, forward, and sideways, as if she were expecting some goblin shape to rise suddenly before her and claim her for its own. They were wretched, uneasy days which followed that visit to Frankfort—days of racking headache to Mrs. Worthington, and days of anxious thought to Hugh, who thus was led in a measure to forget the pain he would otherwise have felt at the memory of Alice's refusal.

CHAPTER XXXII

ADAH AT TERRACE HILL

The next morning was cold and frosty, as winter mornings in New England are wont to be, and Adah, accustomed to the more genial climate of Kentucky, shivered involuntarily as from her uncurtained window she looked out upon the bare woods and the frozen fields covered with the snow of yesterday.

Across the track, near to a dilapidated board fence, a family carriage was standing, the driver unnecessarily, as it seemed to Adah—holding the heads of the horses, who neither sheered nor jumped, nor gave other tokens that they feared the hissing engine. She had not seen that carriage when it drove up before the door, nor yet the young man who had alighted from it; but as she stood there, a loud laugh reached her ear, making her start suddenly, it was so like his—like George's.

"It could not be George," she said; that were impossible, and yet she crept softly out into the hall, and leaning over the banister, listened eagerly to the sounds from the room below, where a crowd of men were assembled.

The laugh was not repeated, and with a dim feeling of disappointment she went back to the window where on Willie's neck she wept the tears which always flowed when she thought of George's desertion. There was a knock at the door, and the baggageman appeared.

"If you please, ma'am," he began, "the Terrace Hill carriage is here. I told the driver how't you wanted to go there. Shall I give him your trunk?"

Adah answered in the affirmative, and then hastened to wrap up Willie, glancing again at the carriage, which, now that it was associated with the gentle Anna, looked far better to her than it had at first. She was ready in a moment and descended to the room where Jim, the driver, stood waiting for her.

"A lady," was his mental comment, and with as much politeness as if she had been Madam Richards herself, he opened the carriage door and held Willie while she entered, asking if she were comfortable, and peering a little curiously in Willie's face, which puzzled him somewhat. "A near connection, I guess, and mighty pretty too. Them old maids will raise hob with the boy,—nice little shaver," thought the kind-hearted Jim.

Once, as Adah caught his good-humored eye, she ventured to say to him:

"Has Miss Anna procured a waiting maid yet?"

There was a comical gleam in Jim's eye now, for Adah was not the first applicant he had taken up to Terrace Hill. He never suspected that this was Adah's business, and he answered frankly:

"No, that's about played out. Madam turned the last one out doors."

"Turned her out doors?" and Adah's face was as white as the snow rifts they were passing.

The driver felt that he had gossiped too much, and relapsed into silence, while Adah, in a paroxysm of terror, sat with clasped hands and closed eyes. Leaning forward, at last she said, huskily:

"Driver, driver, do you think she'll turn me off, too?"

"Turn you off!" and in his surprise at the sudden suspicion which for the first time darted across his mind, Jim brought his horses to a full stop, while he held a parley with the pale, frightened creature, asking so eagerly if Mrs. Richards would turn her off. "Why should she? You ain't going there for that, be you?"

"Not to be turned out of doors, no," Adah answered; "but I—I—I want that place so much. I read Miss Anna's advertisement; but please turn back, or let me get out and walk. I can't go there now. Is Miss Anna like the rest?"

"Miss Anna's an angel," he answered. "If you get her ear, you're all right; the plague is to get it with them two she-cats ready to tear your eyes out. If I'se you, I'd ask to see her. I wouldn't tell my arrent either, till I did. She's sick upstairs; but I'll see if Pamely can't manage it. That's my woman—Pamely; been mine for four years, and we've had two pair of twins, all dead; so I feel tender toward the little ones," and Jim glanced kindly at Willie, who had succeeded in making Adah notice the house standing out so prominently against the winter sky, and looking to the poor woman-girl more like a prison than a home.

It might be pleasant there in the summer, Adah thought; but now, with snow on the roof, snow on the walk, snow on the trees, snow everywhere, it presented a cheerless aspect. Only one part of it seemed inviting—the two crimson-curtained windows opening upon a veranda, from which a flight of steps led down into what must be a flower garden.

"Miss Anna's room," the driver said, pointing toward it; and Adah looked wistfully out, vainly hoping for a glimpse of the sweet face she had in her mind as Anna's.

But only Asenath's grim, angular visage was seen, as it looked from Anna's window, wondering whom Jim could be bringing home.

"It's a handsome trunk—covered, too. Can it be Lottie?" and mentally hoping it was not, she busied herself again with bathing poor Anna's head, which was aching sadly today, owing to the excitement of her brother's visit and the harsh words which passed between him and his sisters, he telling them, jokingly at first, that he was tired of getting married, and half resolved to give it up; while they, in return, had abused him for fickleness, taunted him with their poverty, and sharply reproached him for his unwillingness to lighten their burden, by taking a rich wife when he could get one.

All this John had repeated to Anna in the dim twilight of the morning, as he stood by her bedside to bid her good-by; and she, as usual, had soothed him into quiet, speaking kindly of his bride-elect, and saying she should like her.

He had not told her all of Lily's story, as he meant to do. There was no necessity for that, for the matter was fixed. 'Lina should be his wife, and he need not trouble Anna further; so he had bidden her adieu, and was gone again, the carriage which bore him away bringing back Adah and her boy.

Jim opened the wide door for her, and showing her first into the parlor, but finding that dark and cold, he ushered her next into a little reception-room, where the Misses Richards received their morning calls.

Willie seemed perfectly at home, seating himself upon a little stool, covered with some of Miss Eudora's choicest worsted embroidery, a piece of work of which she was very proud, never allowing anything to touch it lest the roses should be jammed, or the raised leaves defaced. But Willie cared neither for leaves, nor roses, nor yet for Miss Eudora, and drawing the stool to his mother's side, he sat kicking his little heels into a worn place of the carpet, which no child had kicked since the doctor's days of baby-hood. The tender threads were fast giving way to the vigorous strokes, when two doors opposite each other opened simulta-neously, and both Mrs. Richards and Eudora appeared.

"Are you—ah, yes—you are the lady who Jim said wished to see me," Mrs. Richards began, bowing politely to Adah, who had not yet dared to look up, and who when at last she did raise her eyes, withdrew them at once, more abashed, more frightened, more bewildered than ever, for the face she saw fully warranted her ideas of a woman who could turn a waiting maid from her door just because she was a waiting maid.

Something seemed choking Adah and preventing her utter-ance, for she did not speak until Mrs. Richards said again, this time with a little less suavity and a little more hauteur of manner, "Have I had the honor of meeting you before?"—then with a low gasp, a mental petition for help, Adah rose up and lifting to Mrs. Richards' cold, haughty face, her soft, brown eyes, where tears were almost visible, answered faintly: "We have not met before. Excuse me, madam, but my business is with Miss Anna, can I see her please?"

There was something supplicating in the tone with which Adah made this request, and it struck Mrs. Richards unpleasantly. She answered haughtily, though still politely, "My daughter is sick. She does not see visitors. It will be impossible to admit you to her chamber, but I will take your name and your errand."

Adah felt as if she should sink beneath the cold, cruel scrutiny to which she knew she was subjected by the woman on her right and the woman on her left. Too much confused to remember anything distinctly, Adah forgot Jim's injunction; forgot that Pamelia was to arrange it somehow; forgot everything, except that Mrs. Richards was waiting for her to speak. An ominous cough from Eudora decided her, and then it came out, her reason for being there. She had seen Miss Anna's advertisement, she wanted a place, and she had come so far to get it; had left a happy home that she might not be dependent but earn, her bread for herself and her little boy, for Willie. Would they take her message to Anna? Would they let her stay?

"You say you left a happy home," and the thin, sneering lips of Eudora were pressed so tightly together that the words could scarcely find egress. "May I ask, if it was so happy, why you left it?"

There was a flush on Adah's cheek as she replied, "Because it was a home granted at first from charity. It was not mine. The people were poor, and I would not longer be a burden to them."

"And your husband—where is he?"

This was the hardest question of all, and Adah's distress was visible as she replied, "I will be frank with you. Willie's father left me, and I don't know where he is."

An incredulous, provoking smile flitted over Eudora's face as she returned, "We hardly care to have a deserted wife in our family—it might be unpleasant."

"Yes," and the old lady took up the argument, "Anna is well enough without a maid. I don't know why she put that foolish advertisement in the paper, in answer, I believe, to one equally foolish which she saw about 'an unfortunate woman with a child.'"

"I am that woman. I wrote that advertisement when my heart was heavier than it is now, and God took care of it. He pointed it out to Miss Anna. He caused her to answer it. He sent me here, and you will let me see her. Think if it were your own daughter, pleading thus with some one."

"That is impossible. Neither my daughter, nor my daughter-in-law, if I had one, could ever come to a servant's position," Mrs. Richards replied, not harshly, for there was something in Adah's manner and in Adah's eyes which rode down her resentful pride; and she might have yielded, but for Eudora, whose hands had so ached to shake the little child, now innocently picking at a bud.

How she did long to box his ears, and while her mother talked, she had taken a step forward more than once, but stopped as often, held in check by the little face and soft blue eyes, turned so trustingly upon her, the pretty lips once actually putting themselves toward her, as if expecting a kiss. Frosty old maid as she was, Eudora could not harm that child sitting on her embroidery as coolly as if he had a right; but she could prevent her mother from granting the stranger's request; so when she saw signs of yielding, she said, decidedly, "She cannot see Anna, mother. You know how foolish she is, and there's no telling what fancy she might take."

"Eudora," said Mrs. Richards in a low tone, "it might be well for Anna to have a maid, and this one is certainly different from the others who have applied."

"But the child. We can't be bothered with a child. Evidently he is not governed at all, and brother's wife coming by and by."

This last caught Adah's ear and changed the whole current of her thoughts and wishes. Greatly to Mrs. Richards' surprise, she said abruptly, "If I cannot see Miss Anna, I need not trouble you longer. When does the next train go west?"

Adah's voice never faltered, though her heart seemed bursting from her throat, for she had not the most remote idea as to where the next train going west would take her. She had reached a point when she no longer thought or reasoned; she would leave Terrace Hill; that was all she knew, except that in her mind there was a vague fancy or hope that she might meet Irving Stanley again. Not George, she did not even think of him, as she stood before Dr. Richards' mother, who looked at her in surprise, marveling that she had given up so quietly what she had apparently so much desired.

Very civilly she told her when the next train went west, and then added kindly, "You cannot walk. You must stay here till car-time, when Jim will carry you back."

At this unexpected kindness Adah's calmness gave way, and sitting down by the table, she laid her face upon it and sobbed almost convulsively.

"Mamma tie, mam-ma tie," and he pulled Mrs. Richards' skirts vigorously indicating that she must do something for mamma.

Just then the doorbell rang. It was the doctor, come to visit Anna, and both Mrs. Richards and Eudora left the room at once.

"Oh, why did I come here, and where shall I go?" Adah moaned, as a sense of her lonely condition came over her.

"Will my Father in heaven direct me? will He tell me what to do?" she murmured brokenly, praying softly to herself that a way might be opened for her, a path which she could tread.

She could not tell how it was, but a quiet peace stole over her, a feeling which had no thought or care for the future, and it had been many nights since she had slept as sweetly or soundly as she did for one half hour with her head upon the table in that little room at Terrace Hill, Dr. Richards' home and Anna's. She did not see the good-humored face which looked in at her a moment, nor hear the whispering in the hall; neither did she know when Willie, nothing loath, was coaxed from the room and carried up the stairs into the upper hall, where he was purposely left to himself, while Pamelia, the mother of Jim's two pairs of twins, went to Anna's room, where she was to sit for an hour or so, while the ladies had their lunch. Anna's head was better; the paroxysms of pain were leas frequent than in the morning, and she lay upon her pillow, her eyes closed wearily, and her thoughts with Charlie Millbrook. Why had he never written?—why never come to see her?

So intently was she thinking of Charlie that she did not hear the patter of little feet in the hall without. Tired of staying by himself, and spying the open door, Willie hastened toward it, pausing a moment on the threshold as if to reconnoiter. Something in Anna's attitude, as she lay with her long hair falling over the pillow, must have reminded him of Alice, for, with a cry of delight, he ran forward, and patting the white cheek with his soft baby hand, lisped out the word "Arn-tee, arn-tee," making Anna start suddenly and gaze at him in wondering surprise.

"Who is he?" she said, drawing him to her at once and pressing a kiss upon his rosy face.

Pamelia told her what she knew of the stranger waiting in the reception-room, adding in conclusion: "I believe they said you did not want her, and Jim is to take her to the depot when it's time. She's very young and pretty, and looks so sorry, Jim told me."

"Said I did not want her! How did they know?" and something of the Richards' spirit flashed from Anna's eyes. "The child is so beautiful, and he called me 'Auntie,' too! He must have an auntie somewhere. Little dear! how she must love him! Lift him up, Pamelia."

"I must see his mother," Anna said. "She must be above the ordinary waiting maids. Perhaps I should like her. At all events I will hear what she has to say. Show her up, Pamelia; but first smooth my hair a little and arrange my pillows."

Pamelia complied with her request; then leaving Willie with Anna, she repaired to the reception-room, and arousing the sleeping Adah, said to her hurriedly:

"Please, miss, come quick; Miss Anna wants to see you. The little boy is up there with her."

CHAPTER XXXIII

ANNA AND ADAH

For a moment Anna was inclined to think that Pamelia had made a mistake. That beautiful face, that refined, ladylike manner, did not suit well a waiting maid, and Anna's doubts were increasing, when little Willie set her right by patting her cheek again, while he called out: "Mamma, arntee."

The look of interest which Anna cast upon him emboldened Adah to say:

"Excuse him, Miss Richards; he must have mistaken you for a dear friend at home, whom he calls 'Auntie,' I'll take him down; he troubles you."

"No, no," and Anna passed her arm around him. "I love children so much. I ought to have been a wife and mother, my brother says, instead of a useless old maid."

Anna smiled faintly as she said this, while thoughts of Charlie Millbrook flashed across her mind. Adah was too much a stranger to disclaim against Anna's calling herself old, so she paid no attention to the remark, but plunged at once into the matter which had brought her there. Presuming they would rather be alone, Pamelia had purposely left the room, meeting in the lower hall with Mrs. Richards and her daughter, who, in much affright, were searching for the recent occupants of the reception-room. Pamelia quieted them by saying: "The lady was in Miss Anna's room."

"How came she there? She must be a bold piece, upon my word!" she said, angrily, while Pamelia replied:

"The little boy got upstairs, and walked right into Miss Anna's room. She was taken with him at once, and asked who he was. I told her and she sent for the lady. That's how it happened."

Mrs. Richards hurried up to Anna's chamber, where Willie still was perched by Anna's pillow, while Adah, with her bonnet in her lap, sat a little apart, traces of tears and agitation upon her cheeks, but a look of happiness in the brown eyes fixed so wistfully on Anna's fair, sweet face.

"Please, mother," said Anna, motioning her away, "leave us alone a while. Shut the door, and see that no one comes near."

Mrs. Richards obeyed, and Anna, waiting until she was out of hearing, resumed the conversation just where it had been interrupted.

"And so you are the one who wrote that advertisement which I read. Let me see—the very night my brother came home from Europe. I remember he laughed because I was so interested, and he accidentally tore off the name to light his cigar, so I forgot it entirely. What shall I call you, please?"

Adah was tempted to answer her at once, "Adah Hastings"—it

seemed so wrong to impose in any way on that frank, sweet woman; but she remembered Mrs. Worthington's injunction, and for her sake she refrained, keeping silent a moment, and then breaking out impetuously: "Please, Miss Richards, don't ask my real name, for I'd rather not give it now. I will tell you of the past, though I did not ever mean to do that; but something about you makes me know I can trust you." And then, amid a shower of tears, in which Anna's, too, were mingled, Adah told her sad story.

"But why do you wish to conceal?" she asked, after Adah had finished. "Is there any reason?"

"At first there was none in particular, save a fancy I had, but there came one afterward—the request of one who had been, kind to me as a dear mother. Is it wrong not to tell the whole?"

"I think not. You have dealt honestly with me so far, but what shall I call you? You must have a name."

"Oh, may I stay?" Adah asked eagerly, forgetting her late terror of 'Lina.

"Of course you may. Did you think I would turn you away?" was Anna's reply; and laying her head upon the white counterpane of the bed, Adah cried passionately; not a wild, bitter cry, but a delicious kind of cry which did her good, even though her whole frame quivered and her low, choking sobs fell distinctly on Anna's ear.

"Poor child!" the latter said, laying her soft hand on the bowed head. "You have suffered much, but with me you shall find rest. I want you for a companion, rather than a maid. I, too, have had my heart troubles; not like yours, but heavy enough to make me wish I could die."

It was seldom that Anna alluded to herself in this way, and to do so to a stranger was utterly foreign to the Richards' nature. But Anna could not help it. There was something about Adah which interested her greatly. She could not wholly shield her from her mother's and sisters' pride, but she would do what she could.

"Oh, pride, pride," she whispered to herself, "of how much pain hast thou been the cause."

Pride had sent her Charlie over the sea without her; pride had separated her brother from the Lily she was sure he loved, as he could never love the maiden to whom he was betrothed; and pride, it seemed, had been at the root of all this young girl's sorrow. Blessed Anna Richards—the world has few like her—so gentle, so kind, so lovely, and as no one could long be with her and not feel her influence, so Adah, by the touch of the fingers still caressing her, was soothed into peaceful quiet.

When she had grown quite calm, Anna continued: "You have not told me yet what name to give you, or shall I choose one for you?"

"Oh, if you only would!" and Adah looked up quickly.

Anna began to enjoy this mystery, wondering what name she should choose. Adah should be Rose Markham, and she repeated it aloud, asking Adah how it sounded.

"If it did not seem so much like deceiving," Adah said. "You'll tell your family it is not my real name, won't you?"

Anna readily agreed to Adah's proposal, and then, remembering that all this time she had been sitting in her cloak and fur, she bade her lay them aside. "Or, stay," she added, "touch that bell, if you please, and ring Pamelia up. There's a little room adjoining this. I mean to give you that. You will be so near me, and so retired, too, when you like. John—that's my brother—occupied it when a boy. I think it will answer nicely for you."

Obedient to the ring, Pamelia came, manifesting no surprise when told by Anna to unlock the door and see if the little room was in order for "Mrs. Markham."

Pamelia cast a rapid glance at Adah, who winced as she heard the new name, and felt glad when Anna added: "Pamelia, I can trust you not to gossip out of the house. This young woman's name is not Markham, but I choose to have her called so."

Another glance at Adah, more curious than the first, and then Pamelia did as she was bidden, opening the door and saying, as she did so: "I know the room is in order. There's a fire, too; Miss Anna has forgot that Dr. John slept here last night."

"I do remember now," Anna replied. "Mrs. Markham can go in at once. Pamelia, send lunch to her room, and tell your husband to bring up her trunk."

Again Pamelia bowed and departed to do her young mistress' bidding, while Adah entered the pleasant room where Dr. Richards had slept the previous night.

On the marble hearth the remains of a cheerful fire were blazing, while on the mantel over the hearth was a portrait of a boy, apparently ten or twelve years of age, and a young girl, who seemed a few years older. The girl was Anna. But the boy, the handsome, smooth-cheeked boy, in his fancy jacket, with that expression of vanity plainly visible about his mouth. Who was he? Had Adah any knowledge of him? Had they met before? Never that she knew of. Dr. Richards was a stranger to her, for she guessed this was the doctor, 'Lina's betrothed, scrutinizing him closely, and wondering if the man retained the look of the boy. And as she gazed, the features seemed to grow familiar. Surely she had met a face like this, but where she could not guess, and turning from him she inspected the rest of the room, wondering if Alice Johnson were ever in this room.

With thoughts of Alice came memories of Spring Bank, and the wish that they knew all this. How thankful they would be, and how thankful she was for this resting place in the protection of sweet Anna Richards. It was better than she had even dared to hope for, and sinking down by the snowy-covered bed, she murmured inaudibly the prayer of thanksgiving she felt compelled to make to Him who had led her to Terrace Hill. It was thus that Pamelia found her when she came up again, and it did much to establish the profound respect she ever manifested toward the new waiting maid, Rose Markham.

"Your lunch will be here directly," she said to Adah, who little dreamed of the parley which had taken place between Asenath and Dixson, the cook, concerning this same lunch.

Asenath was too proud to discuss the matter with a servant, but when she saw the slices of cold chicken which Dixson was deliberately cutting up, and the little pot of jelly which Pamelia placed upon the salver, she forgot her dignity, and angrily demanded what they were doing.

"Miss Anna ordered lunch, and I'm a-gettin' it," was Dixson's reply.

"Yes, but such a lunch for a waiting woman; and going to send it up. I'd like to know if she's too big a lady to come into the kitchen," and Asenath's sharp shoulders jerked savagely.

"I must say, I think you very foolish indeed, to take a person about whom you know nothing," she said to Anna, as soon as she saw her, but stopped short as Willie ran out from the adjoining room and stood looking at her.

As well as she was capable of doing, Asenath had loved her brother John when a baby; and when he became a prattling active child, like the one standing before her, she had almost worshiped him, thinking there was never a face so pretty or manner so engaging as his. There had come no baby after him, and she remembered him so well, starting now with surprise as she saw reflected in Willie's face the look she never had forgotten.

"Who is he, Anna? Not her child, the waiting woman's, surely."

"Hush—sh," came warningly from Anna, as she glanced toward the open door, and that brought Asenath back from her dream of the past.

It was the waiting woman's child. There was no look like John now. She had been mistaken, and rather rudely pushing him away, she said: "I think you might have consulted us, at least. What are we to do with a child in this house? Here, here, young man," and Asenath started forward just in time to frighten Willie and make him drop and break the goblet he was trying to reach from the stand, "to dink," as he said.

Asenath's purple silk was deluged with the water, and her temper was considerably ruffled as she exclaimed: "You see the mischief he has done, and it was cut glass, too. I hope you'll deduct it from her wages!"

"Asenath," and Anna's voice betrayed her astonishment that her sister should speak so in Adah's presence.

She had hurried out at Asenath's alarm, but the latter did not at first observe her, and when she did, she was actually startled into an apology for her speech.

"I'm sorry Willie was so careless. I'll pay for the goblet cheerfully," Adah said, not to Asenath, but to Anna, who answered kindly: "No matter; it was already cracked across the bottom—don't mind."

But Adah did mind; and once alone in her room, her tears fell in torrents. She had heard the whole about Willie's mischief, heard of the buds torn to pieces, and of the hole kicked in the carpet. She would like to see that hole, and after Willie was asleep, she stole down to the reception-room to see the damage for herself. She found the hole, or what was intended for it, smiling as she examined the few loose threads; and then she hunted for the stool, finding it under the curtain where Eudora had placed it, and finding, too, that letter dropped by Jim. The others were gone, appropriated by Mrs. Richards, who always watched for the western mail and looked it over herself.

Miss Annie Richards,
Snowdown,
Mass.

That was the direction, and the envelope was faced with black. Adah noticed this, together with the heavy seal of wax stamped with an initial; and she was taking the lost epistle to its rightful owner when Mrs. Richards met her, asking what she had.

"I found this beneath the curtain," Adah replied. "It's for Miss Anna; I'll take it to her, shall I?"

"Yes, yes—yes, yes; for Anna," and madam snatched eagerly at that letter from Charlie Millbrook.

Soon recovering herself, she said naturally: "I'll take it myself. Say, girl, what is your name, now that you are to work here? You won't mind righting up the parlors, I presume—sweeping and dusting them, before you go upstairs again?"

It was new business for Adah, sweeping parlors as a servant, but she did it without a murmur; and then, when her task was completed, stopped for a moment by a window, and looked out upon the town, wondering where Alice Johnson's home had been. The house where she once lived would seem like an old friend, she thought, just as Pamelia came in and joined her. At the same moment Adah's eye caught the cottage by the river, and her heart beat rapidly, for that seemed to answer Alice's description of her Snowdon home.

"Whose pretty place is that?" she asked, pointing it out to Pamelia, who replied:

"It was a Mrs. Johnson's, but she's dead, and Miss Alice has gone a long ways off. I wish you could see Miss Alice, the most beautiful and the best lady in the world. She and Miss Anna were great friends. She used to be up here every day, and the village folks talked some that she came to see the doctor. But my," and Pamelia's face was very expressive of contempt, "she wouldn't have him, by a great sight. He's going to be married, though, to a Kentucky belle, with a hundred or more negroes, they say, and mighty big feelin'. But she needn't bring none of her a'rs nor her darkies here!"

"When does she come?" Adah asked, and Pamelia answered:

"In the spring; so you needn't begin to dread her. Why, your face is white as paper," and rather familiarly Pamelia pinched Adah's marble cheek.

Adah did not mean to be proud, but still she could not help shrinking from the familiarity, drawing back so quickly that Pamelia saw the implied rebuke. She did not ask pardon, but she became at once more respectful.

A moment after Anna's bell was heard, but Adah paid no heed, till Pamelia said:

"That was Miss Anna's bell, and it means for you to come."

Adah colored, and hastily left the room, while Pamelia muttered to herself:

"Ain't no more a maid than Miss Anna herself. But why has she come here? That's the mystery. She's been unfortunate."

This was the solution in Pamelia's mind; but the thought went no further than to her better half.

Adah's feelings at being called just as Lulu and Muggins were at home, had been in a measure shared by Anna, who hesitated several minutes ere touching the bell.

"If she is to be my maid, it will be better for us both not to act under restraint," she thought, and so rang out the summons which brought Adah to her room.

It was an awkward business, requiring a menial's service of that ladylike creature, and Anna would have been exceedingly perplexed had not Adah's good sense come to the rescue, prompting her to do things unasked in such a way that Anna was at once relieved from embarrassment, and felt that in Rose Markham she had found a treasure. She did not join the family in the evening, but kept her room instead, talking with Adah and caressing and playing with little Willie, who persisted in calling her "Arntee," in spite of all Adah could say.

"Never mind," Anna answered, laughingly; "I rather like to hear him. No one has ever called me by that name, and maybe never will, though my brother is engaged to be married in the spring. I have a picture of his betrothed there on my bureau. Would you like to see it?"

Adah nodded, and was soon gazing on the dark, haughty face she knew so well, and which, even from the casing, seemed to smile disdainfully upon, her, just as the original had often done.

"What do you think of her?" Anna asked.

Adah must say something, and she replied:

"I dare say people think her pretty."

"Yes; but what do you think? I asked your opinion," persisted Anna; and thus beset Adah replied at last:

"I think her too showily dressed for a picture. She displays too much jewelry."

Anna began to defend her future sister.

"There's rather too much of ornament, I'll admit, but she's a great beauty, and attracts much attention. Why, one of her pictures hangs in Brady's Gallery."

"At Brady's!" and Adah spoke quickly. "I should not suppose your brother would like to have it there where so many can look at it."

Anna tried to shield the heartless 'Lina, never dreaming how much more than herself Adah knew of 'Lina Worthington.

It seemed to Adah like a miserable deceit, sitting there and listening while Anna talked of 'Lina, and she was glad when at last she showed signs of weariness, and expressed a desire to retire for the night.

"Would you mind reading to me from the Bible?" Anna asked.

"Oh, no, I'd like it so much," and Adah read her favorite chapter.

And Anna listening to the sweet, silvery tones reading: "Let not your heart be troubled," felt her own sorrow grow less.

"If you please," Adah said timidly, bending over the sweet face resting on the pillow, "if you please, may I say the 'Lord's Prayer' here with you?"

Anna answered by grasping Adah's hand, and whispering to her:

"Yes, say it, do."

Then Adah knelt beside her, and Anna's fair hand rested as if in blessing on her head as they said together, "Our Father."

Adah's sleep was sweet that night in her little room at Terrace Hill—sweet, not because she knew whose home it was, nor yet because only the previous night he had tossed wearily upon the self-same pillow where she was resting so quietly, but because of a heart at peace with God, a feeling that she had at last found a haven of shelter for herself and her child, a home with Anna Richards, whose low breathings could be distinctly heard, and who once as the night wore on moaned so loudly in her sleep that it awakened Adah, and brought her to the bedside. But Anna was only dreaming and Adah heard her murmur the name of Charlie.

"I will not awaken her," she said, and gliding back to her own room, she wondered who was Anna's Charlie, associating him somehow with the letter she had given, into the care of Mrs. Richards.

CHAPTER XXXIV

ROSE MARKHAM

To Mrs. Richards and her elder daughters Rose Markham was an object of suspicious curiosity, while the villagers merely thought of Rose Markham as one far above her position, saying not very complimentary things of madam and her older daughters when it was known that Rose had been banished from the family pew to the side seat near the door, where honest Jim said his prayers, with Pamelia at his side.

For only one Sabbath had Adah graced the Richards' pew, and then it was all Jim's work. He had driven his wife and Adah first to church, as the day was stormy, and ere returning for the ladies, had escorted Adah up the aisle and turned her into the family pew, where she sat unconscious of the admiring looks cast upon her by those already assembled, or of the indignant astonishment of Miss Asenath and Eudora when they found that for one half day at least they must he disgraced by sitting with their servant. Very haughtily the scandalized ladies swept up the aisle, stopping suddenly at the pew door as if waiting for Adah to leave; but she only drew back further into the corner, while Willie held up to Asenath the picture he had found in her velvet-bound prayer book.

Alas! for the quiet hour Adah had hoped to spend, hallowed by thoughts that the dear ones at Spring Bank were mingling in the same service. She could not even join in the responses at first for the bitterness at her heart, the knowing how much she was despised by the proud ladies beside her.

Very close she kept Willie at her side, allowing him occasionally as he grew tired to stand upon the cushion, a proceeding highly offensive to the Misses Richards and highly gratifying to the row of tittering schoolgirls in the seat behind him. Willie always attracted attention, and numerous were the compliments paid to his infantile beauty by the younger portion of the congregation, while the older ones, they who remembered the doctor when a boy, declared that Willie Markham was exactly like him, when standing in the seat he kept the children in continual excitement by his restless movements and pretty baby ways.

The fire burned brightly in Anna's room when Adah returned from church, and Anna herself was waiting for her, welcoming her back with a smile which went far toward removing the pain still heavy at her heart. Anna saw something was the matter, but it was her sisters who enlightened her as together they ate their Sunday dinner in the little breakfast room where Anna joined them.

"Such impudence," Eudora said. "She had not heard one word of Mr. Howard's sermon, for keeping her book and dress and fur away from that little torment."

Then followed the story in detail, how "Markham had sat in their seat, parading herself up there just for show, while Willie had kissed the picture of little Samuel in Asenath'a book and left thereon the print of his lips. If Anna would have a maid, they did wish she would get one not quite so affected as Markham, one who did not try to attract attention by assuming the airs of a lady," and with this the secret was out.

Adah was too pretty, too stylish, to suit the prim Eudora, who felt keenly how she must suffer by comparison with her sister's waiting maid. Even unsuspicious Anna saw the point, and smiling archly asked "what she could do to make Rose less attractive."

In some things Anna could not have her way, and when her mother and sisters insisted that they would not keep a separate table for Markham, as they called Adah, she yielded, secretly bidding Pamelia see that everything was comfortable and nice for Mrs. Markham and her little boy. There was hardly need for this injunction, for in the kitchen Adah was regarded as far superior to those who would have trampled her down, and her presence among the servants was not without its influence, softening Jim's rough, loud ways, and making both Dixson and Pamelia more careful of their words and manners when she was with them. Much, too, they grew to love and pet the little Willie, who, accustomed to the free range of Spring Bank, asserted the same right at Terrace Hill, going where he pleased, putting himself so often in Mrs. Richards' way, that she began at last to notice him, and if no one was near, to caress the handsome boy. Asenath and Eudora held out longer, but even they were not proof against Willie's winning ways.

It was many weeks ere Adah wrote to Alice Johnson, and when at last she did, she said of Terrace Hill:

"I am happier here than I at first supposed it possible. The older ladies were so proud, so cold, so domineering, that it made me very wretched, in spite of sweet Anna's kindness. But there has come a perceptible change, and they now treat me civilly, if nothing more, while I do believe they are fond of Willie, and would miss him if he were gone."

Adah was right in this conjecture; for had it now been optional with the Misses Richards whether Willie should go or stay, they would have kept him there from choice, so cheery and pleasant he made the house. Adah was still too pretty, too stylish, to suit their ideas of a servant; but when, as time passed on, they found she did not presume at all on her good looks, but meekly kept her place as Anna's maid or companion, they dropped the haughty manner they had at first assumed, and treated her with civility, if not with kindness.

With Anna it was different. Won by Adah's gentleness and purity, she came at last to love her almost as much as if she had been a younger sister. Adah was not a servant to her, but a companion, a friend, with whom she daily held familiar converse, learning from her much that was good, and prizing her more and more as the winter weeks went swiftly by.

Since the morning when Adah confided to her a part of her history, she had never alluded to it or intimated a desire to hear more; but she thought much about it, revolving in her mind various expedients for finding and bringing back to his allegiance the recreant lover.

"If I were not bound to secrecy," she thought one day, as she sat waiting for Adah's return from the post office, "if I were not bound to secrecy, I would tell Brother John, and perhaps he might think of something. Men's wits are sometimes better than women's. When she comes back from the office I mean to see what she'll say."

Adah did not join Anna at once, but went instead to her own room, where she could read and cry alone over the nice long letter from Alice Johnson, telling how much they missed her, how old Sam pined for Willie, how Mrs. Worthington and Hugh mourned for Adah, and how she, Alice, prayed for the dear friend, never so dear as now that she was gone. Many and minute were Alice's inquiries as to whether Adah had yet seen Dr. Richards, when was he expected home, and so forth.

Adah placed her letter in her pocket, and then went to sit with Anna, whose face lighted up at once, for Adah's society was like sunshine to her monotonous life.

"Rose," she said, after an interval of silence had elapsed, "I have been thinking about you all day, and wishing I might do you good. You have never told me the city where you met Willie's father, and I fancied it might be Boston, until I remembered that your advertisement was in the *Herald*. Was it Boston?"

It was a direct question, and Adah answered frankly.

"It was in New York," while Anna quickly rejoined.

"Oh, I'm so glad! for now you'll let me tell Brother John. He has lived there so much he must know everybody, or at all events he may find that man and bring him back. You will have to give his name, of course."

Adah's face was white as ashes, as she replied:

"No, no—oh, no. He could not find him. Nobody can but God. I am willing to wait His time. Don't tell your brother, Miss Anna—don't."

She spoke so earnestly, and seemed so distressed, that Anna answered at once:

"I will not without your permission, though I'd like to so much. He is coming home by-and-by. His wedding day is fixed for April ——, and he will visit us before that time, to see about our preparations for receiving 'Lina. We somehow expected a letter today. Did you get one?"

"Yes, one for your mother—from the doctor, I think," Adah replied, without telling how faint the sight of the handwriting had made her, it was so like George's—not exactly like his, either, but enough so to make her heart beat painfully as she recalled the only letter she ever received from him, the fatal note which broke her heart.

"It is so very long since I had a letter all to myself, that I wonder how it would seem," Anna rejoined. "I have not had one since—since—"

"The day I came there was one for you," said Adah, while Anna looked wonderingly at her, saying, "You are mistaken, I'm sure. I've no remembrance of it. A letter from whom?"

Adah did not know from whom or where. She only knew there was one, and by way of refreshing Anna's memory, she said:

"Jim put it with the others on the table, and it fell behind the curtain, where I found it in the afternoon. I was bringing it to you myself, but your mother took it from me and said she would carry it up while I swept the parlor. Surely you remember now."

No, Anna did not, and she looked so puzzled that Adah, anxious to set the matter right, continued:

"I remember it particularly, because it was spelled A-n-n-i-e instead of Anna."

Adah was not prepared for the sudden start, the look almost of terror in Anna's eyes, or for the color which stained the usually colorless face. In all the world there was but one person who ever called her Annie, or wrote it so, and that person was Charlie. Had he written at last, and if so, why had she never known it? Could it be her proud mother had withheld what would have been life to her slowly dying daughter? It was terrible to suspect such a thing, and Anna struggled to cast the thought aside, saying to Adah. "Was there anything else peculiar about it?"

"Nothing, except that 'twas inclosed in a mourning envelope, sealed with wax, and the letter on the seal was—was—"

"Oh, pray think quick. You have not forgotten. You must not forget," and Anna's soft blue eyes grew dark with intense excitement as Adah tried to recall the initial on that seal.

"She had not noticed particularly, she did not suppose it was important. She was not certain, but she believed—yes, she was nearly sure—the letter was 'M.'"

"Oh, you do not know how much good you have done me," Anna cried, and laying her throbbing head on Adah's neck, she wept a torrent of tears, wrung out by the knowing that Charlie had not forgotten her quite. He had written, and that of itself was joy, even though he loved another.

"The initial was 'M.'—you are sure, you are sure," she kept whispering, while Adah soothed the poor head, wondering at Anna's agitation, and in a measure guessing the truth, the old story, love, whose course had not run smoothly.

"And mother took it," Anna said at last, growing more composed.

"Yes, she said she would bring it to you," was Adah's reply.

For several minutes Anna sat looking out upon the snowy landscape, her usually smooth brow wrinkled with thought, and her eyes gleaming with a strange, new light. There was a shadow on her fair face, a grieved, injured expression, as if her mother's treachery had hurt her cruelly. She knew the letter was withheld, and her first impulse was to demand it at once. But Anna dreaded a scene, and dreaded her mother, too, and after a moment's reflection that her Charlie would write again, and Adah, who now went regularly to the office, would get it and bring it to her, she said:

"Does mother always look over the letters?"

"Not at first," was Adah's reply, "but now she meets me at the door, and takes them from my hand."

Anna was puzzled. Turning again to Adah, she said:

"I wish you to go always to the office, and if there comes another letter for me, bring it up at once. It's mine."

Anna had no desire now to talk with Adah of the recreant lover, or ask that John should hear the story. Her mind was too much disturbed, and for more than half an hour she sat, looking intently into the fire, seeing there visions of what might be in case Charlie loved her still, and wished her to be his wife. The mere knowing that he had written made her so happy that she could not even be angry with her mother, though a shadow flitted over her face, when her reverie was broken by the entrance of Madam Richards, who had come to see what she thought of fitting up the west chambers for John's wife, instead of the north ones.

"I have a letter from him," she said. "They are to be married the —— day of April, which leaves us only five weeks more, as they will start at once for Terrace Hill. Do, Anna, look interested," she continued, rather pettishly, as Anna did not seem very attentive. "I am so bothered. I want to see you alone," and she cast a furtive glance at Adah, who left the room, while madam plunged at once into the matter agitating her so much.

She had fully intended going to Kentucky with her son, but 'Lina had objected, and the doctor had written, saying she must not go.

"I have not the money myself," he wrote, "and I'll have to get trusted for my wedding suit, so you must appeal to Anna's good nature for the wherewithal with which to fix the rooms. She may stay with you longer than you anticipate. It is too expensive living here, as she would expect to live. Nothing but Fifth Avenue Hotel would suit her, and I cannot ask her for funds at once. I'd rather come to it gradually."

And this it was which so disturbed Mrs. Richards' peace of

mind. She could not go to Kentucky, and she might as well have saved the money she had expended in getting her black silk velvet dress fixed for the occasion, while, worst of all, she must have John's wife there for months, perhaps, whether she liked it or not, and she must also fit up the rooms with paper and paint and carpets, notwithstanding that she'd nothing to do it with, unless Anna generously gave the necessary sum from her own yearly income. Anna assented to that, and said she would try to spare the money. Rose could make the carpets, and that would save a little.

"I wish, too, mother," she added, "that you would let her arrange the rooms altogether. She has exquisite taste, besides the faculty of making the most of things. Our house never looked so well as it has since she came. Somehow Eudora and Asenath have such a stiff set way of putting the furniture."

So it was Anna who selected the tasteful carpet for 'Lina's boudoir, and the bedchamber beyond it, but it was Adah who made it, Adah who, with Willie playing on the floor, bent so patiently over the heavy fabric, sometimes wiping away the bitter tears as she thought of the days preceding her own bridal, and of her happiness, even though no fingers were busy for her in the home where they were too proud to receive her. Where was that home? Was it North or South, East or West, and what was it like? She had no idea, though, sometimes fancy had whispered that it might have been like Terrace Hill, that George's haughty mother, who had threatened to turn her from the door, was a second Mrs. Richards, and then an involuntary prayer of thanksgiving escaped her lips for the trial she had escaped.

Frequently doubts crossed her mind as to the future, when it might be known that she came from Spring Bank, and knew the expected bride. Would she not be blamed as a party in the deception? Ought she not to tell Anna frankly that she knew her brother's betrothed? She did not know, and the harassing anxiety wore upon her faster than all the work she had to do.

Anna seemed very happy. Excitement was what she needed, and never since her girlish days had she been so bright and active as she was now, assisting Adah in her labors, and watching the progress of affairs. The new carpets looked beautiful when upon the floor, and gave to the rooms a new and cozy aspect. The muslin curtains, done up by the laundress so carefully, lest they should drop to pieces, looked almost as good as new, and no one would have suspected that the pretty cornice had been made from odds and ends found by Adah in an ancient box up in the lumber-room. The white satin bows which looped the curtains back, were tied by Adah's hands.

And during all this while came there to Adah's heart no suspicion for whom and whose she was thus laboring? No strange interest in the bridegroom, the handsome doctor, so doted upon by mother and sisters? None whatever. She scarcely remembered him, or if she did, it was as one toward whom she was utterly indifferent. He would not notice her. He might not notice Willie, though yes, she rather thought he would like her boy; everybody did, and the young mother bent down to kiss her child, and so hide the blush called up by a remembrance of Irving Stanley's kindness on that sad journey to Terrace Hill.

Rapidly the few days went by, bringing at last the very morning when he was expected. Brightly, warmly the April sun looked in upon Adah, wondering at the load upon her spirits. She did not associate it with the doctor, nor with anything in particular. She did not know for certain that she should even see him. She might and she might not, but if she did perchance stumble upon him, she would a little rather he should see that she was not like ordinary waiting-maids. She would make a good impression!

And so she wore the pretty dark French calico which Anna had given to her, fastened the neat linen collar with a chaste little pin, buttoned her snow-white cuffs, thrust a clean handkerchief into the dainty pocket on the outside of her skirt, and then descended to the drawing-room to see that the fires were burning briskly, for spite of the cheerful sunshine pouring in, the morning was cold and frosty. They had delayed their breakfast until the doctor should come, and in the dining-room the table was laid with unusual care. Everything was in its place, and still Adah fluttered around it like a restless bird, lingering by what she knew was the doctor's chair, taking up his knife, examining his napkin ring, and wondering what he would think of the cheap bone rings used at Spring Bank.

In the midst of her cogitations, the door bell rang, and she heard the tramp of horses' feet as Jim drove around to the stable. The doctor had come and she must go, but where was Willie?

"Willie, Willie," she called, but Willie paid no heed, and as Eudora had said, was directly under foot when she unlocked the door, his the first form distinctly seen, his the first face which met the doctor's view, and his fearless baby laugh the first sound, which welcomed the doctor home!

CHAPTER XXXV

THE RESULT

It was not a disagreeable picture—that chubby, rose-cheeked little boy. Willie had run to the door because he heard the bell. He had not expected to see a stranger, and at sight of the tall figure he drew back timidly and half hid himself behind Mrs. Richards, whom he knew to be the warmest ally he had in the hall.

As the doctor had said to Irving Stanley, he disliked children, but he could not help noticing Willie, and after the first greetings were over he asked, "Who have we here? Whose child is this?"

Eudora and Asenath tried to frown, but the expression of their faces softened perceptibly as they glanced at Willie, who had followed them into the parlor, and who, with one little foot thrown forward, and his fat hands pressed together, stood upon the hearth rug, gazing at the doctor with that strange look which had so often puzzled, bewildered and fascinated the entire Richards' family.

"Anna wrote you that the maid she so much wanted had come to her at last—a very ladylike person, who has evidently seen better days, and this is her child, Willie Markham. He is such a queer little fellow that we allow him more liberties than we ought."

It was Mrs. Richards who volunteered this explanation, while her son stood looking down at Willie, wondering what it was about the child which seemed familiar. Anna had casually mentioned Rose Markham in her letter, had said how much she liked her, and had spoken of her boy, but the doctor was too much absorbed in his own affairs to care for Rose Markham; so he had not thought of her since, notwithstanding that 'Lina had tried many times to make him speak of Anna's maid, so as to calculate her own safety. The sight of Willie, however, set the doctor to thinking, and finally carried him back to the crowded car, the shrieking child, and the young woman to whom Irving Stanley had been so kind.

"I hope I shall not be obliged to see her," he thought, and then he answered his mother's speech concerning Willie. "So you've taken to petting a servant's child, for want of something better. Just wait until my boy comes here."

Eudora tried to blush, Asenath looked unconscious, while Mrs. Richards replied: "If I ever have a grandson one half as pretty or as bright as Willie, I shall be satisfied."

The doctor did not know how rapidly a lively, affectionate child will win one's love, and he thought his proud mother grown almost demented; but still, in spite of himself, he more than once raised his hand to lay it on Willie's head, pausing occasionally in his conversation to watch the gambols of the playful child sporting on the carpet.

"Willie, Willie," called Adah from a distant room, where she was looking for him. "Willie, Willie," and as the silvery tone fell on the doctor's ears he started suddenly.

"Who is that?" he asked, his heart throbs growing fainter as his mother replied: "That is Mrs. Markham. Singularly sweet voice for a person in humble life, don't you think so?"

The doctor's reply was cut short by the entrance of Anna, and in his joy at meeting his favorite sister and the excitement at the breakfast which followed immediately, the doctor forgot Rose Markham, who had succeeded in capturing Willie and borne him to her own room. After breakfast was over he went with Anna to inspect the rooms which Adah had fitted for his bride. They were very pleasant, and fastidious as he was he could find fault with nothing. The carpet, the curtains, the new light furniture, the arm-chair by the window where 'Lina was expected to sit, the fanciful workbasket standing near, and his chair not far away, all were in perfect taste, and passing his arm caressingly about Anna's waist he said: "It's very nice, and I thank my little sister so much; of course, I am wholly indebted to you."

"Not of course. I furnished means, it is true, but another than myself planned and executed the effect," and sitting down in 'Lina's chair, Anna told her brother of Rose Markham, so beautiful, so refined, and so perfectly ladylike. "You must see her, and judge for yourself. Can't I think of some excuse for sending for her?" she said.

It was some evil genius truly which prompted the doctor's reply.

"Never mind. I'm not partial to smart waiting maids. I'd rather talk with you."

And so the golden moment was lost, and Adah was not sent for, while in his bridal rooms the doctor sat, trying to be interested in all that Anna was saying, trying to believe he should be happy when 'Lina was his wife, and trying, oh, so hard, to shut out the vision of another, who should have been there in his own home, instead of lying in some lonesome grave, as he believed she was, with her baby on her bosom. Poor Lily!

It was a great mistake he made when he cast Lily off, but it could not now be helped. No tears, no regrets, could bring back the dear little form laid away beneath the grassy sod, and so he would not waste his time in idle mourning. He would do the best he could with 'Lina. He did believe she loved him. He was almost sure of it, and as a means of redressing Lily's wrongs he would be kind to her.

And where all this while was Adah? Had she no curiosity, no desire to see the man about whom she had heard so much? Doubtless she had, and would have sought an occasion for gratifying it, had not the rather too talkative Pamelia accidentally overheard the doctor's remark concerning "smart waiting maids," and repeated it to her, with sundry little embellishments in tone and manner.

Piqued more than she cared to acknowledge, Adah decided not to trouble him if she could help it, and so kept out of his way, by staying mostly in her own room, where she was busy with sewing for Anna.

Once, as the afternoon was drawing to a close, she felt the hot blood stain her face and prickle the very roots of her hair, as a step, heavier than a woman's, came along the soft, carpeted hall, and seemed to pause opposite her door, which stood partially ajar. She was sitting with her back that way, and so the doctor only saw the outline of her graceful form bending over her work, confessing to himself how graceful, how pliant, how girlish it was. He noted, too, the braids of silken hair drooping behind the well-shaped ears, just as Lily used to wear hers. Dear Lily! Her hair was much like Rose Markham's, not quite so dark, perhaps, or so luxuriant, for seldom had he seen locks so abundant and glossy as those adorning Rose Markham's head.

Slowly the twilight shadows were creeping over Terrace Hill and into the little room, where, with doors securely shut, Adah was preparing for her accustomed walk to the office. But what was it which fell like a thunderbolt on her ear, riveting her to the spot, where she stood, rigid and immovable as a block of granite cut from the solid rock? Between the closet and Anna's room there was only a thin partition, and when the door was open every sound was distinctly heard. The doctor had just come in, and it was his voice, heard for the first time, which sent the blood throbbing so madly through Adah's veins and made the sparks of fire dance before her eyes. She was not deceived—the tones were too distinct, too full, too well remembered to be mistaken, and stretching out her hands in the dim darkness, she moaned faintly: "George! 'tis George!" and she sank upon the floor. She could hear him now saying to Anna, as her moan fell on his ear, "What was that Anna? Are we not alone? I wish to speak my farewell words in private."

"Yes, all alone," Anna replied, "unless—" and stepping to Adah's door she called twice for Rose Markham.

But Adah, though she tried to do so, could neither move nor speak, and Anna failed to see the figure crouching in the darkness, poor, crushed, wretched Adah, who could not dispute her when returning to her brother she said, "There is no one there; Rose has gone to the post office. I heard her as she went out. We are all alone. Was it anything particular you wished to tell me?"

Again the familiar tones thrilled on Adah's ears as Dr. Richards replied: "Nothing very particular. I only wished to say a few words, 'Lina. I want you to like her, to make up, if possible, for the love I ought to give her."

"Ought to give her! Oh, brother, are you taking 'Lina without love? Better never make the vow than break it after it is made."

Anna spoke earnestly, and the doctor, who always tried to

retain her good opinion, replied evasively: "I suppose I do love her as well as half the world love their wives before marriage, but she is different from any ladies I have known; so different from what poor Lily was. Anna, let me talk with you again of Lily. I never told you all—but what is that?" he continued, as he indistinctly heard the choking, gasping, stifled sob which Adah gave at the sound of the dear pet name. Anna answered: "It's only the rising wind. It sounds so always when it's in the east. We surely are alone. What of Lily? Do you wish you were going after her instead of 'Lina?"

Oh, why did the doctor hesitate a moment? Why did he suffer his dread of losing Anna's respect to triumph over every other feeling? He had meant to tell her all, how he did love the gentle girl, the little more than child, who confided herself to him—how he loved even her memory now far more than he loved 'Lina, but something kept the full confession back, and he answered:

"I don't know. We must have money, and 'Lina is rich, while Lily was very poor, and the only friend or relation she knew was one with whom I would not dare have you come in contact, so wicked and reckless he was."

This was what the doctor said, and into the brown eyes, now bloodshot and dim with anguish, there came the hard, fierce look, before which Alice Johnson once had shuddered, when Adah Hastings said:

"I should hate him! Yes, I should hate him!"

And in that dark hour of agony Adah felt that she did hate him. She knew now that what she before would not believe was true. He had not made her a lawful wife, else he had never dared to take another.

She did not hear him now, for with that prayer, all consciousness forsook her, and she lay on her face insensible, while at the very last he did confess to Anna that Lily was his wife. He did not say unlawfully so. He could not tell her that. He said:

"I married her privately. I would bring her back if I could, but I cannot, and I shall marry 'Lina."

"But," and Anna grasped his hand nervously. "I thought you told me once, that you won her love, and then, when mother's harsh letters came, left her without a word. Was that story false?"

The doctor was wading out in deep water, and in desperation he added lie to lie, saying:

"Yes, that was false. I tell you I married her, and she died. Was I to blame for that?"

"No, no. I'd far rather it were so. I respect you more than if you had left her. I am glad, not that she died, but that you are not so bad as I feared. Sweet Lily," and Anna's tears flowed fast.

There was a knock at the door, and Jim appeared, inquiring if the doctor would have the carriage brought around. It was nearly time to go, and with the whispered words to Anna, "I have told you what no one else must ever know," the doctor descended with his sister to the parlor, where his mother was waiting for him. The opening and shutting of the door caused a draught of air, which, falling on the fainting Adah, restored her to consciousness, and struggling to her feet, she tried to think what it was that had happened.

"Oh, George! George!" she gasped. "You are worse than I believed. You have made me an outcast, and Willie—"

George was a greater villain than she had imagined a man could be, and again her white lips essayed to curse him, but the rash act was stayed by the low words whispered in her ear, "Forgive as we would be forgiven."

"If it were not for Willie, I might, but, oh! my boy, my boy disgraced," was the rebellious spirit's answer, when again the voice whispered, "And who art thou to contend against thy God? Know you not that I am the Father of the fatherless?"

There were tears now in Adah's eyes, the first which she had shed.

"I'll try," she murmured, "try to forgive the wrong, but the strength must all be Thine," and then, though there came no sound or motion, her heart went out in agonizing prayer, that she might forgive even as she hoped to be forgiven.

"God tell me what to do with Willie?" she sobbed, starting suddenly as the answer to her prayer seemed to come at once. "Oh, can I do that?" she moaned; "can I leave him here?"

At first her whole soul recoiled from it, but when she remembered Anna, and how much she loved the child, her feelings began to change. Anna would love him more when she knew he was poor Lily's and her own brother's. She would be kind to him for his father's sake, and for the sake of the girl she had professed to like. Mrs. Richards, too, would not cast him off. She thought too much of the Richards' blood, and there was surely enough in Willie's veins to wipe out all taint of hers. Willie should be bequeathed to Anna. It would break her heart to leave him, were it not already broken, but it was better so. It would be better in the end. He would forget her in time, forget the girlish woman he had called mamma, unless sweet Anna told him of her, as perhaps she might. Dear Anna, how Adah longed to fold her arms about her once and call her sister, but she must not. It might not be well received, for Anna had some pride, as her waiting maid had learned.

"A waiting maid!" Adah repeated the name, smiling bitterly as she thought. "A waiting maid in his own home! Who would have dreamed that I should ever come to this, when he painted the future so grandly?"

Then there came over her the wild, yearning desire to see his face once more, to know if he had changed, and why couldn't she? They supposed her gone to the office, and she would go there now, taking the depot on the way.

Apart in the ladies' room at Snowdon depot, a veiled figure sat—Dr. Richards' deserted wife—waiting for him, waiting to look on his face once more ere she fled she knew not whither. He came at last, Jim's voice speaking to his horses heralding his approach.

The group of rough-looking men gathered about the office did not suit his mood, and so he came on to the ladies' apartment, just as Adah knew he would. Pausing for a moment on the threshold, he looked hastily in, his glance falling upon the veiled figure sitting there so lonely and motionless. She did not care for him, she would not object to his presence, so he came nearer to the stove, poising his patent leathers upon the hearth, thrusting both hands into his pockets, and even humming to himself snatches of a song, which Lily used to sing up the three flights of stairs in that New York boarding house.

Poor Adah! How white and cold she grew, listening to that air, and gazing upon the face she had loved so well. It was changed since the night when with his kiss warm on her lips he left her forever, changed, and for the worse. There was a harder, a more reckless, determined expression there, a look which better than words could have done, told that self alone was the god he worshiped.

Once, as he walked up and down the room, passing so near to her that she might have touched him with her hand, she felt an almost irresistible desire to thrust her thick brown veil aside, and confronting him to his face, claim from him what she had a right to claim, his name and a position as his wife—only for Willie's sake, however; for herself she did not wish it.

It was a relief when at last the roll of the cars was heard, and buttoning his coat still closer around him, he turned toward the door, half looking back to see if the veiled figure too had risen. It had, and was standing close beside him, its outside garments sweeping his as the crowd increased, pressing her nearer to him, but Adah passed back into the ladies' room, and opening the rear door was out in the street again almost before the train had left the station. George was gone—lost to her forever! and with a piteous moan for her ruined life, Adah kept on her way till the post office was reached.

There were four letters in the box—one for Mrs. Richards, from an absent brother; one for Eudora, from Lottie Gardner; one for Asenath, from an old friend, and at the bottom, last of all, one for Annie Richards, faced with black, and bearing the initial "M." upon the seal of wax.

Adah saw all this, but it conveyed no meaning to her mind except a vague remembrance that at some time or other, very, very long years it seemed, Anna had bidden her keep from her mother any letter directed to herself in a mourning envelope. Adah retained just sense enough to do this, and separating the letter from the others, thrust it into her pocket, and then took her way back to Terrace Hill.

Willie was asleep; and as Pamelia, who brought him up, had thoughtfully undressed and placed him in bed, there was nothing for Adah to do but think. She should go away, of course; she could not stay there longer; but how should she tell them why she went, and who would be her medium for communication?

"Anna, of course," she whispered; and lighting her little lamp, she sat down to write the letter which would tell Anna Richards who was the waiting maid to whom she had been so kind.

"Dear Anna," she wrote. "Forgive me for calling you so this once, for indeed I cannot help it. You have been so kind to me that if my heart could ache, it would ache terribly at leaving you and knowing it was forever. I am going away from you, Anna; and when, in the morning, you wait for me to come as usual, I shall not be here, I could not stay and meet your brother when he returns. Oh, Anna, Anna, how shall I begin to tell you what I know will grieve and shock your pure nature so dreadfully?

"Anna!—I love to call you Anna now, for you seem, near to me; and believe me, while I write this to you, I am conscious of no feeling of inferiority to any one bearing your proud name. I am, or should have been, your equal, your sister; and Willie!—oh, my boy, when I think of him, the feeling comes and I almost seem to be going mad!

"Cannot you guess?—don't you know now who I am? God forgive your brother, as I asked him to do, kneeling there by the very chair where he sat an hour since, talking to you of Lily. I heard him, and the sound of his voice took power and strength away. I could not move to let you know I was there, for I was, and I lay upon the floor till consciousness forsook me; and then, when I awoke again, you both were gone.

"I went to the depot, I saw him in his face to make assurance sure, and Anna, I—oh, I don't know what I am. The world would not call me a wife, though I believed I was; but they cannot deal thus cruelly by Willie, or wash from his veins his father's blood, for I—I, who write this, I who have been a servant in the house where I should have been the mistress, am Lily—wronged, deserted Lily—and Willie is your brother's child! His father's look is in his face. I see it there so plainly now, and know why that boy portrait of your brother has puzzled me so much. But when I came here I had no suspicion, for he won me, not as a Richards—George Hastings, that was the name by which I knew him, and I was Adah Gordon. If you do not believe me, ask him when he comes back if ever in his wanderings he met with Adah Gordon, or her guardian, Mr. Monroe. Ask if he was ever present at a marriage where this same Adah gave her heart to one for whom she would then have lost her life, erring in that she loved the gift more than the giver; but God punished idolatry, and He has punished me, so sorely, oh so sorely; that sometimes my fainting soul cries out, "'Tis more than I can bear,'"

Then followed more particulars so that there should be no doubt, and then the half crazed Adah took up the theme nearest to her heart, her boy, her beautiful Willie. She could not take him with her. She knew not where she was going, and Willie must not suffer. Would Anna take the child?

"I do not ask that the new bride should ever call him hers," she wrote; "I'd rather she would not. I ask that you should give him a mother's care, and if his father will sometimes speak kindly to him for the sake of the older time when he did love the mother, tell him—Willie's father, I mean—tell him, oh I know not what to bid you tell him, except that I forgive him, though at first it was so hard, and the words refused to come; I trusted him so much, loved him so much, and until I had it from his own lips, believed I was his wife. But that cured me; that killed the love, if any still existed, and now, if I could, I would not be his, unless it were for Willie's sake.

"And now farewell. God deal with you, dear Anna, as you deal with my boy."

Calmly, steadily, Adah folded up the missive, and laying it with the mourning envelope, busied herself next in making the necessary preparations for her flight. Anna had been liberal with her in point of wages, paying her every week, and paying more than at first agreed upon; and as she had scarcely spent a penny during her three months' sojourn at Terrace Hill, she had, including what Alice had given to her, nearly forty dollars. She was trying so hard to make it a hundred, and so send it to Hugh some day; but she needed it most herself, and she placed it carefully in her little purse, sighing over the golden coin which Anna had paid her last, little dreaming for what purpose it would be used. She would not change her dress until Anna had retired, as that might excite suspicion; so with the same rigid apathy of manner she sat down by Willie's side and waited till Anna was heard moving in her room. The lamp was burning dimly on the bureau, and so Anna failed to see the frightful expression of Adah's face, as she performed her accustomed duties, brushing Anna's hair, and letting her hands linger caressingly amid the locks she might never touch again.

It did strike Anna that something was the matter; for when Adah spoke to her, the voice was husky and unnatural. Still, she paid no attention until the chapter was read as usual and "Our Father" said; then, as Adah lingered a moment, still kneeling by the bed, she laid her soft hand on the young head, and asked, kindly, "if it ached."

"No, not my head, not my head," and Adah continued impetuously; "Anna, tell me, have I pleased you?—do you like me? would you, could you love me if I were your equal—love me as I do you?"

Anna noticed that the "Miss" was dropped from her name, that her maid was treating her more familiarly than she had ever done before; and for an instant a flush showed on her cheek, for pride was Anna's besetting sin, the one from which she daily prayed to be delivered. There was an inward struggle, a momentary conflict, such as every Christian warrior has felt at times, and then the flush was gone from the white cheek, and her hand still lay on Adah's head, as she replied: "I do not understand why you question me thus, but I will answer just the same. I do like you very much, and you have always seemed to me much like an equal. I could hardly do without you now."

"And Willie? If I should die, or anything happen to me, would you care for Willie?"

There was something very earnest in Adah's tone as she pleaded for her boy, and had Anna been at all suspicious, she must have guessed there was something wrong. As it was, she merely thought Adah tired and nervous. She had been thinking, perhaps, of the deserted, and she smoothed her hair pityingly as she replied: "Of course I'd care for Willie. He has won a large place in my heart."

"Bless you for that. It has made me very happy," Adah whispered, arising to her feet and adding: "You may think me bold, but I must kiss you once—only once—for it will be pleasant to remember that I kissed Anna Richards."

There was nothing cringing or even pleading in the tone. Adah seemed to ask it as her right, and ere Anna could answer she had pressed one burning kiss upon the smooth, white forehead which a menial's lips had never touched before, and was gone from the room.

"Was she crazy, or what was it that ailed her?" Anna asked herself, wondering more and more, the more she thought of the strange conduct, and lying awake long after the usual hour for sleep.

But wakeful as she was, there was one who kept the vigils with her, knowing exactly when she fell away at last into a slumber all the deeper for the restlessness which had preceded it. Anna slept very soundly as Adah knew she would, and when toward morning a light footstep glided across her threshold she did not hear it. The bolt was drawn, the key was turned, and just as the clock struck three, Adah stood outside the yard, leaning on the gate and gazing back at the huge building looming up so dark and grand beneath the starry sky. One more prayer for Willie and the mother-auntie to whose care she had left him, one more straining glance at the window of the little room where he lay sleeping, and she resolutely turned away, nor stopped again until the Danville depot was reached the station where in less than five minutes after her arrival the night express stood for an instant, and then went thundering on, bearing with it another passenger, bound for—she knew not, cared not whither.

CHAPTER XXXVI

EXCITEMENT

They were not early risers at Terrace Hill, and the morning following Adah's flight Anna slept later than usual; nor was it until Willie's baby cry, calling for mamma, was heard, that she awoke,
and thinking Adah had gone down for something, she bade Willie
come to her. Putting out her arms she lifted him carefully into her
own bed, and in doing so brushed from her pillow the letters left
for her. But it did not matter then, and for a full half hour she lay
waiting for Adah's return. Growing impatient at last, she stepped
upon the floor, her bare feet touching something cold, something
which made her look down and find that she was stepping on a letter—not one, but two—and in wondering surprise she turned
them to the light, half fainting with excitement, when on the back
of the first one examined she saw the old familiar handwriting, and
knew that Charlie had written again!

Anna had hardly been human had she waited an instant ere
she tore open the envelope and learned how many times and with
how little success Charlie Millbrook had written to her since his
return from India. He had not forgotten her. The love of his early
manhood had increased with his maturer years, and he could not
be satisfied until he heard from her that he was remembered and
still beloved.

This was Charlie's letter, this what Anna read, feeling far too
happy to be angry at her mother, and delicious tears of joy flowed
over her beautiful face, as, pressing the paper to her lips, she murmured:

"Dear Charlie! darling Charlie! I knew he was not false, and I
thank the kind Father for bringing him at last to me."

Hiding it in her bosom, Anna took the other letter then, and
throwing her shawl around her, for she was beginning to shiver
with cold, sat down by the window and read it through—read it
once, read it twice, read it thrice, and then—sure never were the
inmates of Terrace Hill thrown into so much astonishment and
alarm as they were that April morning, when, in her cambric night
robe, her long hair falling unbound about her shoulders, and her
bare feet, gleaming white and cold upon the floor, Miss Anna went
screaming from room to room, and asking her wonder-stricken
mother and sisters if they had any idea who it was that had been an
inmate of their house for so many weeks.

"Come with me, then," she almost screamed, and dragging her
mother to her room, where Willie sat up in bed, looking curiously
about him and uncertain whether to cry or to laugh, she exclaimed,
"Look at him, mother, and you, too, Asenath and Eudora!" turning
to her sisters, who had followed. "Tell me who is he like? He is

John's child. And Rose was Lily, the young girl whom you forbade him to marry! Listen, mother, you shall listen to what your pride has done!" and grasping the bewildered Mrs. Richards by the arm, Anna held her fast while she read aloud the letter left by Adah.

Mrs. Richards fainted. She soon recovered, however, and listened eagerly while Anna repeated all her brother had ever told her of Lily.

Poor Willie! He was there in the bed, looking curiously at the four women, none of whom seemed quite willing to own him save Anna. Her heart took him in at once. He had been given to her. She would be faithful to the trust, and folding him in her arms, she cried softly over him, kissing his little face and calling him her darling.

"Anna, how can you fondle such as he?" Eudora asked, rather sharply.

"He is our brother's child. Mother, you will not turn from your grandson," and Anna held the boy toward her mother, who did not refuse to take him.

Asenath always went with her mother, and at once showed signs of relenting by laying her hand on Willie's head and calling him "poor boy." Eudora held out longer, but Anna knew she would yield in time, and satisfied with Willie's reception so far, went on to speak of Adah. Where was she, did they suppose, and what were the best means of finding her.

At this Mrs. Richards demurred, as did Asenath with her.

"Adah was gone, and they had better let her go quietly. She was nothing to them, nothing whatever, and if they took Willie in, doing their best with him as one of the Richards' line, it was all that could be required of them. Had Adah been John's wife, it would of course be different, but she was not, and his marriage with 'Lina must not now be prevented."

This was Mrs. Richards' reasoning, but Anna's was different.

"John had distinctly said, 'I married Lily and she died.' Adah was mistaken about the marriage being unlawful. It was a falsehood he told her. She was his wife, and he must not be permitted to commit bigamy. She would tell John in private. They need not try to dissuade her, for she should go."

This was what Anna said, and all in vain were her mother's entreaties to let matters take their course. Anna only replied by going deliberately on with the preparations for her sudden journey. She was going to find Rose, and blessing her for this kindness to one whom they had liked so much, Dixson and Pamelia helped to get her ready, both promising the best care to Willie in her absence, both asking where she was going first and both receiving the same answer, "To Albany."

Mrs. Richards was too much stunned clearly to comprehend what had happened or what would be the result; and in a kind of apathetic maze she bade Anna good-by, and then went back to where Willie sat upon the sofa, examining and occasionally tearing the costly book of foreign prints which had been given him to keep him still and make him cease his piteous wail for "mamma." It seemed like a dream to the three ladies sitting at home that night and talking about Anna, wondering that a person of her weak nerves and feeble health should suddenly become so active, so energetic, so decided, and of her own accord start off on a long journey alone and unprotected.

And Anna wondered at herself when the excitement of leaving was past and the train was bearing her swiftly along on her mission of duty. She had written a few lines to Charlie Millbrook, telling him of her unaltered love and bidding him come to her in three weeks' time, when she would be ready to see him.

It was very dark and rainy, and the passengers jostled each other rudely as they passed from the cars in Albany and hurried to the boat. It was new business to Anna, traveling alone and in the night, and a feeling akin to fear was creeping over her as she wondered where she should find the eastern train.

"Follow the crowd," seemed yelled out for her benefit, though it was really intended for a timid, deaf old lady, who had anxiously asked what to do of one whose laconic reply was: "Follow the crowd." And Anna did follow the crowd which led her safely to the waiting cars. Snugly ensconced in a seat all to herself, she vainly imagined there was no more trouble until Cleveland or Buffalo at least was reached. How, then, was she disappointed when, alighting for a moment at Rochester, she found herself in a worse babel, if possible, than had existed at Albany. Where were all these folks going, and which was the train? "I ought not to have alighted at all," she thought; "I might have known I never could find my way back." Never, sure, was poor, little woman so confused and bewildered as Anna, and it is not strange that she stood directly upon the track, unmindful of the increasing din and roar as the train from Niagara Falls came thundering into the depot. It was in vain that the cabman nearest to her helloed to warn her of the impending danger. She never dreamed that they meant her, or suspected her great peril, until from out of the group waiting to take that very train, a tall figure sprang, and grasping her light form around the waist, bore her to a place of safety—not because he guessed that it was Annie, but because it was a human being whom he would save from a fearful death.

"Excuse me, madam," he began, but whatever she might have said was lost in the low, thrilling scream of joy with which Anna recognized him.

"Charlie, Charlie! oh, Charlie!" she cried, burying her face in his bosom and sobbing like a child.

There was no time to waste in explanations; scarcely time,

indeed, for Charlie to ask where she was going, and if the necessity to go on were imperative.

"You won't leave me," Anna whispered.

"Leave you, darling? No," and pressing the little fingers twining so lovingly about his own, Charlie replied: "Whither thou goest I will go. I shall not leave you again."

He needed no words to tell him of the letters never received; he knew the truth, and satisfied to have her at last he drew her closely to him, and laying her tired head upon his bosom, gazed fondly at the face he had not seen in many, many years. Curious, tittering maidens, of whom there are usually one or two in every car, looked at that couple near the door and whispered to their companions:

"Bride and groom. Just see how he hugs her. Some widower, I know, married to a young wife."

But neither Charlie nor Anna cared for the speculations to which they were giving rise. They had found each other, and the happiness enjoyed during the two hours which elapsed ere Buffalo was reached more than made amends for all the lonely years of wretchedness they had spent apart from each other. Charlie had told Anna briefly of his life in India—had spoken feelingly, affectionately of his gentle Hattie, who had died, blessing him with her last breath for the kindness he had ever shown to her; of baby Annie's grave, by the side of which he buried the young mother; of his loneliness after that, his failing health, his yearning for a sight of home, his embarkation for America, his hope through all that she might still be won; his letters and her mother's reply, which awakened his suspicions, and his last letter which she received.

Sweetly she chided him, amid her tears, for not coming to her at once, telling how she had waited and watched with an anxious heart, ever since she heard of his return; and then she told him next where she was going, and why, sparing her brother as much as possible, and dwelling long upon poor Lily's gentleness and beauty.

So it was settled that Charlie should go with her, and his presence made her far less impatient than she would otherwise have been, when, owing to some accident, they were delayed so long that the Cleveland train was gone, and there was no alternative but to wait in Buffalo. At Cincinnati there was another detention, and it was not until the very day appointed for the wedding that, with Charlie still beside her, Anna entered the carriage hired at Lexington, and started for Spring Bank, whither for a little we will precede her, taking up the narrative prior to this day, and about the time when 'Lina first returned from New York, laden with arrogance and airs.

CHAPTER XXXVII

MATTERS AT SPRING BANK

It had been a bright, pleasant day in March, when 'Lina was expected home, and in honor of her arrival the house at Spring Bank wore its most cheery aspect; not that any one was particularly pleased because she was coming, unless it were the mother; but it was still an event of some importance, and so the negroes cleaned and scrubbed and scoured, wondering if "Miss 'Lina done fotch 'em anything," while Alice arranged and re-arranged the plainly-furnished rooms, feeling beforehand how the contrast between them and the elegancies to which 'Lina had recently been accustomed would affect her.

Hugh had thought of the same thing, and much as it hurt him to do it, he sold one of his pet colts, and giving the proceeds to Alice, bade her use it as she saw fit.

Spring Bank had never looked one-half so well before, and the negroes were positive there was nowhere to be found so handsome a room as the large airy parlor, with its new Brussels carpet and curtains of worsted brocatelle.

Even Hugh was somewhat of the same opinion, but then he only looked at the room with Alice standing in its center, or stooping in some corner to drive again a refractory nail, so it is not strange that he should judge it favorably. Ad would be pleased, he knew, and he gave orders that the carriage and harness should be thoroughly cleaned, and the horses well groomed, for he would make a good impression upon his sister.

Alas, she was not worth the trouble, the proud, selfish creature, who, all the way from Lexington to the Big Spring station had been hoping Hugh would not take it into his head to meet her, or if he did, that he would not have on his homespun suit of gray, with his pants tucked in his boots, and so disgrace her in the eyes of Mr. and Mrs. Ford, her traveling companions, who would see him from the window. Yes, there he was, standing expectantly upon the platform, and she turned her head the other way pretending not to see him until the train moved on and Hugh compelled her notice by grasping her hand and calling her "Sister 'Lina."

She had acquired a certain city air by her sojourn in New York, and in her fashionably made traveling dress and hat was far more stylish looking than when Hugh last parted from her. But nothing abashed he held her hand a moment while he inquired about her journey, and then playfully added:

"Upon my word, Ad, you have improved a heap, in looks I mean. Of course I don't know about the temper. Spunky as ever, eh?" and he tried to pinch her glowing cheek.

"Pray don't be foolish," was 'Lina's impatient reply, as she drew away from him, and turned, with her blandest smile, to a sprig of a lawyer from Frankfort, who chanced to be there too.

Chilled by her manner, Hugh ordered the carriage, and told her they were ready. Once inside the carriage, and alone with him, 'Lina's tongue was loosened, and she poured out numberless questions, the first of which was, what they heard from Adah, and if it were true, as her mother had written, that she was at Terrace Hill as Rose Markham, and that no one there knew of her acquaintance with Spring Bank?

Yes, he supposed it was, and he did not like it either. "Ad," and he turned his honest face full toward her, "does that doctor still believe you rich?"

"How do I know?" 'Lina replied, frowning gloomily. "I'm not to blame if he does. I never told him I was."

"But your actions implied as much, which amounts to the same thing. It's all wrong, Ad, all wrong. Even if he loves you, and it is to be hoped he does, he will respect you less when he knows how you deceived him."

"Hadn't you better interfere and set the matter right?" asked 'Lina, now really aroused.

"I did think of doing so once," Hugh rejoined, but ere he could say more, 'Lina grasped his arm fiercely, her face dark with passion as she exclaimed:

"Hugh, if you meddle, you'll rue the day. It's my own affair, and I know what I'm doing."

"I do not intend to meddle, though I encouraged Adah in her wild plan of going to Terrace Hill, because I thought they would learn from her just how rich we are. But Adah has foolishly taken another name, and says nothing of Spring Bank. I don't like it, neither does Miss Johnson. Indeed, I sometimes think she is more anxious than I am."

"Miss Johnson," and 'Lina spoke disdainfully, "I'd thank her to mind her own business. Hugh, you are getting a ministerial kind of look, and you have not sworn at me once since we met. I guess Alice has converted you. Well, I only hope you'll not backslide."

'Lina laughed hatefully, and evidently expected an outburst of passion, but though Hugh turned very white, he made her no reply, and they proceeded on in silence, until they came in sight of Spring Bank, when 'Lina broke out afresh.

Such a tumble-down shanty as that. It was not fit for decent people to live in, and mercy knew she was glad her sojourn there was to be short.

"You are not alone in that feeling," came dryly from Hugh.

'Lina said he was a very affectionate brother; that she was glad there were those who appreciated her, even if he did not, and then the carriage stopped at Spring Bank. Mrs. Worthington was hearty in her welcome, for her mother heart went out warmly toward her daughter. Oh, what airs 'Lina did put on, offering the tips of her fingers to good Aunt Eunice, trying to patronize Alice herself, and only noticing Densie Densmore with a haughty stare.

Old Densie had for the last few days been much in 'Lina's mind. She had disliked her at Saratoga, and somehow it made her feel uncomfortable every time she thought of finding her at Spring Bank. Densie had never forgotten 'Lina, and many a time had she recalled the peculiar expression of her black eyes, shuddering as she remembered how much they were like another pair of eyes whose gleams of passion had once thrilled her with terror.

"Upon my word," 'Lina began, as she entered the pleasant parlor, "this is better than I expected. Somebody has been very kind for my sake. Miss Johnson, I'm sure it's you I have to thank," and with a little flash of gratitude she turned to Alice, who replied in a low tone:

"Thank your brother. He made a sacrifice for the sake of surprising you."

Whether it was with a desire to appear amiable in Alice's eyes, or because she really was touched with Hugh's generosity, 'Lina involuntarily threw her arm around his neck, and gave to him a kiss which he remembered for many, many years. At the nicely prepared dinner served soon after her arrival, a cloud lowered on 'Lina's brow, induced by the fact that Densie Densmore was permitted a seat at the table, a proceeding sadly at variance with 'Lina's lately acquired ideas of aristocracy.

Accordingly that very day she sought an opportunity to speak with her mother when she knew that Densie was in an adjoining room.

"Mother," she began, "why do you suffer that woman to come to the table? Is it a whim of Alice's, or what?"

"Oh, you allude to Mrs. Densmore. I couldn't at first imagine whom you meant," Mrs. Worthington replied, going on to say how foolish it was for 'Lina to assume such airs, that Densie was as good as anybody, or at all events was a quiet, well-behaved woman, worthy of respect, and that Hugh would as soon stay away himself as banish her from the table because she had once been a servant.

"Yes, but consider Dr. Richards when he comes. What must he think of us? At the North they recognize white niggers as well as black. I tell you I won't have it, and unless you speak to her, I shall."

'Lina ate her supper exultingly, free from Densie's presence, caring little for the lonely old woman whose lip quivered and whose tears started every time that she remembered the slighting words accidentally overheard.

Swiftly the days went by, bringing callers to see 'Lina; Ellen Tiffton, who received back her jewelry, never guessing that the bracelet she clasped upon her arm was not the same lent so many months ago. Ellen was to be bridesmaid, inasmuch as Alice preferred to be more at liberty, and see that matters went on properly. This brought Ellen often to Spring Bank, and as 'Lina was much with her, Alice was left more time to think. Adah's continued silence with regard to Dr. Richards had troubled her at first, but now she felt relieved. 'Lina had stated distinctly that ere coming to Kentucky, he was going to Terrace Hill, and Adah's last letter had said the same. She would see him then, and if—if he were George—alas! for the unsuspecting girl who fluttered gayly in the midst of her bridal finery, and wished the time would come when she could "escape from that hole, and go back to dear, delightful Fifth Avenue Hotel."

The time which hung so heavily upon her hands was flying rapidly, and at last only one week intervened ere the eventful day. Hugh had gone down to Frankfort on some errand for 'Lina, and as he passed the penitentiary, he thought, as he always did now, of the convict Sullivan. Was he there still, and if so, why could he not see him face to face, and question him of the past?

Three hours later and Hugh Worthington was confronting the famous negro stealer, who gave him back glance for glance, and stood as unflinchingly before him as if there were upon his conscience no Adah Hastings, who, by his connivance, had been so terribly wronged. At the mention of her name, however, his bold assurance left him. There was a quivering of the muscles about his mouth, and his whole manner was indicative of strong emotion as he asked if Hugh knew aught of her since that fatal night, and then listened while Hugh told what he knew and where she had gone.

"To Terrace Hill—into the Richards family; this was no chance arrangement?" and the convict spoke huskily, asking next for the doctor; and still Hugh did not suspect the magnitude of the plot, and answered by telling how Dr. Richards was coming soon to make 'Lina his wife.

Hugh was not looking at his companion then, or he would have been appalled by the livid, fearful expression which for an instant flashed on his face. Accustomed to conceal his feelings, the convict did so now; and asked calmly when the wedding would take place. Hugh named the day and hour, and then asked if Sullivan knew aught of Adah's husband.

"Yes, everything," and the convict said vehemently, "Young man, I cannot tell you now—there is not time, but wait a little and you shall know the whole. You are interested in Adah. The wedding, you say, is Thursday night. My time expires on Tuesday. Don't think me impudent if I ask a list of the invited guests. Will you give it to me?"

Surely there was some deep mystery here, and he made no reply till Sullivan again asked for the list. The original paper on which Hugh had first written the few names of those to be invited chanced to be in his vest pocket, and mechanically taking it out he passed it to the convict, who expressed his thanks, and added: "Don't say that you have seen me, or that I shall be present at that wedding. I shall only come for good, but I shall surely be there."

CHAPTER XXXVIII

THE DAY OF THE WEDDING

Dr. Richards had arrived at Spring Bank. Hugh was the first to meet him. For a moment he scrutinized the stranger's face earnestly, and then asked if they had never met before.

"Not to my knowledge," the doctor replied in perfect good faith, for he had no suspicion that the man eying him so closely was the one witness of his marriage with Adah, the stranger whom he scarcely noticed, and whose name he had forgotten.

Once fully in the light, where Hugh could discern the features plainer, he began to be less sure of having met his guest before, for that immense mustache and those well-trimmed whiskers had changed the doctor's physiognomy materially.

'Lina was glad to see the doctor. She had even cried at his delay, and though no one knew it, had sat up nearly the whole preceding night, waiting and listening by her open window for any sound to herald his approach.

As the result of this long vigil, her head ached dreadfully the next day, and even the doctor noticed her burning cheeks and watery eyes, and feeling her rapid pulse asked if she were ill.

She was not, she said; she had only been troubled because he did not come, and then for once in her life she did a womanly act. She laid her head in the doctor's lap and cried, just as she had done the previous night. He understood the cause of her tears at last, and touched with a greater degree of tenderness for her than he had ever before experienced, he smoothed her glossy black hair, and asked:

"Would you be very sorry to lose me?"

Selfish and hard as she was, 'Lina loved the doctor, and with a shudder as she thought of the deception imposed on him, and a half regret that she had so deceived him, she replied:

"I am not worthy of you. I do love you very much, and it would kill me to lose you now. Promise that when you find, as you will, how bad I am, you will not hate me!"

It was an attempt at confession, but the doctor did not so construe it. Poor 'Lina. It is not often we have seen her thus—gentle, softened, womanly; so we will make the most of it, and remember it in the future.

The bright sunlight of the next morning was very exhilarating, and though the doctor, who had risen early, was disappointed in Spring Bank, he was not at all suspicious, and greeted his bride-elect kindly, noticing, while he did so, how her cheeks alternately paled, and then grew red, while she seemed to be chilly and cold. 'Lina had passed a wretched night, tossing from side to side, bathing her throbbing head and rubbing her aching limbs. The severe cold taken in the wet yard was making itself visible, and she came to the breakfast table jaded, wretched and sick, a striking contrast to Alice Johnson, who seemed to the doctor more beautiful than ever. She was unusually gay this morning, for while talking to Dr. Richards, whom she had met in the parlor, she had, among other things concerning Snowdon, said to him, casually, as it seemed:

"Anna has a waiting maid at last. You saw her, of course?"

Somehow the doctor fancied Alice wished him to say yes, and as he had seen Adah's back, he replied at once:

"Oh, yes, I saw her. Fine looking for a servant. Her little boy is splendid."

Alice was satisfied. The shadow lifted from her spirits. Dr. Richards was not George Hastings. He was not the villain she had feared, and 'Lina might have him now. Poor 'Lina. Alice felt almost as if she had done her a wrong by suspecting the doctor, and was very kind to her that day. Poor 'Lina, we say it again, for hard, and wicked, and treacherous, and unfilial, as she had ever been, she had need for pity on this her wedding day. Retribution, terrible and crushing, was at hand, hurrying on in the carriage bringing Anna Richards to Spring Bank, and on the fleet-footed steed bearing the convict swiftly up the Frankfort pike.

'Lina could not tell what ailed her. Her *hauteur* of manner was all gone, and Mug, who had come into the room to see "the finery," was not chidden or told to let them alone, while Densie, who, at Alice's suggestion, brought her a glass of wine, was kindly thanked, and even asked to stay if she liked while the dressing went on. But Densie did not care to, and she left the room just as the mud-bespattered vehicle containing Anna Richards drove up, Mr. Millbrook having purposely stopped in Versailles, thinking it better that Anna should go on alone.

It was Ellen of course, 'Lina said, and so the dressing continued, and she was all unsuspicious of the scene enacting below, in the room where Anna met her brother alone. She had not given Hugh her name. She simply asked for Dr. Richards, and conducting her into the parlor, hung with bridal decorations, Hugh went for the doctor, amusing himself on the back piazza with the sprightly Mug, who when asked if she were not sorry Miss 'Lina was going off, had naïvely answered:

"No-o—sir, 'case she done jaw so much, and pull my har. I tell you, she's a peeler. Is you glad she's gwine?"

The doctor was not quite certain, but answered: "Yes, very glad," just as Hugh announced "a lady who wished to see him."

Mechanically the doctor took his way to the parlor, while Hugh resumed his seat by the window, where for the last hour he had watched for the coming of one who had said, "I will be there."

Half an hour later, had he looked into the parlor, he would

have seen a frightened, white-faced man crouching at Anna Richards' side and whispering to her as if all life, all strength, all power to act for himself were gone:

"What must I do? Tell me what to do."

This was a puzzle to Anna, and she replied by asking him another question. "Do you love 'Lina Worthington?"

"I—I—no, I guess I don't; but she's rich, and—"

With a motion of disgust Anna cut him short, saying: "Don't make me despise you more than I do. Until your lips confessed it, I had faith that Lily was mistaken, that your marriage was honorable, at least, even if you tired of it afterward. You are worse than I suppose and now you speak of money. What shall you do? Get up and not sit whining at my feet like a puppy. Find Lily, of course, and if she will stoop to listen a second time to your suit, make her your wife, working to support her until your hands are blistered, if need be."

Anna hardly knew herself in this phase of her character, and her brother certainly did not.

"Don't be hard on me, Anna," he said, looking at her in a kind of dogged, uncertain way. "I'll do what you say, only don't be hard. It's come so sudden, that my head is like a whirlpool. Lily, Willie, Willie. The child I saw, you mean—yes, the child—I—saw—did it say he—was—my—boy?"

The words were thick and far apart. The head drooped lower and lower, the color all left the lips, and in spite of Anna's vigorous shakes, or still more vigorous hartshorn, overtaxed nature gave way, and the doctor fainted at last. It was Anna's turn now to wonder what she should do, and she was about summoning aid from some quarter when the door opened suddenly, and Hugh ushered in a stranger—the convict, who had kept his word, and came to tell what he knew of this complicated mystery, about which every invited guest was talking, and which was keeping Ellen Tiffton at home in a fever of excitement to know what it all meant.

"There will be no bridal at Spring Bank tonight, and if the invited guests have any respect for the family, they will remain quietly at home, restraining their curiosity until another day.

"One Who Has Authority."

Such were the contents of the ten different notes left at ten different houses in the neighborhood of Spring Bank that April day, by a strange horseman, who carried them all himself and saw that they were delivered.

The rider kept on his way, reining his panting steed at last before the door of Spring Bank, and casting about him anxious glances as he sprang up the steps. There was nobody in sight but Hugh, who was expecting him, and who, in reply to his inquiries for the doctor, told where he was, and that a stranger was with him.

There was a low, hurried conversation between the two, a partial revelation of the business which had brought Sullivan to the house where were congregated so many of his victims; and at its close Hugh's face was deadly white, for he knew now that he had met Dr. Richards before, and that 'Lina could not be his wife.

"The villain!" he muttered, involuntarily clinching his fist as if to smite the dastard as he followed Sullivan into the parlor, starting back when he saw the prostrate form upon the floor, and heard the lady say: "My brother, sir, has fainted."

She was Anna, then; and Hugh guessed rightly why she was there.

"Madam," he began, but ere another word was uttered, there fell upon his ear a shriek which seemed to cleave the very air and made even the fainting man move in his unconsciousness.

It was Mrs. Worthington, who, with hands outstretched as if to keep him off, stood upon the threshold, gazing in mute terror at the horror of her life, whispering incoherently: "What is it, Hugh? How came he here? Save me, save me from him!"

A look, half of sorrow, half of contempt, flitted across the stranger's face as he answered for Hugh kindly, gently: "Is the very sight of me so terrible to you, Eliza? I am only here to set matters right. Here for our daughter's sake. Eliza, where is our child?"

He had drawn nearer to her as he said this last, but she intuitively turned to Hugh, who started suddenly, growing white and faint as a suspicion of the truth flashed upon him.

"Mother?" he began, interrogatively, winding his arm about her, for she was the weaker of the two.

She knew what he would ask, and with her eye still upon the man who fascinated her gaze, she answered, sadly: "Forgive me, Hugh. He was—my husband; he is—'Lina's father, not yours, Hugh—oh! Heaven be praised, not yours!" and she clung closely to her boy, as if glad one child, at least, was not tainted with the Murdock blood.

The convict smiled bitterly, and said to Hugh himself:

"Your mother is right. She was once my wife, but the law set her free from the galling chain. Will some one call Densie Densmore in? I may need her testimony."

No one volunteered to go for Densie Densmore, and he was about repeating his request, when Alice came tripping down the stairs, and pausing at the parlor door, looked in.

"Anna!" she exclaimed, but uttered no other sound for the terror of something terrible, which kept her silent.

She stood looking from one to the other, until the convict said:

"Young lady, will you call in Densie Densmore? And stay, let the bride know. She is wanted, too. I may as well confront all my victims at once."

Alice never knew what she said to Densie, or 'Lina either. She was only conscious of following them both down the stairs and into that dreadful room. No one had said that she was wanted, but she could not keep away. She must go, and she did, keeping close to Densie, who took but one step, then with a delirious laugh, she darted upon the stranger like a tigress, and seizing his arm, said, between a shriek and hiss:

"David Murdock, why are you here, a wolf in the sheepfold? Tell me, where is my stolen daughter?"

For an instant the convict regarded the raving woman, and then, as if in answer to her question, with a half nod, his glance rested on 'Lina, who, too much terrified to speak, had crept near to her affianced husband, now returning to consciousness. Hugh alone saw the nod, and it brought him at once to 'Lina, where, with his arm upon her chair, he stood as if he would protect her. Noble Hugh! 'Lina never knew one-half how good and generous he was until just as she was losing him.

"Densie," the convict said, trying in vain to shake off the hand which held him so firmly: "Densie, be calm, and wait, as you see the others doing. They all, save one, are interested in me."

"But my daughter, my stolen daughter. I'll have her, or your life!" was Densie's fierce reply.

"Auntie," and Alice glided to Densie's side.

She alone could control that strange being, roused now as she had not been roused in years. At the sound of her voice, and the touch of her fingers on her hand, Densie released her hold and suffered herself to be led to a chair, while Alice knelt beside her.

There was a moment's hesitancy, and his face flushed and paled alternately ere the convict could summon courage to begin.

"Take this seat, sir, you need it," Hugh said, bringing him a chair and then resuming his watch over 'Lina, who involuntarily leaned her throbbing head upon his arm, and with the others listened to that strange tale of sin.

CHAPTER XXXIX

THE CONVICT'S STORY

"**I**t is not an easy task to confess how bad one has been," the stranger said, "and once no power could have tempted me to do it; but several years of prison life have taught me some wholesome lessons, and I am not the same man I was when, Densie Densmore"—and his glance turned toward her—"when I met you, and won your love. Against you first I sinned. You are my oldest victim, and it's meet I should begin with you."

"Yes, with me—me first, and tell me quick of my stolen baby," she faintly moaned.

Her ferocity of manner all was gone, and the poor, white-haired creature sat quietly where Alice had put her, while the story proceeded:

"You know, Densie, but these do not, how I won your love with promises of marriage, and then deserted you just when you needed me most. I had found new prey by that time—was on the eve of marriage with one who was too good for me. I left you and married Mrs. Eliza Worthington. I—"

The story was interrupted at this point by a cry from 'Lina, who moaned:

"No, no, oh no! He is not my father; is he, Hugh? Tell me no. John, Dr. Richards, pray look at me and say it's all a dream, a dreadful dream! Oh, Hugh!" and to the brother, scorned so often, poor 'Lina turned for sympathy, while the stranger continued:

"It would be useless for me to say now that I loved her, Eliza, but I did, and when I heard soon after my marriage that I was a father, I said: 'Densie will never rest now until she finds me, and she must not come between me and Eliza,' so I feigned an excuse and left my new wife for a few weeks. Eliza, you remember I said I had business in New York, and so I had. I went to Densie Densmore. I professed sorrow for the past. I made her believe me, and then laid a most diabolical plan. Money will do anything, and I had more than people supposed. I had a mother, too, at that time, a woman old and infirm, and good, even if I was her son. To her I went with a tale, half false, half true. There was a little child, I said, a little girl, whose mother was not my wife. I would have made her so, I said, but she died at the child's birth. Would my mother take that baby for my sake? She did not refuse, so I named a day when I would bring it. 'Twas that day, Densie, when I took you to the museum, and on pretense of a little business I must transact at a house in Park Row, I left you for an hour, but never went back again."

"No, never back again—never. I waited so long, waited till I almost thought I heard my baby cry, and then went home; but baby was gone. Alice, do you hear me?—baby was gone;" and the poor, mumbling creature, rocking to and fro, buried her bony fingers in Alice's fair hair.

"Poor Densie! poor auntie!" was all Alice said, as she regarded with horror the man, who went on:

"Yes, baby was gone—gone to my mother's, in a part of the city where there was no probability of its being found and I was gone, too. You are shocked, fair maiden, and well you may be," the convict said.

"In course of time there was a daughter born to me and to Eliza; a sweet little, brown-haired, brown-eyed girl, whom we named Adaline."

Instinctively every one in that room glanced at the black eyes and hair of 'Lina, marveling at the change.

"I loved this little girl, as it was natural I should, more than I loved the other, whose mother was a servant. Besides that, she was not so deeply branded as the other; see—" and pushing back the thick locks from his forehead, he disclosed his birthmark, while 'Lina suddenly put her hand where she knew there was another like it.

"At last there came a separation. Eliza would not live with me longer and I went away, but pined so for my child that I contrived to steal her, and carried her to my mother, where was the other one. 'Twas there you tracked me, Densie. You came one day, enacting a fearful scene, and frightening my children until they fled in terror and hid away from your sight."

"I remember, I remember now. That's where I heard the name," 'Lina said, while the convict continued:

"I said you were a mad woman. I made mother believe it; but she never recovered from the shock, and six weeks after your visit, I was alone with my two girls, Densie and Adaline. I could not attend to them both, and so I sent one to Eliza and kept the other myself, hiring a housekeeper, and to prevent being dogged by Densie again, I passed as Mr. Monroe Gordon, guardian to the little child whom I loved so much."

"That was Adah," fell in the whisper from the doctor's lips, but caught the ear of no one.

All were too intent upon the story, which proceeded:

"She grew, and grew in beauty, my fair, lovely child, and I was wondrously proud of her, giving her every advantage in my power. I sent her to the best of schools, and even looked forward to the day when she should take the position she was so well fitted to fill. After she was grown to girlhood we boarded, she as the ward, I as the guardian still, and then one unlucky day I stumbled upon you, Dr. John, but not until you had first stumbled upon my daughter, and been charmed with her beauty, passing yourself as some one else—as George Hastings, I believe—lest your fashionable associates should know how the aristocratic Dr. Richards was in love with a poor, unknown orphan, boarding up two flights of stairs."

"Who is he talking about, Hugh? Does he mean me? My head throbs so, I don't quite understand," 'Lina said, piteously, while Hugh held the poor aching head against his bosom, crushing the orange blossoms, and whispering softly:

"He means Adah."

"Yes, Adah," the convict rejoined. "John Richards fancied Adah Gordon, as she was called, but loved his pride and position more. I'll do you justice, though, young man, I believe at one time you really and truly loved my child, and but for your mother's letters might have married her honorably. But you were afraid of that mother. Your pride was stronger than your love; and as I was determined that you should have my daughter, I proposed a mock marriage."

"Monster! You, her father, planned that fiendish act!" and Alice's blue eyes flashed indignantly upon him, while Hugh, forgetting that the idea was not new to him, walked up before the "monster," as if to lay him at his feet.

"Listen, while I explain, and you will see the monster had an object," returned the stranger, speaking to Alice, instead of Hugh. "There were several reasons why I wished Adah to marry Dr. Richards, and as one of them concerns this scar upon my forehead, I will tell you here its history. You, madam," addressing himself to Anna, "have probably heard how your greatgrandfather died."

"It happened almost a century of years ago, when there was not the difference of position between the proud Richards line and the humble Murdocks that there is now. Your greatgrandfather and mine were friends, boon companions, but one fatal night, when more wine than usual had been drunk, there arose a fearful quarrel between the two, and with a knife snatched from a sideboard standing near, Murdock gave his comrade a blow which resulted in his death. Sobered at once, and nearly beside himself with terror, he rushed frantically to the chamber of his sleeping wife, and laying his blood-wet hands upon her brow, screamed for her to rise, which she did immediately, nearly fainting, it is said, when by the light of the lamp her husband bore, she saw the bloody print upon her forehead. Three months afterward my grandfather was born, and over his left temple was the hated mark which has clung to us ever since, and which a noted clairvoyant predicted would never disappear until the feudal parties came together, and a Murdock wedding with a Richards. The offspring of such union would be without taint or blemish, he said, and I am told, sir, your boy is fair as alabaster."

Dr. Richards, to whom this appeal was made, only stared blankly at him, like one who hears in a dream, but 'Lina, catching at everything pertaining to the doctor, said, quickly:

"His boy! Where is his boy? Oh, what does it all mean?"

"Poor girl!" and the convict spoke sorrowfully. "I did not think she would take it so hard, but the worst is not yet told, and I must hasten. I ingratiated myself at once into John Richards' good graces and when I knew it would answer, I suggested a mock marriage. First, however, I would know something definite of his family as they were then, and so, as a Mr. Morris, who wished to purchase a country seat, I went to Snowdon, and after some inquiries in the village, forced my way to Terrace Hill. The lady listening to me was the only one I saw, and I felt sure she at least would be kind to Adah. On my return to New York, I urged the marriage more pertinaciously than at first, saying, by way of excusing myself, that as I was only Adah's guardian, I could not, of course, feel toward her as a near relative would feel—that as I had already expended large sums of money on her, I was getting tired of it, and would be glad to be released, hinting, by way of smoothing the fiendish proposition, my belief that, from constant association, he would come to love her so much that at last he would really and truly make her his wife. He did hesitate—he did seem shocked, and if I remember rightly, called me a brute, an unnatural guardian, and all that; but little by little I gained ground, until at last he consented, and I hurried the matter at once, lest he should repent.

"I had an acquaintance, I said, who lived a few miles from the city—a man who, for money, would do anything, and who, as a feigned justice of the peace, would go through with the ceremony, and ever after keep his own counsel. I wonder the doctor did not make some inquiries concerning this so-called justice, but I think I am right in saying that he is not remarkably clear-headed, and this weakness saved me much trouble, and after a long time I arranged the matter with my friend, who was a lawful justice, staying with his brother, at that time absent in Europe. This being done, I decided upon Hugh Worthington for a witness, as being the person, of all the world, who should be present at Adah's bridal. He had recently come to New York. I had accidentally made his acquaintance, acquiring so strong an influence over him that I could almost mold him to my will. I did not tell him what I wanted until I had tempted him with drugged wine, and he did not realize what he was doing. He knew enough, however, to sign his name and to salute the bride, who really was a bride, as lawful a one as any who ever turned from the altar where she had registered her vows."

"Oh, joy, joy!" and Alice sprang at once to her feet, and hastening to the doctor's side, said to him, authoritatively:

"You hear, you understand, Adah is your wife, your very own, and you must go back to her at once. She's in your own home as Rose Markham. She went from here, Adah Hastings, whose husband's name was George. You do understand me?" and Alice grew very earnest as the doctor failed to rouse up, as she thought he ought to do.

Appealing next to Anna, she continued:

"Pray, make him comprehend that his wife is at Terrace Hill."

Very gently Anna answered:

"She was there, but she has gone. He knows it; I came to tell him, but she fled immediately after recognizing my brother, and left a letter revealing the whole."

It had come to 'Lina by this time that Dr. Richards could never be her husband, and with a bitter cry, she covered her face with her hands, and went shivering to the corner where Mrs. Worthington sat, as if a mother's sympathy were needed now, and coveted as it had never been before.

"Oh, mother," she sobbed, laying her head in Mrs. Worthington's lap, "I wish I had never been born."

Sadly her wail of disappointment rang through the room, and then the convict went on with his interrupted narrative.

"When the marriage was over, Mr. Hastings took his wife to another part of the city, hiding her from his fashionable associates, staying with her most of the time, and appearing to love her so much that I thought it would not be long before I should venture to tell him the truth. I went South on a little business which a companion and myself had planned together—the very laudable business of stealing negroes from one State and selling them in another. Some of you know that I was caught in my traffic, and that the negro stealer Sullivan, was safely lodged in prison, from which he was released but two days since. Fearing there might be some mistake, I wrote from my prison home to Adah herself, but suppose it did not reach New York till after she had left it. My poor, dear little girl, thoughts of her have helped to make me a better man than I ever was before. I am not perfect now, but I certainly am not as hard, as wicked, or bad as when I first wore the felon's dress."

A casual observer would have said that Densie Densmore had heard less of that strange story than any one else, but her hearing faculties had been sharpened, and not a word was missed by her—not a link lost in the entire narrative, and when the narrator expressed his love for his daughter, she darted upon him again, shrieking wildly:

"And that child whom you loved was the baby you stole, and I shall see her again—shall hear that blessed name of mother from her own sweet lips."

A little apart from the others, his eyes fixed earnestly upon the convict, stood Hugh. His mind, too, had gathered in every fact, but he had reached a widely different conclusion from what poor Densie had.

"Answer her," he said, gravely, as the convict did not reply. "Tell her if Adah be her child, or—'Lina—which?"

Had a clap of thunder cleft the air around her, 'Lina could not have started up sooner than she did. The convict took his eyes away from her, pitying her so much, while Densie's bony hand was raised as if to thrust her off, and Densie's voice exclaimed: "Not this, not this. She despises me, a white nigger. I will not be her mother. The other one—Densie, I named her—she is mine—"

The convict shook his head. "No, Densie, not Adah, I kept her, my lawful child, and sent the other back. It was a bold move, and I wonder it was not questioned, but Adaline's eyes were not so black then as they are now, and though six months older than the other, she was small for her age, and cannot now be so tall as Adah. The mark, too, must have strengthened the deception, as I knew it would, and eighteen months sometimes changes a child materially; so Eliza took it for granted that the girl she received as Adaline, and whose real name was Densie, was her own; but Adah Hastings is her daughter and Hugh's half sister, while this young woman is—the child of myself and Densie Densmore!"

Alice, Anna, and the doctor looked aghast, while Mrs. Worthington murmured audibly: "Adah, Adah, darling Adah, she always seemed near to me; and Willie, precious Willie—oh, I want them here now!"

One mother had claimed her own, but alas, the fond cry of welcome to sweet Adah Hastings was a death knell to 'Lina, for it seemed to shut her out of that gentle woman's heart. There was no place for her, and in her terrible desolation she stood alone, her eyes wandering wistfully from one to another, but turning very quickly when they fell on the white-haired Densie, her mother. She would not have it so; she could not own the woman she had affected to despise, that servant for her mother, that villain for her father, and worse—oh, infinitely worse than all—she had no right to be born! A child of sin and shame, disgraced, disowned, forsaken. It was a terrible blow, and the proud girl staggered beneath it.

"Will no one speak to me?" she said, at last; "no one break this dreadful silence? Has everybody forsaken me? Do you all loathe and hate the offspring of such parents? Won't somebody pity and care for me?"

"Yes, 'Lina," and Hugh—the one from whom she had the least right to expect pity—Hugh came to her side; and winding his arm around her, said, with a choking voice: "I will not forsake you, 'Lina; I will care for you the same as ever, and so long as I have a home you shall have one, too."

"Oh, Hugh, I don't deserve this from you!" was 'Lina's faint response, as she laid her head upon his bosom, whispering: "Take me away—from them all—upstairs—on the bed I am so sick, and my head is bursting open!"

Hugh was strong as a young giant, and lifting gently the

yielding form, he bore it from the room—the bridal room, which she would never enter again, until he brought her back—and laid her softly down beneath the windows, dropping tears upon her white, still face, and whispering:

"Poor 'Lina!"

As Hugh passed out with his burden in his arms, the bewildered company seemed to rally; but the convict was the first to act. Turning to Mrs. Worthington he said:

"Eliza, I am here tonight for my children's sake; and now that I have done what I came to do, I shall leave you, only asking that you continue to be a mother to the poor girl who is really the only sufferer. The rest have cause for joy; you in particular," turning to the doctor, who suddenly seemed to break the spell which had bound him, and springing to his feet, exclaimed:

"Yes, Lily shall be found, Lily shall be found; but I must see my boy first. Anna, can't we go now, tonight?"

That was impossible, Alice said; and as hers was the only clear head in the household, she set herself at once to plan for everybody. To the convict and the doctor she paid no heed; but the tired Anna was conducted at once to her own room, and made to take the rest she so much needed. Densie too was cared for kindly, soothingly; for the poor old woman was nearly crushed with all she had heard; and Alice, as she left her upon the bed, heard her muttering deliriously to herself:

"She wouldn't let her own mother eat with her. She compared me to a white nigger; and can I receive her now? No, no; and she don't wish it. Yet I pitied her when her heart snapped to pieces there in the middle of the room; poor girl, poor girl!"

When Alice returned again to the parlor, the convict had gone. There had been a short consultation between himself and the doctor, an engagement to meet in Cincinnati to arrange their plan of search; and then he had turned again to his once wife, still sitting in her corner, motionless, white, and paralyzed with nervous terror.

"You need not fear me, Eliza," he said, kindly, "I shall probably never trouble you again; and though you have no cause to believe my word, I tell you solemnly that I will never rest until I have found our daughter, and sent her back to you. Be kind to Densie Densmore; she was more sinned against than sinning. Good-by, Eliza, good-by."

He did not offer her his hand; he knew she would not touch it; but with one farewell look of contrition and regret, he left her, and mounting the horse which had brought him there, he dashed away from Spring Bank, just as Colonel Tiffton reined up to the gate.

Nell would give him no peace until he went over to see what it all meant and if there really was to be no wedding. It was Alice who met him in the hall, explaining to him as much as she thought necessary, and asking him, on his return, to wait a little by the field gate, and turn back any other guest who might be on the road.

The colonel promised compliance with her request, and thus were kept away two carriage loads of people whose curiosity had prompted them to disregard the contents of the note brought to them so mysteriously.

Spring Bank was not honored with wedding guests that night; and when the clock struck eight, the appointed hour for the bridal, only the bridegroom sat in the dreary parlor, his head bent down upon the sofa arm, and his chest heaving with the sobs he could not repress as he thought of all poor Lily had suffered since he left her so cruelly. Hugh had told him what he did not understand before. He had come into the room for his mother, whom 'Lina was pleading to see; and after leading her to the chamber of the half delirious girl, he had returned to the doctor, and related to him all he knew of Adah, dwelling long upon her gentleness and beauty, which had won from him a brother's love, even though he knew not she was his Sister.

"I was a wretch, a villain!" the doctor groaned. Then looking wistfully at Hugh, he said: "Do you think she loves me still? Listen to what she says in her farewell to Anna," and with faltering voice, he read: "That killed the love and now, if I could, I would not be his except for Willie's sake.' Do you think she meant it?"

"I have no doubt of it, sir. How could her love outlive everything? Curses and blows might not have killed it, but when you thought to ruin her good name, to deny your child, she would be less than woman could she forgive. Why, I hate and despise you myself for the wrong you have done my sister," and Hugh's tall form seemed to take on an increased height as he stood, gazing down on one who could not meet his eye, but cowered and hid his face.

It was the first time Hugh had called Adah "my sister," and it seemed to fill every nook and corner of his great heart with unutterable love for the absent girl. "Sister, sister," he kept repeating to himself, and as he did so, his resentful indignation grew toward the man who had so cruelly deceived her, until at last he abruptly left the room, lest his hot temper should get the mastery, and he knock down his dastardly brother-in-law, as he greatly wished to do.

It was a sad house at Spring Bank that night, and only the negroes were capable of any enjoyment. Terrified at first at what by dint of listening they saw and heard, they assembled in the kitchen, and together rehearsed the strange story, wondering if none of the tempting supper prepared with so much care would be touched by the whites. If not, they, of course, had the next best right, and when about midnight Mrs. Worthington passed hurriedly through the dining-room, the table gave evidence that somebody had partaken of the marriage feast, and not very sparingly either. But she did not care, her thoughts were divided between the distant Adah, her daughter—her own—the little brown-eyed child she had been so proud of years ago, and the moaning, wretched girl upstairs, 'Lina, tossing distractedly from side to side; now holding her throbbing head, and now thrusting out her hot, dry hands, as if to keep off some fancied form, whose hair, she said, was white as snow, and who claimed to be her mother.

The shock had been a terrible one to 'Lina—terrible in more senses than one. She did love Dr. Richards; and the losing him was enough of itself to drive her mad; but worse even than this, and far more humiliating to her pride, was the discovery of her parentage, the knowing that a convict was her father, a common servant her mother, and that no marriage tie had hallowed her birth.

"Oh, I can't bear it!" she cried. "I can't. I wish I might die! Will nobody kill me? Hugh, you will, I know!"

But Hugh was away for the family physician, for he would not trust a gossiping servant to do the errand. Once before that doctor had stood by 'Lina's bedside, and felt her feverish pulse, but his face then was not as anxious as now. He did not speak of danger, but Hugh, who watched him narrowly, read it in his face, and following him down the stairs, asked to be told the truth.

"She is going to be very sick. She may get well, but I have little to hope from symptoms like hers."

That was the doctor's reply, and with a sigh Hugh went back to the sick girl, who had given him little else than sarcasm and scorn.

CHAPTER XL

POOR 'LINA

Drearily the morning dawned, but there were no bridal slumbers to be broken, no bridal farewells said. There were indeed good-byes to be spoken, for Anna was impatient to be gone. But for Adah, who must be found, and Willie, who must be cared for, and Charlie, who was waiting for her, she would have tarried longer, and helped to nurse the girl whom she pitied so much. But even Alice said she had better go, and so at an early hour she was ready to leave the house she had entered under so unpleasant circumstances.

"I would like to see 'Lina," she said to Alice, who carried the request to the sick room.

But 'Lina refused. "I can't," she said; "she hates, she despises me, and she has reason. Tell her I was not worthy to be her sister; tell her anything you like; but the doctor—oh, Alice, do you think he'll come, just for a minute, before he goes?"

It was not a pleasant thing for the doctor to meet 'Lina now face to face, for of course she wished to reproach him for his treachery. But she did not—she thought only of herself; and when at last, urged on by Anna and Alice, he entered into her presence, she only offered him her hand at first, without a single word. He was shocked to find her so sick, for a few hours had worked a marvelous change in her, and he shrank from the bright eyes fixed so eagerly on his face.

"Oh Dr. Richards," she began at last, "if I loved you less it would not be so hard to tell you what I must. I did love you, bad as I am, but I meant to deceive you. It was for me that Adah kept silence at Terrace Hill. Adah, I almost hate her for having crossed my path."

There was a fearfully vindictive gleam in the bright eyes now, and the doctor shudderingly looked away, while 'Lina, with a soft tone, continued: "You believed me rich, and whether you loved me afterward or not, you sought me first for my money. I kept up the delusion, for in no other way could I have won you. Dr. Richards, if I die, as perhaps I may, I shall have one less sin for which to atone, if I confess to you that instead of the heiress you imagined me to be, I had scarcely money enough to pay my board at that hotel. Hugh, who himself is poor, furnished what means I had, and most of my jewelry was borrowed. Do you hear that? Do you know what you have escaped?"

She almost shrieked at the last.

"Go," she continued, "find your Adah. It's nothing but Adah now. I see her name in everything. Hugh thinks of nothing else, and why should he? She's his sister, and I—oh! I'm nobody but a beggarly servant's brat. I wish I was dead! I wish I was dead! and I will be pretty soon."

This was their parting, and the doctor left her room a soberer, sadder man than he had entered it. Half an hour later, and he, with Anna, was fast nearing Versailles, where they were joined by Mr. Millbrook, and together the three started on their homeward route.

Rapidly the tidings flew, told in a thousand different ways, and the neighborhood was all on fire with the strange gossip. But little cared they at Spring Bank for the storm outside, so fierce a one was beating at their doors, that even the fall of Sumter failed to elicit more than a casual remark from Hugh, who read without the slightest emotion the President's call for seventy-five thousand men. Tenderer than a brother was Hugh to the sick girl upstairs, staying by her so patiently that none save Alice ever guessed how he longed to be free and join in the search for Adah. To her it had been revealed by a few words accidentally overheard. "Oh, Adah, sister, I know that I could find you, but my duty is here."

This was what he said, and Alice felt her heart throb with increased respect for the unselfish man, who gave no other token of his impatience to be gone, but stayed home hour after hour in that close, feverish room, ministering to all of 'Lina's fancies, and treating her as if no word of disagreement had ever passed between them. Night after night, day after day, 'Lina grew worse, until at last, there was no hope, and the council of physicians summoned to her side said that she would die. Then Densie softened again, but did not go near the dying one. She could not be sent away a second time, so she stayed in her own room, which witnessed many a scene of agonizing prayer, for the poor girl passing so surely to another world.

"God save her at the last. God let her into heaven," was the burden of shattered Densie's prayer, while Alice's was much like it, and Hugh, too, more than once bowed his head upon the burning hands he held, and asked that space might be given her for repentance, shuddering as he recalled the time when, like her, he lay at death's door, unprepared to enter in. Was he prepared now? Had he made a proper use of life and health restored? Alas! that the answer conscience forced upon him should have wrung out so sharp a groan. "But I will be," he said, and laying his own face by 'Lina's, he promised that if God would bring her reason back, so they could tell her of the untried world her feet were nearing, he would henceforth be a better man, and try to serve the God who heard and answered that earnest prayer.

It was many days ere the fever abated, but there came a morning in early May when the eyes were not so fearfully bright as they had been, while the wild ravings were hushed, and 'Lina lay quietly upon her pillow.

"Do you know me?" Alice asked, bending gently over her, while Hugh, from the other side of the bed, leaned eagerly forward for the reply.

"Yes, Alice, but where am I? This is not New York—not my room. Have I—am I sick, very sick?" and 'Lina's eyes took a terrified expression as she read the truth in Alice's face. "I am not going to die, am I?" she continued, casting upon Alice a look which would have wrung out the truth, even if Alice had been disposed to withhold it, which she was not.

"You are very sick," she answered, "and though we hope for the best, the doctor does not encourage us much. Are you willing to die, 'Lina?"

Neither Hugh nor Alice ever forgot the tone of 'Lina's voice as she replied:

"Willing? No!" or the expression of her face, as she turned it to the wall, and motioned them to leave her.

For two days after that she neither spoke nor gave other token of interest in anything passing around her, but at the expiration of that time, as Alice sat by her, she suddenly exclaimed:

"Forgive us our trespasses as we forgive those who trespass against us. I wish He had said that some other way, for if that means we cannot be forgiven until we forgive everybody, there's no hope for me, for I cannot, I will not forgive Densie Densmore for being my mother, neither will I forgive Adah Hastings for having crossed my path. If she had never seen the doctor I should have been his wife, and never have known who or what I was. I hate them both, Densie and Adah, so you need not pray for me. I heard you last night, and even Hugh has taken it up, but it's no use. I can't forgive."

'Lina was very much excited—so much indeed, that Alice could not talk with her then; and for days this was the burden of her remarks. She could not forgive Densie and Adah, and until she did, there was no use for her or any one else to pray. But the prayers she could not say for herself were said for her by others, while Alice omitted no proper occasion for talking with her personally on the subject she felt to be all-important. Nor were these efforts without their effect; the bitter tone when speaking of Densie ceased at last, and Alice was one day surprised at 'Lina's asking to see her, together with Mrs. Worthington. Timidly, Densie approached the bed from which she had once been so angrily dismissed. But there was nothing to fear now from the white, wasted girl, whose large eyes fastened themselves a moment on the wrinkled face; then with a shudder, closed tightly, while the lip quivered with a grieved, suffering expression. She did not say to poor old Densie that she acknowledged her as a mother, or that she felt for her the slightest thrill of love. She was through with deception; and when, at last, she spoke to the anxiously waiting woman, it was only to say:

"I wanted to tell you that I have forgiven you; but I cannot call you mother. You must not expect it. I know no mother but this one," and the white hand reached itself toward Mrs. Worthington, who took it unhesitatingly and held it between her own, while 'Lina continued: "I've given you little cause to love me, and I know how glad you must be that another, and not I, is your real daughter. I did not know what made me so bad, but I understand it now. I saw myself so plainly in that man's eyes; it was his nature in me which made me so hateful to Hugh. Oh, Hugh! the memory of what I've been to him is the hardest part of all," and covering her face with the sheet, 'Lina wept bitterly; while Hugh, who was standing behind her, laid his warm hand on her head, smoothing her hair caressingly, as he said:

"Never mind that, 'Lina; I, too, was bad to you. If 'Lina can forgive me, I surely can forgive 'Lina."

There was the sound of convulsive sobbing; and then, uncovering her face, 'Lina raised herself up, and laying her hand on Hugh's bosom, answered through her tears:

"I wish I had always felt as I do now. Hugh, you don't know how bad I've been. Why, I used to be ashamed to call you brother, if any fine people were near."

There was a sparkle of indignation in Alice's blue eyes.

"You have no cause to be ashamed of Hugh," she said, quickly, the tone of her voice coming like a revelation to 'Lina, who scanned her face eagerly, and then, turning, looked curiously up to Hugh.

"I'm glad, I'm glad," she whispered, "for I know now you are worthy even of her."

"You are mistaken, 'Lina," Hugh said, huskily, while 'Lina continued; "And, Hugh, I must tell you more, how bad I've been. You remember the money you sent to Adah last summer in mother's letter. I kept the whole. I burned the letter, and mother never saw it. I bought jewelry with Adah's money. I did so many things, I—I—it goes from me now. I can't remember all. Oh, must I confess the whole, everything, before I can say, 'Forgive us our trespasses?'"

"No, 'Lina. Unless you can repair some wrong, you are not bound to tell every little thing. Confession is due to God alone," Alice whispered to the agitated girl, who looked bewildered, as she answered back: "But God knows all now, and you do not; besides, I can't feel sorry toward Him as I do toward others. I try and try, but the feeling is not there—the sorry feeling, I mean, as sorry as I want to feel."

"God, who knows our feebleness, accepts our purposes to do better, and gives us strength to carry them out," Alice whispered, again bending over 'Lina, on whose pallid, distressed face a ray of hope for a moment shone.

"I have good purposes," she murmured; "but I can't, I can't. I don't know as they are real; maybe, if I get well, they would not last, and it's all so dark, so desolate—nothing to make life desirable—no home, no name, no friends—and death is so terrible. Oh, Hugh, Hugh! don't let me go. You are strong; you can hold me back, even from Death himself; and I can be good to you; I can feel on that point, and I tell you truly that, standing as I am with the world behind and death before, I see nothing to make life desirable, but you, Hugh, my noble, my abused brother. To make you love me, as I hope I might, is worth living for. You would stand by me, Hugh—you, if no one else, and I wish I could tell you how fast the great throbs of love keep coming to my heart. Dear Hugh, Hugh, Brother Hugh, don't let me die—hold me fast."

With an icy shiver, she clung closer to Hugh, as if he could indeed do battle with the king of terror stealing slowly into that room.

"Somebody say 'Our Father,'" she whispered, "I can't remember how it goes."

"Do you forgive and love everybody?" Alice asked, sighing as she saw the bitter expression flash for an instant over the pinched features, while the white lips answered: "Not Adah, no, not Adah."

Alice could not pray after that, not aloud at least, and a deep silence fell upon the group assembled around the deathbed. 'Lina slept at last, slept quietly on Hugh's strong arm, and gradually the hard expression on the face relaxed, giving way to one of quiet peace, and Densie, watching her anxiously, whispered beneath her breath: "See, the Murdock is all gone, and her face is like a baby's face. Maybe she would call me mother now."

Poor Densie! Eagerly she waited for the close of that long sleep, her eye the first to note that it was ended, and 'Lina awake again. Still the silence remained unbroken, while 'Lina seemed lost to all else save the thoughts burning at her breast—thoughts which brought a quiver to her lips, and forced out upon her brow great drops of sweat, which Densie wiped away, unnoticed, it may be, or at least unrebuked. The noonday sun of May was shining broadly into the room, but to 'Lina it was night, and she said to Alice, now kneeling at her side: "It's growing dark; they'll light the street lamps pretty soon, and the band will play in the yard, but I shall not hear them. New York and Saratoga are a great ways off, and so is Terrace Hill. Tell him I meant to deceive him, but I did love him. Tell Adah I do forgive her, and I would like to see her, for she is my half sister. The bitter is all gone. I am in charity with everybody, everybody. May I say 'Our Father' now? It goes and comes, goes and comes, forgive our trespasses, my trespasses; how is it, Hugh? Say it with me once, and you, too, mother."

She did not look toward Densie, but her hand fell off that way, and Densie, with a low cry began with Hugh the soothing prayer in which 'Lina joined feebly, throwing in ejaculatory sentences of her own.

"I forgive Densie Densmore; I forgive Adah, Adah, everybody. Forgive my trespasses then as I forgive those that trespass against me. Bless Hugh, dear Hugh, noble Hugh. Forgive us our trespasses, forgive us our trespasses, our trespasses, forgive my trespasses, me, forgive, forgive."

It was the last word which ever passed 'Lina's lips, "Forgive, forgive," and Hugh, with his ear close to the lips, heard the faint murmur even after the hands had fallen from his neck where in the last struggle they had been clasped, and after the look which comes but once to all had settled on her face. That was the last of 'Lina, with that cry for pardon she passed away, and though it was but a deathbed repentance, and she, the departed, had much need for pardon, Alice and the half acknowledged mother clung to it as to a ray of hope, knowing how tender and full of compassion was the blessed Savior, even to those who turn not to Him until the river of death is bearing them away. Very gently Hugh laid the dead girl back upon the pillow, and leaving one kiss on her white forehead, hurried away to his own room, where, unseen to mortal eye, he could ask for knowledge to give himself aright to the God who had come so near to them.

There were no noisy outbursts among the negroes when told their young mistress was dead, for 'Lina had not been greatly loved. The sight of Alice's swollen eyes and tear-stained face affected Mug, it is true, but even she could not cry until she had coaxed old Uncle Sam to repeat to her, for the twentieth time, the story of Bethlehem's little children slain, by order of the cruel Herod. This story, told in old Sam's peculiar way, had the desired effect, and the tears which refused to start even at the sight of 'Lina dead, flowed freely for the little ones over whom Rachel wept, refusing to be comforted.

"I can cry dreffully now, Miss Alice, I'se sorry, Miss 'Lina is dead, very sorry. She never can come back any more, can she?" Mug sobbed, running up to Alice, and hiding her face in her dress.

And this was about as real as any grief expressed by the blacks for 'Lina. Poor 'Lina, she had taken no pains to win affection while she was living, and she could not expect to be missed much when she was gone. Hugh mourned for her the most, more even than his mother or Densie Densmore—the latter of whom seemed crazier than ever, shutting herself entirely in her room, and refusing to be present at the funeral. 'Lina had been ashamed of her, she said, and she would not disgrace her by claiming relationship now that she was dead, so with eyes whose blackness was dimmed by tears, she watched from her window the procession moving from the yard, across the fields, and out to the hillside, where the Spring Bank dead were buried, and where on the last day of blooming, beautiful

May, they laid 'Lina to rest, forgetting all her faults, and speaking only kindly words of her as they went slowly back to the house, from which she had gone forever.

CHAPTER XLI

TIDINGS

A few days after 'Lina's burial, there came three letters to Spring Bank, one to Mrs. Worthington from Murdock, as he now chose to be called, saying that though he had looked, and was still looking everywhere for the missing Adah, he could only trace her, and that but vaguely, to the Greenbush depot, where he lost sight of her entirely, no one after that having seen a person bearing the least resemblance to her. After a consultation with the doctor, he had advertised for her, and he inclosed a copy of the advertisement, as it appeared in the different papers of Boston, Albany, and New York.

"If A—— H—— will let her whereabouts be known to her friends, she will hear of something to her advantage."

This was the purport of Murdock's letter, if we except a kind of inquiry after 'Lina, of whose death he had not heard.

The second, for Alice, was from Anna Richards, who was also ignorant as yet of 'Lina's decease. After inquiring kindly for the unfortunate girl, she wrote:

"I have great hopes of my erring brother, now that I know how his whole heart goes toward his beautiful boy, our darling Willie. I wish poor, dear Lily could have seen him when, on his arrival at Terrace Hill, he not only bent over, but knelt by the crib of his sleeping child, waking him at once, and hugging him to his bosom, while his tears dropped like rain. I am sure she would have chosen to be his wife, for her own sake as well as Willie's.

"You know how proud my mother and sisters are, and it would surprise you, as it does me, to see them pet, and spoil, and fondle Willie, who rules the entire household, mother even allowing him to bring wheelbarrow, drum, and trumpet into the parlor, declaring that she likes the noise, as it stirs up her blood. Willie has made a vast change in our once quiet home, and I fear I shall meet with much opposition when I take him away, as I expect to do next month, for Lily gave him to me, and brother John has said that I may have him until the mother is found, while Charlie is perfectly willing; and thus, you see, my cup of joy is full.

"Brother is away now, hunting for Adah, and I am wicked enough not to miss him, so busy am I in the few preparations needed by the wife of a poor missionary."

Then, in a postscript. Anna added: "I forgot to tell you that Charlie and I are to be married some time in July, that the Presbyterian Society of Snowdon has given him a call to be their pastor, that he has accepted, and what is best of all, has actually rented your old home for us to live in. I don't know how it will seem to stop on Sundays at the meeting house instead of keeping on to our dear, old St.

Luke's. I love the service dearly, but I love my Charlie more, notwithstanding that he calls me his little heretic, and accuses me of proselytizing intentions towards himself. I have never confessed it before, but, seriously, I have strong hopes of seeing him yet in surplice and gown; but till that time comes, I shall be a real good Presbyterian, or orthodox, as they are called here in Massachusetts.

"Perhaps you may have heard that mother was once much opposed to Charlie. I must say, however, that she has done well at the last, for when I told her I had found him, and that we were to be married, she said she was glad on the whole, as it relieved her of a load, and she hoped I would be happy."

Anna did not explain to Alice that the load of which her mother was relieved was mostly Charlie's hidden letters, given up with a full confession of the pains taken to conceal them, and a frank acknowledgment of wrong to Anna, who, as her letter indicated, was far too happy to be angry for a single moment. With a smile, Alice finished the childlike letter, so much like Anna. Then feeling that Hugh would be glad to hear from Willie, she went in quest of him, finding him at the end of the long piazza, where he sat gazing vacantly at the open letter in his hand—Irving Stanley's letter, which he passed at once to Alice in exchange for Anna's given to him.

Glancing at the name at the bottom of the page, Alice blushed painfully, feeling rather than seeing that Hugh was watching her, and guessing of what he was thinking. Irving did not know of 'Lina's death. From Dr. Richards, whom he had accidentally met on Broadway, he had heard of her sudden illness, and apparently accepted that as the reason why the marriage was not consummated. Intuitively, however, he felt that there must be something behind, but he was far too well-bred to ask any idle questions, and in his letter he merely inquired after 'Lina, as after any sick friend, playfully hoping that for the sake of the doctor, who looked very blue, she would soon recover and make him the happiest man alive. Then followed some allusions to the relationship existing between himself and Hugh, with regrets that more had not been made of it, and then he said that having decided to accompany his sister and Mrs. Ellsworth on her tour to Europe, whither she would go the latter part of July, and having nothing in particular to occupy him in the interim, he would, with Hugh's permission, spend a few days at Spring Bank. He did not say he was coming to see Alice Johnson, but Hugh understood it just the same, feeling confident that his sole object in visiting Kentucky was to take Alice back with him, and carry her off to Europe.

Some such idea flitted across Alice's mind as she read that letter, and for a single instant her eyes sparkled with delight at the thought of wandering over Europe in company with Mrs. Ellsworth and Irving Stanley; but when she looked at Hugh, the bright vision faded, and with it all desire to go with Irving Stanley, even should he ask her. Hugh needed her more than Irving Stanley. He was, if possible, more worthy of her. His noble, unselfish devotion to 'Lina had finished the work begun on that memorable night, when she said to him: "I may learn to love you," and from the moment when to 'Lina's passionate cry, "Will no one pity me?" he had answered, "Yes, 'Lina, I will care for you," her heart had been all his own, and more than once as she watched with him by 'Lina's bedside, she had been tempted to wind her arm around his neck and whisper in his ear:

"Hugh, I love you now, I will be your wife."

But propriety had held her back and made her far more reserved toward him than she had ever been before. Terribly jealous where she was concerned, Hugh was quick to notice the change, and the gloomy shadow on his face was not caused wholly by 'Lina's sad death, as many had supposed. Hugh was very unhappy. Instead of learning to love him, as he had sometimes hoped she might, Alice had come to dislike him, shunning his society, and always making some pretense to get away if, by chance, they were left alone; and now, as the closing act in the sad drama, Irving Stanley was coming to carry her off forever.

Hugh's heart was very sore as he sat there waiting for Alice to finish that letter, and speak to him about it. What a long, long time it took her to read it through—longer than it needed, he was sure, for the handwriting was very plain and the letter very brief.

Alice knew he was waiting for her, and after hesitating a while, she went up to him, and laying her hand on his shoulder, as she had not done in weeks, she said:

"You will be glad to see your cousin?"

"Yes; I suppose so. Shall you?"

He turned partly around, so he could look at her; and this it was which brought the blood so quickly to her face, making her stammer as she replied:

"Of course I shall be glad. I like him very much; but—"

Here she stopped, for she did not know how to tell Hugh that she was not glad in the way which he supposed.

"But what?" he asked, "What were you going to say?" and in his eyes there was a look which drove Alice's courage away, and made her answer:

"It's queer the doctor did not tell him anything except that 'Lina was sick."

"There are a great many queer people in this world," Hugh replied, rather testily, while Alice mildly rejoined.

"The letter has been delayed, and he will be here day after tomorrow. Did you notice?"

"Yes; and as I am impatient to go for Adah, the sooner he comes the better, for the sooner it will leave me at liberty. Would it be very impolite for me to go at once, and leave you to entertain him?"

"Of course it would," said Alice. "Adah's claim is a strong one, I'll admit; but the doctor and Mr. Murdock are doing their best; and I ask, as a favor, that you remain at home to meet Mr. Stanley."

Now Hugh knew that nothing could have tempted him to leave Spring Bank so long as Irving Stanley was there; but as he was just in a mood to be unreasonable, he replied that, "if Alice wished it, he should remain at home until Mr. Stanley's visit was ended."

Alice felt exceedingly uncomfortable, for never had Hugh been so provokingly distant and cool, and she was really glad when at last a carriage appeared across the fields, and she knew the "city cousin," as Hugh called him, was coming.

CHAPTER XLII

IRVING STANLEY

He had come, and up in the chamber where 'Lina died, was making the toilet necessary after his hot dusty ride. Hugh, heartily ashamed of his conduct for the last two days, had received him most cordially, meeting him at the gate, and holding him by the hand, as they walked together to the house, where Mrs. Worthington stood waiting for him, her lips quivering, and tears dimming her eyes, as she said to him: "Yes, 'Lina is dead."

Irving had heard as much at the depot, and heard, too, a strange story, the truth of which he greatly doubted. Mrs. Worthington had been 'Lina's mother, he believed, and his sympathy went out toward her at once, making him forget that Alice was not there to meet him, as he half expected she would be, although they were really comparative strangers.

It was not until a rather late hour that Alice joined him, sitting upon the cool piazza, with Hugh as his companion. In summer Alice always wore white, and now, as she came tripping down the long piazza, her muslin dress floating about her like a snowy mist, her fair hair falling softly about her face and on her neck, a few geranium leaves twined among the glossy curls, and her lustrous eyes sparkling with excitement, both Irving Stanley and Hugh held their breath and watched her as she came, the one jealously and half angry that she was so beautiful, the other admiringly and with a feeling of wonder at the beauty he had never seen surpassed.

Alice was perfectly self-possessed, and greeted Mr. Stanley as she would have greeted any friend—and she was glad to see him—spoke of Saratoga, and then inquired for Mrs. Ellsworth about whom poor 'Lina had talked so much.

Mrs. Ellsworth was well, Irving said, though very busy with her preparations for going to Europe, adding "it was not so much pleasure which was taking her there as by the hope that by some of the Paris physicians her little deformed Jennie might be benefited. She had secured a gem of a governess for her daughter, a young lady whom he had not yet seen, but over whose beauty and accomplishments his staid sister Carrie had really waxed eloquent."

Hugh cared nothing for that governess, and after a little, thinking he was not wanted, stole quietly away, and being moodily inclined, rambled off to 'Lina's grave, half wishing, as he stood there in the moonlight, that he, too, was lying beside it.

"Were I sure of heaven, it would be a blessed thing to die," he thought, "for this world has little in it to make me happy. Oh, Alice, Golden Hair, I could almost wish we had never met, though, as I told her once, I would rather have loved and lost her than never have loved her at all."

Poor Hugh! He was mistaken with regard to Alice. She was not listening to love words. She was telling Irving Stanley as much of 'Lina's sad story as she thought necessary, and Irving, though really interested, was, we must confess, too intent on watching the changing expressions of her beautiful face to comprehend it clearly in all its complicated parts.

He understood that 'Lina was not, and that a certain Adah Hastings was, Mrs. Worthington's child; understood, too, that Adah was the wife of Dr. Richards—that she had at some time, not quite clear to him, been at Terrace Hill, but he somehow received the impression that she eventually fled from Spring Bank after recognizing the doctor, and never once thought of associating her with the young woman to whom, many months previously, he had been so kind in the crowded car, and whose sad, brown eyes had haunted him at intervals ever since.

Irving Stanley was not what could well be called fickle. He admired ladies indiscriminately, respected them all, liked some very much, and next to Alice was more attracted by and pleased with Adah's face than any he had ever seen save that of "the Brownie," which seemed to him much like it. He had thought of Adah often, but had as often associated her with some tall, bewhiskered man, who loved her and her little boy as she deserved to be loved. With this idea constantly before him, Adah had gradually faded from his mind, leaving there only the image of one who had made the strongest impression upon him of any whom he yet had met. Alice Johnson, she was the star he followed now, hers the presence which would make that projected tour through Europe all sunshine. Irving had decided to be married; his mother said he ought; Augusta said he ought; Mrs. Ellsworth said he ought; and so, as Hugh suspected, he had come to Kentucky for the sole purpose of asking Alice to be his wife. At sight, however, of Hugh, so much improved, so gentlemanly, and so fine looking, his heart began to misgive him, and Hugh would have been surprised could he have known that Irving Stanley was as jealous of him as he was of Irving Stanley. Yet, such was the fact, and it was a hard matter to tell which was the more miserable of the two, Irving or Hugh, when at last the latter returned from 'Lina's grave, and seated himself upon the moon-lighted piazza, a little apart from the lovers, as he believed Irving and Alice to be.

By mutual consent the conversation turned upon the war, and Alice could scarcely forbear laying her hand in Hugh's in token of approbation as she watched the glow of enthusiasm kindling in his cheek, and the fire of patriotism flashing from his dark, handsome eyes.

"I wonder, with your strong desire to punish the South, that you are not in the field," Irving said, a little dryly, for though not a sympathizer with the rebellion, he was a Baltimorean, and not yet quite as much aroused as Hugh, who replied at once:

"And so I should have been, but for circumstances I could not control. I shall soon start in quest of my sister, and when she is found I shall volunteer at once, fighting like a blood-hound, until some ball strikes me down."

This he said savagely, and partly for Alice's benefit; never, however, glancing at her, and so he failed to see the sudden pallor on her cheek, as she heard, in fancy, the whizzing of the ball which was to lay that stalwart form in the dust.

"No, sir," Hugh continued fiercely, "it's not for lack of will that I am not with them today; and, I assure you, nothing could take me to Europe at such a time as this, unless I went to be rid of the trouble," and springing from his chair, Hugh strode up and down the piazza, chafing like a caged lion, while Irving Stanley's face flushed faintly at the insinuation he could not help understand, and Alice looked surprised that Hugh should so far have forgotten his position as host.

The same thought came to Hugh at last, and turning suddenly in his walk, he confronted Irving Stanley, and offering him his hand, said:

"Forgive me, sir, for my rudeness. When I get upon the war, I grow too much excited. I knew you were from Baltimore, and I was fearful you might uphold that infernal mob which murdered the brave Massachusetts boys. I could lay that city in ashes."

Irving took the offered hand, and answered, good humoredly:

"That would punish the innocent as well as the guilty, so I am not with you there, though, like you, I recoil in horror from the perpetration of that fiendish attack upon peaceable troops. I was there myself, and did what I could to quiet the tumult, receiving more than one brickbat for my interference. One word more, Cousin Hugh, I am not going to Europe to be rid of the trouble, or for pleasure either, but as my sister's escort. I do not yet see that my country needs me; when I do I shall come home and join the Union army. We may meet yet on some battlefield, and if we do you will see I am no coward or traitor either."

Alice's face was white now as marble, and her breath came hurriedly. The war, before so far off, seemed very near—a terrible reality, when those two young men talked of standing side by side on some field of carnage. Hugh noticed her now, and attributing her emotions wholly to her fears for Irving Stanley, wrung the hand of the latter and then walked away, half wishing that the leafy woods beyond the distant fields were so many human beings and he was one of them, marching on to duty.

In this quiet way two days went by, Irving Stanley, quiet, pleasant, gentlemanly, and winning all hearts by his extreme suavity of manner; Hugh, silent, fitful, moody; Alice, artificially gay, and even merry, trying so hard to make up Hugh's deficiencies, that she led poor Irving astray, and made him honestly believe she might be won. It was on the morning of the third day that he resolved to end the uncertainty, and know just how she regarded him. Hugh had gone to Frankfort, he supposed; Mrs. Worthington was suffering from a nervous headache, while Densie, as usual, sat in her own room, mostly silent, but occasionally whispering to herself, "White nigger, white nigger—that's me!" Apparently it was the best opportunity he could have, and joining Alice in the large, cool parlor, he seated himself beside her, and with the thought that nothing was gained by waiting, plunged at once into his subject.

"Alice," he began, "I must leave here tomorrow, and the business on which I came is not yet transacted. Can't you guess what it is? Has not my manner told you why I came to Kentucky?"

Alice was far too truthful to affect ignorance, and though it cost her a most painful effort to do so, she answered, frankly: "I think I can guess."

"And you will not tell me no?" Irving said, involuntarily winding his arm around her, and drawing her drooping head nearer to him.

Just then a shadow fell upon them, but neither noticed it, or dreamed of the tall form passing the window and pausing long enough to see Irving Stanley's arm around Alice's neck, to hear Irving Stanley as he continued: "Darling Alice, you will be my wife?"

The rest was lost to Hugh, who had not yet started for Frankfort, as Irving supposed. With every faculty paralyzed save that of locomotion, he hurried away to where Rocket stood waiting for him, and mounting his pet, went dashing across the fields, conscious of nothing save that Golden Hair was lost forever. In his rapid walk down the piazza he had not observed Old Sam, seated in the door, nor heard the mumbled words, "Poor Massa Hugh! I'se berry sorry for him, berry! I kinder thought, 'fore t'other chap comed, Miss Ellis was hankerin' after him a little. Poor Massa Hugh!"

Old Sam, like Hugh, had heard Irving Stanley's impassioned words, for the window nearby was opened wide; he had seen, too, the deadly pallor on Hugh's face, and how for an instant he staggered, as from a blow, covering his eyes with his hands and whispering as he passed the negro, "Oh, Alice, Golden Hair!"

All this Sam had witnessed, and in his sympathy for "Massa Hugh" he failed to hear the rest of Irving's wooing, or Alice's low-spoken answer. She could not be Irving Stanley's wife. She made him understand that, and then added, sadly: "I am sorry I cannot love you as I ought, for I well know the meed of gratitude I owe to one who saved my life, and I have wanted so much to thank you, only you did not seem to remember me at all."

In blank amazement Mr. Stanley asked her what she meant,

while Alice, equally amazed, replied: "Surely, you have not forgotten me? Can I be mistaken? I am the little girl whom Irving Stanley rescued from drowning, when the *St. Helena* took fire, several years ago."

"I was never on a burning boat, never saw the *St. Helena*," was Mr. Stanley's reply; and then for a moment the two regarded each other intently, but Irving was the first to speak.

"It was Hugh," he said. "It must have been Hugh, for I remember now that when he was a lad, or youth, his uncle sometimes called him Irving, which is, I think, his middle name."

"Yes, Yes, H.I. Worthington. I've seen it written thus, but never thought to ask what 'I.' was for. It was Hugh, and I mistook that old man for his father. I understand it now," and Alice spoke hurriedly, her fair face coloring with excitement as the truth flashed upon her that she was Golden Hair.

Then the bright color faded away, and alarmed at the pallor which succeeded it, Irving Stanley passed his arm supportingly around her, asking if she were faint. Old Sam, moving away from the door, saw her as she sat thus, but did not hear her reply: "It takes me so by surprise. Poor Hugh, how he must have suffered."

She said this last more to herself than to Irving Stanley, who, nevertheless, saw in it a meaning; and looking her earnestly in the face, said to her: "Alice, you cannot be my wife, because your heart is given to Hugh Worthington. Is it not so?"

Alice would not deceive him, and she answered, frankly: "It is," while Irving replied: "I approve your choice, although it makes me very wretched. You will be happy with him. Heaven bless you both."

He dared not trust himself to say another word, but hurrying from her presence, sought the shelter of the woods, where alone he could school himself to bear this terrible disappointment.

Hugh did not return until evening, and the first object he saw distinctly as he galloped to the house, was Alice, sitting near to Irving upon the pleasant piazza, just as it was natural that she should sit. He did not observe that his mother was there with them; he did not think of anything as he rode past them with nod and smile, save that life henceforth was but a dreary, hopeless blank to him.

Leaving Rocket in Claib's care, he sauntered to the back piazza, where Sam was sitting, and taking a seat beside him startled him by saying that he should start on the morrow in quest of his missing sister.

"Yes, massah," was Sam's quiet reply, for he understood the reason of this sudden journey.

Old Sam pitied Hugh, and after a moment's silence his pity expressed itself in words. Laying his dark hand on Hugh's bowed head, he said:

"Poor Massah Hugh. Sam kin feel for you ef he is black. Niggers kin love like the white folks does."

"What do you mean? What do you know?" Hugh asked, a little haughtily, while Sam fearlessly replied:

"'Scuse me, massah, but I hears dem dis mornin'—hears de city chap sparkin' Miss Ellis, and seen his arm spang round her, too, with her sweet face, white as wool, lyin' in his buzzum."

"You saw this after I was gone?" Hugh asked, eagerly, and Sam replied:

"Yes, massah, strue as preachin', and I'se sorry for massah. I prays that he may somewhar find anodder Miss Ellis, only not quite so nice, 'cause he can't."

Hugh smiled bitterly, as he rejoined:

"Pray rather that I may find Adah, that is the object now for which I live; and, Sam, keep what you have seen to yourself. Be faithful to Miss Johnson and kind to mother. There's no telling when I shall return. I may join the Federal Army, but not a word of this to any one."

"Oh, massah," Sam began, but Hugh left him ere he finished, and compelled himself to join the group on the front side of the building, startling them as he had Sam by announcing his determination to start on the morrow for New York.

Alice's exclamation of surprise was lost as Irving rejoined:

"Then we may travel together, as I, too, leave in the morning."

Hugh gave him a rapid, searching glance, and then his eye fell on Alice, whose white face he jealously fancied was caused by the prospect of parting so soon with her affianced husband. He could not guess whether she were going to Europe or not. A few weeks seemed so short a time in which to prepare, that he half believed she might induce Mr. Stanley to defer the trip till autumn. But he would not ask. She would surely tell him at the last, he thought. She ought, at least, to trust him as a brother, and say to him:

"Hugh, I am engaged to Mr. Stanley, and when you return, if you are long gone, I shall probably not be here."

But she said to him no such thing, and only the whiteness of her face and the occasional quivering of her long eyelashes, showed that she felt at all, as at an early hour next morning she presided at the breakfast prepared for the travelers. There was no tremor in her voice, no hesitancy in her manner, and a stranger could not have told which of the young men before her held her heart in his possession, or which had kept her wakeful the entire night, revolving the propriety of telling him ere he left that the Golden Hair he loved so much was willing to be his.

"Perhaps he will speak to me. I'll wait," was the final decision, as, rising from her sleepless pillow, she sat down in the gray dawn of the morning and penned a hasty note, which she thrust into his hand at parting, little dreaming how long a time would intervene ere they would meet again.

He had not said to her or to his mother that he might join the army, gathering so fast from every Northern city and hamlet; only Sam knew this, and so the mother longing for her daughter was pleased rather than surprised at his abrupt departure, bidding him Godspeed, and lading him with messages of love for Adah and the little boy. Alice, too, tried to smile as she said good-by, but it died upon her lips and a tear trembled on her cheek, when Hugh dropped the little hand he never expected to hold again just as he held it then.

Feeling intuitively that Irving and Alice would rather say their parting words alone, Hugh drew his mother with him as he advanced into the midst of the sobbing, howling negroes assembled to see him off. But Alice had nothing to say which she would not have said in his presence. Irving Stanley understood better than Hugh, and he merely raised her cold hand to his lips, saying as he did so:

"Just this once; I shall never kiss it again."

He was in the carriage when Hugh came up, and Alice stood leaning against one of the tall pillars, a deep flush now upon her cheek, and tears filling her soft blue eyes. In another moment the carriage was rolling from the yard, neither Irving nor Hugh venturing to look back, and both as by mutual consent avoiding the mention of Alice, whose name was not spoken once during their journey together to Cincinnati, where they parted company, Irving continuing his homeward route, while Hugh stopped in the city to arrange a matter of business with his banker there. It was not until Irving was gone and he alone in his room that he opened the little note given him by Alice, the note which would tell him of her approaching marriage, he believed. How then was he surprised when he read:

"Dear Hugh: I have at last discovered the mistake under which, for so many years, I have been laboring. It was not Irving Stanley who saved me from the water, but your own noble self, and you have generously kept silent all this time, permitting me to expend upon another the gratitude due to you.

"Dear Hugh, I wish I had known earlier, or that you did not leave us so soon. It seems so cold, thanking you on paper, but I have no other opportunity, and must do it here.

"Heaven bless you, Hugh. My mother prayed often for the preserver of her child, and need I tell you that I, too, shall never forget to pray for you? The Lord keep you in all your ways, and lead you safely to your sister.

"Alice"

Many times Hugh read this note, then pressing it to his lips thrust it into his bosom, but failed to see what Alice had hoped he might see, that the love he once asked for was his, and his alone. He was too sure that another was preferred before him to reason clearly, and the only emotions he experienced from reading her note were feelings of pleasure that she had been set right at last, and that Irving had not withheld from her the truth.

"That ends the drama," he said. "I don't quite believe she is going with him to Europe, but she will be his when he returns; and henceforth my duty must be to forget, if possible, that ever I knew I loved her. Oh, Golden Hair, why did I ever meet, or meeting you, why was I suffered to love her so devotedly, if I must lose her at the last!"

There were great drops of sweat about Hugh's lips and on his forehead, as, burying his face in his hands, he laid both upon the table, and battled manfully with his love for Alice Johnson, a love which refused at once to surrender its object, even though there seemed no longer a shadow of hope in which to take refuge.

"God, help me in my sorrow," was the prayer which fell from the quivering lips, but did not break the silence of that little room, where none, save God, witnessed the conflict, the last Hugh ever fought for Alice Johnson.

He could give her up at length; could think, without a shudder, of the time when another than himself would call her his wife; and when, late that afternoon, he took the evening train for Cleveland, not one in the crowded car would have guessed how sore was the heart of the young man who plunged so energetically into the spirited war argument in progress between a Northern and Southern politician. It was a splendid escape valve for his pent-up feelings, and Hugh carried everything before him, taking by turns both sides of the question, and effectually silencing the two combatants, who said to each other in parting: "We shall hear from that Kentuckian again, though whether in Rebeldom or Yankeeland we cannot tell."

CHAPTER XLIII

LETTERS FROM HUGH AND IRVING STANLEY

Claib had brought two letters from the office, one for Mrs. Worthington from Hugh, and one for Alice from Irving Stanley. This last had been long delayed, and as she broke the seal a little nervously, reading that his trip to Europe had been deferred on account of the illness of his sister's governess, but that he was going on board the ship that day, July tenth, and that his sister was there with him and the governess, "A modest, sweet-faced body," he wrote, "who looks very girl-like from the fact that her soft, brown hair is worn short in her neck."

Alice had a tolerably clear insight into Irving Stanley's character, and immediately her mind conjured up visions of what might be the result of a sea voyage and months of intimate companionship with that sweet-faced governess, "who wore her soft, brown hair short in her neck."

"I hope it may be so," she thought; and folding up her letter, she was about going out to the rustic seat beneath a tall maple where Mug sat, whispering over the primer she was trying so hard to read, when a cry from Mrs. Worthington arrested her attention and brought her at once to the side of the half fainting woman.

"What is it?" Alice asked, in much alarm, and Mrs. Worthington replied: "Oh, Hugh, Hugh, my boy! he's enlisted, joined the army! I shall never see him again!"

Could Hugh have seen Alice then he would not for a moment have doubted the nature of her feelings toward himself. She did not cry out, nor faint, but her face turned white as the dress she wore, while her hands pressed so tightly together, that her long, taper nails left the impress in her flesh.

"God keep him from danger and death," she murmured; then, winding her arms around the stricken mother, she wiped her tears away; and to her moaning cry that she was left alone, replied: "Let me be your child till he returns, or, if he never does—"

She could get no further, for the very idea was overwhelming, and sinking down beside Hugh's mother, she laid her head on her lap, and wept bitterly. Alas, that scenes like this should be so common in our once happy land, but so it is. Mothers start with terror and grow faint over the boy just enlisted for the war; then follow him with prayers and yearning love to the distant battlefield; then wait and watch for tidings from him; and then too often read with streaming eyes and hearts swelling with agony, the fatal message which says their boy is dead.

It was a sad day at Spring Bank when first the news of Hugh's enlistment came, sadder even than when 'Lina died, for Hugh seemed as really dead as if they all had heard the hissing shell or whizzing ball which was to bear his young life away. It was nearly two months since he left home, and he could find no trace of Adah, though searching faithfully for her, in conjunction with Murdock and Dr. Richards, both of whom had joined him in New York.

"If Murdock cannot find her," he wrote, "I am convinced no one can, and I leave the matter now to him, feeling that another duty calls me, the duty of fighting for my country."

It was just after the disastrous battle of Bull Run, when people were wild with excitement, and Hugh was thus borne with the tide, until at last he found himself enrolled as a private in a regiment of cavalry gathering in one of the Northern States. There had been an instant's hesitation, a clinging of the heart to the dear old home at Spring Bank, where his mother and Alice were; a thought of Irving Stanley, and then, with an eagerness which made his whole frame tremble, he had seized the pen and written down his name, amid deafening cheers for the brave Kentuckian. This done, there was no turning back; nor did he desire it. It seemed as if he were made for war, so eagerly he longed to join the fray. Only one thing was wanting, and that was Rocket. He had tried the "Yankee horses," as he called them, but found them far inferior to his pet. Rocket he must have, and in his letter to his mother he made arrangements for her to send him northward by a Versailles merchant, who, he knew, was coming to New York.

Hugh and Rocket, they would make a splendid match, and so Alice thought, as, on the day when Rocket was led away, she stood with her arms around his graceful neck, whispering to him the words of love she would fain have sent his master. She had recovered from the first shock of Hugh's enlistment. She could think of him now calmly as a soldier; could pray that God would keep him, and even feel a throb of pride that one who had lived so many years in Kentucky, then poising almost equally in the scale, should come out so bravely for the right, though by that act he called down curses on his head from those at home who favored rebellion, and who, if they fought at all, would cast in their lot with the seceding States. She had written to Hugh a kind, sisterly letter, telling him how proud she was of him, and how her sympathy and prayers would follow him everywhere. "And if," she had added, in concluding, "you are sick, or wounded, I will come to you as a sister might do. I will find you wherever you are."

She had sent this letter to him three weeks before, and now she stood caressing the beautiful Rocket, who sometimes proudly arched his long neck, and then looked wistfully at the sad group gathered around him, as if he knew that was no ordinary parting. Colonel Tiffton, who had heard what was going on, had ridden over to expostulate with Mrs. Worthington against sending Rocket North. "Better keep him at home," he said, "and tell Hugh to come back, and let those who had raised the muss settle their own difficulty."

The old colonel, who was a native of Virginia, did not know exactly where he stood. "He was very patriotic," he said, "very, but hanged if he knew which side to take—both were wrong. He didn't go Nell's doctrine, for Nell was a rabid Secesh; neither did he swallow Abe Lincoln, and he'd advise Alice to keep a little more quiet, for there was no knowing what the hotheads might do. He'd heard of Harney's threatening vengeance on all Unionists, and now that Hugh was gone he might pounce on Spring Bank any night."

"Let him!" and Alice's blue eyes flashed brightly, while her girlish figure seemed to expand and grow higher as she continued: "he will find no cowards here. I never touched a revolver in my life. I am quite as much afraid of one that is not loaded as of one that is, but I'll conquer the weakness. I'll begin today. I'll learn to handle firearms. I'll practice shooting at a mark, and if Hugh is killed I'll—oh, Hugh! Hugh—"

She could not tell what she would do, for the woman conquered all other feelings, and laying her face on Rocket's silken mane, she sobbed aloud.

"There's pluck, by George!" muttered the old colonel. "I most wish Nell was that way of thinking."

It was time now for Rocket to go, and 'mid the deafening howls of the negroes and the tears of Mrs. Worthington and Alice he was led away, the latter watching him until he was lost to sight beyond the distant hill, then, falling on her knees, she prayed, as many a one has done, that God would be with our brave soldiers, giving them the victory, and keeping one of them, at least, from falling.

Sadly, gloomily the autumn days came on, and the land was rife with war and rumors of war. In the vicinity of Spring Bank were many patriots, but there were hot Secessionists there also, and bitter contentions ensued. Old friends were estranged, families were divided, neighbors watched each other jealously, while all seemed waiting anxiously for the result. Toward Spring Bank the aspersions of the Confederate adherents were particularly directed. That Hugh should go North and join the Federal army was taken as an insult, while Mrs. Worthington and Alice were closely watched, and all their sayings eagerly repeated. But Alice did not care. Fully convinced of the right, and that she had yet a work to do, she carried out her plan so boldly announced to Colonel Tiffton, and all through the autumn months the frequent clash of firearms was heard in the Spring Bank woods, where Alice, with Mug at her side, like her constant shadow, "shot at her marks," hitting once Colonel Tiffton's dog, and coming pretty near hitting the old colonel himself as he rode leisurely through the woods.

After that Alice confided her experiments to the open fields, where she could see whatever was in danger, and Harney, galloping up and down the pike, stirring up dissension and scattering his opinions broadcast through the country, saw her more than once at her occupation, smiling grimly as he muttered to himself: "It's possible I may try a hand with you at shooting some day, my fair Yankee miss."

Blacker, and darker, and thicker the war clouds gathered on our horizon, but our story has little to do with that first year of carnage, when human blood was poured as freely as water, from the Cumberland to the Potomac. Over all that we pass, and open the scene again in the summer of '62, when people were gradually waking to the fact that Richmond was not so easily taken, or the South so easily conquered.

CHAPTER XLIV

THE DESERTER

There had been a desertion from a regiment on the Potomac. An officer of inferior rank, but whose position had been such as to make him the possessor of much valuable information, and whose perfect loyalty had been for some time suspected, was missing from his command one morning, and under such circumstances as to leave little doubt that his intention was to reach the enemy's lines if possible. Long and loud were the invectives against the traitor, and none were deeper in their denunciations than Captain Hugh Worthington, as, seated on his fiery war horse, Rocket, he heard from Irving Stanley the story of Dr. Richards' disgrace.

"He should be pursued, brought back, and shot!" he said, emphatically, feeling that he would like much to be one of the pursuers, already on the track of the treacherous doctor, who skillfully eluded them all, and just at the close of a warm summer day, when afar, in his New England home, his Sister Anna was reading, with an aching heart, the story of his disgrace, he sat in the shadow of the Virginia woods, weary, footsore and faint with the pain caused from his ankle, sprained by a recent fall.

He had hunted for Adah until entirely discouraged, and partly as a panacea for the remorse preying so constantly upon him, and partly in compliance with Anna's entreaties, he had at last joined the Federal army, and been sworn in with the full expectation of some lucrative office. But his unlucky star was in the ascendant. Stories derogatory to his character were set afloat, and the final result of the whole was that he found himself enrolled in a company where he knew he was disliked, and under a captain whom he thoroughly detested, for the fraud practiced upon himself. In this condition he was sent to the Potomac, and while on duty as a picket, grew to be on the most friendly terms with more than one of the enemy, planning at last to desert, and effecting his escape one stormy night, when the watch were off their guard. Owing to some mistake, the aid promised by his Rebel friends had not been extended, and as best he could he was making his way to Richmond, when, worn out with hunger, watchfulness and fatigue, he sank down to die, as he believed, at the entrance of some beautiful woods which skirted the borders of a well-kept farm in Virginia. Before him, at the distance of nearly a quarter of a mile, a large, handsome house was visible, and by the wreath of smoke curling from the rear chimney, he knew it was inhabited, and thought once to go there, and beg for the food he craved so terribly. But fear kept him back—the people might be Unionists, and might detain him a prisoner until the officers upon his track came up. Dr. Richards was cowardly, and so with a groan, he laid his head upon the grass, and half wished that he had died ere he came to be the miserable wretch he was. The pain in his ankle was by this time intolerable, and the limb was swelling so fast that to walk on the morrow was impossible, and if he found a shelter at all, it must be found that night.

Midway between himself and the house was a comfortable-looking barn, whither he resolved to go. But the journey was a tedious one, and brought to his flushed forehead great drops of sweat, wrung out by the agony it caused him to step upon his foot. At last, when he could bear his weight upon it no longer, he sank upon the ground, and crawling slowly upon his hands and knees, reached the barn just as it was growing dark, and the shadows creeping into the corners made him half shrink with terror lest they were the bayonets of those whose coming he was constantly expecting. He could not climb to the scaffolding, and so he sought a friendly pile of hay, and crouching down behind it, ere long fell asleep for the first time in three long days and nights.

The early June sun was just shining through the cracks between the boards when he awoke, sore, stiff, feverish, burning with thirst, and utterly unable to use the poor, swollen foot, which lay so helplessly upon the hay.

"Oh, for Anna now," he moaned; "if she were only here; or Lily, dear Lily, she would pity and forgive, could she see me now."

But hark, what sound is it which falls upon his ear, making him quake with fear, and, in spite of his aching ankle, creep farther behind the hay? It is a footstep—a light, tripping step, and it comes that way, nearer, nearer, until a shadow falls between the open chinks and the bright sunshine without. Then it moves on, around the corner, pausing for a moment, while the hidden coward holds his breath, and listens anxiously, hoping nothing is coming there. But there is, and it enters the same door through which he came the previous night—a girlish figure, with a basket on her arm—a basket in which she puts the eggs she knows just where to find. Not behind the hay, where a poor wretch was almost dead with terror. There was no nest there, and so she failed to see the ghastly face, pinched with hunger and pain, the glassy eyes, the uncombed hair, and soiled tattered garments of him who once was known as one of fashion's most fastidious dandies.

She had secured her eggs for the morning meal, and the doctor hoped she was about to leave, when there was a rustling of the hay, and he almost uttered a scream of fear. But the sound died on his lips, as he heard the voice of prayer—heard that young girl as she prayed, and the words she uttered stopped, for an instant, the pulsations of his heart, and partly took his senses away. First for her baby boy she prayed, asking that God would be to him father and mother both, and keep him from temptation. Then for her country, her distracted, bleeding country, and the doctor, listening to her, knew it was no Rebel tongue calling so earnestly on God to save the Union, praying so touchingly for the poor, suffering soldiers, and coming at last even to him, the miserable outcast, whose bloodshot eyes grew blind, and whose brain grew giddy and wild, as he heard again Lily's voice, pleading for George, wherever he might be. She did not say: "God send him back to me, who loves him still." She only asked forgiveness for the father of her boy, but this was proof to the listener that she did not hate him, and forgetful of his pain he raised himself upon his elbow, and looking over the pile of hay, saw her where she knelt. Lily, Adah, his wife, her fair face covered by her hands, and her soft, brown hair cut short and curling in her neck.

Twice he essayed to speak, but his tongue refused to move, and he sank back exhausted, just as Adah arose from her knees and turned to leave the barn. He could not let her go. He should die before she came again; he was half dying now, and it would be so sweet to breathe out his life upon her bosom, with perhaps her forgiving kiss upon his lips.

"Adah!" he tried to say; but the quivering lips made no sound, and Adah passed out, leaving him there alone. "Adah, Lily, Anna," he gasped, hardly knowing himself whose name he called in his despair.

She heard that sound, and started suddenly, for she thought it was her old, familiar name which no one knew there at Sunny Mead. For a moment she paused; but it came not again, and so she turned the corner, and her shadow fell a second time on the haggard face pressed against that crevice in the wall, the opening large enough to thrust the long fingers through, in the wild hope of detaining her as she passed.

"Adah!"

It was a gasping, bitter cry; but it reached her, and looking back, she saw the pale hand beckoning, the fingers motioning feebly, as if begging her to return. There was a moment's hesitation, and then conquering her timidity, Adah went back, shuddering as she passed the still beckoning hand, and caught a glimpse of the wild eyes peering at her through the crevice.

"Adah!"

She heard it distinctly now, and with it came thoughts of Hugh. It must be he; and her feet scarcely touched the ground in her eagerness to find him. Over the threshold, across the floor, and behind the hay she bounded; but stood aghast at the spectacle before her. He had struggled to his knees; and with his sprained limb coiled under him, his ashen lips apart, and his arms stretched out, he was waiting for her. But Adah did not spring into those trembling arms, as once she would have done. She would never willingly rest in their embrace again; and utter, overwhelming surprise was the only emotion on her face as she recognized him, not so much by his looks as by the name he gave her.

"George, oh, George, how came you here?" she asked, drawing backward from the arm reached out to touch her.

He felt that he was repulsed, and, with a wail which smote painfully on Adah's heart, he fell forward on his face, sobbing: "Oh, Adah, Lily, pity me, pity me, if you can't forgive! I have slept for three nights in the woods, without once tasting food! My ankle is sprained, my strength is gone, and I wish that I were dead!"

She had drawn nearer to him, while he spoke, near enough to recognize her country's uniform, all soiled and tattered though it was. He was a soldier, then—Liberty's loyal son—and that fact awoke a throb of pity.

"George," she said, kneeling down beside him, and laying her hand upon his ragged coat, "tell me how came you here, and where is your company?"

He would not deceive her, though tempted to do so, and he answered her truthfully: "Lily, I am a deserter. I am trying to join the enemy!"

He did not see the indignant flash of her eyes, or the look of scorn upon her face, but he felt the reproach her silence implied, and dared not look up.

"George," she began at last, sternly, very sternly, "but for Him who bade us forgive seventy times seven, I should feel inclined to leave you here to die; but when I remember how much He is tried with one, I feel that I am to be no one's judge. Tell me, then, why you have deserted; and tell me, too—oh, George, in mercy—tell me if you know aught of Willie?"

The mother had forgotten all the wrongs heaped upon the wife, and Adah drew nearer to him now, so near, indeed, that his arm encircled her at last, and held her close; but the ragged, dirty, fallen creature did not dare to kiss her, and could only press her convulsively to his breast, as he attempted an answer to her question.

"You must be quick," she said, suddenly remembering herself; "it is growing late, Mrs. Ellsworth will be waiting for her breakfast; and since the stampede of her servants, two old negroes and myself are all there are left to care for the house. Stay," she added, as a new thought seemed to strike her; "I must go, or they will look for me; but after breakfast I will return, and do for you what I can. Lie down again upon the hay."

She spoke kindly to him, but he felt it was as she would have spoken to any one in distress, and not as once she had addressed him. But he knew that he deserved it, and he suffered her to leave him, watching her with streaming eyes as she hurried along the path, and counting the minutes, which seemed to him like hours, ere he saw her returning. She was very white when she came back, and he noticed that she frequently glanced toward the house, as if haunted by some terror. Constantly expecting detection, he grasped her arm, as she bent to bathe his swollen foot, and whispered huskily: "Adah, there's something on your mind—some evil you fear. Tell me, is any one after me!"

Adah nodded; while, like a frightened child, the tall man clung to her neck, saying, piteously: "Don't give me up! Don't tell; they would hang me, perhaps!"

"They ought to do so," trembled on Adah's lips, but she suppressed the words, and went on bandaging up the ankle, and handling it as carefully as if it had not belonged to a deserter.

He did not feel pain now in his anxiety, as he asked: "Who is it, Adah? who's after me?" but he started when she replied, with downcast eyes and a flush upon her cheek: "Major Irving Stanley. You were in his regiment, the—— th New York Volunteers."

Dr. Richards drew a relieved breath. "I'd rather it were he than Captain Worthington, who hates me so cordially. Adah, you must hide me; I have so much to tell. I know your parents, your brother, your husband; and I am he. It was not a mock marriage. It has been proved real. It was a genuine justice who married us, and you are my lawful wife. Oh, pray, please don't hurt me so." He uttered a scream of pain as Adah's hands pressed heavily now upon the hard, purple flesh.

She scarcely knew what she was doing as she listened to his words and heard that she was indeed his wife. Two years before, such news would have overwhelmed her with delight, but now for a single instant a fierce and almost resentful pang shot through her heart as she thought of being bound for life to one for whom she had no love, and whose very caresses made her loathe him more and more. But when she thought of Willie, and how the stain upon his birth was washed away, the hard look left her eyes, and her hot tears dropped upon the ankle she was bandaging.

"You are glad?" he asked, looking at her curiously, for her manner puzzled him.

"Yes, very glad for Willie," she replied, keeping her face bent down so he could not see its expression.

Then when her task was done, she seemed to nerve herself for some powerful task, and sitting down upon the hay, out of reach of his arms, she said:

"Tell me now all that has happened since I left Terrace Hill; but first of Willie. You say Anna has him?"

"Yes, Anna—Mrs. Millbrook," he replied, and was about to say more, when Adah interrupted him with:

"It may spare you some pain if I tell you first what I know of the tragedy at Spring Bank. I know that 'Lina is dead, and that the fact of my existence prevented the marriage. So much I heard Mr. Stanley tell his sister. I had just come to her then. She was prouder toward me than she is now, and with a look silenced him from talking in my presence, so that was all I ever knew, as I dared not question her lest I should be suspected. Go on, you spoke of my parents, my brother. Who are they?"

Her manner perplexed him greatly, but he controlled himself, while he repeated rapidly the story known already to our readers, the story which made Adah reel where she sat, and turn so white that he attempted to reach her, and so keep her from falling. But just the touch of his hand had power to arouse her, and drawing back she laid her face in the hay, and moaned:

"That gentle woman, my mother; that noble Hugh, my brother! it's more than I ever hoped. Oh, Heavenly Father, accept my thanks for this great happiness. A mother and a brother found."

"And husband, too," chimed in the doctor, eagerly, "thank Him for me, Adah. You are glad to find me?"

There was pleading in his tone—earnest pleading, for the terrible conviction was fastening itself upon him, that not as they once parted had he and Adah met. For full five minutes Adah lay upon the hay, her whole soul going out in a prayer of thankfulness for her great joy, and for strength to bear the bitterness mingling with her joy. Her face was very white when she lifted it up at last, but her manner was composed, and she questioned the doctor calmly of Spring Bank, of Alice, of Hugh, of Anna, but could not trust herself to say much to him of Willie, lest her calmness should give way, and a feeling spring up in her heart of something like affection for Willie's father. Alas, for the miserable man. He had found his wife, his Adah, but there was between them a gulf which his own act had built, and which he never more might pass. He began to suspect it, and ere she had finished the story of her wanderings, which at his request she told, he knew there was no pulsation of her heart which beat for him. He asked her where she had been since she fled from Terrace Hill, and how she came to be in Mrs. Ellsworth's family.

There was a moment's hesitancy, as if she were deciding how much to tell him of the past, and then resolving to keep nothing back which he might know, she told him how, with a stunned heart and giddy brain, she had gone to Albany, and mingling with the crowd had mechanically followed them down to a boat just starting for New York. That, by some means, she never knew how, she found herself in the saloon, and seated next to a feeble, deformed little girl, who lay upon the sofa, and whose sweet, childish voice said to her pityingly:

"Does your head ache, lady, or what makes you so white?"

She had responded to that appeal, talking kindly to the little girl, between whom and herself the friendliest of relations were established and whose name she learned was Jenny Ellsworth. The mother she did not then see, as, during the journey down the river she was suffering from a nervous headache, and kept her room.

From the child and child's nurse, however, she heard that Mrs. Ellsworth was going ere long to Europe, and was anxious to secure some young and competent person to act in the capacity of Jenny's governess. Instantly Adah's decision was made. Once in New York she would by letter apply for the situation, for nothing then could so well suit her state of mind as a tour to Europe, where she would be far away from all she had ever known. Very adroitly she ascertained Mrs. Ellsworth's address, wrote to her a note the day following her arrival in New York, and the day following that, found her in Mrs. Ellsworth's parlor at the Brevoort House, where for a few days she was stopping. She had been greatly troubled to know what name to give, but finally resolved to take her own, the one by which she was known ere George Hastings crossed her path. Adah Maria Gordon was, as she supposed, her real name, so in her note to Mrs. Ellsworth she signed herself "Maria Gordon," omitting the Adah, which might lead to her being recognized. From her little girl Mrs. Ellsworth had heard much of the sweet young lady, who was so kind to her on the boat, and was thus already prepossessed in her favor.

Adah did not tell Dr. Richards, and perhaps she did not herself know how surprised and delighted Mrs. Ellsworth was with the fair, girlish creature, announced to her as Miss Gordon, and who won her heart before five minutes were gone, making her think it of no consequence to inquire concerning her at Madam ——'s school, where she said she had been a pupil.

"My sister must have been there at the same time," Mrs. Ellsworth had said. "Perhaps you remember her, Augusta Stanley?"

Yes, Miss Gordon remembered her well, but added modestly:

"She may have forgotten me, as I was only a day scholar, and—not—not quite her circle. I was poor."

Charmed with her frankness, Mrs. Ellsworth decided in her own mind to take her, but, for form's sake, she would write to her sister Augusta, recently married, and living in Milwaukee.

"Your first name is Maria," she said, taking out her pencil to write it down.

Adah could not tell a lie, and she replied unhesitatingly:

"No, ma'am; my name is Adah Maria, but I prefer being called Maria."

Mrs. Ellsworth nodded, wrote down "Adah Maria Gordon," but in the letter sent that day to Augusta, merely spoke of her governess in prospect as a Miss Gordon, who had been at the same school with Augusta, asking if she remembered her.

Yes, Augusta remembered Miss Gordon, well, a brown-eyed, sweet-faced, conscientious little creature whom she liked so much, and whose services her sister had better secure.

Mrs. Ellsworth hesitated no longer, and ten days after the

receipt of this letter, Adah was duly installed as governess to the delighted little Jennie, who learned to love her gentle teacher with a love almost amounting to idolatry.

"You were in Europe then, and that is the reason why we could not find you," Dr. Richards said, adding, after a moment: "And Irving Stanley went with you—was your companion all the while?"

"Yes, all the while," and Adah's cold fingers worked nervously at the wisp of hay she was twisting in her hand. "I had seen him before—he was in the cars when Willie and I were on our way to Terrace Hill. Willie had the earache, and he was so kind to us both."

Adah looked fixedly now at the craven doctor, who could not meet her glance, for well he remembered the dastardly part he had played in that scene, where his own child was screaming with pain, and he sat selfishly idle.

"She don't know I was there, though," he thought, and that gave him some comfort.

But Adah did know, and she meant he should know she did. Keeping her calm brown eyes still fixed upon him, she continued:

"I heard Mr. Stanley talking of you once to his sister, and among other things he spoke of your dislike for children, and referred to an occasion in the cars, when a little boy, for whom his heart ached, was suffering acutely, and for whom you evinced no interest, except to call him a brat, and wonder why his mother did not stay at home. I never knew till then that you were so near to me."

"It's true, it's true," the doctor cried, tears rolling down his soiled face; "but I never guessed it was you. Lily, I supposed it some ordinary woman."

"So did Irving Stanley," was Adah's quiet, cutting answer; "but his heart was open to sympathy, even for an ordinary woman."

The doctor could only moan, with his face still hidden in his hands, until a sudden thought like a revelation flashed upon him, and forgetting his wounded foot, he sprang like a tiger to the spot where Adah sat, and winding his arm firmly around her, whispered hoarsely:

"Adah, Lily, tell me you love this Irving Stanley. My wife loves another than her husband."

Adah did not struggle to release herself from his close grasp. It was punishment she ought to bear, she thought, but her whole soul loathed that close embrace, and the loathing expressed itself in the tone of her voice, as she replied:

"Until within an hour I did not suppose you were my husband. You said you were not in that letter; I have it yet; the one in which you told me it was a mock marriage, as, by your own confession, it seems you meant it should be."

"Oh, darling, you kill me, yet I deserve it all; but, Adah, I have suffered enough to atone for the dreadful past; and I tried so hard to find you. Forgive me, Lily, forgive," and falling again on his knees, the wretched man poured forth a torrent of entreaties for her forgiveness, her love, without which he should die.

Holding fast her cold hands, he pleaded with all his eloquence, until, maddened by her silence, he even taunted her with loving another, while her own husband was living.

Then Adah started, and pushing him away, sprang to her feet, while the hot blood stained her face and neck, and a resentful fire gleamed from her brown eyes.

"It is not well for you to reproach me with faithlessness," she said, "you, who have dealt so treacherously by me; you, who deliberately planned my ruin, and would have effected it but for the deeper-laid scheme of one you say is my father. No thanks to you that I am a lawful wife. You did not make me so of your own free will. You did to me the greatest wrong a man can do a woman, then cruelly deserted me, and now you would chide me for respecting another more than I do you."

"Not respecting him, Adah, no, not for respecting him. You should do that. He's worthier than I; but, oh, Adah, Lily, wife, mother of my boy, do you love Irving Stanley?"

He was sobbing bitterly, and the words came between the sobs, while he tried to clutch her dress. Staggering backward against the wooden beam, Adah leaned there for support, while she replied:

"You would not understand if I should tell you the terrible struggle it was for me to be thrown each day in the society of one as noble, as good as Irving Stanley, and not come at last to feel for him as a poor governess ought never to feel for the handsome, gifted brother of her employer. Oh, George, I prayed against it so much, prayed to be kept from the sin, if it were a sin, to have Irving Stanley mingled with every thought. But the more I prayed, the more the temptation seemed thrust upon me. The kinder, gentler, more attentive, grew his manners toward me. He never treated me as a mere governess. It was more like an equal at first, and then like a younger sister, so that few strangers took me for a subordinate, so kind were both Mrs. Ellsworth and her brother."

"And he," the doctor gasped, looking wistfully in her face, "does he—do you think he loves you?"

Adah colored crimson, but answered frankly:

"He never told me so; never said to me a word which a husband should not hear; but—sometimes I've fancied, I've feared, I've left him abruptly lest he should speak, for that I know would bring the crisis I so dreaded. I must tell him the whole then, and by my dread of doing this, I knew he was more than a friend to me. I was fearful at first that he might recognise me, but I was much thinner than when I saw him in the cars, while my hair, purposely worn short, and curling in my neck, changed my looks materially, so that he only wondered whom I was so much like, but never suspected the truth."

There was silence, a moment, and then the doctor asked: "How is all this to end?"

The question brought into Adah's eyes a fearful look of anguish, but she did not answer, and the doctor spoke again.

"Have I found Lily only to lose her?"

Still there was no reply, and the doctor continued: "You are my wife, Adah. No power can undo that, save death, and you are my child's mother. For Willie's sake, oh, Adah, for Willie's sake, forgive."

When he appealed to her as his wife, Adah seemed turning into stone; but the mention of Willie touched the mother within that girlish woman, and the iceberg melted at once.

"For Willie, my boy," she gasped, "I could do almost anything; I could die so willingly but—but—oh, George, that ever we should come to this. You a deserter, a traitor to your country—lamed, disabled, wholly in my power, and begging of me, your outcast wife, for the love which surely is dead—dead. No, George, I do forgive, but never, never more can I be to you a wife."

There was a rising resentment now in the doctor's manner, as he answered reproachfully: "Then surrender me at once to the lover hunting for me. Let him take me back where I can be shot and that will leave you free."

Adah raised her hand deprecatingly, and when he had finished, rejoined: "You mistake Major Stanley, if you think he would marry me, knowing what I should tell him. It's not for him that I refuse. It's for myself. I could not bear it. I—"

"Stay, Adah, Lily, don't say you should hate me;" and the doctor's voice was so full of anguish that Adah involuntarily advanced toward him, standing quite near, while he begged of her to say if the past could not be forgotten. His family were ready, were anxious to receive her. Sweet Anna Millbrook already loved her as a sister, while he, her husband, words could not tell his love for her. He would do whatever she required; go back to the Federal army if she said so; seek for the pardon he was sure to gain; fight for his country like a hero, periling life and limb, if she would only give him the shadow of a hope.

"I must have time to think. I cannot decide alone," Adah answered, while the doctor clutched her dress, half shrieking with terror:

"You surely will not consult him, Major Stanley?"

"No," and Adah spoke reverently, "there's a mightier friend than he. One who has never failed me in my need. He will tell me what to do."

The doctor knew now what she meant, and with a moan he laid his head again upon the hay, wishing, oh, so much, that the lessons taught him when in that little attic chamber, years ago, he knelt by Adah's side, and said with her, "Our Father," had not been all forgotten. When he lifted up his face again, Adah was gone, but he knew she would return, and waited patiently while just outside the door, with her fair face buried in the sweet Virginia grass, and the warm summer sunshine falling softly upon her, poor half crazed Adah fought and won the fiercest battle she had ever known, coming off conqueror over self, and feeling sure that God had heard her earnest cry for help, and told her what to do. There was no wavering now; her step was firm; her voice steady, as she went back to the doctor's side, and bending over him, said:

"I will nurse you, my husband, till you are well; then you must go back whence you came, confess your fault, rejoin your regiment, and by your faithfulness wipe out the stain of desertion. Then, when the war is over, or you are honorably discharged, I will—be your wife. I may not love you at first as once I did, but I shall try, and He, who counsels me to tell you this, will help me, I am sure."

It was almost pitiful now to see the doctor, as, spaniel-like, he crouched at Adah's feet, kissing her hands and blessing her 'mid his tears. "He would be worthy of her, and they should yet be so happy."

Adah suffered him to caress her for a moment, and then told him she must go, for Mrs. Ellsworth would wonder at her long absence, and possibly institute a search. Pressing one more kiss upon her hand the doctor crept back to his hiding place, while Adah went slowly to the house where she knew Irving Stanley was anxiously waiting for her. She dared not meet him alone now, for latterly each time they had so met, she knew she had kept at bay the declaration trembling on his lips, and which now must never be listened to. So she stayed away from the pleasant parlor where all the morning he sat chatting with his sister, who guessed how much he loved the beautiful and accomplished girl, whom, by way of his sister Augusta he now knew as the Brownie he had once seen at Madam ——'s school, in New York.

Right-minded and high-principled, Mrs. Ellsworth had conquered any pride she might at first have felt—any reluctance to her brother's marrying her governess, and now like him was anxious to have it settled. But Adah gave him no chance that day, and late in the afternoon he rode back to his regiment, wondering at the change in Miss Gordon, and why her face was so deadly white, and her voice so husky, as she bade him good-by.

Poor Adah! Hers was now a path of suffering, such as she had never known before. But she did her duty to the doctor faithfully, nursing him with the utmost care; but never expressing to him the affection she did not feel. It was impossible to keep his presence there a secret from the two old negroes, and knowing she could trust them, she told them of the wounded Union soldier, enlisting their sympathies for him, and thus procuring for him the care of older and more experienced people than herself.

He was able at length to return, and one pleasant summer night, just three weeks after his arrival at Sunnymead, Adah walked with him to the woods, and kneeling with him by a running stream, whose waters farther away would yet be crimson with the blood of our slaughtered brothers, she commended him to God. Through the leafy branches the moonbeams were shining, and they showed to Adah the expression of the doctor's wasted face as he said to her at parting: "I have kissed you many times, my darling, but you have never returned it. Please do so once, dear Lily, for the sake of the olden time. It will make me a better soldier."

She kissed him once for the sake of the olden time, and when he whispered, "Again for Willie's sake," she kissed him twice, and then she bade him leave her, herself buttoning about him the soldier coat which her own hands had cleaned and mended and made respectable. She was glad afterward that she had done so; glad, too, that she had kissed him and waited by the tree, where, looking backward, he could see the flutter of her white dress until a turn in the forest path hid her from his view.

CHAPTER XLV

THE SECOND BATTLE OF BULL RUN

The second disastrous battle at Bull Run was over, and the shadow of a summer night wrapped the field of carnage in darkness. Thickly upon the battlefield lay the dead and dying, the sharp, bitter cries of the latter rising on the night wind, and adding tenfold to the horror of the scene. In the woods, not very far away, more than one brave soldier was weltering in his lifeblood, just where, in his rapid flight, he had fallen, the grass his pillow, and the leafy branches of the forest trees his only covering.

Side by side, and near to a running brook, two wounded men were lying, or rather one was supporting the other and trying to stanch the purple gore, pouring darkly from a fearful bullet wound in the region of the heart. The stronger of the two, he who wore a major's uniform, had come accidentally upon the other, writhing in agony, and muttering at intervals snatches of the prayer with which he once had been familiar, and which seemed to bring Lily back to him again, just as she was when in the attic chamber she made him kneel by her, and say "Our Father." He tried to say it now, and the whispered words caught the ear of Irving Stanley, arresting his steps at once.

"Poor fellow! it's gone hard with you," he said, kneeling by the sufferer, whom he recognized as the deserter, Dr. Richards, who had returned to his allegiance, had craved forgiveness for his sins, and been restored to the ranks, discharging his duties faithfully, and fighting that day with a zeal and energy which did much in reinstating him in the good opinion of those who witnessed his daring bravery.

But the doctor's work was done, and never from his lips would Lily know how well his promise had been kept. Giddy with pain and weak from the loss of blood, he had groped his way through the woods, fighting back the horrid certainty that tomorrow's sun would not rise for him, and sinking at length exhausted upon the grass, whose freshness was now defaced by the blood which poured so freely from his wound.

It was thus that Irving Stanley found him, starting at first as from a hissing shell, and involuntarily clasping his hand over the place where lay a little note, received a few days before, a reply to the earnest declaration of love he had at last written to his sister's governess, Maria Gordon. There was but one alternative, and Adah met it resolutely, though every fiber of her heart throbbed with keen agony as she told to Irving Stanley the story of her life. She was a wife, a mother, the sister of Hugh Worthington, they said, the Adah for whom Dr. Richards had sought so long in vain, and for whom Murdock, the wicked father, was seeking still for aught she knew to the contrary. Even the story of the doctor's secretion in the barn at Sunnymead was confessed. Nothing was withheld except the fact that even as he professed to love her, so she in turn loved him, or had done so before she knew it was a sin. Surprise had, for a few moments, stifled every other emotion, and Irving Stanley had sat like one suddenly bereft of motion, when he read who Maria Gordon was. Then came the bitter thought that he had lost her, mingled with a deep feeling of resentment toward the man who had so cruelly wronged the gentle girl, and who alone stood between him and happiness. For Irving Stanley could overlook all the rest. His great warm heart, so full of kindly sympathy and generous charity for all mankind could take to its embrace the fair, sweet woman he had learned to love so much, and be a father to her little boy, as if it had been his own. But this might not be. There was a mighty obstacle in the way, and feeling that it mattered little now whether he ever came from the field alive, Irving Stanley, with a whispered prayer for strength to bear and do right, had hidden the letter in his bosom, and then, when the hour of conflict came, plunged into the thickest of the fight with a fearlessness born of keen and recent disappointment, which made life less valuable than it had been before.

It is not strange, then, that he should start and stagger backward when he came so suddenly upon the doctor, or that the first impulse of weak human nature was to leave the fallen man, but the second, the Christian impulse, bade him stay, and forgetting his own slight but painful wound, he bent over Adah's husband, and did what he could to alleviate the anguish he saw was so hard to bear. At the sound of his voice, a spasm of pain passed over the doctor's pallid face, and the flash of a sudden fire gleamed for a moment in his eye, as he, too, remembered Adah, and thought of what might be when the grass was growing over his untimely grave.

The doctor knew that he was dying, and yet his first question was:

"Do you think I can live? Did any one ever recover with such a wound as this?"

Eagerly the dim eyes sought the face above them, the kind, good face of one who would not deceive him. Irving shook his head as he felt the pulse, and answered frankly:

"I believe you will die."

There was a bitter moan, as all his misspent life came up before him, followed closely by the dark future, where there shone no ray of hope, and then with the desperate thought, "It's too late now for regrets. I'll meet it like a man," he said:

"It may as well be I as any one, though it's hard even for me to die; harder than you imagine;" then, growing excited as he talked, he raised himself upon his elbow, and continued: "Major Stanley, tell me truly, do you love the woman you know as Maria Gordon?"

"I did love her once, before I knew I must not—but now—I—yes, Dr. Richards, my heart tells me that never was she so dear to me as now when her husband lies dying at my side."

Irving Stanley hardly knew what he was saying, but the doctor—the husband, understood, and almost shrieked out the words:

"You know then that she is Adah, a wife, a mother, and that I am her lawful husband?"

"I know the whole," was the reply, as with his hand Irving dipped water from the brook and laved the feverish brow of the dying man, who went on to speak of Adah as she was when he first knew her, and of the few happy months spent with her in those humble lodgings.

"You don't know my darling," he whispered. "She's an angel, and I might have been so happy with her. Oh, if I could only live, but that can't be now, and it is well. Come close to me, Major Stanley, and listen while I tell you that Adah promised if I would do my duty to my country faithfully, she would live with me again, and all the while she promised, her heart was breaking, for she did not love me. It had all died out for me. It had been given to another; can you guess to whom?"

Irving made no reply, except to chafe the hands which clasped his so tightly, and the doctor continued:

"I am surely dying—I shall never see her more, or my boy, my beautiful boy. I was a brute in the cars; you remember the time. That was Adah, and those little feet resting on my lap were Willie's, baby Willie's, Adah's baby."

The doctor's mind was wandering now, and he kept on disconnectedly:

"She's been to Europe with him. She's changed from the shy girl into a queenly woman. Even the Richards line might be proud of her bearing, and when I'm gone, tell her I said you might have Willie, and—and—it grows very dark; the noise of the battle drowns my voice, but come nearer to me, nearer—tell her—tell Adah, you may have her. She needn't mourn, nor wait; but carry me back to Snowdon. There's no soldier's grave there yet. I never thought mine would be the first. Anna will cry, and mother and Asenath and Eudora; but Adah, oh Lily, darling. She's coming to me now. Don't you hear that rustle in the grass?" and the doctor listened intently to a sound which also caught Irving's ear, a sound of a horse's neigh in the distance, followed by the tramp of feet.

"Hush-sh," he whispered. "It may be the enemy," but his words were not regarded, or understood.

The doctor was in Lily's presence, and in fancy it was her hand, not Irving's which wiped the death-sweat from his brow, and he murmured words of love and fond endearment, as to a living, breathing form. Fainter and fainter grew the pulse, weaker and weaker the trembling voice, until at last Irving could only comprehend that some one was bidden to pray—to say "Our Father."

Reverently, as for a departing brother, he prayed over the dying man, asking that all the past might be forgiven, and that the erring might rest at last in peace.

"Say Amen for me, I'm too weak," the doctor whispered; then, as reason asserted her sway again, he continued: "I see it now; Lily's gone, and I am dying here in the woods, in the dark, in the night, on the ground; cared for by you who will be Lily's husband. You may, you may tell her I said so; tell her kiss my boy; love him, Major Stanley; love him as your own, even though others shall call you father. Tell her—I tried—to pray—"

He never spoke again; and when next the thick, black, clotted blood oozed up from the gaping wound, it brought with it all there was of life; and there in those Virginia woods, in the darkness of the night, Irving Stanley sat alone with the dead. And yet not alone, for away to his right, and where the neigh of a horse had been heard, another wounded soldier lay—his soft, brown locks moist with dew, and his captain's uniform wet with the blood which dripped from the terrible gash in the fleshy part of the neck, where a murderous ball had been. One arm, the right one, was broken, and lay disabled upon the grass; while the hand of the other clutched occasionally at the damp grass, and then lifting itself, stroked caressingly the powerful limbs of the faithful creature standing guard over the prostrate form of his master.

Hugh and Rocket! They had been in many battles, and neither shot nor shell had harmed them until today, when Hugh had received the charge which sent him reeling from his horse, breaking his arm in the field, and scarcely conscious that two of his comrades were leading him from the field. How or by what means he afterward reached the woods, he did not know, but reach them he had, and unable to travel farther, he had fallen to the ground, where he lay, until Rocket came galloping near, riderless, frightened, and looking for his master. With a cry of joy the noble brute answered that master's faint whistle, bounding at once to his side, and by many mute but meaning signs, signifying his desire that Hugh should mount as heretofore.

But Hugh was too weak for that, and after several ineffectual efforts to rise, fell back half fainting on the turf; while Rocket took his stand directly over him, a powerful and efficient guard until help from some quarter should arrive. Patiently, faithfully he stood, waiting as quietly as if he knew that aid was coming, not far away, in the form of an old man, whose hair was white as snow, and whose steps were feeble with age, but who had the advantage of knowing every inch of that ground, for he had trodden it many a time, with a homesick heart which pined for "old Kentuck," whence he had been stolen.

Uncle Sam! He it was whose uncertain steps made Rocket prick up his ears and listen, neighing at last a neigh of welcome, by which he, too, was recognized.

"De dear Father be praised if that be'nt Rocket hisself. I've found him, I've found my Massah Hugh. I tole Miss Ellis I should, 'case I knows all de way. Dear Massuh Hugh, I'se Sam, I is," and with a convulsive sob the old negro knelt beside the white-faced man, who but for this timely aid could hardly have survived that fearful night.

CHAPTER XLVI

HOW SAM CAME THERE

It is more than a year now since last we looked upon the inmates of Spring Bank, and during that time Kentucky had been the scene of violence, murder, and bloodshed. The roar of artillery had been heard upon its hills. Soldiers wearing the Federal uniform had marched up and down its beaten paths, encamping for a brief season in its capital, and then departing to other points where their services were needed more.

Morgan, with his fierce band of guerillas, had carried terror, dismay, and sometimes death, to many a peaceful home; while Harney, too, disdaining open, honorable warfare, had joined himself, it was said, to a horde of savage marauders, gathered, some from Texas, some from Mississippi, and a few from Tennessee; but none, to her credit be it said, none from Kentucky, save their chief, the Rebel Harney, who despised and dreaded almost equally by Unionist and Confederates, kept the country between Louisville and Lexington in a constant state of excitement.

At Spring Bank, well known as the home of stanch Unionists, nothing as yet had been harmed, thanks to Alice's courage and vigilance, and the skill with which she had not only taught herself to handle firearms, but also taught the negroes, who, instead of running away, as the Wendell Phillips men of the North seem to believe all negroes will do, only give them the chance, remained firmly at their post, and nightly took turns in guarding the house against any attack from the guerillas.

Toward Spring Bank Harney had a peculiar spite, and his threats of violence had more than once reached the ears of Alice, who wisely kept them from the nervous, timid Mrs. Worthington. At her instigation, Aunt Eunice had left her home in the cornfield, and come to Spring Bank, so that the little garrison numbered four white women, including crazy Densie, and twelve negro servants.

As the storm grew blacker, it had seemed necessary for Colonel Tiffton openly to avow his sentiments, and not "sneak between two fires, for fear of being burned," as Harney wolfishly told him one day, taunting him with being a "villainous Yankee," and hinting darkly of the punishment preparing for all such.

The colonel was not cowardly, but as was natural he did lean to the Confederacy. "Peaceful separation, if possible," was his creed; and fully believing the South destined to triumph, he took that side at last, greatly to the delight of his high-spirited Nell, who had been a Rebel from the first. The inmates of Spring Bank, however, were not forgotten by the colonel, and regularly each morning he rode over to see if all were safe, sometimes sending there at night one or two of his own field hands as body guard to Alice, whose courage and intrepidity in defending her side of the question he greatly admired.

One night, near the middle of summer, Jake, a burly negro, came earlier than usual, and seeking Alice, thrust into her hand a note from Colonel Tiffton. It read as follows:

"Dear Alice: I have a suspicion that the villainous scamps, headed by Harney, mean to steal horses from Spring Bank tonight, hoping by that means to engage you in a bit of a fight. In short, Harney was heard to say, 'I'll have every horse from Spring Bank before tomorrow morning; and if that Yankee miss appears to dispute my claim, as I trust she will, I'll have her, too;' and then the bully laid a wager that 'Major Alice,' as he called you, would be his prisoner in less than forty-eight hours.

"I hope it is not true, but if he does come, please keep quietly in the house, and let him take every mother's son of a horse. I shall be around watching, but hanged if it will do to identify myself with you as I wish to do. They'd shoot me like a dog."

To say that Alice felt no fear would be false. There was a paling of the cheek and a sinking of the heart as she thought of what the fast-falling night might bring. But her trust was not in her own strength, and dismissing Jake from her presence, she bent her face upon the piano lid and prayed most earnestly to be delivered from the approaching peril, to know just what to do, and how to act; then summoning the entire household to the large sitting-room, she explained to them what she had heard, and asked what they must do.

"Shall we lock ourselves inside the house and let them have the horses, or shall we try to keep them?"

It took a few minutes for the negroes to recover from their fright, and when they had done so Claib was the first to speak.

"Please, Miss Ellis, Massa Hugh's last words to me was: 'Mind, boy, you takes good keer of de hosses.' Massa Hugh sot store by dem. He not stay quiet in de chimbly corner and let Sudden 'Federacy stole 'em."

"Dem's my theology, Miss Ellis," chimed in Uncle Sam, rising and standing in the midst of the dark group assembled near the door. "I'se for savin' de horses."

"An' I'se for shootin' Harney," interrupted the little Mug, her eyes flashing, and her nostrils dilating as she continued: "I knows it's wicked, but I hates him, an' I never tole you how I seen him in de woods one day, an' he axes me 'bout my Miss and Mars'r Hugh—did they writ often, an' was they kinder sparkin'? I told him none of his bizness, and cut and run, but he bawl after me and say how't he steal Miss Ellis some night and make her be his wife. I flung a rock at him, big rock, too, and cut again. Ugh!"

Mug's face, expressive as it was, only reflected the feelings of the others and Alice's decision was taken. They would protect

Hugh's horses. But how? That was a perplexing question until Mug suggested that they be brought into the kitchen, which adjoined the house, and was much larger than Southern kitchens usually are. It was a novel idea, but seemed the only feasible one, and was acted upon at once. The kitchen, however, would not accommodate the dozen noble animals, Claib's special pride, and so the carpet was taken from the dining-room floor, and before the clock struck ten every horse was stabled in the house, where they stood as quietly as if they, too, felt the awe, the expectancy of something terrible brooding over the household.

It was Alice who managed everything, giving directions where each one of her subordinates was to stay, and what they were to do in case of an attack. Every door and window was barricaded, every possible precaution taken, and then, with an unflinching nerve, Alice stole up the stairs, and unfastening a trapdoor which led out upon the roof, stood there behind a huge chimney top, scanning wistfully the darkness of the woods, waiting, watching for a foe, whose very name was in itself sufficient to blanch a woman's cheek with fear.

"Oh, what would Hugh say, if he could see me now?" she murmured, a tear starting to her eye as she thought of the dear soldier afar in the tented field, and wondered if he had forgotten his love for her, as she sometimes feared, or why, in his many letters, he never breathed a word of aught save brotherly affection.

She was his mother's amanuensis, and as she could not follow her epistles, and see how, ere breaking the seal, Hugh's lips were always pressed to the place where her fingers had traced his name, she did not guess how precious they were to him, or how her words of counsel and sympathy kept him often from temptations, and were molding him so fast into the truly consistent Christian man she so much wished him to be. He had in one letter, expressed his surprise that she did not go to Europe, while she had replied to him: "I never thought of going;" and this was all the allusion either had made to Irving Stanley since the day that Hugh left Spring Bank. Gradually, however, the conviction had crept over Hugh that in his jealousy he acted hastily, that Irving Stanley had sued for Alice's hand in vain, but he would not seek an explanation yet; he would do his duty as a soldier, and when that duty was done, he might, perhaps, be more worthy of Alice's love. He would have had no doubt of it now could he have seen her that summer night, and known her thoughts as she stood patiently at her post, now starting with a sudden flutter of fear, as what she had at first taken for the distant trees seemed to assume a tangible form; and again laughing at her own weakness, as the bristling bayonets subsided into sleeping shadows beneath the forest boughs.

"Miss Ellis, did you hear dat ar?" came in a whisper from the opening of the roof, and with a suppressed scream Alice recognized Muggins, who had followed her young mistress, and for the last half hour had been poising herself, first on one foot and then upon the other, as she stood upon the topmost narrow stairs, with her woolly head protruding just above the roof, and her cat-like ears listening for some sound.

"How came you here?" Alice asked, and Mug replied:

"I thinks dis the best place to fire at Mas'r Harney. Mug's gwine to take aim, fire, bang, so," and the queer child illustrated by holding up a revolver which she had used more than once under Alice's supervision, and with which she had armed herself.

Alice could not forbear a smile, but it froze on her lips, as clutching her dress Mug whispered:

"Dar they comes," pointing at the same time toward the woods where a band of men was distinctly visible, marching directly upon Spring Bank.

"Will I bang 'em now?" Mug asked, but Alice stopped her with a sign, and leaning against the chimney, stood watching the advancing foe, who, led by Harney, made straight for the stables, their suppressed voices reaching her where she stood, as did their oaths and imprecations when they found their booty gone.

There was a moment's consultation and then Harney, dismounting, came into the yard and seemed to be inspecting the dark, silent building, which gave no sign of life.

"We'll try the cabins first. We'll make the negroes tell where the horses are," Alice heard him say, but the cabins were as empty as the stalls, and in some perplexity Harney gave orders for them to see, "if the old rookery were vacant too."

"Mr. Harney, may I ask why you are here?"

The clear, silvery tones rang out on the still night and startled that guerilla band almost as much as would a shell dropped suddenly in their midst. Looking in the direction whence the voice had come they saw the girlish figure clearly defined upon the housetop, and one, a burly, brutal Texan, raised his gun, but Harney struck it down, and involuntarily lifting his cap, replied:

"We are here for horses, Miss Johnson. We know Mr. Worthington keeps the best in the country, and as we need some, we have come to take possession, peaceably if possible, forcibly if need be. Can you tell us where they are?"

"I can," and Alice's voice did not tremble a particle. "They are safely housed in the kitchen and dining-room and the doors are barred."

"The fair Alice will please unbar them," was Harney's sneering reply, to which came back the answer: "The horses are not yours; they are Captain Worthington's, and we will defend them, if need be, with our lives!"

"Gritty, by George! I didn't know as Yankee gals, had such splendid pluck," muttered one of the men, while Harney continued: "You say 'we.' May I ask the number of your forces?"

Ere Alice could speak old Sam's voice was heard parleying with the marauders.

"That's a nigger, shoot him!" growled one, but the white head was withdrawn from view just in time to escape the ball aimed at it.

There was a rush, now for the kitchen door, a horrid sound of fearful oaths, mingled with the cries of the negroes, the furious yells of Rover, whom Lulu had let loose, and the neighing of the frightened steeds. But amid it all Alice retained her self-possession. She had descended from her post on the housetop, and persuading Mrs. Worthington, Aunt Eunice, and Densie to remain quietly in her own room, joined the negroes below, cheering them by her presence, and by her apparent fearlessness keeping up their sinking courage.

"We's better gin dem de hosses, Miss Ellis," Claib said, entreatingly, as blow after blow fell upon the yielding door—"'cause dey's boun' to hab 'em."

"I'll try argument first with their leader," Alice replied, and ere Claib suspected her intention she was undoing the fastenings of a side door, bidding him bolt it after her as soon as she was safely through it.

"Is Miss Ellis crazy?" shrieked Sam. "Dem men has no 'spect for female wimmen," and he was forcibly detaining her, when the sharp ring of a revolver was heard, accompanied by a demoniacal shriek as a tall body leaped high in the air and then fell, weltering in its blood.

A moment more and a little dusky figure came flying down the stairs, and hiding itself behind the astonished Alice, sobbed hysterically: "I'se done it, I has! I'se shooted old Harney!" and Mug, overcome with excitement, rolled upon the floor like an India rubber ball.

It was true, as Mug had said. Secreted by the huge chimney she had watched the proceedings below, keeping her eye fixed on him she knew to be Harney; and, at last, when a favorable opportunity occurred, had sent the ball which carried death to him and dismay to his adherents, who crowded around their fallen leader, forgetful now of the prey for which they had come, and anxious only for flight. Possibly, too, their desire to be off was augmented by the fact that from the woods came the sound of voices and the tramp of horses' feet—Colonel Tiffton, who, with a few of his neighbors, was coming to the rescue of Spring Bank. But their services were not needed to drive away the foe, for ere they reached the gate, the yard was free from the invaders, who, bearing their wounded leader, Harney, in their midst, disappeared behind the hill, one of them, the brutal Texan, who had raised his gun at Alice, lingering behind the rest, and looking back to see the result of his infernal deed. Secretly, when no one knew it, he had kindled a fire at the rear of the wooden building, which being old and dry caught readily, and burned like tinder.

Alice was the first to discover it, and "Fire! fire!" was echoed frantically from one to the other, while all did their best to subdue it. But their efforts were in vain; nothing could stay its progress, and when the next morning's sun arose it shone on the blackened, smoking ruins of Spring Bank, and on the tearful group standing near to what had been their happy home. The furniture mostly had been saved, and was scattered about the yard just where it had been deposited. There had been some parley between the negroes as to which should be left to burn, the old secretary at the end of the upper hall, or a bureau which stood in an adjoining and otherwise empty room.

"Massah done keep his papers here. We'll take dis," Claib had said, and so, assisted by other negroes and Mug, he had carried the old worm-eaten thing down the stairs, and bearing it across the yard, had dropped it rather suddenly, for it was wondrously heavy, and the sweat stood in great drops on the faces of the blacks, as they deposited the load and turned away so quickly as not to see the rotten bottom splintering to pieces, or the yellow coin dropping upon the grass.

Making the circuit of the yard in company with Colonel Tiffton, Alice's eye was caught by the flashing of something beneath the bookcase, and stooping down she uttered a cry of surprise as she picked up and held to view a golden guinea. Another, and another, and another—they were thick as berries on the hills, and in utter amazement she turned to the equally astonished colonel for an explanation. It cams to him after a little. That bookcase, with its false bottom and secret drawers, had been the hiding place of the miserly John Stanley's gold. In his will, he had spoken of that particularly, bidding Hugh be careful of it, as it had come to him from his grandfather, and this was the result. What had been a mystery to the colonel was explained. He knew what John Stanley had done with all his money, and that Hugh Worthington's poverty was now a thing of the past.

"I'm glad of it—the boy deserves this streak of luck, if ever a fellow did," he said, as he made his rapid explanations to Alice, who listened like one bewildered, while all the time she was gathering up the golden coin, which kept dropping from the sides and chinks of the bookcase.

There was quite a little fortune, and Alice suggested that it should be kept a secret for the present from all save Mrs. Worthington, a plan to which the colonel assented, helping Alice to recover and secrete her treasure, and then going with her to Mrs. Worthington, who sat weeping silently over the ruins of her home.

"Poor Hugh, we are beggars now," she moaned, refusing at

first to listen to Alice's attempts at consolation.

They told her at last what they had found, proving their words by occular demonstration, and proposing to her that the story should go no further until Hugh had been consulted.

"You'll go home with me, of course," the colonel said, "and then we'll see what must be done."

This seemed the only feasible arrangement, and the family carriage was brought around to take the ladies to Mosside—the negroes, whose cabins had not been burned, staying at Spring-Bank to watch the fire, and see that it spread no farther. But Alice could not remain in quietness at Mosside, and early the next morning she rode down to Spring Bank, where the negroes greeted her with loud cries of welcome, asking her numberless questions as to what they were to do, and who would go after "Massah Hugh."

It seemed to be the prevailing opinion that he must come home, and Alice thought so, too.

"What do you think, Uncle Sam?" she asked, turning to the old man, who replied:

"I thinks a heap of things, and if Miss Ellis comes dis way where so many can't be listen in', I tella her my mind."

Alice followed him to a respectable distance from the others, and sitting down upon a chair standing there, waited for Sam to begin.

Twirling his old straw hat awkwardly for a moment, he stammered out:

"What for did Massah Hugh jine de army?"

"Because he thought it his duty," was Alice's reply, and Sam continued:

"Yes, but dar is anodder reason. 'Scuse me, miss, but I can't keep still an' see it all agwine wrong. 'Scuse me 'gin, miss, but is you ever gwine to hev that chap what comed here oncet a sparkin'—Massah Irving, I means?"

Alice's blue eyes turned inquiringly upon him, as she replied: "Never, Uncle Sam. I never intended to marry him. Why do you ask?"

"'Cause, miss, when a young gal lets her head lay spang on a fellow's buzzum, and he a kissin' her, it looks mighty like somethin'. Yes, berry like;" and in his own way Sam confessed what he had seen more than a year ago, and told, too, how Hugh had overheard the words of love breathed by Irving Stanley, imitating, as far as possible, his master's manner as he turned away, and walked hurriedly down the piazza.

Then he confessed what, in the evening, he had repeated to Hugh, telling Alice how "poor massah groan, wid face in his hands, and how next day he went off, never to come back again."

In mute silence, Alice listened to a story which explained much that had been strange to her before, and as she listened, her resolve was made.

"Sam," she said, when he had finished, "I wish I had known this before. It might have saved your master much anxiety. I am going North—going to Snowdon first, and then to Washington, in hopes of finding him."

In a moment Sam was on his knees, begging to go with her.

"Don't leave me, Miss Ellis. Take me 'long. Please take me to Massah Hugh. I'se quite peart now, and kin look after Miss Ellis a heap."

Alice could not promise till she had talked with Mrs. Worthington, whose anxiety to go North was even greater than her own. They would be nearer to Hugh, and by going to Washington would probably see him, she said, while it seemed that she should by some means be brought near to her daughter, of whom no tidings had been received as yet. So it was arranged that Mrs. Worthington, Alice and Densie, together with Lulu and Sam, should start at once for Snowdon, where Alice would leave a part of her charge, herself and Mrs. Worthington going on to Washington in hopes of meeting or hearing directly from Hugh. Aunt Eunice and Mug were to remain with Colonel Tiffton, who promised to look after the Spring Bank negroes.

Accordingly, one week after the fire, Alice found herself at the same station in Lexington where once Hugh Worthington, to her unknown, had waited for her coming. The morning papers were just out, and securing one for herself, she entered the car and read the following announcement:

"DIED, at his country residence, from the effect of a shot received while dastardly attacking a house belonging to Unionists, Robert Harney, Esq., aged thirty-three."

With a shudder Alice pointed out the paragraph to Mrs. Worthington, and laying her head upon her hand prayed silently that there might come a speedy end to the horrors entailed by the cruel war.

CHAPTER XLVII

FINDING HUGH

Sweet Anna Millbrook's eyes were dim with tears, and her heart was sore with pain when told that Alice Johnson, was waiting for her in the parlor below. Only the day before had she heard of her brother's disgrace, feeling as she heard it, how much rather she would that he had died ere there were so many stains upon his name. But Alice would comfort her, and she hastened to meet her. Sitting down beside her, she talked with her long of all that had transpired since last they met; talked, too, of Adah, and then of Willie, who was sent for, and at Alice's request taken by her to the hotel, where Mrs. Worthington was stopping. He had grown to be a most beautiful and engaging child, and Mrs. Worthington justly felt a thrill of pride as she clasped him to her bosom, weeping over him passionately. She could scarcely bear to lose him from her sight, and when later in the day Anna came down for him, she begged hard for him to stay. But Willie was rather shy of his new grandmother, and preferred returning with Mrs. Millbrook, who promised that he should come every day so long as Mrs. Worthington remained at the hotel.

As soon as Mrs. Richards learned that Mrs. Worthington and Alice were in town, she insisted upon their coming to Terrace Hill. There was room enough, she said, and her friends were welcome there for as long a time as they chose to stay. There were the pleasant chambers fitted up for 'Lina, they had never been occupied, and Mrs. Worthington could have them as well as not; or better yet—could take Anna's old chamber, with the little room adjoining, where Adah used to sleep. Mrs. Worthington preferred the latter, and removed with Alice at Terrace Hill, while at Anna's request Densie went to the Riverside Cottage, where she used to live, and where she was much happier than she would have been with strangers.

Not long could Mrs. Worthington stay contentedly at Snowdon, and after a time Alice started with her and Lulu for Washington, taking Sam also, partly because he begged so hard to go, and partly because she did not care to trouble her friends with the old man, who seemed a perfect child in his delight at the prospect of seeing "Massah Hugh." But to see him was not so easy a matter. Indeed, he seemed farther off at Washington than he had done at Spring Bank, and Alice sometimes questioned the propriety of having left Kentucky at all. They were not very comfortable at Washington, and as Mrs. Worthington pined for the pure country air, Alice managed at last to procure board for herself, Mrs. Worthington, Lulu and Sam, at the house of a friend whose acquaintance she had made at the time of her visit to Virginia. It was some distance from Washington, and so near to Bull Run that when at last the second disastrous battle was fought in that vicinity, the roar of the artillery was distinctly heard, and they who listened to the noise of that bloody conflict knew just when the battle ceased, and thought with tearful anguish of the poor, maimed, suffering wretches left to bleed and die alone. They knew Hugh must have been in the battle, and Mrs. Washington's anxiety amounted almost to insanity, while Alice, with blanched cheek and compressed lip, could only pray silently that he might be spared, and might yet come back to them. Only Sam thought of acting.

"Now is the time," he said to Alice, as they stood talking together of Hugh, and wondering if he were safe. "Something tell me Massah Hugh is hurted somewhar, and I'se gwine to find him. I knows all de way, an' every tree around dat place. I can hide from de 'Federacy. Dem Rebels let ole white-har'd nigger look for young massah, and I'se gwine. P'raps I not find him, but I does somebody some good. I helps somebody's Massah Hugh."

It seemed a crazy project, letting that old man start off on so strange an errand, but Sam was determined.

He had a "'sentiment," as he said, that Hugh was wounded, and he must go to him.

In his presentiment Alice had no faith; but she did not oppose him, and at parting she said to him, hesitatingly:

"Sam, if you do find your master wounded, and you think him dying, you may tell him—tell him—that I said—I loved him; and had he ever come back, I would have been his wife."

"I tells him, and that raises Massah Hugh from de very jaws of death," was Sam's reply, as he departed on his errand of mercy, which proved not to be a fruitless one, for he did find his master, and falling on his knees beside him, uttered the joyful words we have before repeated.

To the faint, half dying Hugh, it seemed more like a dream than a reality—that familiar voice from home, and that dusky form bending over him so pityingly. He could not comprehend how Sam came there, or what he was saying to him. Something he heard of burning houses, and ole miss and Snowdon, and Washington; but nothing was real until he caught the name of Alice, and thought Sam said she was there.

"Where, Sam—where?" he asked, trying to raise himself upon his elbow. "Is Alice here, did you say?"

"No, massah; not 'zactly here—but on de road. If massah could ride, Sam hold him on, like massah oncet held on ole Sam, and we'll get to her directly. They's kind o' Secesh folks whar she is, but mighty good to her. She knowed 'em 'fore, 'case way down here is whar Sam was sold dat time Miss Ellis comed and show him de road to Can'an. Miss Ellis tell me somethin' nice for Massah Hugh, ef he's dyin'—suffin make him so glad. Is you dyin', massah?"

"I hardly think I am as bad as that. Can't you tell unless I am near to death?" Hugh said; and Sam replied:

"No, massah; dem's my orders. 'Ef he's dyin', Sam, tell him I'—dat's what she say. Maybe you is dyin', massah. Feel and see!"

"It's possible," and something like his old mischievous smile played around Hugh's white lips as he asked how a chap felt when he was dying.

"I'se got mizzable mem'ry, and I don't justly 'member," was Sam's answer; "but I reckons he feel berry queer and choky—berry."

"That's exactly my case, so you may venture to tell," Hugh said; and getting his face close to that of the young man, Sam whispered: "She say, 'Tell Massah Hugh—I—I—' You's sure you's dyin'?"

"I'm sure I feel as you said I must," Hugh, continued, and Sam went on: "'Tell him I loves him; and ef he lives I'll be his wife.' Dem's her very words, nigh as I can 'member—but what is massah goin' to do?" he continued in some surprise, as Hugh attempted to rise.

"Do? I'm going to Alice," was Hugh's reply, as with a moan he sank back again, too weak to rise alone.

"Then you be'nt dyin', after all," was Sam's rueful comment, as he suggested: "Ef massah only clamber onto Rocket."

This was easier proposed than done, but after several trials Hugh succeeded; and, with Sam steadying him, while he half lay on Rocket's neck, Hugh proceeded slowly and safely through the woods, meeting at last with some Unionists, who gave him what aid they could, and did not leave him until they saw him safely deposited in an ambulance, which, in spite of his entreaties, took him direct to Georgetown. It was a bitter disappointment to Hugh, so bitter, indeed, that he scarcely felt the pain when his broken arm was set; and when, at last, he was left alone in his narrow hospital bed, he turned his face to the wall and cried, just as many a poor, homesick soldier had done before him, and will do again.

Twenty-four hours had passed, and in Hugh's room it was growing dark again. All the day he had watched anxiously the door through which visitors would enter, asking repeatedly if no one had called for him; but just as the sun was going down he fell away to sleep, dreaming at last that Golden Hair was there—that her soft, white hands were on his brow, her sweet lips pressed to his, while her dear voice murmured softly: "Darling Hugh!"

There was a cry of pain from a distant corner, and Hugh awoke to consciousness—awoke to know it was no dream—the soft hands on his brow, the kiss upon his lips—for Golden Hair was there; and by the tears she dropped upon his face, and the mute caresses she gave him, he knew that Sam had told him truly. For several minutes there was silence between them, while the eyes looked into each other with a deeper meaning than words could have expressed;

then, smoothing back his damp brown hair, and letting her fingers still rest upon his forehead, Alice whispered to him: "Why did you distrust me, Hugh? But for that we need not have been separated so long."

Winding his well arm around her neck, and drawing her nearer to him, Hugh answered:

"It was best just as it is. Had I been sure of your love, I should have found it harder to leave home. My country needed me. I am glad I have done what I could to defend it. Glad that I joined the army, for Alice, darling, Golden Hair, in my lonely tent reading that little Bible you gave me so long ago, the Savior found me, and now, whether I live or not, it is well, for if I die, I am sure you will be mine in heaven; and if I live—"

Alice finished the sentence for him.

"If you live, God willing, I shall be your wife. Dear Hugh, I bless the Good Father, first for bringing you to Himself, and then restoring you to me, darling Hugh."

CHAPTER XLVIII

GOING HOME

The Village hearse was waiting at Snowdon depot, and close beside it stood the carriage from Terrace Hill; the one sent there for Adah, the other for her husband, whose lifeblood, so freely shed, had wiped away all stains upon his memory, and enshrined him in the hearts of Snowdon's people as a martyr. He was the first dead soldier returned to them, his the first soldier's grave in their churchyard; and so a goodly throng were there, with plaintive fife and muffled drum, to do him honor. His major was coming with him, it was said—Major Stanley, who had himself been found, in a half fainting condition watching by the dead—Major Stanley, who had seen that the body was embalmed, had written to the wife, and had attended to everything, even to coming on himself by way of showing his respect. Death is a great softener of errors; and the village people, who could not remember a time when they had not disliked John Richards, forgot his faults now that he was dead.

It seemed a long-time-waiting for the train, but it came at last, and the crowd involuntarily made a movement forward, and then drew back as a tall figure appeared upon the platform, his stylish uniform betokening an officer of rank, and his manner showing plainly that he was master of ceremonies.

"Major Stanley," ran in a whisper through the crowd, whose wonder increased when another, and, if possible, a finer-looking man, emerged into view, his right arm in a sling, and his face pale and worn, from the effects of recent illness. He had not been expected, and many curious glances were cast at him as, slowly descending the steps, he gave his well hand to the lady following close behind, Mrs. Worthington; they knew her, and recognized also the two young ladies, Alice and Adah, as they sprang from the car. Poor Adah! how she shrank from the public gaze, shuddering as on her way to the carriage she passed the long box the men were handling so carefully.

Summoned by Irving Stanley, she had come on to Washington to meet, not a living husband, but a husband dead, and while there had learned that Mrs. Worthington, Hugh, and Alice were all in Georgetown, whither she hastened at once, eager to meet the mother whom she had never yet met as such. Immediately after the discovery of her parentage, she had written to Kentucky, but the letter had not reached its destination, consequently no one but Hugh knew how near she was; and he had only learned it a few days before the battle, when he had, by accident, a few moments' conversation with Dr. Richards, whom he had purposely avoided. He was talking of Adah, and the practicability of sending for her, when she arrived at the private boarding house to which he had been removed.

The particulars of that interview between the mother and her daughter we cannot describe, as no one witnessed it save God; but Adah's face was radiant with happiness, and her soft, brown eyes beaming with joy when it was ended, and she went next to where Hugh was waiting for her.

"Oh, Hugh, my noble brother!" was all she could say, as she wound her arms around his neck and pressed her fair cheek against his own, forgetting, in those moments of perfect bliss, all the sorrow, all the anguish of the past.

Nor was it until Hugh said to her: "The doctor was in that battle. Did he escaped unharmed?" that a shadow dimmed the sunshine flooding her pathway that autumn morning.

At the mention of him the muscles about her mouth grew rigid, and a look of pain flitted across her face, showing that there was yet much of bitterness mingled in her cup of joy. Composing herself as soon as possible she told Hugh that she was a widow, but uttered no word of complaint against the dead, and Hugh, knowing that she could not sorrow as other women have sorrowed over the loved ones slain in battle, drew her nearer to him, and after speaking a few words of poor 'Lina, told her of the golden fortune which had so unexpectedly come to him, and added: "And you shall share it with me. Your home shall be with me and Golden Hair—Alice—who has promised to be my wife. We will live very happily together yet, my sister."

Then he asked what Major Stanley's plan was concerning the body of her husband, and upon learning that it was to bury the doctor at home, he announced his determination to accompany them, as he knew he should be able to do so.

Hugh had no suspicion of the truth, but Alice guessed it readily, and could scarcely forbear throwing her arms around Adah's neck and whispering to her how glad she was. She had said to her softly: "I am to be your sister, Adah—are you willing to receive me?" and Adah had only answered by a warm pressure of the hand she held in hers and by the tears which shone in her brown eyes.

It was a great trial to Adah to face the crowd they found assembled at the depot, but Irving, Hugh, and Alice all helped to screen her from observation, and almost before she was aware of it she found herself safe in the carriage which effectually hid her from view. Slowly the procession moved through the village, the foot passengers keeping time to the muffled drum, whose solemn beats had never till that morning been heard in the quiet streets. The wide gate which led into the grounds of Terrace Hill was opened wide, and the black hearse passed in, followed by the other carriages, which wound around the hill and up to the huge building where badges of mourning were hung out—mourning for the only son, the youngest born, the once pride and pet of the stately woman who watched the coming of that group with tear-dimmed eyes, holding upon her lap the little boy whose father they were bringing in, dead, coffined for the grave. Not for the world would that high-bred woman have been guilty of an impropriety, and so she sat in her own room, while Charlie Millbrook met the bearers in the hall and told them where to deposit their burden.

In the same room where we first saw him on the night of his return from Europe, they left him, and went their way, while to Dixson and Pamelia was accorded the honor of first welcoming Adah, whom they treated with as much deference as if she had never been with them in any capacity save that of mistress. She had changed since they last saw her—was wonderfully improved, they said to each other as they left her at the door of the room, where Mrs. Richards, with her two older daughters, was waiting to receive her. But if the servants were struck with the air of dignity and cultivation which Adah acquired during her tour in Europe, how much more did this same air impress the haughty ladies waiting for her appearance, and feeling a little uncertain as to how they should receive her. Any doubts, however, which they had upon this subject were dispelled the moment she entered the room, and they saw at a glance that it was not the timid, shrinking Rose Markham with whom they had to deal, but a woman as wholly self-possessed as themselves, and one with whose bearing even their critical eyes would find no fault. She would not suffer them to patronize her; they must treat her fully as an equal or as nothing, and with a new-born feeling of pride in her late son's widow, Mrs. Richards arose, and putting Willie from her lap, advanced to meet her, cordially extending her hand, but uttering no word of welcome. Adah took the hand, but her eyes never sought the face of her lady mother. They were riveted with a hungry, wistful, longing look on Willie, the little boy, who, clinging to his grandmother's skirts, peered curiously at her, holding back at first, when, unmindful of Asenath and Eudora, who had not yet been greeted, she tried to take him in her arms.

"Oh, Willie, darling, don't you know me? I am poor mamma," and Adah's voice was choked with sobs at this unlooked-for reception from her child.

He had been sent for from Anna's home to meet his mother, because it was proper; but no one at Terrace Hill had said to him that the mamma for whom sweet Anna taught him daily to pray was coming. She was not in his mind, and as eighteen months had obliterated all memories of the gentle, girlish creature he once knew as mother, he could not immediately identify that mother with the lady before him.

It was a sad disappointment to Adah, and without knowing what she was doing, she sank down upon the sofa, and involuntarily laying her head in Mrs. Richards' lap, cried bitterly, her tears bringing answering ones from the eyes of all three of the ladies, for they half believed her grief, in part, was for the lifeless form in the room below.

"Poor child, you are tired and worn. It is hard to lose him just as there was a prospect of perfect reconciliation with us all," Mrs. Richards said, softly smoothing the brown tresses lying on her lap, and thinking even then that curls were more becoming to her daughter-in-law than braids had been, but wondering why, now she was in mourning, Adah had persisted in wearing them.

"Pretty girl, pretty turls, is you tyin'?" and won by her distress, Willie drew near, and laid his baby hand upon the curls he thought so pretty.

"That's mamma, Willie," Asenath said; "the mamma Aunt Anna said would come some time—Willie's mamma. Can't he kiss her?"

The child could not resist the face which, lifting itself up, looked eagerly at him, and he put up his little hands for Adah to take him, returning the kisses she showered upon him and clinging to her neck, while he said:

"Is you mam-ma sure? I prays for mam-ma—God take care of her, and pa-pa too. He's dead. They brought him back with a dum. Poor pa-pa, Willie don't want him dead;" and the little lip began to quiver.

Never before since she knew she was a widow had Adah felt so vivid a sensation of something akin to affection for the dead, as when her child and his mourned so plaintively for papa; and the tears which now fell like rain were not for Willie alone, but were given rather to the dead.

"Mrs. Richards has not yet greeted us," Asenath said; and turning to her at once, Adah apologized for her seeming neglect, pressing both her and Eudora's hands more cordially than she would have done a few moments before.

"Where is Anna?" she asked; and Mrs. Richards replied:

"She's sick. She regretted much that she could not come up here today;" while Willie, standing in Adah's lap, with his chubby arm around her neck, chimed in.

"You don't know what we've dot. We've dot 'ittle baby, we has."

Adah knew now why Anna was absent, and why Charlie Millbrook looked so happy when at last he came in to see her, delivering sundry messages from his Anna, who, he said could scarcely wait to see her dear sister. There was something genuine in Charlie's greeting, something which made Adah feel as if she were indeed at home, and she wondered much how even the Richards race could ever have objected to him, as she watched his movements and heard him talking with his stately mother.

"Yes, Major Stanley came," he said, in reply to her questions, and Adah was glad it was put to him, for the blushes dyed her cheek at once, and she bent over Willie to hide them, while Charlie continued: "Captain Worthington came, too, Adah's brother, you know. He was in the same battle with the doctor, was wounded rather seriously and has been discharged, I believe."

"Oh," and Mrs. Richards seemed quite interested now, asking where the young men were, and appearing disappointed when told that, after waiting a few moments in hopes of seeing the ladies, they had returned to the hotel, where Mrs. Worthington and Alice were stopping.

"I fully expected the ladies here; pray, send for them at once," she said, but Adah interposed:

"Her mother would not willingly be separated from Hugh, and as he of course would remain at the hotel, it would be useless to think of persuading Mrs. Worthington to come to Terrace Hill."

"But Miss Johnson surely will come," persisted Mrs. Richards.

Adah could not explain then that Alice was less likely to leave Hugh than her mother, but she said: "Miss Johnson, I think, will not leave mother alone," and so the matter was settled.

It was a terribly long day to Adah, for Mrs. Richards and her daughter kept their darkened room, seeing no one who called, and appearing shocked when Adah stole out from their presence, and taking Willie with her, sought the servants' sitting-room, where the atmosphere was not so laden with restraint. Once the elder lady rang for Pamelia, asking where Mrs. Richards was, and looking a little distressed when told she was in the garden playing with Willie.

"Why, do you want her?" was Pamelia's blunt inquiry, to which her mistress responded with an aggrieved sigh:

"No-o, only I thought perhaps she was with her dead husband; but, poor thing, it is not her nature, I presume, to take it much to heart."

Pamelia didn't believe she did "take it much to heart." Indeed, she didn't see how she could, but she said nothing, and Adah was left to play with Willie until Alice was announced as being in the reception-room. She had driven around, she said, to call on Mrs. Richards, and after that take Adah with her to the cottage, where Anna, she knew, was anxious to receive her. At first Mrs. Richards demurred, fearing it would be improper, but saying: "my late son's wife is, of course, her own mistress, and can do as she likes."

Very adroitly Alice waived all objections, and bore Adah off in triumph.

"I knew you must be lonely up there," she said, as they drove slowly along, "and there can be no harm in visiting one's sick sister."

Anna surely did not think there was, as her warm, welcoming

kisses fully testified.

"I wanted so much to see you today," she said, "that I have worked myself into quite a fever; but knowing mother as I do, I feared she might not sanction your coming;" then proudly turning down the blanket, she disclosed the red-faced baby, who, just one week ago, had come to the Riverside Cottage.

"Isn't he a beauty?" she asked, pressing her lips upon the wrinkled forehead. "A boy, too, and looks so much like Charlie, but—" and her soft, blue eyes seemed more beautiful than ever with the maternal love-shining for them, "I shall not call him Charlie, nor yet John, though mother's heart is set on the latter name. I can't. I loved my brother dearly, and never so much as now that he is dead, but my baby boy must not bear his name, and so I have chosen Hugh, Hugh Richards. I know it will please you both," and she glanced archly at Alice, who blushingly kissed the little boy who was to bear the name dearest to her of all others.

Hugh—they talked of him a while, and then Anna spoke of Irving Stanley, expressing her fears that she could not see him to thank him for his kindness and forbearance to her erring brother.

"He must be noble and good," she said, then turning to Adah, she continued: "You were with him a year. You must know him well. Do you like him?"

"Yes," and Adah's face was all ablaze, as the simple answer dropped from her lips.

For a moment Anna regarded her intently, then her eyes were withdrawn and her white hand beat the counterpane softly, but nothing more was said of Irving Stanley then.

The next day near the sunsetting, they buried the dead soldier, Mrs. Richards and Adah standing side by side as the body was lowered to its last resting place, the older leaning upon the younger for support, and feeling as she went back to her lonely home and heard the merry laugh of little Willie in the hall that she was glad her son had married the young girl, who, now that John was gone forever from her sight began to be very dear to her as his wife, the Lily whom he had loved so much. In the dusky twilight of that night when alone with Adah she told her as much, speaking sadly of the past, which she regretted, and wishing she had never objected to receiving the girl about whom John wrote so lovingly.

"Had I done differently he might have been living now, and you might have been spared much pain, but you'll forgive me. I'm an old woman, I am breaking fast, and soon shall follow my boy, but while I live I wish for peace, and you must love me, Lily, because I was his mother. Let me call you Lily, as he did," and the hand of her who had conceded so much rested entreatingly upon the bowed head of the young girl beside her. There was no acting there, Adah knew, and clasping the trembling hand she involuntarily whispered:

"I will love you, mother, I will."

"And stay with me, too?" Mrs. Richards continued, her voice choked with the sobs she could not repress, when she heard herself called mother by the girl she had so wronged. "You will stay with him, Lily. Anna is gone, my other daughters are old. We are lonely in this great house. We need somebody young to cheer our solitude, and you will stay, as mistress, if you choose, or as a petted, youngest daughter."

This was an unlooked for trial to Adah. She had not dreamed of living there at Terrace Hill, when Hugh and her own mother could make her so happy in their home. But Adah had never consulted her own happiness, and as she listened to the pleading tones of the woman who surely had some heart, some noble qualities, she felt that 'twas her duty to remain there for a time at least, and so she replied at last:

"I expected to live with my own mother, but for the present my home shall be here with you."

"God bless you, darling," and the proud woman's lips touched the fair cheek, while the proud woman's hand smoothed again the soft short curls, pushing them back from the white brow, as she murmured: "You are very beautiful, my child, just as John said you were."

It was hard for Adah to tell Mrs. Worthington that she could not make one of the circle who would gather around the home fireside Hugh was to purchase somewhere, but she did at last, standing firmly by her decision and saying in reply to her mother's entreaties: "It is my duty. They need me more than you, who have both Hugh and Alice."

Adah was right, so Hugh said, and Alice, too, while Irving Stanley said nothing. He must have found much that was attractive about the little town of Snowdon, for he lingered there long after there was not the least excuse for staying. He did not go often to Terrace Hill, and when he did, he never asked for Adah, but so long as he could see her on the Sabbath days when, with the Richards' family she walked quietly up the aisle, her cheek flushing when she passed him, and so long as he occasionally met her at Mrs. Worthington's rooms, or saw her riding in the Richards' carriage, so long was he content to stay. But there came a time when he must go, and then he asked for Adah, and in the presence of her mother-in-law invited her to go with him to her husband's grave. She went, taking Willie with her, and there, with that fresh mound between them, Irving Stanley told her what he had hitherto withheld, told what the dying soldier had said, and asked if it should be so.

"Not now, not yet," he continued, as Adah's eyes were bent upon that grave, "but by and by, will you do your husband's bidding—be my wife?"

"I will," and taking Willie's hand Adah put it with hers into the broad, warm palm which clasped them both, as Irving whispered: "Your child, darling, shall be mine, and never need he know that I am not his father."

It was arranged that Alice should tell Mrs. Richards, as Adah would have no concealments. Accordingly, Alice asked a private interview with the lady, to whom she told everything as she understood it. And Mrs. Richards, though weeping bitterly, generously exonerated Adah from all blame, commended her as having acted very wisely, and then added, with a flush of pride:

"Many a woman would be glad to marry Irving Stanley, and it gives me pleasure to know that to my son's widow the honor is accorded. He is worthy to take John's place, and she, I believe, is worthy of him. I love her already as my daughter, and shall look upon him as a son. You say they are in the garden. Let them both come to me."

They came, and listened quietly, while Mrs. Richards sanctioned their engagement, and then, with a little eulogy upon her departed son, said to Adah: "You will wait a year, of course. It will not be proper before."

Irving had hoped for only six months' probation, but Adah was satisfied with the year, and they went from Mrs. Richards' presence with the feeling that Providence was indeed smiling upon their pathway, and flooding it with sunshine.

The next day Major Stanley left Snowdon, but not until there had come to Hugh a letter, whose handwriting made Mrs. Worthington turn pale, it brought back so vividly the terror of the olden times. It was from Murdock, and it inclosed for Densie Densmore the sum of five hundred dollars.

"Should she need more, I will try and supply it," he wrote, "for I have wronged her cruelly." Then, after speaking of his fruitless search for Adah, and his hearing at last that she was found and Dr. Richards dead, he added: "As there is nothing left for me to do, and as I am sure to be playing mischief if idle, I have joined the army, and am training a band of contrabands to fight as soon as the government comes to its senses, and is willing for the negroes to bear their part in the battle."

The letter ended with saying that he should never come out of the war alive, simply because it would last until he was too old to live any longer.

It was a relief for Mrs. Worthington to hear from him, and know that he probably would not trouble her again, while Adah, whose memories of him were pleasanter, expressed a strong desire to see him.

"We will find him by and by, when you are mine," Irving said playfully; then, drawing her into an adjoining room where they could be alone, he said his parting words, and then with Hugh went to meet the train which took him away from Snowdon.

CHAPTER XLIX

CONCLUSION

The New England hills were tinged with that peculiar purplish haze so common to the Indian summer time, and the warm sunlight of November fell softly upon Snowdon, whose streets this morning were full of eager, expectant people, all hurrying on to the old brick church, and quickening their steps with every stroke of the merry bell, pealing so joyfully from the tall, dark tower. The Richards' carriage was out, and waiting before the door of the Riverside Cottage, for the appearance of Anna, who was this morning to venture out for a short time, and leaving her baby Hugh alone. Another, and far handsomer carriage, was standing before the hotel, where Hugh and his mother were yet stopping, and where, in a pleasant private room, Adah Richards helped Alice Johnson make her neat, tasteful toilet, smoothing lovingly the rich folds of grayish-colored silk, arranging the snowy cuffs and collar, and then bringing the stylish hat of brown Neapolitan, with its pretty face trimmings of blue, and declaring it a shame to cover up the curls of golden hair falling so luxuriously about the face and neck of the blushing bride. For it was Alice's wedding day, and in the room adjoining, Hugh Worthington stood, waiting impatiently the opening of the mysterious door which Adah had shut against him, and wondering if, after all, it were not a dream that the time was coming fast when neither bolts nor locks would have a right to keep him from his wife.

It seemed too great a joy to be true, and by way of reassuring himself he had to look often at the crowds of people hurrying by, and down upon old Sam, who, in full dress, with white cotton gloves drawn awkwardly upon his cramped distorted fingers, stood by the carriage, bowing to all who passed, himself the very personification of perfect bliss. Sam was very happy, inasmuch as he took upon himself the credit of having made the match, and was never tired of relating the wondrous story to all who would listen to it.

"Massah Hugh de perfectest massah," he said, "and Miss Ellis a little more so;" adding that though "Canaan was a mighty nice place, he 'sumed he'd rather not go thar jist yet, but live a leetle longer to see them 'joy themselves. Thar they comes—dat's miss in gray. She knows how't orange posies and silks and satins is proper for weddin' nights; but she's gwine travelin', and dat's why she comed out in dat stun-color, Sam'll be blamed if he fancies." And having thus explained Alice's choice of dress, the old negro held the carriage door himself, while Hugh, handing in his mother, sister and his bride, took his seat beside them, and was driven to the church.

Twenty minutes passed, and then the streets were filled again; but now the people were going home, talking as they went of the beauty of the bride and of the splendid-looking bridegroom, who looked so fondly at her as she murmured her responses, kissing her first himself when the ceremony was over, and letting his arm rest for a moment around her slender form. No one doubted its being a genuine love match, and all rejoiced in the happiness of the newly-married pair, who, at the village depot, were waiting for the train which would take them on their way to Kentucky, for that was their destination.

In the distracted condition of the country, Hugh's presence was needed there; for, taking advantage of his absence, and the thousand rumors afloat touching the Proclamation, one of his negroes had already run away in company with some half dozen of the colonel's, who, in a terrible state of excitement, talked seriously of emigrating to Canada. Hugh's timely arrival, however, quieted him somewhat, though he listened in sorrow, and almost with tears, to Hugh's plan of selling the Spring Bank farm and removing with his negroes to some New England town, where Alice, he knew, would be happier than she had been in Kentucky. This was one object which Hugh had in view in going to Kentucky then, but a purchaser for Spring Bank was not so easily found in those dark days; and so, doing with his land the best he could, he called about him his negroes, and giving to each his freedom, proposed that they stay quietly where they were until spring, when he hoped to find them all employment on the farm he went to buy in New England.

Aunt Eunice, who understood managing blacks better than his timid mother or his inexperienced wife, was to be his housekeeper in that new home of his, where the colonel and his family would always be welcome; and having thus provided for those for whom it was his duty to care, he bade adieu to Kentucky, and returned to Snowdon in time to join the Christmas party at Terrace Hill, where Irving Stanley was a guest, and where, in spite of the war clouds darkening our land, and in spite of the sad, haunting memories of the dead, there was much hilarity and joy—reminding the villagers of the olden time when Terrace Hill was filled with gay revelers. Anna Millbrook was there, more beautiful than in her girlhood, and almost childishly fond of her missionary Charlie, who she laughingly declared was perfectly incorrigible on the subject of surplice and gown, adding that as the mountain would not go to Mahomet, Mahomet must go to the mountain; and so she was fast becoming an out-and-out Presbyterian of the very bluest stripe.

Sweet Anna! None who looked into her truthful, loving face, or knew the beautiful consistency of her daily life, could doubt that whether Presbyterian or Episcopal in sentiment, the heart was right and the feet were treading the narrow path which leadeth unto life eternal.

It was a happy week spent at Terrace Hill; but one heart ached to its very core when, at its close, Irving Stanley went back to where duty called him, trusting that the God who had succored him thus far, would shield him from future harm, and keep him safely till the coming autumn, when, with the first falling of the leaf, he would gather to his embrace his darling Adah, who, with every burden lifted from her spirits, had grown in girlish beauty until others than himself marveled at her strange loveliness.

On the white walls of a handsome country seat just on the banks of the Connecticut, the light of the April sunset falls, and the soft April wind kisses the fair cheek and lifts the golden curls of the young mistress of Spring Bank—for so, in memory of the olden time, have they named their new home—Hugh and Alice, who, arm in arm, walk up and down the terraced garden, talking softly of the way they have been led, and gratefully ascribing all praise to Him who rules and overrules, but does nought save good to those who love Him.

Down in the meadow land and at the rear of the building, dusky forms are seen—the negroes, who have come to their Northern home, and among them the runaway, who, ashamed of his desertion, has returned to his former master, resenting the name of contraband, and dismissing the ultra-abolitionists as humbugs, who deserved putting in the front of every battle. Hugh knows it will be hard accustoming these blacks to Northern usages and ways of doing things, but as he has their good in view as well as his own, and as they will not leave him, he feels sure that in time he will succeed, and cares but little for the opinion of those who wonder what he "expects to do with that lazy lot of niggers."

On a rustic seat, near a rear door, white-haired old Sam is sitting, listening intently, while dusky Mug reads to him from the book of books, the one he prizes above all else, stopping occasionally to expound, in his own way, some point which he fancies may not be clear to her, likening every good man to "Massah Hugh," and every bad one to the leader of the "Suddern 'Federacy," whose horse he declares he held once in "ole Virginny," telling Mug, in an aside, "how, if 'twasn't wicked, nor agin' de scripter, he should most wish he'd put beech nuts under Massah Jeffres' saddle, and so broke his fetched neck, 'fore he raise sich a muss, runnin' calico so high that Miss Ellis 'clar she couldn't 'ford it, and axin' fifteen cents for a paltry spool of cotton."

In the stable yard, Claib, his good-humored face all aglow with pride, is exercising the fiery Rocket, who arches his neck as proudly as of old, and dances mincingly around, while Lulu leans over the gate, watching not so much him as the individual who holds him. And now that it grows darker, and the ripple of the river sounds more like eventide, lights gleam from the pleasant parlor, and thither Hugh and Alice repair, still hand in hand, still looking love into each other's eyes, but not forgetting others in their own great happiness.

Very pleasantly Alice smiles upon Mrs. Worthington and Aunt Eunice sitting by the cheerful fire just kindled on the marble hearth; and then, withdrawing her hand from Hugh's, trips up the stairs and knocking at a door, goes in where Densie sits, watching the daylight fade from the western sky, and whispering to herself of the baby she could not find when she went back to her home in the far-off city. Without turning her head, she puts to Alice the same question she puts to every one:

"Have you children, madam?" and when Alice answers no, she adds: "Be thankful then, for they will never call you a white nigger, as 'Lina did her mother. Poor 'Lina, she died, though saying 'Our Father.' Will you say that with me?"

"Yes, Densie, it's almost time to say our evening prayer, I came for you," Alice rejoins, and taking the crazed creature's hand, she leads her gently down to the parlor below, where, ere long, the blacks are all assembled, and kneeling side by side, they follow with stammering tongues, but honest hearts, their beloved master as he says first the prayer our Savior taught, and then with words of thankful praise asks God to bless and keep him and his in the days to come, even as He has blessed and kept them in the days gone by.

THE END

www.ingramcontent.com/pod-product-compliance
Lightning Source LLC
Chambersburg PA
CBHW020647030726
47498CB00002B/412